Elizabeth Moon joined the US Marine Corps in 1968, reaching the rank of 1st Lieutenant during active duty. She has also earned degrees in history and biology, run for public office and been a columnist on her local newspaper. She lives near Austin, Texas, with her husband and their son.

Find out more about Elizabeth Moon and other Orbit authors by registering for the free monthly newsletter at www.orbitbooks.co.uk

D0320430

SPORTING CHANCE

Book Two of
The Serrano Legacy

Elizabeth Moon

www.orbitbooks.co.uk

An *Orbit* Book

First published in Great Britain by Orbit 1999
Reprinted 1999, 2001, 2003, 2005

Copyright © 1994 by Elizabeth Moon

The moral right of the author has been asserted.

A CIP catalogue record for this book
is available from the British Library.

ISBN 1 85723 882 6

Printed and bound in Great Britain by
Mackays of Chatham PLC, Chatham, Kent

Orbit
An imprint of
Time Warner Book Group UK
Brettenham House
Lancaster Place
London WC2E 7EN

Dedication

For all the great-aunts—Jessie, Ruth, and Grace—who showed generations of young people that age is a rich gift to be savoured, not feared. And for those gifted therapists who recognise the individual, the person, obscured by disability.

Acknowledgments

Among the people who made this project possible were the Usual Crew at home . . . the new horse, who ensured that I didn't waste time riding by bucking me off and breaking some ribs . . . Richard and Michael, who know when to quietly sneak away and come back with pizza . . . the people on Main Street who tell me to quit talking about it, and go finish the (ahem) book. Thanks to Mary Morell, a very old friend who said the right things at the right time, and also to Judy D'Albini Tuley for the same reason. Margaret Ball, for help with names and references. Nancy McGibbon, for assistance with the theory and practice of hippotherapy—especially of controversies in the field and ideas about its future. The use I've made of them is all mine; none of it represents her views.

"Still. We'd be safer to leave now. I haven't forgotten that smugglers were using your ship. Somewhere there's a very unhappy criminal waiting for delivery of whatever was in the scrubber. And I'd expect the smugglers to come looking for us, eventually. It's not as if we'd be hard to find; everyone knew where you were going from Takomin Roads, and we've filed the trip to Rockhouse in Bunny's computer—and with the Crown Minister."

"Good point. I'll mention that to the Crown Minister, and of course he already has the names of your crew. I assume that until the courts-martial, they were all considered loyal servants of the Crown?"

"As far as I know. If they weren't, they could have lost us some battles."

"Fine, then. You set up our departure as you wish; I'll deal with the political end later."

Heris looked after her employer and shook her head. She had not expected Cecelia—who had seemed to have a one-track mind firmly aimed at horses—to be so effective politically. Of course, she came from a political family, but every family had its black sheep. Heris shivered suddenly. She was, in her own way, the black sheep of her family. *Two black sheep don't make a white*, she thought, and shivered again.

In the flurry of preparation, it was hard to remember the last few days with Petris. He was now aboard, supervising the resupply, and (at Heris's suggestion) tucking away the new weaponry before Cecelia decided they didn't need it.

"Nothing for the ship, I notice," he'd said to her over a secure comlink.

"No. Not stocked locally. I know; I've already talked to Lady Cecelia about it."

"Um. Crew rotations?"

"Well . . . you'll all be on your secondary specialties. We'll have to reorganize quite a bit. Civilian regulations divide the responsibilities a bit differently. There's a manual on it—"

"I found that one," Petris said. She wished she could see

him face-to-face, but she needed to be downside just a few hours longer. "But I haven't had the returning crew list from Hospitality Bay yet. Sirkin's the only one staying from the shift up here. You were right, by the way; she's a nice girl and very competent."

"Glad you agree," said Heris. "About that crew list—it was supposed to have been there yesterday. I wonder what's going on? I'll find out."

When she tried calling the crew hostel at Hospitality Bay, none of her crew answered. That seemed odd; she had sent word several days before that they would be leaving Sirialis shortly. Someone should have been there, ready to take any messages from her. She wished she could dump the whole lot of them and replace them with qualified people. She left an urgent message, and asked the hostel clerk when they were expected back.

"Sometime tonight, I 'spect, ma'am," the clerk said. "They rented a cat and took it out to Shell Island."

"Without a comunit aboard?" Heris asked.

"Well, there is one, but the charge to relay is pretty high. That Mr. Gavin said you might call, and to say they'd be back tonight." Heris grimaced, but it wouldn't help to yell at the hostel clerk.

"Tell Mr. Gavin to call here at once when he gets in, whatever the hour," she said. Should she threaten? No. Wait and see what was really going on, she reminded herself.

Gavin's call, relayed to her in the drawing room the green hunt favored, revealed a plot as spiritless as he himself. On the tiny screen of the drawing-room communications niche, he looked sunburnt and nervous.

"I'm not coming back, Captain," he said. "You'll have to find another chief engineer." It sounded almost smug, but she ignored that. She didn't need him.

"And the others?" she asked.

"They don't want to . . . they're not coming either. Not without Lady Cecelia changing . . . I mean, they're not coming."

Now his expression was defiant. Heris took a long breath, conscious of the need to control her expression in a roomful of curious and intelligent observers. They couldn't hear what was said, but they could certainly see her reactions.

"Would you care to explain, Mr. Gavin?" she asked. The edge of steel in her voice cut through his flabby resistance.

"Well, it's just . . . we . . . they . . . we don't want you for our captain." That last phrase came out all in a rush. "We're not coming back. You don't have a crew. We want to talk to Lady Cecelia. She has to find someone else, or we won't come back to her." When Heris said nothing, momentarily silenced by fury, he blundered on. "It's—you're not fair, that's what it is. You got poor Iklind killed, and you're so rigid and all you do is criticize and you don't—you don't *respect* us." It was so outrageous, so ridiculous, that Heris found herself fighting back a sudden incongruous laugh as well as a tirade. The unborn laugh moderated her tone.

"I see you don't know the situation," she said without even a hint of anger. That seemed to make Gavin even more nervous.

"I don't—It doesn't matter," he said, almost stammering. "It doesn't matter what happened—what you say; we're not coming back as long as you're the captain."

"I see," Heris said. "Perhaps I'd better let you speak to Lady Cecelia." She waved her employer over, and stepped away from the comunit, out of its pickup range, for a moment. In brief phrases, she explained Gavin's message, and watched almost amused as Lady Cecelia went white with fury and then red.

"Damn them!"

"No . . . think a moment. They're incompetent, lazy, and we wanted to get rid of them anyway. Now they're also in legal jeopardy—and you have the reins. They don't know what's happened over here—none of it. They don't know you have a crew already. Have fun, milady!" Heris grinned, and after a last glower, Lady Cecelia grinned, too. She beckoned Heris to join her at the comunit niche.

Gavin's self-pitying whine had scarcely begun when Lady Cecelia cut him off with a terse and almost certainly inaccurate description of his ancestry, his progeny, his intellect, and his probable destination. Heris decided that foxhunting offered unique opportunities for invective, and found her own anger draining away as Cecelia continued her tirade.

"And I shall certainly file suits for breach of contract," she wound down, "and I daresay Lord Thornbuckle will be investigating you to see if you're involved in this other affair."

"But Lady Cecelia," whined Gavin. "What other affair? And why—I mean, we've served you—" She cut him off, and turned to face Heris, breathing heavily.

"How was that?"

"Fine. And since we know you had one smuggler in the group, I would carry through on that threat to have them investigated."

"I certainly will," Cecelia said. She stalked off, her tall angularity expressing indignation with every twitch of her formal skirt. Heris excused herself early and went upstairs to contact Petris again.

"So we're going out short-crewed," Heris said. She was not unhappy about it. "By civilian standards, that is. And overcrewed on the house-staff side, considering Lady Cecelia's guests this round." The prince had his own set of servants, and Cecelia insisted on adding another cook.

"Looks adequate to me, Captain," Petris said. He had worked up a crew rotation. "We could use two or three more, but—"

"But you're right, this is adequate. If we don't run into trouble, and if everyone works at Fleet efficiency. Which I expect you will. Something to consider is that we can hire replacements to fill out the list at Rockhouse Major. And we might think of hiring ex-Fleet personnel, while we're about it."

"Are you looking for trouble, Captain?" Petris's dark eyes twinkled.

"No. But I expect it anyway." A tap at her door interrupted. "Oh—that'll be Bunny's daughter Bubbles, I expect." She had forgotten, thanks to Gavin, that she'd agreed to talk to Bubbles after she went up to her room. "She's insisted on talking to me." Petris grinned at her expression.

"What—do you think she wants to come along?"

"Yes, and I can't let her. And I don't like the role she's casting me in."

"You'll do her no harm," Petris said.

"That's what her father told me," Heris said, shaking her head. "I'll get back to you shortly." She closed the uplink, and turned to the door of her suite. The blonde girl she'd first seen passed out drunk on a couch in the yacht had changed beyond recognition, and although being in mortal danger changed most people, this was exceptional.

"Captain Serrano," the young woman said. She stood stiffly, as if in a parody of military formality.

"Yes—do come in. We had a small crisis aboard, and I was just dealing with it."

"I—if this is a bad time—" She had flushed, which made her look younger.

"Not at all. Between crises is an excellent time." Heris led the way to a pair of overstuffed chairs beneath the long windows, and gestured as she sat in one of them. "Have a seat."

The girl sat bolt upright, not her usual posture, and looked like a young officer at a first formal dinner. Heris wondered again what this was about. Her father had refused to give any hints; Heris's own experience was that when young people preferred to talk to a relative stranger, the topic was usually embarrassing—at least for the youngster. But she didn't know what, in the current state of the aristocracy, would be likely to provoke embarrassment. What "rules" could such a girl have broken—or be planning to break—when most of society's rules didn't affect her at all?

"I want to change my name," the girl said, all in a rush, as if it were a great confession. Heris blinked. She would never have allowed herself to be called Bubbles in the first place, and she could understand why the girl would want to change . . . but not why anyone would object. Was this the big problem? Surely there was more.

"Bubbles doesn't really fit you," she said cautiously.

"No, not now." The girl waved that off as if it were trivial—which is what Heris thought it. "My full name's Brunnhilde Charlotte, and Raffa and I thought Brun would be a good version. But that's not the whole problem."

"Oh?"

"No—my parents are willing to give up Bubbles, though Mother would prefer some other variation, but it's the other part . . ."

The other part meaning what, Heris wondered. She sat and waited; youngsters usually told you more if you did.

"It's . . . the family name." Aha. That would cause a row, she could see. "I haven't told them yet, but I know they won't like it." They would more than "not like it" if she wanted to give up her family name; they would, Heris suspected, be furious and hurt. The girl—Brun, she tried to think of her now—went on. "It's just that I've always been Bubbles, Bunny's daughter—Lord Thornbuckle's daughter—and not myself. I feel—different now. When we were in the cave—" Ah, thought Heris. The rapid personal maturation by danger has left behind the social immaturity. "—I realized I didn't feel like who I was. I mean, I felt different, and it didn't match." She took a deep breath and rushed through the rest. "I want to change my name and go into the Regular Space Service and learn how to really do things and find out who I am."

Heris blinked again, remembering her own impulse (quickly squashed) to change her name and apply to the Academy not as a Serrano but purely on her own merits. She had even made up a name and practiced the signature. The silly romanticism of youth—or, if you looked at it another way, the integrity and courage.

"And you thought I could help you?" she said, keeping her reactions to herself.

"Yes. You know how things work—and you could take me to someplace I could enlist."

Now the problem was how to say no without shutting the girl off completely.

"How old are you?" Heris asked. "And what kind of background would you offer the Fleet?" She already suspected the answers. Brun was too old to enlist with the skills she could reasonably claim—having been taught marksmanship by your father didn't count, even if he was a renowned hunter—and lacking any education the Fleet would recognize. At least, under an assumed name. "Which will get you in trouble anyway," Heris explained. "After all, plenty of people the Fleet doesn't want would like to get in. Falsifying one's identity is fairly common—and nearly always detected, and when detected is always justification for rejection."

"But I thought if I explained that I just don't want to use my father's privilege—"

"To whom would you explain? A recruiting officer? That would get you sent for psychiatric and legal evaluation—are you impersonating a member of your father's family? And if not, what's wrong with you that you don't enjoy your privilege? No—" She held up her hand. "I see your point, and I admire you for wanting to make your own way, but you cannot sneak into the Fleet that way. Not with our methods of certifying identity. You'd do better, if you're intent on a dangerous military career, to travel as a tourist outside the Familias Regnant and take service with some planetary ruler. Don't try to be fancy—just say you're running away from family problems. Someplace like Aethar's World or the Compassionate Hand would probably hire you."

"But Aethar's World is all . . . those hulks, isn't it?"

"Soldiers can't afford prejudice," Heris said with an internal grin. She'd thought that would get a reaction. "Aethar's World always needs soldiers. Admittedly, that's because the

Fatherland uses them up in bloody and unnecessary battles, but they do give you a glorious funeral, I hear. And yes, they're all big-boned and fair-haired—one reason they might hire you—and they have anachronistic ideas about warrior women—another reason they might hire you. But they do pay on time, if you survive."

"And the . . . the Compassionate Hand?" asked Brun, her brow furrowed.

"Not an accurate name, but you don't want to call them the Black Scratch unless you've got a battle group behind you. A *large* battle group. You may not have heard of them; the Familias discourages trade that way. We have a border incident every few years, though. They would like to control Karyas and the nearby jump points."

"Black Scratch . . . Compassionate Hand?"

"Well, you know about protection rackets, don't you?" Brun nodded, but still looked puzzled. "The motto of the families that settled Corus IV-a was 'You scratch my back, and I'll scratch yours.' They referred to this as being a compassionate hand—a helping hand. But the first colony they raided, on Corus V, called it the 'black scratch.' They now control the Corus system, with heavy influence in two nearby systems, and their official designation is 'The Benignity of the Compassionate Hand.' They hire offworlders for mercenary actions, often against underground groups who still call them the Black Scratch."

"But they're—illegal," said Brun.

"Not by their laws, and they're not part of our legal system. From what I read of Old Earth history, their ancestors ran the same kinds of rackets there and no one ever converted them to what we call law and order. Actually, if you're on an official visit, it looks like a model government. I've known a few people who had served in their military—said it wasn't bad, if you followed the rules exactly, but they have no tolerance for dissent."

"You're saying I can't really do what I was talking about,"

Brun said. "If my choices run to the barbarians of Aethar's World or the Compassionate Hand—"

"There are others. But I'm not exactly sure what you're looking for. A military career? If so, leading to what? Coming back to your family someday, or retiring on your own independent savings? How much adventure—otherwise known as danger—do you really want? Do you have something against your family which would prevent your adventuring within its canopy?"

"Mmm." Brun looked thoughtful; Heris was glad to see that she could calm down and think. "I suppose—I want change. Change from what I was, and from what people think of me." She looked up at Heris, who said nothing. Let the girl work it out for herself; then she'd believe it. "Lady Cecelia crossed her family—but—she did use her own money—"

"Makes it easier," said Heris. "And there's no reason to do things the hard way if you don't have to."

"I don't know what, really," Brun said. "I guess I just want to serve notice to my family—to others—that I'm not the bubblehead they think—that I'm not the designated blonde sure to marry someone like the odious George." She grinned then. "And you're saying there are easier ways to do that than get myself killed by barbarians with blond braids or a knife in the ribs from the . . . er . . . Compassionate Hand."

"I didn't say it," Heris said. "You did. I'd think you'd had enough adventure for a while . . . although . . . if you liked that, there's training that would help you survive other . . . adventures."

Brun's face lit. "That's what I'd like—what bothered me most wasn't the danger, but not knowing what to do. But I thought you could only get that training in the military."

"No—in fact, not everyone in the military does. There are other sources, if that's what you want. Tell you what, I'll give you a list of skills and places I know you can get training . . . and then you can find a use for that training. How about that?"

"I'd love it. Can't I come to Rockhouse with you? I already know about Mr. Smith, of course."

"No—I'm sorry. We're overloaded, with the required escorts for Mr. Smith. But if you're going back there, you can start to acquire some of the things I'm talking about—"

"Tell me what sorts of things," Brun interrupted, eyes bright.

"Well . . . the more you know about all the technology we use for transportation and communication, the better. Not just classroom theory but practical stuff like being able to maintain and repair the equipment. Lady Cecelia's taken an interest in her yacht now, and she's finding it very helpful. I wish we had time for you to meet Brigdis Sirkin—my Nav First. She's done it all by formal schooling, but she's taken every opportunity to expand her skills and knowledge on the job, too."

From the look on Brun's face, she wanted to *be* Brigdis Sirkin. Heris wondered if Sirkin would return the favor, if she imagined the opulence and privilege of Brun's background. Probably not. That very practical young woman was headed exactly where she wanted to go—perhaps a narrow goal, but one she knew she could attain. Brun had so many choices it must be hard to make them.

"Do you like space travel?" Heris asked.

"Yes—but I don't know if I'd like to spend all my time in space." And this was someone who had thought of joining Fleet! "What I really like—liked—was thinking up elaborate pranks, but of course there's no place for that in the real world."

Was there not! Heris cocked her head. "What kind of pranks?"

"Oh—you know—like when we were kids on that island, and having mock wars." She had flushed again, clearly embarrassed to put her childhood mock wars up against the real thing, even in imagination. "I got pretty good at ambushes. And at school, my first term . . . they never did figure out who had reprogrammed the water supply so all the hot was cold and vice versa. Silly stuff. Except about Lucianne—keeping her away from her uncle when he came to visit was serious enough, but necessary."

It really was too bad that they couldn't take Brun along with them. She might have resources to match the prince's—she might keep Ronnie amused—and it would be fun to find out if she really did have a knack for innovative tactics. In Heris's experience, the people who created interesting pranks for the pranks' sake (not just to inconvenience people) often had good luck in real-life tactical situations. They just needed to be kept busy. For a moment her mind toyed with the idea of Brun as part of her crew—of talking Cecelia into some clandestine adventure somewhere—but she pushed it away. Getting the prince back to his father in one piece, and Ronnie with him, was enough to deal with for the moment.

"Tell you what," she said. "After we finish this mission, you might ask Lady Cecelia if she'd let you come along on a voyage or two. That's *if* you've been working on the things I'll list."

"Yes!" Brun grinned broadly. "I will—and thanks."

And what did I just get myself into? Heris asked herself. The girl's father had asked her to give advice—it wasn't as if she was going behind anyone's back—but she still felt odd about it. She made a note to herself to come up with that list of skills and resources before they left.

Their final head count came to forty-nine. Heris had had to accept a couple of Bunny's militia, and two crew from his personal yacht, to satisfy the Crown Minister that the prince would be travelling safely. When the *Sweet Delight* eased away from the peculiar eye-twisting space station, it had its holds stuffed with supplies enough for a year-long voyage. Heris had had plenty of time to complete her list for Brun while waiting for the last luxuries to be ferried up from Sirialis.

Once the ship was on its way out of the system, Heris released the prince from his suite. She expected a tantrum, but the young man smiled at her, and asked the way to the gym. Heris wondered why he hadn't looked it up on his deskcomp, but perhaps princes didn't ever look things up for themselves.

Dinner that first night surpassed anything Lady Cecelia's cook had produced on the voyage out. Cecelia wore her amber and ivory lace; Ronnie and the prince both appeared in semi-formal dress. Heris had to admit they were handsome, as decorative as young roosters. She preferred Ronnie, whose recent adventures seemed to have settled him a bit. At least he never rose to the prince's obvious attempts to tease. The prince . . . she had not really been around him in the days of his captivity, and his brief appearance at the Hunt Dinner had given her no feel for his real personality. Now, at the dinner table, he looked the very picture of a prince, and yet she felt something missing. Not quite the same as Ronnie and George, who had been so difficult on the voyage out, but whose spoilt manners clearly overlay interesting minds. The prince, aside from a hectic energy that emerged as one stale joke after another, was . . . to put it plainly . . . boring. Heris, imagining him as a king in the future, could form only a blurry vision of someone dull and stolid, with an eye for the girls and a taste for wine and game, a stout middle-aged fellow who elbowed his cronies in the ribs but never quite got the point of stories.

Four days into the voyage back to Rockhouse, Ronnie brought up the prince's intellectual gaps in a private conversation with Heris and Cecelia. He looked earnest and worried. "Did you know the prince was stupid?"

Heris nearly choked, and Cecelia let out an unladylike snort before she controlled herself and glared at her nephew.

"You are not going to start quarrelling with him. I forbid it."

Ronnie waved that away. "I'm not quarrelling. It's not like that. But I just realized—he's really stupid."

"Perhaps," his aunt said, looking down her longish nose, "you would care to explain that discourteous comment."

"That's why I'm here." Ronnie settled into his chair, leaning forward, hands clasped tensely. "I think something's wrong. We have to do something."

"That is not an explanation," Cecelia said crisply. "Please get to it."

"Yes. All right." He took a deep breath, and began. "We haven't been in the same classes or anything for years, or I'm sure I'd have noticed. He's just not very smart."

Heris repressed a smile. She had never expected royalty to be overburdened with brains. "Probably he never was very smart. Children can't really tell about each other—" But a memory lifted through her mind like a bubble . . . that boy who had been so brilliant in primary: she had known that, and so had all the other kids. She herself had been smart, but he had been something far more.

"He *was*," Ronnie said, with a return of his old sullenly stubborn expression. "He was, and now he's not. If I didn't know it was Gerel, I wouldn't believe it was the same person."

Cecelia sat up suddenly. "If you didn't know—how *do* you know it's the same person?"

Ronnie looked at her blankly. "Well, of course it is—how could it be anyone else? He's too well known."

"Now he is. But a child?"

"Gene types," Heris said, cutting off that wild idea. "It would be impossible to switch someone else; surely he has annual physicals. And it could be checked so easily . . ."

"That's right. He's a Registered Embryo." Ronnie wrinkled his nose. "And that's odd, too. Registered Embryos are at least one sig above average IQ." Heris looked at him; he turned red. "All right, we don't all act it, but we have the brains, if we learn to use them. Gerel wasn't stupid in childhood, and he's near that now. Something's happened to him."

Heris had an unpleasant crawling sensation in her midsection; she recognized fear of the unknown in the ancient form. Her forebrain didn't like it, either. Something to make princes stupid: it had been done before, and never with good intent.

"Someone must have noticed," she said slowly, wanting it to be false. But already she believed. Despite the physical beauty, the athletic body, the energy, the prince was dull.

"Some people wouldn't notice on principle," Cecelia said. "But his parents, surely . . . Kemtre wasn't that dim the last time I chatted with him. Admittedly that was ten years or so ago; I hate social functions where people expect me to be up on the latest Court gossip and I feel like a fool fresh off the farm. But we had a nice talk about the expansion of agricultural trade into the Loess Sector, and he seemed quite knowledgeable. Velosia, of course, was immersed in the gossip and wondered why I didn't spend more time with my sisters. I could believe this meant she was a dullard, except that she and Monica played dual-triligo and were ranked in the top ten. I never could understand the rules beyond primary level, so if they're stupid, I'm worse."

"Ten or twelve years ago, Gerel was just starting school outside the home for the first time," Ronnie pointed out. "What if something happened there, something that took a while to show up? We were only together for three or four years, then they shifted him to Snowbay and I stayed at Fallowhill." The names meant nothing to Heris, but Cecelia nodded.

"Or it could've started at Snowbay. I remember there was some concern about sending him so far away, to such a strict headmaster. But Nadrel had gotten in all that trouble—" Heris blinked again. She knew—it had been her business to know—the names of the various members of the Royal Family, but she wasn't used to anyone calling them by first names. Nadrel, the second son, had died when he eluded his Security protection and got himself into a brawl with someone who didn't worry about the niceties of aristocratic duelling. Before that, he had been considerably wilder than the current prince.

"I hadn't realized," Ronnie said, looking at his hands. "I feel . . . bad about it. It's sort of indecent, I mean—our quarrel, when he's not—not like he was. Like the time George had that virus or whatever, and nearly flunked everything for a month; we started out teasing him, but it wasn't funny."

"It's indecent that it happened, if you're right. The quarrel's beside the point, although I expect it influenced him." Heris fought her way through Cecelia's logic in that and by the time she had it figured out both aunt and nephew were off on another tangent. Whom to tell, and how, and when.

"Better not tell anyone," she said, interrupting them. "It's dangerous knowledge." They stared back at her.

"But I must," Cecelia said. "He's the only surviving prince. If his father doesn't know—"

"Then someone doesn't want him to know. Someone who will be glad to eliminate you. His father probably does know, after all, and I doubt very much he wants it widely recognized or talked about."

"I'm not a gossip. Everyone knows that." Cecelia looked exasperated. "It's not something I can ignore. If I do, and he knows, then he'll suspect—it will be worse than telling him."

"But it's dangerous," said Heris. Surely Cecelia could see that; it was like taking a light escort straight into a suspicious scanfield. They needed to know more before anyone said anything. Her mind tickled her with something Ronnie had just said about George. George had had a month of being stupid? A virus? Or the same thing that affected the prince? But Cecelia, sticking to her own main interest, was talking again.

"They need to know. Even if it's dangerous, it's more dangerous to have him like this, unrecognized. Dangerous to everyone, not just to me. It can't be hidden much longer anyway; he's getting to an age where he'll be expected to take on some Crown functions. The sooner it's known, the sooner we—" This time the *we* clearly meant those who managed things, the great families of the realm, "—can change our plans and adjust. If it's permanent, for instance, he can't take the throne later. Then there's the Rejuvenant/Ageist split; this could change the balance in Council."

"But it'll be terribly embarrassing, Aunt Cecelia," said Ronnie. "Maybe Captain Serrano is right—"

But Heris could tell from the stubborn set of Cecelia's jaw that they weren't getting anywhere. Maybe later. They were still a long way from Rockhouse. She could talk to Ronnie about George's experience in private.

The ship itself functioned smoothly. Sirkin had looked startled the first time she heard Oblo say "Aye, sir" to Heris, but she soon got used to the preponderance of military backgrounds. Heris thought it improved the tone a lot; it seemed a comfortable compromise between military formality and civilian casualness. Bunny's yacht crew, efficient enough, held themselves slightly aloof from Lady Cecelia's; she didn't mind, since they'd be going back to Bunny's from Rockhouse.

Her relationship with Petris, however, seemed as uneven as the foxhunting fields. She had understood the prohibition of relationships between commanders and their subordinates as preventing both sexual harassment of subordinates and favoritism . . . it had not occurred to her that there was any intrinsic problem with the relationship if both desired it. She learned differently.

"I don't know," Petris said one late watch, when they had expected a pleasant evening in bed, and instead found themselves less interested in bed than talk. "It's not the past, really. I'd been crazy about you for a long time, and once I found a way—but on this ship—"

"It's the teal and lavender," Heris said, trying to make light of it.

"No. It's—how can I say this and not sound like a barbarian?—it's the authority. Here, you're in charge—you have to be. And—" Heris waited out a long silence as he worked his way through it. "When we were back on that island, you weren't. You were hurting, and I could help. I had the choices to make."

"Mmm. An authority block?"

"I suppose. Except I've never resented your authority, you know. Not with the ship. It never has bothered me who captained a ship, so long as they were good at it. I knew early on I never would . . . didn't really want to." That surprised her.

"Didn't you?"

"No. Not all enlisted are lusting for command, you know.

Commanders maybe, but not command itself. It's damned scary; I can see that in your eyes. Maybe I feel that way here—it's scary, because I'm stepping out of my role, with the commander. It didn't bother me off the ship . . ."

"And it's not something I can command," Heris said. Some did; she knew that. But she couldn't. "How about we pretend this isn't the ship?"

"I'll try." It seemed to be working—Heris had felt the shifts in her own breathing that went with great pleasure long deferred—when the intercom intruded.

"Captain Serrano—there's something on the screen—" She lunged across Petris to answer it, and he cursed.

By the time she'd been to the bridge, where the image onscreen had vanished, and gotten back to her quarters, Petris was gone. Heris didn't call him back. Later. There would be time enough later.

✧ Chapter Two

Nothing had been settled—not about the prince, not about Petris—when the *Sweet Delight* made its last jump. They came out of the anomalous status of jump space precisely where Sirkin had intended, for which Heris gave her a nod of approval. She wished Sirkin hadn't had a lover waiting at Rockhouse Major—she'd have liked to keep her as crew.

"Somebody flicked our ID beacon," Oblo said. "Stripped it clean and fast: R.S.S., I'd say, remembering the other side . . ."

"We're not fugitive," Heris said. "And they'd be looking for the *Sweet Delight*, considering . . ."

"Mmm. Wish we had better longscans and a decoder that could do the same. Feels all wrong to have someone stripping our beacon when we can't strip theirs."

"Mass sensors show a lot of ships," Sirkin put in. "And the delays are too long to tell me where they are now—"

"That's what I meant," Oblo said. "Now in the Fleet, we've got—" He broke off suddenly as Heris cleared her throat, and looked up at her. "Sorry, Captain. I'm used to being on the inside of security, not outside."

"We'd all best be careful, if we want to stay outside a prison, and not inside," Heris said. The only bad thing about Sirkin—and Bunny's crew—was this tension between what the ex-military crew knew and what they weren't supposed to know and couldn't share with shipmates. It would have been easier if they'd all been her former crew members.

She had sent off a message when they first dropped out of FTL, with the codes given them by the Crown Minister. Now the system's outer beacons blipped the first response.

"Captain, *Sweet Delight*, proceed on R.S.S. escort course—" and the coordinates followed.

Oblo whistled. "They're putting us down the dragon's throat, all right."

"What?" Sirkin asked.

"Escort course is the fastest way insystem; eats power and makes a roil everyone in the whole system can pick up. Hardly what I'd call discreet. All other traffic gives way, and we're snagged by a tug that could stop a heavy cruiser, in a counterburn maneuver. Plus, we go past the heavy guns and damn near every piece of surveillance between us and Rockhouse."

Heris glared at him, and Oblo actually flushed. He knew better, and she had already warned him. Sirkin wasn't military, had never been military, wasn't ever going to be military, and he had no business explaining Fleet procedure to her. But he had a thing for neat-framed dark-haired girls, whether they liked men or not, and he had taken a liking to Sirkin.

They were only halfway home, as Cecelia put it, when the escorts pulled up on either side. R.S.S., both of them; Heris got an exterior visual and grinned. She had once captained one of these stubby, peculiar-looking ships; ridiculously overpowered, designed for fast maneuvers within a single system, their small crews prided themselves on "flair." On distant campaigns, they traveled inside podships, even though they mounted FTL drives.

The voicecom board lit. Heris flicked the lit buttons, and then a sequence which informed the caller that she had no secured channel.

"Ahoy, *Sweet Delight*. R.S.S. Escort *Adrian Channel* calling—"

"Captain Serrano, *Sweet Delight*," Heris said.

"You don't have any kind of secure com?" At least that showed some discretion; she'd been afraid they'd ask in clear if she had the prince aboard.

"Negative."

"Well . . ." A pause, during which Heris amused herself by imagining the comments passing between the two escorts and their base. Then the voice returned. "We understand you have urgent need for priority docking at Rockhouse Major. Is that correct?"

"Yes, it is," Heris said. "The relevant enabling codes were in my initial transmission—"

"Yes, ma'am. Well, ma'am, we're here just to see you make a safe transit, and chase any boneheaded civvie that doesn't listen to his Traffic Control updates out of your way. Our instruments show you on course—" Oblo scowled at that; with him on the board there was no question of being off course.

The counterburn maneuver, when it came, strained the resources of the *Sweet Delight's* artificial gravity; dust shimmered in the air and made everyone on the bridge cough. For one moment Heris felt nausea, then her stomach ignored the odd sensations. Others were not so lucky. She saw a medic light go on in the prince's stateroom, and in the galley.

Then the internal gravity stabilized again; the tug's grapple snagged the yacht's bustle, and Petris shut down their drive. Far faster than a commercial tug, the R.S.S. ship shoved them toward Rockhouse Major, and put them in a zero-relative motion less than 100 meters away from the docking bay. Visuals, boosted several magnifications, showed the Royal Seal above their assigned bay, and the gleaming sides of a Royal shuttle and a larger, deepspace yacht twice the size of *Sweet Delight*. Grapples shot out, homing on magnetic patches on the yacht's hull. These would stabilize, but not change, their inward drift under docking thrusters. Heris had always enjoyed docking maneuvers, and the chance to show off at a Royal berth delighted her. She eased the yacht in, with neither haste nor delay, until the grapples were fully retracted and the hull snugged against the access ports.

Until this moment, she had spoken with the Rockhouse Major Sector Landing Control—a professional exactly like any other landing control officer—and their exchanges were limited to the necessary details of bringing the yacht in. Now another channel lit on the board. Heris took a steadying breath. This would be a very different official, she was sure—and even after hours reading everything Cecelia's library had on Royal protocol, she wasn't sure she would get it right. Once, she could have relied on the military equivalent, but as a civilian captain—

"Royal Security to the captain of *Sweet Delight*—"

"Captain Serrano here," she said.

"We need to establish a secure communications link before your passengers debark; we'll need hardwire access. Open the CJ-145 exterior panel next to the cargo access, please."

At least he'd said "please." For a moment she was surprised that they knew which panel to use, but of course they would: the yacht was a standard design, built at a well-known yard. They'd had weeks to get all the specs.

"Just a moment, please," she said. She nodded at Oblo, who put the relevant circuits up on a screen, and cut out all but the communications input. No reason to give them easy access to Cecelia's entire system, just in case they were of a mind to strip that, too. When he grinned at her, she popped the latch and waited while Security set the link up.

And after all that, the formalities were no different than docking at any fairly large Fleet base. Mr. Smith—the prince—had spoken to Security from his suite, she presumed in some code. She herself admitted the Royal Security team (one technician in gray, the others in dress blues, a major commanding) who would escort the prince down to the planet. No one seemed to expect any protocol from her that she didn't already understand.

But when the prince came into the lounge, Lady Cecelia was with him. Her maid followed, with a small travel case in her hand. The prince's servants, behind the maid, filled the passage with luggage.

"I'm going with him," Cecelia said. Heris, who hadn't

expected this, stared at her. Cecelia pulled herself to her full height, and looked every millimeter the rich, titled lady she was. "The Crown Minister gave me the responsibility—"

"But madam . . . we're Royal Security." The major looked unhappy, as well he might.

"Very well. Then you can make sure that I also reach groundside safely."

"But our orders were to take . . . er . . . Mr. Smith . . ."

The red patches of incipient temper darkened on Cecelia's cheekbones. "Your sacred charge, young man, is the personal safety, the life itself, of your prince. If you think *I* endanger it, you are sadly mistaken about the source of danger. I suggest you need to have a long talk with the Crown Council. I went out of my way, at my own expense, to bring this young man safely home from a life-threatening situation. It might be asked where you, the Royal Security, were when he was being shot at!"

"Shot at!" Clearly this man had not heard the whole story. Heris wished Cecelia had not said so much; she'd assumed they would know already. "But he was on a training mission, with military guard—"

Cecelia glared. "Perhaps your superior will, if you prove discreet, tell you the full truth later. Suffice it to say that my honor, and my family's honor, are involved in this, and I will witness Mr. Smith's return to his father myself. You will find that his father agrees, should you care to take it that far."

"Yes, madam." The Security man still looked unhappy, but resigned. Exactly what she wanted.

"I will not require my maid's attendance, since I expect to travel directly to my brother's residence once I've spoken to the king. I am ready." She glanced back, to find Gerel and his luggage in the passage behind her, took her small case from her maid, and stepped forward.

The Royal shuttle eased into atmosphere with hardly a shiver in its silken ride. Four Royal Aerospace Service single-seaters flanked it, and another pair led it in. The prince sprawled in a wide seat, looking glum. Cecelia divided her glances between the viewports—she had always liked watching planetfall—and the Security men, who avoided meeting her gaze. She enjoyed the excellent snack a liveried waiter served her. The prince, she noticed, waved it away, and the Security men drank only water.

Two flitters waited on the landing field. Both dark blue, both with the Crown Seal in gold and scarlet. Honor guards stood by both. Cecelia snorted to herself. It wasn't going to work; she would see to that.

Sure enough, Security steered the prince toward one flitter, and attempted to lead her to the other. She strode on after the prince.

"Gerel—wait a moment." He paused, and looked back almost blankly.

"Yes, Lady Cecelia?"

"You're too fast for an old woman," she said, grinning at him. "Ronnie knows to slow down for me."

He smiled. She saw no malice in his smile, but no great intelligence either. What had gone wrong? How could the king not know? "I'm sorry," he said. "I was just thinking of being home."

"But sir," one of the Security men said. "We're supposed to take you home, and Lady Cecelia to her—"

"I told you," Cecelia said, still smiling, "I'm going with Gerel. It is a matter of honor." To her surprise, Gerel nodded.

"Yes, it is. A matter of honor." And he held out his arm for her. Whatever had blunted his intelligence had not ruined his manners. Here, she saw no sign of the hectic energy, the tension that had led him to such stupid outbreaks at Sirialis. Through the flitter ride, he sat quietly, not fidgeting, and when they arrived at the palace landing field, he gave her his arm again on the way in. Although she had believed Ronnie before, Cecelia found herself even more worried about the prince now.

❖   ❖   ❖

"So, you see, I felt it necessary to come to you myself," Cecelia said, watching the king's face for any reaction. He had offered her one of the scarlet and gold striped chairs in his informal study, where she was both amused and delighted to see a picture of herself among the many others on one wall. It was one of her favorites, too, one the king had taken himself just as her horse sailed over a big stone wall.

The king looked tired. Rejuv had smoothed his skin, but he still had deep discolored pouches beneath his eyes. "I'm glad you did," he said. "Do you have any idea how many other people have noticed?"

"I'm not sure." Heris had warned her not to answer this question; she felt a warning flutter in her diaphragm. But this was the king; she had known him from boyhood. Surely she could trust him, though not his ministers. "I would guess that plenty of people know he can act like a silly young ass—but then so do many of them, my nephew Ronnie included."

"It's a difficult situation," the king said, toying with a stylus.

"You did . . . know something." Cecelia made that not quite a question. The king looked at her.

"We knew something. But—you will forgive me—it's not something I want to discuss."

Cecelia felt herself reddening. His tone, almost dismissive, irritated her. She was not some old busybody. Just because she hadn't accepted rejuvenation, he shouldn't assume her brain had turned to sand. It was this kind of attitude that made Ageists out of people who simply didn't want rejuv. He smiled, a gentle smile for a man of such power, and interrupted what she might have said.

"I do appreciate your coming to tell me yourself. It was thoughtful of you; I know you won't spread this around. And you're right, we must do something, soon. But at the moment, I'm not ready to discuss it outside the family. In the meantime, let's talk about you. You have a new captain and crew for that yacht of yours, I understand . . . and you've infected the

captain with your enthusiasm for horses . . ." Cecelia smiled
back, well aware that she had no way to force him to confi-
dences he didn't want to give. They chatted a few more minutes, then she took her leave.

The king stared at the picture of Lady Cecelia he had taken.
She was a good fifteen years older than he; he had taken that
picture in his youthful enthusiasm for photography, before he
realized that kings have no time for hobbies—especially not
hobbies that reveal so much about their interests and priorities. He had grown up a lot since then; the adolescent who
had admired her so openly, who had taken that picture and
sent her a print with a letter whose gushing phrases he still
recalled, had learned to mask his feelings—had almost learned
to feel only what suited the political reality.

She had not matured the same way, he thought. She still
rode her enthusiasms as boldly as she had ridden horses; she
said what she thought, and damn the consequences. She felt
what she felt, and didn't care who knew it. Immature, really. A
slow comfort spread through him, as he finally grasped the
label that diminished her concern to a childish fretfulness, an
undisciplined outburst of the sort he had long learned to forego.
Deep inside, his mind nagged: she's not stupid. She's not crazy.
She's right. But he smothered that nagging voice with ease; he
had quit listening to his conscience a long time ago.

Heris had plenty to do while waiting to hear from her
employer, but she could not banish the chill she felt. She had
to get all the crew properly identified for Royal Security; not
even Bunny's crewmen, who had been there before, and were
only passing through on the way downplanet, could leave the
Royal Docks without a pass. Heris put them first in the identification queue, and within a few hours they were on their
way downplanet to Bunny's estate on Rockhouse. Then there
was the usual post-docking business: arranging for tank
exchange, for recharging depleted 'ponics vats, for lines to

the Station carbon-exchange tanks (waste) and water (supply). It would be hours yet before Cecelia's shuttle would land, before she could reach the king, before whatever would happen could happen.

But the knot in her belly remained; she barely picked at the delicious lunch the two cooks produced. Something would go wrong. She knew it. She just couldn't figure out what it would be.

By the time Cecelia called, Heris had dug herself into a nest of clerical work. She had almost forgotten why she was so tense. Cecelia called up from the surface, with such a cheerful, calm expression that Heris had to believe everything had gone well. She did not, on a commercial communications channel, mention the prince. Instead, she chattered about refitting.

"I've discussed matters with the family, and my sister has agreed not to be offended if I have *Sweet Delight* redecorated to fit my tastes instead of hers. It really was generous of her to do it before, but as you know, lavender and teal are not colors I'm fond of. We've had a dividend payout, from some business, and I can easily afford to redo it. I'll be up in a few days; you'll have to move the ship to a refitting dock over on the far side of Major—at least that's the one I'm leaning towards. Even though I didn't like the colors, they did a good job last time. I'll bring the preliminary plans with me, and if you'd supervise—"

"Of course," Heris said. For a moment her original estimate of rich old ladies resurfaced. How could she think only of redecoration at such a time? But something about Cecelia's eyes reassured her. Something else was going on than changing the color of carpet and upholstery. "Have any idea how long it will take?"

"A few weeks, last time. Presumably about the same this time, although restocking the solarium may take longer. I've missed my miniatures—"

"Ummm . . . but milady, you said you wanted to be at Zenebra for the horse trials . . ."

"I know, but if I have a choice between missing the Trials one time and living with that lavender for the weeks between here and there, and then however long it takes to get to refitting, I'm willing to miss the Trials. And we'll have plenty of time to make the big race meetings after the Trials. A friend has asked me to look for replacement bloodstock."

"Ah. I see. Very well, milady, as you ask. If you could tell me when to expect you back . . . ?"

"Not tomorrow or the next day. Perhaps the day after. I'll put a message on the board for you; I should be able to find my way from the shuttledock to the ship by myself."

Unwise, Heris thought. Very unwise. But she could have an escort there if Cecelia told her which shuttle she was taking. "If you're going to delay for redecoration, milady, there are a few other equipment changes I'd like to suggest."

Cecelia didn't even ask questions. "Quite all right. Whatever you want. This time let's do it all, so there's nothing to worry about for *years.*"

Heris wondered if she'd gotten a refund from Diklos & Sons—or would it be the insurance? She wasn't sure just how the refitters would be made to pay for that fraudulent, almost-fatal job they didn't do, but Cecelia could get solid credits out of them if anyone could. She somehow didn't believe in the dividend payout—not at this odd time of year. Cecelia probably didn't realize that midlevel officers could have investment experience too. When Cecelia cut the link, Heris turned to Petris and Oblo.

"You heard that. You know what we need. Go find me the best deals on it, will you? I spent too much of her money buying those small arms on Sirialis."

"Good weapons, though," Petris said. He had, of course, tried them out. "Fancied up, but quality."

"Well, now I want quality without any fancying up. Whatever's legal—"

"Legal!" That was Oblo, of course. Then he sobered. "You mean, not stolen?"

"I mean legal, as in 'will pass inspection.'" Heris found she could not maintain the severity she wanted. A grin puckered the corner of her mouth. "All right . . . you know what I mean. Don't cause us trouble, but get us what we need."

"Yes, sir." Oblo saluted in the old way, and retreated from her office. Petris stayed.

"Is Lady Cecelia all right?" he asked.

"I hope so. I don't think she half understands the danger she could be in." Heris's uneasiness had not faded, despite Cecelia's assurances.

"Of course," the Crown Minister said, "if someone had to notice, Lady Cecelia de Marktos is the safest . . . she's not a gossip like most of them."

His sister, demure in her long brocaded gown, said nothing. True, Lady Cecelia was not a gossip. Her danger lay in other directions. Perhaps Piercy would figure it out for himself.

"It's a nuisance, though. If she did take it into her head to mention it to someone, they might pay attention, precisely because she's known to be no gossip." Ah. He had realized the danger. "I wonder if that scamp Ronnie knows. The king didn't say—"

"If Ronnie knew, Cecelia would have told the king," his sister said. Always argue the point you oppose; people believe what they think up for themselves.

"I suppose. He might not have told me, though. And the idiot—" Only here, in this carefully shielded study, did the Crown Minister allow himself to speak of the king this way. Here it had begun to seem increasingly natural; his sister radiated neither approval nor disapproval, merely acceptance. "That idiot didn't even record the conversation. Said it would have been a breach of manners and trust. Said of course Lady Cecelia was loyal. And she is, I've no doubt." But people said "I've no doubt" when their doubts were just surfacing. He knew that now. His sister had taught him, gently, over the years.

"It must have been upsetting for her, and yet exciting in a way," she said. At his quizzical expression, she explained, her delicate voice never rising. "Of course she worried—she has a warm heart under her gruff manner, as we all know. Look at the way she took on young Ronnie after his . . . troubles. But at the same time . . . she's always thrived on excitement. To be the one who brings important news—even bad news—must have made her feel important. And it's been so long since she won any of those horse trials."

"Well, but Lorenza, she's over eighty. And she won't take rejuvenation."

"Quite so." Lorenza studied her fingernails, exquisitely patterned in the latest marbleized silver and pale pink. Piercy would, in time, realize the problem and its necessary solution. He wasn't stupid; he just had the soft heart of a man whose every comfort had been arranged for years by a loving and very efficient sister.

Ordinarily, she never intervened; she felt it was important for him to feel, as well as appear, independent of any influence from his family. She had her own life, her own social activities, which kept her out and about. But in this instance, she might do him a favor, indulge his softheartedness by taking on the task—not in this instance unpleasant at all—of removing the threat of Lady Cecelia de Marktos and her unbridled tongue.

You stupid old bitch, she thought, making sure to smile as she thought it. *I always knew the time would come . . . and now you're mine.* Still smiling, still silent, she poured Piercy a cup of tea and admired the translucency of the cup, the aroma, the grace of her own hand.

"Here you are," she said, handing it to him. He smiled at her, approving. He had never seen her contempt for him; he never would. If necessary he would die, but he would die still believing in her absolute devotion. That small kindness she had promised him. She promised none to Cecelia. Already her mind lingered on possibilities . . . which would be best for her? Which would be worst for that arrogant loud-mouthed old bitch who had humiliated her all those years ago?

"I can't believe you're not taking this more seriously," Piercy said, reaching for a sandwich from the tray.

"Oh, I do, Piercy. But I know you and the king are quite competent to deal with any problems that might arise. Although, perhaps—I could keep my ear to the ground, among the ladies?"

"Bless you, Lorenza." He smiled at her. "If there's any gossip, you'll hear it."

There won't be, she thought. *Until they're all talking about what happened to poor dear Cecelia.*

"I want you to meet my captain, Heris Serrano," Lady Cecelia said. She wore tawny silk, a flowing gown with a flared collar, low boots, and jewels Heris hadn't seen before. She had arrived at the shuttleport in high good humor, and insisted that they go straight to the most prestigious of the yacht refitters. The woman behind the desk of Spacenhance flicked Heris a glance.

"Pleased, Captain Serrano."

"She's my agent for this project," Lady Cecelia said. "I have too much business groundside to be on call for the questions that always come up." Her puckish grin took the sting out of that. "I've told her what I want, and she knows the ship's capacity. You two settle everything, and let me know when it's done."

"Very well, milady," the woman said. "But we must have your authorization for credit—"

"Of course." Cecelia handed over her cube. "Heris has my power of attorney if you need more."

Heris tried not to stare . . . power of attorney? What was Cecelia up to? Or did rich people typically give power of attorney to ship captains when they didn't want to be bothered?

"Well, then," the woman said. "You're fortunate that you called when you did . . . we happen to have a slot open at the moment. Bay 458-E, North Concourse. Do you have a storage company in mind, Captain Serrano, or shall I schedule removal and storage with one of our regulars?"

Heris had no idea which storage company was reputable; she wished Cecelia had given her more warning of what to expect. "Schedule it, please; if you would just tell me what you require—"

"It's in our brochure. We do ask specifically that the owner remove all valuables, organic and inorganic, under private seal. We ourselves seal all electronics components. Depending on the owner's decisions, some service areas may be sealed off and left intact. Quite often owners choose to leave the galley and food storage bays the same."

Heris took the datacards, the hardcopies (the cover of one, she noted, showed the *Sweet Delight*'s earlier redecoration, unless teal and lavender and spiky metal sculptures were everyone's taste).

"Let's have lunch at Shimo's," Cecelia said cheerily, as they swept out of the Spacenhance office. The last thing Heris wanted was a fancy meal at that most expensive and exclusive of Rockhouse Major restaurants. If she was supposed to move the ship, and prepare for storage of all the furniture and personal items, she needed to get back aboard. And where would the crew stay? But from the look on Cecelia's face, she would get no more information until her employer had some food.

Shimo's was just what she feared: fashionably dressed ladies of all ages, and a few obviously wealthy men, all tucked into the intricate alcoves that surrounded a lighted stage on which live musicians played something that made Heris's nerves itch. Cecelia fussed over the menu far more than usual, and finally settled on what Heris thought of as typical ladies' luncheon fare. It was very unlike her. She waited, less patient than she seemed, for Cecelia to explain what was going on.

"The Crown is paying for it; it's my reward for bringing the prince home. That's why there's a berth open at Spacenhance." Cecelia spoke softly, between mouthfuls

of the clear soup she had ordered. Heris sipped her own
warily, wondering why Cecelia had chosen this public
place to talk about it. The alcoves had privacy shields,
but she doubted they were effective against anything but
the unaided ears of those in the next alcove. "I told them
I didn't want a reward, but Council doesn't want an unpaid
debt to my family right now. I'm not sure what's going
on . . . but Ronnie's father isn't happy. Meanwhile, I'm
undoing the damage done during the annual business
meeting—changing my registered proxy, moving assets
around." She grinned at Heris. "Nothing for you to worry
about. I don't walk down dark alleys at night; I'm spending hours in business offices, and then going home to my
sister's town house."

"But you don't have anyone with you."

"Only lawyers, accountants, clerks, the odd section head,
salespeople when I shop, and the entire staff of the house.
And the family." From the sound of Cecelia's voice, these were
annoyances.

"Milady." Heris waited until she was sure Cecelia had caught
the tone. "Considering what Ronnie said about Mr. Smith—
and if anyone should care if it's known, you're the one most
likely to have noticed—don't you think some precaution is
warranted?"

Cecelia huffed out a lungful of air, and looked thoughtful. Heris waited. In this place where anyone might have
heard what they said, she dared not press her argument.
Finally Cecelia shook her head. "I think not. And if I should
fall dead of a heart attack or even a street assault, I would
prefer you consider that the natural end of a long, eventful
life. I am, after all, over eighty—all original parts, no rejuv.
There is no advantage to be gained by killing me. I'm not
political. For all that I grumbled about my proxy, and made
some changes, I have little to do with the family business,
and they know it. I have no children whose plans would
change were I a hostage. Besides, if—and I think it's

unlikely, remember—*if* someone has designs on me, there is no way to tell without awaiting a move."

"You could wear a tagger."

"Detectable, is it not, by anyone with the right equipment? Which means that the very persons you most fear would be first to know, and—should they wish—disable it."

That was true. Yet Heris was sure that Cecelia didn't realize her peril; she had lived her entire life in privilege, safely sheltered from any violence she didn't herself choose. That she had chosen a dangerous hobby still did not prepare her for attack. She could say she wasn't political, but what else could her report to the king be called?

"You are coming back to the ship this afternoon, aren't you? Perhaps we can talk—"

"No." That was firm enough; the red patches on her cheeks gave additional warning. "No . . . I think it best that I not come aboard right now."

"But—"

"Captain Serrano—" That formality stung; Heris stared and got back a warning look. "Please. Do this my way. I am not stupid, and I have my reasons."

Did this mean she was worried about the Crown's response, or was something else going on? Heris couldn't tell, and she realized Cecelia was not about to discuss it. They finished the meal in near silence.

"Captain Serrano?" Heris looked up; she had headed back to the yacht's berth still concentrating on Lady Cecelia's odd behavior. The woman who'd spoken had a soft voice and sleepy green eyes. Her hair, chopped short by some unpracticed hand, had once been honey gold, and her face might have been attractive before something cut a broad slash down one side. But it was the voice that stopped Heris in her tracks.

"Methlin Meharry—Sergeant Meharry!" Petris had not known what had happened to the women who'd been court-martialed, although he'd heard rumors. And none of them had contacted Heris after the amnesty Cecelia had arranged. Until now.

"Didn't know if you'd remember," the woman said. She held herself with the same pride as always, but she wasn't in uniform, and Heris couldn't read her expression. Did she know that Heris hadn't known about the courts-martial, or was she still as angry as Petris had been? "Arkady Ginese said you would—"

"Of course I do. But—I was told you'd all been reinstated, with back pay and all—"

Meharry spat. "If they can screw us once, they can do it again. I've got sixty days to think about it, and what I think is I never want to see the inside of another Fleet brig, thank you very much. Arkady said you were hiring."

Heris's mind scrambled. She couldn't hire everyone who had suffered on her behalf; not even Cecelia had that much money, or that large a ship. But Meharry—an unusual set of specialties, she'd started with ground troops and gone on to shipboard weapons systems. "I need a weapons specialist, yes. Ideally someone who can do bodyguard work on Stations or onplanet. And ideally a woman, since Lady Cecelia's the one who'll need guarding. Was that what you wanted?"

Meharry shrugged. "Sounds good to me. Anything would, after that. You know, Captain, we were upset with you." Upset was a ludicrously mild expression. Heris nodded.

"So you should have been. I thought I was keeping you out of worse trouble, and all I did was take my protection away from you. Biggest mistake I ever made."

Meharry cocked her head. "Not really, Captain. Biggest was being born a Serrano, begging your pardon. I should know, given my family." The Meharry family was almost as prominent in Fleet enlisted ranks as the Serranos in the officer corps. "Families get your judgment all scrambled sometimes. But that's over with. Point is, I don't want to go back in, and if you trust me, I'll trust you. You're not a bad commander." Heris almost laughed at the impudence. This was the perfect bodyguard for Lady Cecelia, if only she could persuade her employer.

"Right. Why don't you come aboard and look at what we've got. You may not like a yacht once you've seen it."

Meharry grinned; the scar rippled on her cheek and gave her a raffish look. "Why not? It's built on a good hull, Arkady says, and you're giving it some teeth."

"True, but not for publication. Come on, then, and let's see what you think."

On one side of her mind, Heris thought how glad she was to be out of that ridiculous purple uniform—she could just imagine Meharry's reaction to that garish outfit. On the other side, she thought of the balance of her crew. With Methlin Meharry to back Arkady Ginese, she would need only one more person to serve the ship's weapons in a short combat—the only kind she intended to be involved in. Ships the size of *Sweet Delight* didn't get into slugfests with other ships—not if their captains had sense. But she wouldn't have to depend on Bunny's loans, even though they seemed happy enough to be with her. Yet—the ship was becoming more Fleet with every change she made. And she wasn't sure Cecelia would like it.

Back at the ship, Meharry grinned at Petris and Oblo, who just happened to be lurking around the access tube.

"Found her, did you?" Petris said to Heris.

"Was I looking?" Heris asked mildly. She had the feeling she'd been outmaneuvered by all of them, a feeling intensified when Arkady happened to be in the passage between the bridge and the number four storage bay. He grinned at her, too.

"I hope you don't mind, Captain," he began. Courteous always, even when cutting your throat, one of his former commanders had said. "I happened to see Meharry's name on a list of those returning from . . . er . . . confinement—"

"Glad you did," Heris said. "And I remember you two worked well together. Why don't you show her around, and let her find out if she wants to stay."

An hour later, on the bridge, Meharry and Ginese were deep in consultation on the control systems of the weapons already installed. Heris called Petris into her office.

"Suppose you tell me just how many more little surprises you people have cooked up. I'm delighted about Meharry, but there's a limit, you know."

"If we crewed entirely with former R.S.S. personnel, we wouldn't have to worry about the official secrets people jumping on us," he said. Heris frowned; she was always wary when Petris went indirect. It meant he was trying to outflank her somewhere.

"Numbers," she said, flicking her fingers at him. "I'm not objecting to former Fleet personnel, but I do need numbers."

"I was going to ask you that," he said. "What do you think we need, for what Lady Cecelia's going up against? These smugglers—how likely are they to attack and with what force? What kind of protection do we need to be able to give her where she visits? Can't plan the necessary force until we know the mission."

"I wish I knew," Heris said. "One of the things bothering me is lack of good information. I know there are information networks in the civilian world, but I haven't made my connections yet. And I'm used to having Fleet intelligence to work with—bad as it sometimes was."

"Ummm. You might want to switch Oblo over from Navigation to Communications—reorganize the roster that way—and let him poke around. You know his talents."

She did indeed. They did not appear on any official list of occupational skills.

"He wants to put in some . . . er . . . equipment he sort of found the other day."

Heris felt the hair rising on the back of her neck.

"Found?"

"In a manner of speaking. In return for . . . mmm . . . certain services." That could mean anything, up to and including a discreet killing. "Good stuff," Petris went on, with a wicked grin that made her want to clout him. "Navigational aids. Communication enhancements. He'd like to put it in when no civilians—I mean, those who've always been—are aboard. Just in case."

She couldn't ask if it was stolen Fleet equipment, not directly. Petris would have to answer, and she'd have to do something about it—or he'd have to lie, which would be another problem.

"How much is it costing Lady Cecelia?" she asked instead. Might as well find out.

"Nothing. It's between Oblo and . . . er . . . someone who wanted him to do something. A private donation, you might call it. Are you hiring Meharry?"

"If she wants to come. We need another weapons specialist."

"Good. And how are you going to get hooked into the civilian network?"

"By checking in with the Captains' Guild," Heris said. "If that's a hint." She'd spend some time browsing the general databases, too. Her understanding of politics had been limited to what impinged on the military—on funding, on procurement, on what the admirals optimistically called grand strategy. She'd never heard of some of the groups Cecelia and Ronnie had mentioned. Ageists? Rejuvenants? The meanings seemed obvious, but what did these groups actually do?

✧ Chapter Three

Her new uniform clashed with the lavender and teal, but no longer made Heris feel like an exotic bird. Severely plain midnight blue suited her, and the captain's rings on her sleeves were enough proof of her rank. Her pass to the royal docking sector hung from one lapel. She'd been advised to wear it even on the public concourse.

"Isn't that conspicuous?" she'd asked.

"Yes . . . but they'll expect you to be monitored, so they won't ask," the Royal Security officer said. "And by the way, you *are* being monitored. It's in the tag, so don't leave it somewhere or we'll have to do a full investigation, and we hate that." His tone said they'd take it out of her hide somehow.

"Fine with me," Heris said. It wasn't, but it wouldn't do any good to argue. What she intended to do was aboveboard anyway. She wanted to report her dismissal of some former crew to the employment agency, with her reasons, and find out if Sirkin's friend had registered for employment yet. She would like to keep Sirkin, but that meant hiring her partner. She needed to check in with the Captains' Guild. And she needed to consult her banker; she didn't know if Cecelia had paid her salary yet. It had not seemed a good time to ask Cecelia directly.

Once out of the royal sector, she took the slideway past the exclusive shops and transferred to the tubetram for the ride to the outer rims. It was midshift of the second watch . . . the tram was half-empty, its other occupants a pair of obvious tourists, rich kids, and four quiet middle-aged men who looked like off-duty crew from a royal shuttle. Possibly they were.

They got off at Three, the tourists at Four, and she rode out to Six in splendid solitude.

Six, Sector Orange: back where she'd started, when she left Fleet. Now it didn't bother her the same way at all . . . not in the new uniform, not with the new understanding of what being Cecelia's captain meant. She stopped by the Captains' Guild, paid her onstation fee, smiled at the Warden.

"Do you want to list for posting?" he asked, his hand hovering over the board.

"No, I'm still with Lady Cecelia," she said. "Is there much demand?"

"There's always a demand for those with a clean record," he said. "Lots of people want to retire here. Anything to report?"

"No." Guild members were supposed to inform the Guild of unusual occurrences, including those that they might not want to report to the Fleet or other law enforcement. If you paid the pirates off, Fleet would want to be sure it wasn't a plot; the Captains' Guild simply wanted to know where the pirates had been and how they'd trapped you. Heris had considered whether to tell the Guild about the smugglers' operation on *Sweet Delight*—but Olin was a Guild member, too.

The Warden's brow rose, and he stared pointedly at her royal pass. *That* certainly wasn't the Guild's business. Heris smiled until he shrugged. "Want a room here?" he asked then.

"No, thank you. I'm staying aboard. But—can you tell me if Sagamir Olin is listed here?" She didn't expect the *Sweet Delight*'s former captain would cooperate with her, but she would try.

"Olin?" His eyes shifted aside. "You hadn't heard—? No, that's right; you left so fast. Olin . . . died. A . . . er . . . random assault."

"Random assault" didn't get that expression or that mumble. Heris felt her hairs prickling. Olin had been killed . . . why? Because he hadn't delivered the goods, or because he'd lost that handy ship, or both?

"When?" she asked.

"Oh . . . let me see." He muttered at his console, and then turned to her. "Five weeks after you left. He had been drinking, the militia said. A bar fight spilled over; someone got him on the way home. They said."

And you don't believe it, Heris thought, but you aren't going to explain it to me.

"Thanks anyway," she said. "I'd have bought him a drink . . . here, put this in the memorial fund."

His eyes widened, then he relaxed. "Ah . . . ex-Fleet. You people do that, don't you, whether you know someone or not?"

"That's right," Heris said cheerfully. "Hear of a death, put something in . . . there's always someone needs it."

"Well . . . thank you. It's very kind. I suppose we'd do well to follow that habit ourselves, but . . ."

"Never mind. I couldn't do any less." With a wave, she went back out before he could say more. Her mind was working too hard; he would see it on her face if she stayed. Where could she find out what had really happened without making herself conspicuous? She went on toward the banker and the employment agency. Chores first, fun later.

The employment agency turned out to be fun in its own way. Now that she wasn't a suppliant, the gray and white decor merely looked functional, not cold and threatening. The receptionist might have been sniffy, but not once he saw that Royal Sector pass. Ser Bryn could see her in an hour; perhaps she would prefer to come back? No? Then the private lounge . . . Heris accepted this offer, and settled into a comfortable chair to wait. The viewscreen and cube reader were supplemented by glossy hardcopies of periodicals.

"Captain Serrano." She looked up from an article advising prudent investors to be wary of unregistered companies offering investment in heavy-metal mining operations on worlds like Chisholm and Sakati. The article argued pure finance; Heris, who had been to Chisholm once, thought the influence of the Compassionate Hand there was more reason to keep clear of it. The only profits out of Chisholm would go straight to the Black Scratch. But the man standing at the door, she reminded herself, could as easily be a Compassionate Hand agent. Who *were* the smugglers?

"Ser Bryn?" She stood and extended her hand. He shook hers; she did not let herself glance down to see if he had the telltale tattoo on the thumb web. He wouldn't, not in this position. If he'd ever had it, it would have been redone in flesh tones when he was chosen for a position on Rockhouse.

"What can we do for you, Captain?" he asked, his voice cordial and his eyes guarded.

Heris smiled at him. "I needed to speak to you about Lady Cecelia's former employees." His eyes flickered; he didn't like the sound of that. And, of course, with the security measures on the Royal Docks, he wouldn't have heard about the new crew. "It's rather a long story," she said. "Perhaps we could discuss it privately?" The lounge where she'd been waiting had no one else in it, but she knew it would have full monitoring.

"Ah . . . yes, Captain. Do come along to my . . . er . . . private office." He led the way into a spacious, luxurious office, where Heris suspected wealthy clients gave their requirements for employees. It didn't look anything like the office where she'd been interviewed.

"I brought along a data cube with their records and my reports on them," she said. "But for the obvious reasons there are some details which I'd prefer not to have on cube, and which you need to know."

"Ah." That seemed to be his favorite response to possibly upsetting news. Safe enough.

"As you may or may not know, Ser Bryn, before I departed, I asked this office for any additional details on the qualifications of Lady Cecelia's existing crew. I was told there were none, and furthermore I was told that private employers such as Lady Cecelia were furnished with—I won't say *dregs*, because that would be insulting—but let's say with less quali- fied personnel than, for example, a major commercial

employer. The reasons I understood, if I didn't approve them."
She paused to see if he had any response. Beyond a tightening around his eyes, he gave none. She continued.

"With that, I had to be content. Unfortunately, events on
the voyage revealed how . . . imprudent . . . that policy was.
You may have heard from Takomin Roads about the death of
one environmental tech, Iklind?" At this he nodded, but still
said nothing. "Presumably you also heard that Iklind was considered to be responsible for the contraband found on the
ship. I myself am not sure that he alone was responsible. Surely
Captain Olin knew that the maintenance had not been per-
formed; I had intended to pursue his responsibility, but the
Guild tells me he's dead."

"Er . . . yes. Random assault, the militia said."

"Perhaps." Heris steepled her fingers and waited for the
twitch of muscles beside his mouth before she went on. "At
Takomin Roads, I found it necessary to relieve the pilot of his
duties—no great hardship, since a ship that size doesn't require
one, if the captain is qualified." She let that sink in, too—she
knew that the agency's recommendation on crewing had cost
Lady Cecelia at least two extra salaries. "You, of course, are
not responsible for the crew's astonishing lack of training or
fitness—that would be the captain's responsibility, and the
captain involved is dead. But at Sirialis, most of the remaining
employees tried to stage a mutiny."

"What!" That got a reaction. "What did you do to them?"

"I did nothing. They chose not to return to the ship after
spending time at Hospitality Bay—need I explain Hospitality Bay?" He shook his head; as she expected, such an
elite agency would know all about the amenities of Bunny's
planet. "They didn't want to work with an ex-military captain; they felt my precautions were excessive—and this after
the death of one crew member and the near death of
another. You are probably not aware that a simultaneous
crisis on Sirialis made Lord Thornbuckle suspect that they
might be politically motivated. Lady Cecelia accepted their

applications to terminate employment and they are currently in custody on Sirialis, where they will be tried for conspiracy."

"But—but who's crewing the ship now?" She could see the flicker of greed in his eyes. Surely she'd need more crew, and if she didn't get it here, she would enrich some other employment agency.

"I should mention," she went on, "that I'm extremely pleased with one former employee, Brigdis Sirkin. *That* young woman has what I consider adequate qualifications, and to the extent that Lady Cecelia wishes to make crew changes, that is the level of qualification I shall insist on." She waited until she saw that take effect, and then answered his question. "Presently, the crew consists of former R.S.S. personnel . . . I am not at liberty to discuss the exact way they . . . er . . . became employed. Only that it has both Fleet and Crown approval. However—none of them presently have civilian licenses. I shall be sending them here, where you can arrange for the transfer of skills registration and the appropriate civilian licensure into specialties . . . for your standard fee, of course. Unless you have some objection?"

Ser Bryn gulped. Her meaning was clear to both of them. He could get his firm the minimal profit involved in transferring registered military skills to civilian ones—the paper pushers' fees—in return for a chance to regain some chance of providing Lady Cecelia with employees later. Or, he could be difficult, and see that influence vanish—and possibly, considering who she was, more business vanish at the same time. Heris watched the glisten of perspiration on his forehead.

"We . . . we are always glad to help Lady Cecelia in any way we can," he said finally. "I hope, Captain Serrano, that you do not think *we* had any suspicion whatsoever that any persons we supplied would become involved in . . . er . . . illegal acts of any nature. We do our best to supply only the most qualified and responsible personnel."

Heris gave him her best grin, and watched him flinch from

it. "I'm sure you didn't," she said. "But from this time, Lady Cecelia will be understandably more . . . selective . . . in her dealings with you. She may be only one old lady, on one small yacht, but she pays well and deserves to have the best crew. So I've explained to her." She gave a short nod and turned to her second topic. "Now. Do you have a young woman named Yrilan—Amalie Yrilan—registered with the firm?"

"Just a moment." He slid out a drawer that Heris assumed contained a deskcomp link and poked at it. His next glance at her showed honest confusion. "Yrilan—yes, but—but she's not what you're looking for—not if what you just said—"

Heris turned her hands over. "Ser Bryn, even for me there are occasional personal matters that impinge on business. I assume from your statements that she is not as supremely qualified as, say, Sirkin?"

"By no means," he said.

"Would you have sent her to Lady Cecelia a year ago?"

"Well . . ." He had the grace to flush. "We might have. As an entry-level tech. It's not a demanding job, after all—" Not with the ship heavily overcrewed and underutilized.

"Then send me her application file, and send her for an interview. To the ship. I meant what I said, and I doubt I'll hire her if she's not up to my standards, but I might hear of another slot . . . and of course I would inform you, first." That got a nod of understanding and approval. "Thank you, then, Ser Bryn. I'll have the military personnel report to your office next mainshift—is that convenient?"

"Er . . . yes. And thank you, Captain Serrano."

From there, Heris decided to begin opening contacts with other ships' officers. Some of her former acquaintances in the R.S.S. would still speak to her, she thought, and the sooner she began networking again, the better.

Bryssum had always been a mixed bar, a place respectable officers of both Fleet and civilian ships could eat and drink in proximity if not friendship. Sometimes it was friendship, of sorts. She remembered, as a young officer, being treated to dinner by the captain of a great liner who had owed favors to Fleet. Now she was the civilian, finding a table on the civilian side, but not too near the windows. She didn't recognize any of the Fleet officers. It didn't matter. Her heart pounded, and she argued it back to a normal rhythm. It really did not matter. She had her ship; she had her place.

"Service, Captain?" Bryssum also had human service, unless you requested otherwise. She liked it.

"Yes," she said. "Mainshift menu." She glanced at the display, flinched inwardly at the prices, and chose a simple meal from among the day's specials.

"Heris!" She looked across to the tables kept by tradition for Fleet officers. A woman a few years her junior waved at her; she had clearly just walked in. Constanza D'Altini, she remembered. The man with her gave Heris an uncertain look. Who would that be, she wondered. Constanza always had someone . . . Heris grinned and nodded, but didn't rise. She couldn't appear too eager. Besides, Constanza had curiosity enough for the whole Intelligence department. After a quick conversation with her table partner, she came over to Heris. The man sat down alone, looking grumpy.

"I hate it that you're out," Constanza said. Along with curiosity, she had the tact and directness of a toppling tree. "It had to be a frame-up; rumor says Admiral Lepescu. Was it?"

"I can't talk about it," Heris said. Constanza's black eyes glinted.

"Not even to me?"

"Not even to you. But thanks for coming over."

"Word is you got amnesty, you and all the rest—"

"That are alive," Heris said. Until she said it, she had not expected to say it, or with that bitterness. But that was Constanza's effect on most people.

"Ah." A careful look. "So that's why you're not coming back?"

Heris made herself grin. "Connie, I've got a cushy job working for a very rich old lady in a beautiful yacht—why should I come back and get myself in more trouble?"

Constanza snorted. "You'll get yourself in trouble, Heris, wherever you are. It's your nature, perhaps the one thing you inherited from your family." She leaned closer. "What do you think of him?" *Him* had to be the man at the table, now pointedly ignoring them.

"He's handsome," Heris said. "Not my type, though."

"He's exec on a heavy cruiser," Constanza said. That was explanation enough; Heris could read her insignia and knew from experience what limited facilities escorts had . . . besides, cruiser duty helped more at promotion time than it was supposed to. Constanza still hadn't made Sub-commander and had only one more Board to do it.

"Good luck, Connie," Heris said. She meant it. Constanza was a good officer whose slow promotion had more to do with her tactlessness than anything that mattered. "Don't queer your chances by hanging around with me."

"I'm not. I'll just tell him you're involved in something you can't talk about." And she was gone, with a last grin and wave. Heris wanted to wring her neck, and felt a moment of compassion for those officers who had given her less than stellar fitness reports.

The rest of her meal passed without incident. She reviewed her personal finances with a link to her banker, and discovered that Cecelia had indeed transferred her salary to her account—a quarter's worth. She called up her investment files, and allowed herself to order an expensive dessert in celebration. Her guesses had once more outperformed the market as a whole.

"This is Amalie," Sirkin said with the unmistakable tone that meant *my lover*. Amalie looked nervous, and well she might. Heris had reviewed her records, and she was nowhere near as qualified as Brigdis Sirkin. Moreover, her credentials, such as they were, overlapped an area Heris had filled with her former crewmates. She didn't really need a third-rate engineering technician.

But she did need a superb navigator, if she could keep her. "Amalie Yrilan," she said. "And you're considering small-ship work, too?"

"Since Brigdis found this . . . and she likes it." Amalie, smaller and rounder than Sirkin, had a deeper voice. Heris knew that meant nothing. "But we quite understand if you don't have an opening in engineering."

"You have a minor in environmental systems—"

"Yes, ma'am, but I'm not really—" Her voice trailed away. She didn't have to say that; her test scores showed it. She had barely made the lower limit of certification.

"You've applied to other places, of course," Heris said, wishing that the scores would go up by themselves.

"I . . . talked to the same agency Brig used," Amalie said. "They . . . said to talk to you." They had said, no doubt, that someone with her scores could whistle for a job and she had better start doing it. Linked with Sirkin, she might get a job, but more likely they'd both fail. Heris sighed.

"You do understand that your scores aren't very good."

"Oh . . . yes, but I'm just not very good at tests. I know more than that, really. Brig can tell you."

Sirkin flushed. In the months under Heris's command, she had continued to develop in her field, and contact with other ships' officers at Sirialis had shown her how much more was possible. Whatever she had thought of Amalie's ability earlier, now she knew better. Heris noted the flush, and spoke first. No need to humiliate her in front of a friend.

"Sirkin has been aboard more than a standard year now; your scores are your best witness. Test anxiety, you say? Didn't you ever take the Portland treatments?"

"Well, yes, ma'am, but they . . . but I was just so busy sometimes, you know. Working part-time . . ."

She had not worked part-time for the first two years, and her scores had been no better then. Sirkin, whose record also showed employment during school, had finished in fewer terms with top scores. Either ability or effort was missing here; Heris wasn't sure which.

"Sirkin's an outstanding junior officer, as I'm sure you know; if it weren't for that, I wouldn't be considering your application. I've got a full crew in engineering, and while I could use someone in environmental, I don't want slackers. I won't tolerate anything but excellence."

The tension around the young woman's eyes said it all, as far as Heris was concerned. This one didn't want to work that hard, and would always find excuses for herself. Too bad for Sirkin; irresponsibility made for bad lovers as well as bad shipmates. But she would give it a try, for the time they'd be onstation, just in case.

"I can understand that, ma'am, but—"

Heris held up her hand. "Tell you what. According to the owner, we're going to be here awhile, doing some work on the yacht. I'll hire you as general labor—mostly environmental work, some powerplant engineering—on a thirty-day temp contract. You and Sirkin can job hunt together in your off-shift time. If you satisfy me, and don't find something you like better, I may offer you a longer contract then. But I won't promise anything. How's that?"

That didn't satisfy Amalie, though she forced a smile, but Sirkin was relieved. She had clearly expected refusal.

"We'll be installing quite a bit of replacement electronics," Heris went on. "And a new backup set of powerplant control systems. The environmental system was overhauled thoroughly only a few months ago, but given the state of the former system, I want a complete baseline calibration."

"Yes, ma'am," Amalie said. At least she had that part right. Heris nodded.

"Sirkin, take her over to engineering, and introduce her to Haidar and Kulkul—they're the Environmental first, and Engineering second, Yrilan. I'll post the relevant orders on the comp for them."

Amalie started to open her mouth; Sirkin got there first

with "Thank you, ma'am," and pulled her friend along by the
arm. Heris shook her head once they were out of sight. What
a shame that a brilliant young person like Sirkin had fallen for
a loser. She was sure Amalie was a loser; she had seen too
many of that type.

Over the next few days, Nasiru Haidar reported that Amalie
Yrilan was reasonably willing when supervised, but lacked the
expertise she should have had and wouldn't stick to a job without constant supervision. Padoc Kulkul agreed, and added that
he would rather have a dumbot—the lowest level of robotic
assistant—than a fluffheaded girl who kept humming popular music off-key.

"About what I thought," Heris said. "Can you perk her up?
Maybe that school—"

"I can try," Nasiru said. "But how much do you want to risk
on her? She'll never go beyond third class on the exams, I'd
bet my last credit chip. Half the work would do twice as much
with a good candidate." Padoc simply shook his head.

"Well, we're not in the service anymore," Heris said. "We
don't have an endless supply of recruits. I was hoping—"

"I'll work on it." Nasiru sounded not quite grumpy. "But I
won't promise anything. I know Sirkin's good, but young love
doesn't last forever."

Heris snorted. "Don't try to tell them that. We have to
remember, we're all a lot older, and with real experience." By
real, of course, she meant military.

"That one'll get herself killed, and maybe her friends," Padoc
said. "You know we all like young Sirkin, but—Amalie's like
that cute little kid back on *Fisk*." Heris raised her brows, but
he didn't back down. The cute little kid on *Fisk* had been
someone important's nephew, and he had hit the wrong control in combat and—luckily—died along with those his idiocy
killed. Turned out his uncle had known about the addiction
problem, but concealed it in the hopes that life on a ship would
straighten him out.

"Well, if she's that bad, we don't want her," Heris said. "I know that. But as long as we're in dock, she can't hurt us that much, and we just might pull off a miracle."

"There's a slight chance that you may have some trouble dockside," Heris said. She had called the crew together before giving them Station liberty. "Those of you who were aboard at the time know about the smugglers' stash. If they choose to retaliate for its loss—"

"But they've already killed Olin," Petris said.

"Wouldn't they go after Lady Cecelia?" asked Nasiru. "Or the ship itself?"

"They might. But they also might make an example of a crew member." She knew her ex-military crew would know how to handle any invitations to criminality, but Sirkin and Yrilan were young and vulnerable, bait for everything from gambling sharks to smugglers. "I suggest you travel in pairs, at least, and keep your eyes open. You're not children, to be coddled and watched over, but as long as we don't know what the danger is, you're vulnerable. I'm not sure just how far they'll go to express their displeasure. If you want to indulge in any-thing mind-altering, be sure you're in a safe place."

"If there's trouble, how about weapons?" Oblo, as usual with a fight even remotely in view, looked both sleepy and happy. The sleepiness was entirely deceptive.

"No. Not on Station. We don't need legal trouble as well as illegal. And given Lady Cecelia's . . . mmm . . . connections, we could even have political trouble. Fight if you have to, but call for the gendarmes right away."

"Yes, ma'am." That with a heavy-lidded look that meant he would interpret it in his own way. Petris gave him a sharp glance, and Heris told herself to talk to Petris about Oblo before he had a shift off. His formidable brawling skills should be reserved for times they needed them, not wasted on casual displays.

✧ Chapter Four

Under the supervision of Nasiru Haidar, Yrilan earned her pay. Heris had to respect her for coming back, shift after shift, to face the grudging acceptance of the rest of the crew. Sirkin, she noticed, stayed clear of Yrilan during work hours, but she was looking increasingly tense. Heris assumed that meant they hadn't found a joint berth on some other ship. Sirkin would be facing a hard decision soon enough; Heris didn't try to offer advice she was sure the younger woman would resent.

On the day they completed the new installations, which would be sealed again when the yacht entered the refitting docks, Heris gave the crew a half-shift bonus off. She gave Ginese the standing watch, and finished the interminable forms necessary to clear the Royal Docks and transfer the ship around the station on the next mainshift but one. She hated the thought of letting a tug do the shift but those were the rules. She expected all the off-duty crew to be gone by the time she finished, but as it happened she left the ship just behind Sirkin and Yrilan. They were not quite holding hands as they hurried through the Royal sector to the public concourse beyond. She wondered if they'd job hunt or spend the extra time another way.

They seemed to be headed the same direction she was. Once in the transit car, they shared a seat at the far end. Heris hung back at the exit, hoping they wouldn't think she was following them, but traffic was light, just before shiftchange. In another half hour, all transit tubes would be crowded. She dawdled, glancing at a shop window down the concourse from the Captain's Guild, until they were nearly out of sight around the curve.

Heris turned into the Captains' Guild, mentally shaking her head. When she'd been that young, she hadn't been unlucky enough to fall that far in love. Sirkin and Yrilan were together, but it could hardly be called alert awareness of possible danger. Yet it would do no good to suggest anything to them; they might try, but in twenty paces they'd be back to concentrating on each other. At least Sirkin had basic good sense, and they had promised to bunk aboard until the decorators took the ship over. Surely they wouldn't get in much trouble. After all, Oblo had the history of dockside and planetside brawls.

The Captains' Guild rooms had begun to look familiar, and the Warden knew her now. She posted her daily report, and looked over the news. Here again, the different format had begun to make sense. Which ships were in, with which captains, reporting changes they'd noted in their routes. She was looking specifically for anything to suggest what Captain Olin had been doing in the regions where he'd hung about as if looking for a rendezvous. So far, she'd found no comment helpful. After all, if another captain was up to the same game, she could hardly expect an honest report to the Captains' Guild.

"Captain Serrano's following us," Yrilan said. "We're off duty—she doesn't have to—"

"Captains' Guild's down this way," Sirkin said. "Don't get paranoid, Amalie. She isn't bothering us."

"Just wish she'd mind her own—" Yrilan glanced over her shoulder and turned back. "Or catch up. Something."

Sirkin laughed. "What've you done or not done that you think she'll scold you for? You're trying, aren't you?"

Yrilan nodded. "'Course I am, but it's a lot harder than school. That Haidar is so picky. I swear he watches me every second, and he wants everything to be just so."

"But you're learning," Sirkin said. "And we're together." For how long? she asked herself. She had overheard some of Haidar's comments, and even more from Kulkul. They didn't think the captain should hire Yrilan permanently. She forced herself not to think about it. They had a full three-shift off, and for once the money to enjoy it. "Where shall we eat?" she asked. "Why not a dinner-dance place like Califa's?"

Yrilan grinned at her, the grin she had first fallen for, and gave a little skip-step. "Great—but why not Uptop first, to get in the mood?"

"I'm already in the mood," Sirkin said, and ran a finger down Yrilan's arm.

"Patience is a virtue," Yrilan said, tossing her head, and Sirkin had to laugh. They both knew who had the patience. She wished Yrilan didn't like noisy taverns like Uptop, but she'd have put up with worse for the evening to come.

By the time they reached Uptop, it was crammed with mainshift rush hour business, vibrating to the beat of its music. Sirkin saw a sonic cop check her meter from across the corridor, shrug, and go on. Well-bribed, perhaps. She inserted her own filters, and followed Yrilan inside. They stood with a clump of others waiting for space at the bar or booths; Sirkin saw merchant ship patches on some arms, nothing on others. Uptop had never been a favorite of either Fleet or Royals, which made it more popular with other groups. Remembering the captain's warning, she tried to notice anything out of the ordinary, but she didn't like this kind of place anyway. How could she tell if the big, scar-faced man in front of her was really from Pier's Company #35 or not? Against her hip, she felt Yrilan's hip twitch to the music. She wouldn't be wearing sonic filters; she liked it this loud. Sirkin had to admit that the bass resonances dancing up her bones from heel to spine were exciting, but she wished the higher tones didn't tangle her eardrums in the middle of her skull.

Two seats finally opened at a large table. Yrilan nodded before Sirkin had a chance to see everyone clearly, but she shrugged and followed the flashing arrow on the floor. Two women in matching gray with a yellow stripe: Lyons, Inc., but probably not ship crew, since they were hunched over a digipad poking at it with styluses. Probably accountants. A man in rusty black; Sirkin was glad he sat on the far side of the table. A woman and two men in nondescript blue, playing some sort of game on the table's projector. An elegant woman, hair streaked with silver, whose silui-silk suit probably cost more than all the other clothes at the table. The empty seats were between her and the Lyons, Inc. women.

Yrilan edged in beside the older woman. She would, Sirkin thought, amused. She had a passion for jewels, the classic case of champagne tastes on a beer budget, and the woman wore jewelry as costly and elegant as her clothes. Sirkin wondered what she was doing there . . . she wasn't much like the rest of Uptop's clientele. She herself squeezed in beside Yrilan and looked at the table's display. She wanted wine with dinner; she really didn't want anything now.

"Let's have a mixed fry as well," Yrilan said in her ear. "Or will it spoil your appetite?"

The tickle distracted her from the question for a moment. "If we're going to eat a good dinner, why . . . ?"

"Oh . . . there's no hurry, is there? I think I just want to cram it all in, love, all the things we like. I can see the signs as well as you can. Your Captain Serrano isn't going to hire me, and this may be our last chance to celebrate together."

Implicit in that was the understanding that she, Sirkin, wasn't going to quit the *Sweet Delight* to work wherever Yrilan found a berth. Nor would Yrilan wait. Her eyes stung; she hadn't admitted it to herself yet, but it was true. She drew a breath, trying to think how to say what she really felt.

"Don't spoil it, now," Yrilan said, punching her arm lightly. "Let's just party and enjoy it." She reached out and entered an order for both of them. Sirkin didn't cancel it; right then she didn't care.

The mixed fries, hot and spicy, gave her an excuse for watering eyes; the first gulp of her drink took the edge off both spice and emotion. Was Yrilan trying to anesthetize her, or what? She glanced sideways, and saw that Yrilan was smiling at the elegant older woman. Fine. Drag her into a place like this and then ignore her.

"Amalie—" That got a quick sidelong look, a nudge. "Look—maybe we should go somewhere and talk—"

"No . . . talk's the last thing we need." Yrilan shook her head decisively, and reached for more fries. Sirkin shrugged and sat back. Even with filters, her ears hurt. On her right, the conversation between the two women she thought of as accountants consisted of sequences of numbers with exclamations like "But of *course* the rate's pegged to the Green List!" She knew the Green List had something to do with investments, but had no idea what. Glancing that way, she saw their display covered with intersecting lines that flicked from one pattern to another. "All profit," one of them was saying. "See, the first shipment makes up the difference between—"

Yrilan poked her. "Wake *up*, Brig. Kirsya here has asked us to dine with her."

Sirkin peered around Yrilan at the elegant woman, startled out of her mood and into wariness. Had Yrilan known her before? But she was explaining.

"I met Kirsya while waiting for *Sweet Delight* to arrive—I wanted you to meet her before, but we've been so busy—"

Was this her replacement? But she had to say something; Kirsya was reaching around to shake her hand. Sirkin forced herself to smile. "Glad to meet you," she said. At least she didn't have to say how much she'd heard, since she'd heard nothing. Surely Yrilan could have mentioned her.

"And I." Kirsya had a lovely voice, surprisingly clear through the music and the filters. "I asked Amalie to let me be a surprise . . . I hope it doesn't bother you."

Bother was the wrong word. Sirkin felt that she was somehow in the wrong when she hadn't done anything. Yet.

"I'm Amalie's therapist," Kirsya said. Sirkin glanced at Yrilan, whose cheeks were slightly flushed.

"Therapist? What's wrong?" Immediately she knew that was the wrong thing to say, even before both sets of eyebrows went up. "I'm sorry," she said quickly, but too late. "I know— it doesn't mean anything's wrong—it's just—" Just that unless Amalie was going to confront her laziness, there was nothing she really needed to change. Not to please Sirkin, anyway.

"I was really miserable, waiting for you," Yrilan said, not quite apologetically. "I got into a little . . . mess, sort of. And they recommended therapy."

"Who?" asked Sirkin, her heart sinking right to the floor. Mess? She hadn't mentioned any mess, and they'd always shared everything before. What kind of "mess" got a recommendation of therapy, and how had she concealed that from Captain Serrano? Sirkin felt a sudden desire to bolt from the tavern, straight back to *Sweet Delight*.

"The . . . uh . . . Station police. They said no charges might be filed if I agreed to short-term therapy . . ." Yrilan's voice had the pleading tone which had always worked before. Now it sawed on Sirkin's nerves almost like the music. "And . . . Kirsya really helped me. We got to be friends—"

In the short time that Yrilan had had to wait, of course. Friends. Sirkin bit back all she was thinking, and simply nodded. Memories flooded her: the day she'd first seen Amalie Yrilan in the registration line, fumbling with a stack of forms and data cubes. What had it been, the look in her green eyes or the quick toss of her hair? The study dates, the walks by the lake, the long intense discussions of their future.

"It's not what you think," Yrilan was saying now, with a worried look. Kirsya's face was composed. So it well might be, Sirkin thought, finally recognizing her own anger. She with her good clothes and jewels— "Of course I still love you," Yrilan went on. "I always will—" The necessary *but* hung in the air, battered by the music.

"I see," said Sirkin, just to stop the process, whatever it was. She had to have time, space, silence. She couldn't deal with all this now. She made herself meet the older woman's eyes. "Is this meeting your idea?"

Kirsya smiled. It was a very mature smile. "A meeting, certainly. But Uptop was Amalie's idea. In my experience, meetings should take place where the client is comfortable—not that Amalie is my client anymore, of course."

"Of course," Sirkin echoed.

"I certainly wasn't planning to intrude on your . . . evening together." Again, a missing word hung in the air; she had not quite said *last* evening together. "I did want to meet the person who has been so important in Amalie's life. Perhaps we could chat a bit another time, where it's quieter?"

"Of course," Sirkin said, though she couldn't think what about. Perhaps this woman thought she would come for therapy, too. *Never*, she thought, and hoped it didn't show on her face. She struggled for lightness in her tone, and turned to Yrilan. "Well, Amalie, just what kind of mess did you get into? Or is that confidential now?"

"Oh—I was playing Goorlah and I sort of . . . well . . . overdid it."

Gambling again. She'd promised to quit, and since she hadn't shown up broke or in debt, Sirkin thought maybe she'd really reformed. "How bad?" she asked now.

"No worry. I got a temp job with Kirsya's help, and paid it off. And I know, I shouldn't have gambled at all. I promised you. But it was only that once."

It wouldn't have been only that once, Sirkin knew, but it would be useless to argue. She found herself cataloguing the things she had loved about Amalie Yrilan from the beginning, from the color of her hair to the sound of her laugh, as she would have catalogued the attractions of a navigating system she would never use again. Already Amalie belonged to the past, although she sat there, eyes wide and excited. Sirkin felt a cold lump in her belly, and wished she could evaporate like the spilled drinks.

Kirsya, with an understanding look that Sirkin wanted to

remove from her face with a blaster, turned to Yrilan. "Well—what have you two planned for the evening?" Yrilan answered eagerly, her voice already showing the effects of the drinks she'd had.

"Califa's for dinner, maybe some dancing, then a party wherever we find one. We're in the mood for fun, aren't we, Brig?"

Sirkin forced a smile to meet Kirsya's. She would not, absolutely not, show that cradle-robbing sleaze what she felt. "Celebration," she said, surprising herself with the sound of her own voice. It held none of the pain she felt, but considerable force. Kirsya looked confused a moment, then smiled widely and pushed back her chair.

"Then I'd better get along and let you enjoy it. By the way—if you didn't happen to see the announcement, they've closed the F-way slides for repair, so if you're going to Califa's, it's shorter from here to use the Number 11 bounce-tube and that shortcut through Avery Park than go all the way back to the G-way slides."

"Thank you," said Sirkin. Shortcut through Avery Park, indeed. She had more sense than that, and she'd bet that Kirsya never went there—not dressed in silk and jewels, anyway. "We're in no hurry," she said. "There's a shop on G-way that I'd like to visit anyway." She had meant to buy Yrilan a certain piece of jewelry there. Now . . . she didn't know, but she certainly didn't want to follow Kirsya's suggestion. The older woman shrugged, gave Yrilan a smile that seemed entirely too warm, and squeezed past other chairs on her way out. She had an elegant back, long and supple, and Sirkin saw how many others noticed it.

"She really helped me," Yrilan said. "I hoped you'd like her."

"I'm glad," Sirkin said to the first part of that. She couldn't deal with the second part. Her throat had closed; she didn't want any more of the spicy fries. "Are you ready?" It sounded churlish even to her.

"Look—" Yrilan glanced around and leaned closer. "I know

you're upset, but let's not spoil the evening. Maybe I'm wrong; maybe Serrano will hire me. If she does, I'll do anything I can to stay on her good side. At least we can enjoy this."

"Right." Sirkin tried to push the depression and grumpiness away. "But I'm really not in the mood for more fries—and you're not eating them now—so could we please go somewhere that the music doesn't split my brain?"

"All right." Yrilan twitched her shoulders and pushed away from the table. Sirkin followed her out, sighing internally.

But out in the open, Yrilan seemed to relax, and they walked together as they always had. They stopped to look in shop windows—Yrilan thought a blue-and-violet wrap would look good on Sirkin, and Sirkin shrugged and agreed to try it on. The shop wasn't much out of their spending range, though they both agreed the wrap didn't look that good on. Sirkin felt her own nerves settling as they came out of the shop. Maybe it would be all right this time—maybe. She was still thinking that when Yrilan turned toward the Number 11 bounce-tube entrance.

"Hey—let's go back to G-way slides. There's a place I wanted to show you—"

"Maybe after dinner." Yrilan scowled. "I saw the look on your face—you're just afraid of Avery Park. And that's silly at this time of day. It's not that far past shiftchange rush, and it's only second shift anyway." Sirkin glanced around. Traffic had eased, but it was busy enough; the bounce-tube entrance had a short line. If they waited until after dinner, and then Amalie insisted on testing her courage, the park would be even more dangerous.

"Eh, Amalie!" The man wore ordinary spacers' coveralls, but no ship patch. He had appeared suddenly in the park, just when Sirkin had been thinking how empty it was, how silly it had been to object to the shortcut. Sirkin felt the twitch in Yrilan's hand. Someone she knew, then, and someone she didn't really want to see. An ordinary face, perhaps a bit paler than average, with lank gray-brown hair. "That your friend you told us about? Handsome, she is."

"Back off, Curris." Yrilan sounded cross and scared both. "We're not interested in your games."

"Games of your own, eh?" He laughed, and so did his companions. Sirkin did not like the looks of the three men and two women. All, like him, wore spacers' coveralls with not a ship patch among them. Bad sign, that. Station dwellers didn't wear spacers' clothes; they had their own styles that didn't offer as many hiding places for weapons. "She looks a bit nervous, Amalie—didn't you tell her about the party?"

"We're not coming," Yrilan said. "That's why I came up here—to tell you. We've got other plans."

"Now that's not friendly, hon," the man said. "Y'know what we agreed. Just a party, that's all, just a chance to chat with your friend there."

"No." Sirkin realized suddenly that Yrilan was really scared, not just nervous. That the tension of the past hour or so had had little to do with her, and a lot to do with this man and the "party" he mentioned.

"Kirsya knows about it," Yrilan said. She was bluffing, whatever that was supposed to mean. Sirkin had known her too long to be fooled by that tone. And the man must recognize it, too. "She approved the change of plans."

"I don't think so," the man said. "You're as bad at lying as you are at gambling, Amalie."

"You—" Yrilan began. Sirkin touched her arm.

"Let's go, Amalie. No sense talking."

"Now there you're wrong," the man said, switching his gaze to her face. Sirkin tried not to shiver visibly. She had known they shouldn't come this way; now she wondered how far away a Security alarm was. "There's a lot of sense talking, when the alternatives are . . . less pleasant."

A gleam, in his hand. In another hand or two, in that group. All Captain Serrano's warnings came back to her, and everything her former crew had added. But she didn't have that training; she had no idea what to do when faced with people like this in a shadowy corner where she should never have come. Yet she couldn't have let Amalie come this way alone, could she?

"We have nothing to talk about," Sirkin said, hoping her voice didn't sound as scared as she felt. "We're meeting friends—"

"I don't think so," the man said again, in the same tone he'd used to Yrilan. "That's not what we heard from Kirsya. She says you two were planning a quiet little farewell dinner . . . but Amalie really prefers a party, don't you? Quite a party girl, our Amalie." He bared his teeth in an expression nothing at all like a normal smile. "Now we'll have us a nice chat, and you'll find us a friendly bunch."

"No," Sirkin said, before she had time to think how scared she was.

"Brig—" Yrilan's hand closed over hers. "Don't—"

She didn't have to say more. There were the weapons, the bulbous snout of a very illicit sonic pulser, familiar from entertainment cubes, and several plasteel knives. Sirkin felt her mouth go dry. The advice she'd had—never go with the attacker, the place you're accosted is the most dangerous for the attacker, and the place he takes you is safer for him—now seemed impossible to follow. Her imagination leaped ahead to the effects of sonic pulser and knife . . . she saw blood, felt the pain. What could they do? She tried to look around without moving her head, but saw nothing helpful, no one she could call for help.

"Come on," the man said, gesturing with the sonic pulser. "It's party time, girls." Behind him, the others grinned and moved forward.

"You're going to spoil their fun," Methlin Meharry said. Oblo shook his head.

"Not me. If they find a nice room and spend the night

together, fine—but that's not the mood Yrilan's in. She's out for trouble of some kind. I know that look."

Methlin gave him a poke. "You should. You're always out for trouble . . ."

"Captain'll be upset if we let Sirkin get trashed because of Yrilan's foolishness. You know what she thinks—and besides, the girl's worth working on; she could have been Fleet." High praise, for Oblo. "And they'll never know we're watching, 'less something goes sour."

"I can think of things I'd rather do on my off shift—"

"Fine. Let me do it."

"Not you alone . . . I know better."

They lounged in the doorway of Uptop, drinking pirate chasers from the outside bar. "Classy one sitting with 'em," Oblo said. "Doesn't fit here."

"Don't like her looks. Actin' like a shill. Let's check 'er out." Methlin pulled out her very illicit Fleet data-capture wand. Oblo grinned.

"Good idea." Methlin pointed it at the overdressed woman for a moment, capturing her image, then looked around for a public dataport. "Go on," said Oblo. "I'll wait here."

Methlin found a 'port two shops down, and it even had a privacy shield. Her wand stabbed into the port and overrode the usual restriction codes, sucking the data she wanted out of the station computers. When she slid the wand into the 'port of her handcomp, the display showed everything the station personnel files knew about Kirsya, Melotis Davrin.

"A therapist," she murmured to Oblo.

"Wipe your hand," Oblo said. "Never."

"Says. Licensed and all that. Does work for the Station militia, mostly addicts up for minor stuff. Has interesting friends."

"Oh?"

"That agency." They both knew which agency; Heris had told them her suspicions about the employment agency before sending them over to get their civilian licenses and ratings. It had smelled as rotten to them as it had to Heris. "Finds jobs for clients, sometimes."

"Ah." Oblo sucked his teeth noisily, drained the rest of his drink, and grinned. "Sounds whole to me. Got?"

"Got. Who?"

"The kids. We'll stay with the kids, but put a ferret on the tinker." They retreated across the corridor. Methlin slid the wand into another public connection, and transmitted both the data on Kirsya and Oblo's request to the *Sweet Delight*.

"Ah—there she goes." Oblo grunted. "Huh. Just passed a signal, too. Wonder who that was?"

"I didn't see . . . oh, yes. Classy rear view the lady has."

"Keep your mind on business."

When Sirkin and Yrilan came out, Oblo could tell that they were at odds. He and Meharry dropped back a little. No need to embarrass Sirkin if she suddenly stormed back this way.

"Just a little chat," the man said. "Just a suggestion your friend wasn't confident enough to take."

"I don't need to chat with you," Sirkin said. "If Amalie didn't want to do it, I don't either."

"Unwise," the man said. "You're smart enough to know she's not. And we're offering an unusual opportunity here. We'd pay well for a contact aboard the *Sweet Delight*. No risk worth mentioning, and a profit—and no harm done your employer, if that bothers you."

"No risk?" Sirkin was glad to find her voice didn't shake. "Like Captain Olin?"

"He didn't follow instructions," the man said. "He upset the old lady, got himself fired—and then we hear that Iklind died and the goods were discovered because he was trying to double his profit with a payoff to the refitters. He double-crossed us . . . we couldn't let that pass."

"I suppose not." Sirkin had been hoping someone would come into the park, but no one did. Had these people somehow cut it off from the corridors? Had they bribed the Station militia?

"Don't hurt her!" Yrilan's voice was shrill.

"Convince her, then," said the man.

"No—let her alone. It's not her fault. She had nothing to do with it, any of it."

"Get out of the way." His voice had flattened, utter menace.

"No." Yrilan, stubborn, was immovable. He lifted the weapon, his finger tightening, and Yrilan launched herself in useless rage and love. Sirkin grabbed for her lover and missed, but it was already too late. Yrilan screamed as the sonic pulser focused its lethal vibrations on her; she curled into the agony, still screaming. Sirkin, on the edge of that cone, felt as if someone had stabbed her brain with a needle; tears burst from her right eye and she lurched sideways. The man strode forward, but somehow Yrilan grabbed at his leg and tripped him. Sirkin, fighting off the dizziness of the sonic attack, managed to knock the weapon out of his hand before he could turn it on Yrilan again.

The others joined the melee then, knives and fists and boots. Sirkin tried to get to Yrilan, but one of them slammed an elbow into her face, and another kicked her legs out from under her. She hit someone hard enough to make him grunt, then a blow in the belly took all her breath. And Yrilan—she couldn't see. She couldn't hear anything but curses, grunts, the slam of boots and fists. A hand came over her mouth, and she twisted her head and bit, hard. A curse, a blow to the head that made her eyes water—someone yanking her arms up behind her—then more yells and the feeling that someone else had arrived.

Gasping, Sirkin tried to break the armhold and find a way to strike back. Another kick, this one in the ribs—she felt something crunch—and then someone fell on top of her, hard knees and elbows and too much weight. She couldn't breathe . . . she couldn't complain about not breathing . . . her vision grayed out, and the next blow sent her into darkness.

"Captain Serrano!" That was the Warden, with quiet urgency. She wondered why he hadn't simply buzzed her carrel until she saw his face. He was gray around the lips, his eyes showing too much white. She came at once, ignoring a few surprised glances from other captains who had noticed the Warden's unusual invasion of the inner rooms.

Heris didn't bother to ask; she simply followed him back to the reception area. He almost scurried. Waiting for them were two uniformed Station Security Police, faces grim. Heris felt her heart begin to pound, a great hammer. If they had come, instead of asking her to visit one of the waitstations, whatever had happened was serious—even fatal.

"Captain Serrano?" asked the shorter one. "I'm Detective Morin Cannibar. We have a problem concerning your crew."

"Who is it?" asked Heris. Oblo came automatically to mind, but he ought to be busy installing that semipirated bit of navigational electronics he had come back with the day before. He had wanted to do it himself, when Sirkin and Yrilan were not aboard. That thought struck a chill in her— those two?

"We aren't sure, Captain Serrano. The—uh—body carried identification as a member of your crew, but—uh—"

Heris felt herself going cold, the protective freeze of emotion that would carry her through any necessary action. "Do you need me to identify the body?"

"It's—it's not going to be easy, ma'am. She's a young woman, that's all we can tell. Hit with a sonic pulser, then . . . pretty well beaten to a pulp."

Let it not be Sirkin, Heris thought, then hated herself for thinking that. Yrilan might be a bit lazy and not overbright, but she had not deserved anything that would put that expression on the faces of police officers.

She nodded shortly. "I'll come now. I have two young female

crew members, and they are both off duty at present. Can you tell me something about it?"

The taller one shrugged. "Someone wanted her dead. Messily. Either of them have enemies you know about?"

Heris looked at him sharply. "You know I filed a report when we arrived that my crew might be the target of retaliation from some criminal organization. And that I had been contacted, subsequently, by someone whose credentials worried me."

"Yes, but you didn't know many details. Made it hard for us to help you."

"True—nonetheless, my guess is this young woman ran afoul of that group, not an enemy of her own. Neither of them had been on this station very long. One arrived with my ship, and the other met her here after finishing her technical training. I don't suppose you know where the other is—"

"No, ma'am. If it's some group like you're thinking of, and they were together, then I'd expect both . . ."

"So would I." She walked along between them, trying not to feel trapped. "Where are we going? The morgue?"

"No, ma'am. We'd like you to see the . . . body . . . in place. In case you can help figure out what happened."

In place meant in a corner of Rockhouse she'd never known about. "It's a park, actually," one of the men said. "Reasonably safe during shift changes, because it's a shortcut from a concentration of civilian housing units to two big employers. There's a primary school that uses it during mainshift for recreation and exercise. But it's a bit out of the way—especially midshift on Second. And the usual patrol had a domestic disturbance call and missed two rounds through here."

"Planned?" Heris asked. She could see the cluster of people working ahead, under brilliant lighting.

"Maybe. Can't tell—it's a family with a history. This time they'll be split up for a while, see if that settles them."

Then they were close enough for Heris to see the bodies under the lights.

✧ Chapter Five

She recognized Yrilan by the hair and clothes. The young woman's face was disfigured by parallel knife slashes, the skin reddened by the sonic pulser wound. "That's mine," she said, pointing. The man beside her nodded.

"Right—do you know which?"

"Amalie Yrilan, on temporary contract. She left the ship today about when I did, and that's what she was wearing. Also the hair—" That ginger-colored hair, once fluffy and now matted with blood.

"You don't seem—that upset by . . . the other . . ." the man said. She could hear the suspicion in his voice.

"My background's Fleet," she said. "Regular Space Service." Let them think she was a coldhearted military bitch . . . easier than explaining that her feelings would come later, when she felt safe. That she would have the right number of nightmares about the ruin of Amalie Yrilan's face, enough to prove her own humanity. She braced herself for criticism, but the man merely nodded.

"Right. You've seen combat trauma, then." It wasn't a question. "This was sonic pulser plus, I suspect, being on the ground in the midst of a major brawl. We think the knife wounds were after death, maybe accidental; the autopsy will check for that."

Heris stared at the parallel wounds across Yrilan's face, and the deep gash between thumb and first finger on both hands. Did the militia not recognize those wounds? Or did they wonder if she did? Better to be honest.

"Those marks—the last time I saw something like that, it was a Compassionate Hand action."

"Ah. I wondered if you'd know."

"We were called to Chisholm once." They could look that up in her service record, the public part. "They had trouble with their ore haulers being hijacked between the insystem Stations and the jump-point insertion." They had had more trouble than that, but the rest was classified.

"Two of the dead bodies had C.H. marks on the thumb web," the man said. "Did Yrilan?"

"Certainly not. Not overt, anyway. But you're right, that hand cut's usually given to traitor members, not stray associates." And where was Sirkin, her mind insisted? Was she, too, a Compassionate Hand victim?

"You recognize any of the others?"

None of the others had mutilated faces, beyond a bruise or two. She knew none of them. But something about the pattern of injuries on two—she frowned. "No. But—" Suddenly it came clear. The time she had had to get Oblo out of trouble . . . the miners he'd felled had exactly the same marks. "But none of them are my crew," she said, finishing smoothly. "We've been staying close to the ship, most of the time, getting it ready to leave the Royal Docks—"

"I know." He had checked, then. "I didn't really think you would recognize them, but it was a chance." He paused, then asked, "And you say this—Yrilan, was it?—usually had a companion?"

"Yes—she did tonight. Brigdis Sirkin, my Navigator First. They'd known each other at school, and Yrilan had hoped I'd hire her. Unfortunately, she wasn't nearly as qualified."

"Was Sirkin going to leave your crew?"

"I'm not sure. I had hoped not, but they were close. She had a tough decision coming up. I hope—" It was stronger than that, a plea to whatever powers ran the universe. "I hope Sirkin's not a prisoner or anything."

"We can't tell." The man frowned. "Five dead, including your crew member. This Sirkin must be some kind of fighter if she didn't have help. Someone badly wounded got away that direction—" He pointed to smears of blood heading to the far end of the little park. "There's all too many ways out down there, though we're looking. But two bounce tubes, and a slideway."

Heris looked again at the dead she already thought of as "enemy." She couldn't see the thumb-web marks from here—probably they were flesh-colored tattoos, designed to fluoresce under UV light. But the pattern—again she thought of Oblo. One of the dead had been hit by someone shorter, she thought, but this wasn't her field of expertise. Shorter than Oblo would be most of her crew, but her mind drifted to her weapons specialists. Arkady Ginese? No; Arkady, even onstation, would have carried something that left distinctive marks. No one had ever broken him of the habit. Besides, he had the standing watch; he wouldn't have been here. Methlin Meharry, perhaps? Those sleepy green eyes had fooled more than one, but her unarmed combat skills topped even Arkady's. And the two of them could have got Sirkin away—somewhere. Where?

"Ah—Captain Serrano?" That was another of the investigating militia. She turned to him. "Urgent message from your ship. Shall I put it on the local tapline?"

She hoped that meant they'd gotten Sirkin back to the ship safely. She nodded, and stepped over to the little communications booth set up for the investigators. The headset they gave her hissed a bit—no doubt from the offtake tape spool—but Petris's voice was clear enough.

"Captain? Hate to bother you, but we've got a problem here."

"Ah, yes, Mr. Petris." That should warn him. "I'm dealing with one here, too. It seems Yrilan has been killed by thugs, and the investigating officers have found no sign of Sirkin."

"Right. I'm at the Royal Security office, at the access. The officer in charge prefers your personal authorization before passing some of our crew members who . . . have had an accident. The scanners picked up bloodstains."

"How many?" Heris asked, mentally crossing her fingers.

"Mr. Vissisuan, Ms. Meharry, and Ms. Sirkin," Petris said. "With injuries." Such formality could only mean trouble. No one had called Oblo "Mr. Vissisuan" since his second tour. At least Sirkin was alive.

"Would it help if I spoke to Royal Security?"

"Maybe," Petris said cautiously. "Here's Major Defrit."

Major Defrit sounded as frosty and formal as Heris would have in his place. She explained that she was on the site of a murder, with the station militia.

"Your crew seems to have a talent for trouble," Major Defrit said.

"I hardly think that justified," Heris said, in the same tone. Actually Oblo had more than a talent for it—genius, more like—but it wasn't something to brag about. "Are any of my crew injured?"

"Ms. Sirkin seems to have some injuries, but I would judge them not serious. She is conscious and her vital signs appear within normal limits." He sounded entirely too certain; Heris trusted the worry in Petris's voice.

"I'd prefer to have Sirkin evaluated by medical personnel. You are not, I gather, a physician?"

"Well no, but—"

"Since one of my crew died from a murderous assault, and Sirkin is injured, it would be prudent to have her examined, don't you think?"

"But that would mean admitting her to this Sector—unless you want her sent to the central clinic—" His resolution wavered; she could hear it in his voice, a faint whine.

"Major, Sirkin has a valid Royal Docks pass, as have my other crew members. You have no real reason to exclude them. I can understand that you might want to escort them to medical care—"

"But—"

"I will be there as soon as possible," Heris interrupted. "And I expect to find my crew members receiving adequate medical treatment." Watching her, the militia communications tech raised his eyebrows; Heris winked, and they went up another notch. "Let me speak to my second in command."

Petris came back on the line. "Yes, Captain?"

"I believe the major understands the need for Sirkin to receive immediate medical evaluation and treatment. I'd like you to stay with her. If Mr. Vissisuan is not injured, I'd like him to meet me at the access area on my return. Ms. Meharry can return to the ship if she needs no medical care, and I'll speak to her there. Clear?"

"Clear, Captain."

Heris came out of the little booth shaking her head. "Well, my other crew member has shown up, wounded apparently, at the Royal Docks access station. I don't know if she was trying to get help or what. I know you'll need to talk to her, but I think her medical care should come first."

"I'll come with you," Cannibar said. "Want to leave now? What about the disposition of your crew member's remains after autopsy?"

"I'm not sure—I'll have to check my files aboard." She would have to ask Sirkin, most likely. Anything but token cremation would be impossibly expensive; most who died aboard went into the carbon-cycle tanks. But it was always possible that Yrilan had taken out a burial insurance policy that would pay for shipping her body to a planet for "real" burial. Heris felt guilty that she had not known even this about the girl.

At the Royal Docks Access, Oblo and the Royal Security major waited in unamiable silence. Oblo had a ripening bruise on his forehead and his hands bore the marks of a good fight. But his expression was that of a large predatory mammal fully fed and satisfied. Heris spared him only a glance, then met the major's angry gaze. Before he could say anything she introduced the Station militia captain.

"—investigating the death of Amalie Yrilan, a temporary-contract crew member."

"I suppose you'll want in to interview the others," the major said sourly, transferring his glare to the militia captain.

"As a matter of fact, yes." Heris had warmed to the captain already, and she liked his tone now. Not a trace of arrogance or obsequiousness either: he simply stated the obvious in a voice that meant to be obeyed. The major shrugged, and handed over a clip-on pass.

"Very well. This is a forty-eight-hour pass; if you need an extension, just give us a call."

"How's Sirkin?" Heris asked Oblo. He looked less smug.

"She caught part of a sonic blast, and a couple of knife slashes. I think she's got some broken ribs, but this officer thinks it's just bruising. Some heavy people landed on her, and she got some hard kicks I know of, one in the head."

"Unconsciousness?"

"Yes, for a bit, but the one that landed on her weighed enough it could have been that."

Heris thought of all she'd like to ask him, but not in front of Royal Security and Station militia officers. Why had he waited so long to come into the fight? Why had he brought Sirkin back here rather than the nearest militia station? Why had he been on the scene in the first place?

"Could I talk to you now?" said the militia captain. It wasn't really a question.

"Sure, sir," said Oblo, rubbing his hands over his head and trying to look innocent. It didn't work. He had the face and hands of the experienced brawler, and the bruise was like a rose on a rosebush—a fitting decoration.

"I'm going to see Sirkin," Heris said. "Oblo—when you've finished here, I'll see you aboard."

Sirkin had been through the diagnostics when Heris got to the clinic. She lay in a bed, in a bright-patterned gown Heris thought had been chosen to disguise bloodstains and other marks. Her face looked lopsided—she had swollen bruises down one side, and the other was discolored with the sunburn flush of the sonic pulser that had burst small blood vessels. That eye, too, was bloodshot. If Heris hadn't seen the medical report, she'd have worried, but the eye had escaped real damage. She looked drowsy and said nothing when Heris came into the room. That would be the concussion the scans had shown.

Petris rose from a chair at the bedside. "Captain. Meharry's gone back to the ship, as you asked. Oblo?"

"He's talking to the militia captain in charge of the investigation. I still haven't heard what happened. Have you?"

"Sirkin and Yrilan were out for a night, and took a shortcut through that park; they were jumped by a gang. Oblo and Meharry were following them, but trying to be discreet. They tried to deal quietly with someone who tried to keep them from entering the park—maybe part of the gang—and that took enough time that the row had started when they caught up. Yrilan was down, probably dead or dying, and Sirkin was fighting. They both think the gang was trying to capture Sirkin at that point—someone had cuffs out."

"And they brought her out of the park because they weren't sure if more trouble would arrive, or who it was—I can understand that," Heris said. "But they should have called the ship, at least."

"No time, Oblo said. But you know him—he hates to call for help."

"True." Heris looked down at Sirkin. So far she hadn't spoken; her expression hadn't changed. How badly was she really hurt—not physically, but emotionally? How would she react when she woke fully and realized that her lover was dead? "Brigdis," she said, touching the young woman's bandaged hand. "How are you feeling?"

"Captain?" Her voice was blurred; that could be the injuries or the drugs used to treat them. "You . . . came."

"Yes." No use to explain who had come when, not until her mind cleared. But tears rose in the younger woman's eyes.

"Amalie . . . she screamed . . ."

"I'm sorry, Brigdis," Heris said.

"Is she dead?" That sounded rational enough.

"Yes. I'm sorry. The sonic pulser got her at close range—you barely escaped."

"She—jumped in front of me," Sirkin said. "She—died for me." Her body trembled, as if she were trying to cry but was too exhausted. Probably those ribs, Heris thought. They wouldn't want to put her in the regeneration tank for the ribs until her concussion had stabilized.

"She was very brave," Heris said. It never hurt to praise the dead, and Amalie Yrilan could be brave and foolish both. Many people were.

"But . . . she had gambled." Heris wondered what that was about. Sirkin took a cautious breath. "She got in some trouble. I don't know what. There was this woman." All short sentences, carried on one difficult breath after another.

"You don't have to talk now," Heris said. "You're safe here. We'll stay with you, Petris or I."

"But I want to." Sirkin's face had a stubborn expression now, someone forcing herself past a margin of discomfort for her own reasons. "She died. She saved me. But that woman said go there." What woman? What was Sirkin talking about? Heris glanced at Petris, who shrugged.

"Brigdis, you've had a sonic charge to half your face, and some blows to the other half . . . I really think you shouldn't try to talk now. You're not clearheaded."

"But—I thought she loved me. And then I thought she didn't. And then she died. For me. So she must have—" Sirkin's expression was pleading now. Heris wished she was still small and young enough to pick up and hug—that's what she needed, medicine be damned.

"She did love you," she said firmly. "I could see that. She loved you enough to try to qualify for deep-space work, to follow you here. Whatever happened, she did love you. And she proved it at the end." She had long suspected that Yrilan would never have chosen a career aboard ships if Sirkin hadn't

been so intent on one. That face and attitude belonged somewhere else, though Heris didn't know where.

"You're sure?" Sirkin asked.

"I'm sure." Heris stroked her head. "Now you get some
sleep. I know you feel sick and hurt all over, but you're alive,
and you have friends to help you." Sirkin closed her eyes, and
in a few minutes was snoring delicately. Heris looked at Petris.
"I should go back to the ship and check on Meharry and Oblo.
Can you stay with her for now, and I'll be back later?"

"Of course. If you'd just speak to the staff here, and let
them know—they wanted to throw me out, earlier."

"Right. She shouldn't be alone, and I want to be notified at
once if the militia or Royal Security tries to talk to her."

Shiftchange chimed as Heris headed for the *Sweet Delight*.
She would be up three shifts running, probably, and she hated
to admit that it got harder every year. At her former rank in
the R.S.S., she'd have been up for automatic rejuvenation
treatment within the next few years, but as a civilian she'd
have to pay for it herself. She wondered if she could afford it.
Lady Cecelia claimed not to want rejuvenation; would she
disapprove of her captain taking it?

In the access tube, Issigai Guar waited for her. "Captain,
Oblo's not back yet, but Meharry's here . . . how's Brigdis?"

Heris shook her head. "She's got reparable physical injuries, but Yrilan's death is going to shake her badly. I'm going
back there after I debrief Meharry—any messages?"

"No, Captain, not since you've been back to this side of the
dock. Station militia called here earlier, and I told 'em you'd
headed for the Captains' Guild. But that was hours ago. Ginese
is on the bridge, of course."

"Let me know, then. I'm going to talk to Meharry and I
may put in a call to Lady Cecelia." Heris went on into the ship.
The lavender plush didn't look quite as bad to her now, especially since it was all going to disappear in the next few weeks.
Lady Cecelia had chosen crisp blues and greens with white

for her new scheme, over the protests of the decorator, who insisted that the very latest colors were peach, cream, and something called sandfox. With accents of hot coral and hunter green. Feminine, the decorator had said, and flattering to mature complexions. Cecelia's complexion had turned red at that, and she'd muttered that she could take her business to a place that would do what she wanted.

Meharry was outside her office, obviously fresh from a shower and change of clothes. She had a few visible bruises, but no worse damage.

"Sirkin's in the clinic—the ribs are broken, and she does have a concussion," Heris said before the other could ask. "They're trying some new drug on the concussion—supposed to counter diffuse damage and reduce swelling—and they'll put her in regen for the ribs when that's done. I'm going back later; Petris is with her now."

"Tough kid," Meharry said. "We'd been showing her some things, but I wouldn't have expected her to use them that well her first time out."

"Tell me about it," Heris said. The story from Meharry's viewpoint took longer than it had when Petris gave her the short form, and began with her pointing out to Oblo that even if Sirkin had been learning how to fight, when she was with Yrilan she wasn't really alert.

"I thought Oblo was installing that . . . navigational equipment."

"Well, ma'am, he was. But those two didn't leave right away—they spent awhile in Sirkin's cabin—and Oblo was just about nearly finished when they did. We just didn't want anything to happen . . . like it did."

"I didn't see you," Heris said. "And they were ahead of me."

Meharry's green eyes twinkled. "You weren't exactly looking, ma'am. You's looking at them, and we's looking at you . . . and them. They saw you, didn't see us. . . . classic, y'know?"

"So?"

"So," Meharry said, with an eloquent shrug, "they went to

this bar." Here she fished out the datawand. Heris felt her own brows rise. "You might want to read this off, Captain. We sent the main stuff back here already, but there's a bit more hasn't gone in the computer yet."

"You have a *Fleet* wand?"

"It's not Fleet now." The green eyes had gone muddy, like stagnant water. "It gives us that edge in networking you were talking about." If no one caught her with it. If it wasn't traced back to Heris.

"Still accesses Fleet nets?"

Meharry cocked her head. "Don't know, really. Haven't tried that yet. Be really risky to try it, if it doesn't." A mild way of putting it. "But it sucks strings out of civilian nets, no problem. Take a look."

Heris brought the data up on her desk screen. The picture of the woman in the silk suit and jewels was clear enough for recognition.

"Enhanced by her database identification," Meharry said, leaning over Heris's shoulder. "That's what she was wearing in the bar, but the face has been cleaned up by the ID subroutines. We didn't have a picmic to overhear what they said—the noise level in there was really bad and there were sonic cops out in the concourse, who'd have detected anything good enough to filter voices."

"Therapist," said Heris thoughtfully. "And Sirkin said something about Yrilan gambling—could the girl have had a gambling problem and seen a therapist?"

"Yrilan got crosswise and got mandatory counseling instead of a hotspot in records," Meharry said. "Pulled that out of this lady's office files, once I knew where. But Oblo and I think she's working for someone else. She definitely—definitely—signalled to these guys—" She pointed to the display again. "—when she came out. Then she fell off our scanners like a rock off a cliff. Had to be counterscan, had to be illegal." Meharry sounded righteous about that.

"Meharry, *your* scans are illegal," Heris said, trying not to laugh.

"Well, sure, but that's how I know her counterscans were. Legal citizen-type scans aren't worth the space in your pockets. Anybody can privacy-shield from them. We had to have something that'd work." Meharry shrugged that off and pointed to the display.

"Her accounts, now . . . look at what she spends just on clothes. Public service therapists don't make that much."

"Investment income, it says," Heris commented, not mentioning that sucking data from the banking nets was even more illegal than the rest of it.

"Yeah, but what investment? I grant you dividend income, but I wonder about the companies. You have investments, don't you? Why don't you check this stuff out, Captain?"

Heris laughed aloud. "In what spare time? I suppose I could ask about—uh—Siritec, since it seems to be paying her the most, but without knowing her initial investment there's no way to tell . . . and no, I'm not about to stick a wire into investment accounts myself. What you've got is interesting—I wish I could figure out a way to let the militia in on it without compromising you."

"You said Sirkin mentioned Yrilan's gambling. Maybe just that?"

"I'll think about it; I don't want her catching any more trouble if we can help it. Now—about the fight itself—"

Meharry grinned. "Like I said, the kid was tough. Yrilan was down when we got around the corner, one of 'em leaning over her—probably making her that C.H. pattern—and Sirkin was fighting hard, but not hard enough. 'Course, she was outnumbered, and they were armed." From the tone, she was making excuses she didn't think would have to be made for her. "They weren't trying to kill her, though. Somebody was on top of her, trying to cuff her, when Oblo 'bout took his head off. After that—" She gave a surprisingly detailed account of the brawl, interspersed with her assessment of the enemy's

ability and training. "And it was after they were all down, that
we saw Yrilan's face and hands. That's when we figured it was
Compassionate Hand business, and we'd better get Sirkin back
to safety—"

"Eh, Captain." That was Oblo, free surprisingly early
from the militia captain. Heris had thought he'd be much
later.

"Well—let's hear it from you." Oblo gave Meharry an
oblique glance and settled into a seat. His clothes still had the
marks of the fight, though he had daubed at the bloodstains
somewhere along the line. His version was even racier than
Meharry's. She hadn't bothered to mention the delay at the
park entrance; they hadn't wanted to kill any of their oppo-
nents at that point, but his description of the action made her
wonder why the militia hadn't found more inert bodies. Heris
heard him out, then sent them off to rest. She was a little
surprised that no more calls had come in for her, but she told
Guar to patch them to the clinic if they did come. After a look
at the time cycle where Cecelia was, she decided not to wake
her.

When she called later, she found that Cecelia was in a mood
Heris privately considered ridiculous. She was in a raging fury
about some point of family politics, and threatening to throw
things. Her reaction to Heris's news was just as strong and no
more helpful.

"*Just* what I needed," she snapped. "You can't even keep
things straightened out up there. Why I ever thought you were
more efficient than the prissy officious managers down here, I
cannot now recall." Heris tried not to get angry in return.
"Another dead body . . . and that nice girl Sirkin injured . . .
and that overpaid lot in the clinic will probably charge me
double."

"As a matter of fact, no." Heris broke in with quiet satisfaction. "Since Sirkin is the victim of a crime, and it's quite clear
that she bears no responsibility for what happened, no charges

apply to your employee accounts, and it will not affect your medical-tax rates in the future."

"Oh. Well." Heris could practically see the boiling temper settling down again. "Well, of course I care most about Sirkin and . . . whoever."

"Sirkin will be fine, they tell me. In fact, while it's a selfish thought at such a time, we're more likely to keep her now. Her lover, Yrilan, wasn't really qualified and I could not have justified offering her a long-term contract. Sirkin might or might not have stayed with us, if it meant separation from Yrilan."

"That's sad." Now Cecelia sounded like herself again. Heris was glad she had the experience to know that the harsh, biting voice was only an expression of mood, not basic personality. "What a price to solve a dilemma."

"True. Now, both Royal Security and the Station militia prefer that we remain docked here until Sirkin is out of the clinic and back aboard. That means we'll be late to the Spacenhance slot, but I've already contacted them and they're holding it for you. I'll be very careful arranging accommodations for the crew during the time the ship won't be habitable."

"Of course," Cecelia said. "And I'm sorry if I sounded off at first. It's just that you haven't been having to deal with the flat-footed *idiots*—" Her voice rose again. "—who messed up my perfectly clear instructions and landed me with a lot of low-grade bonds. These people who rejuvenate too often end up with brains like babies—no sense at all."

Heris shook her head, and tried not to grin. For a woman who claimed to know and care about nothing but horses and good food, Lady Cecelia had strong opinions about the minutiae of investing.

Three days later, Sirkin was finally cleared for the regen tanks, and her broken ribs responded with the alacrity of youth. "She's still not completely recovered from the concussion," the doctors warned Heris. "Don't expect rapid calculations, or long concentration—you're not going to make jump points any time soon, are you?"

"No. We're going in for redecorating—she'll have plenty of time to recover."

"Good. We'll want to see her every ten days until the scans are completely normal. Immediately, of course, if you notice any changes in behavior that might be the result of head injury. I know she's lost a close friend, and grief can produce some of the same symptoms—so be alert."

Heris walked back to the ship access with Sirkin. The sparkle she had enjoyed was gone; the younger woman looked pale and sad. Natural, of course. Heris knew from experience that nothing she said would really help. In time, she'd work through her grief, but right now she needed time and privacy to react. As they came aboard the yacht, Sirkin turned to her.

"Can you tell me what—where Amalie's—where they put . . . her?"

"In the morgue, awaiting instructions. The necropsy's finished; the sonic pulser killed her. Do you know what her wishes would have been?"

Sirkin frowned. "She didn't have burial insurance . . . I suppose it'll have to be the usual. But I wanted to see her."

Heris started to say *Better not*, then thought again. Would she have shielded a military youngster that way? Sirkin had earned a right to choose the difficult.

"Would you like me to come with you?"

"You'd do that?" Naked relief on her face. Heris nodded.

"Of course I will—and so will Petris. Oblo and Meharry, too, if you don't mind."

"I thought—I'd have to go alone," Sirkin said. Heris could see her determination to do just that if necessary, and her relief that she would have friends beside her.

"It's what shipmates are for," she said. "But you're just out of the clinic. If you'll take my advice, you'll get cleaned up, eat a good meal, and then go. By then I'll have called them to schedule a visit."

"Is it all right to wait? They won't . . . do anything?"

"Not without legal clearance."

"Then . . . I think I'd like to lie down a bit . . ." Sirkin looked even paler; Heris got an arm around her before her knees gave way, and helped her to her quarters.

"You'll be better in a few hours," she said. She hoped it would be true.

On the way to the morgue, next mainshift, Sirkin said "I suppose I should find out about Amalie's things. Or would the militia have done that?"

"They'll have looked in her lodgings. I haven't asked about that, but we can find out. Anything in particular?"

"Not really." It was the tone that meant yes, of course.

"Did she have a will?"

"Not . . . yet. We hadn't thought . . . you know . . . that she could die. Yet." That complicated things, but not too badly. If Sirkin wanted a keepsake, something not too valuable, Heris was sure she could get it.

At the morgue, Heris called in to the militia headquarters to ask about Yrilan's belongings. Cannibar wasn't in; she spoke to his assistant.

"Her stuff's in storage already, Captain Serrano, but if your crew has a legal claim—"

"No—she said Yrilan had made no will. I suspect they'd exchanged gifts, keepsakes—"

A long bored sigh in her ear. "Younglings. I wish she'd thought of this before we sealed the storage cube."

"She had a concussion," Heris said. "She was under medical treatment, remember?"

"Oh. Right. Well . . . she has to come by here for an interview anyway, doesn't she? I suppose, if you're willing to sit in, so I don't have to waste someone else's time—and it can't be anything of substantive value. Does your—uh—Sirkin have the next-of-kin names and addresses?"

"I'll find out," Heris said. "Right now we're at the morgue."

"Young idiot," said the voice, but with a tinge of humanity this time. "When can we expect you?"

"An hour or so, I expect, from here to there. She's not supposed to ride drop-tubes for a few more days. I'll call back if it's longer."

"If she comes apart," said the voice, this time full of resignation.

"Have you caught the ones who got away?" asked Heris. Time to put the voice on the defensive.

"Not yet. I'd figured from the blood that at least one would show up in some medical facility, but no such luck. Maybe he died and they put the body in the tanks." Heris opened her mouth, but the voice went on. "And before you ask, no, we can't do the kind of analysis you could on a Fleet ship—this Station's too big for that. We've always got some unauthorized recycs garbaging our figures."

"Too bad," Heris said. She glanced over and saw that Sirkin was about to go through a door into the viewing area. "Talk to you later," she said, and punched off.

Oblo and Meharry stood on either side of Sirkin as she waited in the viewing area. It was cold and a sharp odor made Heris's nose itch. A waist-high bar separated them from the polished floor on which the wheeled trays slid out from a wall of doors. Sirkin punched in the numbers she'd been given at the front desk. A door snicked open, and a draped form emerged so smoothly it seemed magical. The tray unfolded wheeled legs as it cleared the door, and rolled along tracks sunk in the floor until it stopped in front of their group. Heris glanced past to see an arrangement of visual baffles and sound-proofing that would allow several—she could not tell how many—viewings at once. With a thin buzz, the bar lifted to let them through.

Rituals for the dead varied; Heris had no idea what Sirkin felt necessary for Yrilan. Slowly, the young woman folded back the drape, and stared at the face. Morgues were nothing like the funeral hostels of those religions that thought it important to make the dead look "lifelike." No one had worked on Yrilan's face with paint or powder, with clay or gum or needle to reshape and recolor it. Her dead body looked just that: dead. Heris guessed that under the rest of the sheet the marks of the fight and the autopsy both would be even more shocking. Sirkin had given one sharp gasp, as the reality of it hit her. Heris touched her shoulder, lightly.

"It's so . . . ugly," Sirkin said. Heris saw Oblo's eyelids flicker. This was far from ugly, as they had both seen ugly death . . . but it was Sirkin's first, maybe. "Her hair's all dirty and bloody—" She touched it, her hands shaking.

"She had beautiful hair," Meharry said. Heris glanced at her. She hadn't expected Meharry to notice, or to comment now. But Meharry was watching Sirkin. "Lovely hair it was, and if you cut yourself a lock—over on this side, it's just as clean and lovely as ever . . ."

Sirkin's hand went out again, then she turned and grabbed for a hand, anyone's hand. Heris took it, and put an arm around her shoulders. "I'm sorry," she said, and meant it. "You've seen enough now, haven't you? Do you have a picture, the way she was?"

"I—yes—but that's not the point." Sirkin, trembling, was still trying to stay in control. "She died for me; the least I can do is look."

Heris was surprised in spite of herself. She'd been impressed with Sirkin before, but death spooked a lot of people. Sirkin pushed herself away from Heris, but Oblo intercepted her.

"There's a right way," he said. "You loved her; we all respect her body. You take that corner; let the captain take this."

What lay beneath the drape met Heris's expectations. None of Yrilan's beauty remained, nor any clue to her personality. In slow procession across the inside of Heris's eyelids passed the dead she had seen in all her years, one blank face after another. She, too, always looked—and she had never yet become inured to it. Sirkin, only a fine tremor betraying her, stared blankly at the evidence of a violent death, and then, with Heris's help, stretched the drape across the body once more. A last stroke of the hand on that fire-gold hair, and she turned away, mouth set. Meharry, Heris noted, had clipped a single curl and folded it into a tissue: Sirkin might want it later. Or might not—she trusted Meharry to know whether to offer it or not.

◊ Chapter Six

Shifting the *Sweet Delight* from the Royal Docks to the decorators took only a few hours, but Heris felt she'd put in a full shift's work by the time they had linked with their new docking site. First there'd been the formalities of leaving the Royal Sector, with a double inventory of all badges issued, and multiple inspections of the access area. That had made them half an hour late in departure. Then the captain of the tug designated to move the yacht, angry because of the delay, took out his frustrations with several abrupt attitude changes that strained *Sweet Delight's* gravity compensators. Heris had to be almost rude to get him to stop. Finally, even the docking at Spacenhance presented problems. Although Heris had given them the yacht's specifications as soon as the contract was signed, the slot had been left "wide" for the much larger vessel just completed. Heris had to hold the yacht poised, just nuzzling the dock, while the expansion panels eased out to complete the docking seal.

"They probably thought you'd tear up their space if they resized it ahead of time," Petris pointed out. Heris wanted to grumble at him but there was no time. Somewhere on the dock, the moving and storage crews would be racking up time charges. Her crew would supervise the packing and removal of all the yacht's furnishings, and the sealing of essential systems from whatever chemicals the decorators used.

At least the lavender plush was about to disappear. Heris wondered if they'd roll it up and sell it to someone else. Perhaps that's why they'd tried to argue Cecelia into yet another color scheme she didn't like. It would save energy and resources to reuse all that material. She led the crew to the access tube and looked around for the decorator's representative.

The decorator's dockside looked nothing like the luxurious offices in which Cecelia had made her choices of color and texture. A vast noisy space, in which rows of shipping containers looked like children's blocks on the floor of a large room, gaped around them. Machinery clanked and grumbled; something smelled oily and slightly stale. A crew in blue-striped uniforms, presumably from the moving and storage company, lounged near the shipping containers.

"Ah . . . Captain Serrano." That was a tall, gangling man in a formal gray suit. "Are we ready to get started?"

"Quite," said Heris. He had an ID tag dangling from his lapel, with the firm's logo in purple on peach. Typical, she thought. He turned and waved to the moving and storage crew.

"You do understand that everything must be removed or sealed? Not that there's any question of contamination . . ." He laughed, three very artificial ha-ha-has, and Heris wondered what ailed him. "But we want no questions. I am Ser Schwerd, by the way, the director on this project. I suppose the owner is still determined on that . . . unfortunate color scheme?"

"If you mean green and white, yes."

"Pity. We can do so much more when given a free hand. Really, if clients would only realize that we know much more about decorating than they do. However, the client's satisfaction is more important than any other consideration; though if we could strike a blow for artistic integrity—"

"Lady Cecelia," Heris said, "is quite sure what she wants."

He sighed. "They always are, Captain Serrano. All these old ladies are sure they know what they want, and really they have no idea. But let's not waste our time lamenting what can't be changed. Always think positively, that's my motto. If the lady is unsatisfied with this redecoration, perhaps next time she'll trust the judgment of someone with real expertise."

Heris managed not to laugh at him. Anyone who knew Lady Cecelia knew that she had no doubts about her own desires; she would not likely change her mind because someone else claimed to have better taste. Ser Schwerd introduced the movers' supervisor, a thickset bald man with twinkling brown eyes.

"Gunson," he said. "Quite reliable." Gunson's expression said he could prove that without Schwerd's commentary. Heris liked him at once, and they exchanged handshakes.

A steady stream of packers and movers moved through the ship. Cecelia's belongings disappeared into padded containers, which then fit into the larger storage/shipping containers. With all the crew to help, the inventory checkoffs went more quickly than usual—according to Gunson. Cecelia's own quarters, the guest quarters, the public areas of the ship, crew quarters. Furniture, the contents of built-in storage, clothing, decorations—everything.

"What about this?" Gunson asked, opening the galley door.

"Nothing—seal it off," Heris said. Schwerd grimaced.

"It needs something—"

"No . . . Lady Cecelia has a very exacting cook. He's got it just the way he wants it, and if you'll look at the contract, it specifies absolutely no change in the galley or pantries."

"But foodstuff should be removed—"

"Why?" Heris asked, surprised. "These are staples; they won't deteriorate in the few weeks you'll be working. If the galley's sealed, there's no danger of contamination from any paint fumes or whatever. Besides, we were told initially that there was no need to remove anything from compartments that could be sealed and were not to be worked on."

He looked unhappy, but nodded. The decorators had provided coded seals for compartments not part of the contract. Heris had her crew seal the hatches under his supervision; she wasn't sure she trusted the decorators not to try something fancy where it wasn't wanted. The bridge, for example, and the ships' systems compartments. The garden sections of hydroponics were all empty now, but the gas-exchange tanks remained operational, the bacterial cultures on maintenance nutrients. She didn't want to take the time to recharge them all later.

At last everything was off the ship, and all the crew had their personal gear loaded on carryalls. Heris sent them ahead to the lodgings she'd arranged. She and Ser Schwerd had to do the final inspection, checking both the seals to areas not being worked on and the areas that were supposed to be clear.

"Someone always leaves something," Schwerd said. "Always. Sometimes it's valuable—once, I recall, a distinguished lady's diamond-and-ruby brooch, lying there in the middle of the owner's stateroom. Why someone hadn't stepped on it and broken it, I never knew. More often it's some little thing the movers can't believe is important, but it has sentimental value. A child's soft toy, an unimportant trophy." He strode through the passages with an expression of distaste, glancing quickly into each compartment.

"Ah . . ." This was in Cecelia's quarters, the study which looked so different with its antique books and artwork removed. Sure enough, a squashed and dusty arrangement of faded ribbons, which Heris realized, after Schwerd smoothed it with his hands, had once been a rosette of some sort. "One of Lady Cecelia's earlier triumphs, I would say." He held it out; Heris could just make out ". . . hunter pony . . ." in flaking black letters on the purplish ribbon. "It would have been a first place blue," Schwerd said. "Those letters were originally gold or silver ink. And I'm sure she'd notice if it were gone." He handed it to Heris, ceremoniously, and she brushed off the rest of the dust, folded it, and tucked it into her jacket. Perhaps Cecelia would notice, perhaps not, but she would keep it safe.

Back at the hostel, Heris checked on her crew. Transient crew housing had few amenities; the ship had been far more comfortable. But they had settled in, having arranged adjoining cubicles. She had decided to stay here, with them, rather than at the Captains' Guild. She worried about the next few weeks—how to keep them busy and out of trouble until they could go back aboard. With the Compassionate Hand looking for revenge—and despite the militia's assurances, she knew they would be looking for revenge—all were in danger until something else distracted that organization. Perhaps she could schedule some training in civilian procedures.

Petris signalled her with raised eyebrows. Did she want to—? Of course, though she'd like to have a long uninterrupted sleep first. With the ship now the responsibility of the decorating firm, she could reasonably sleep late into the next shift. Surely her crew could cope by themselves for a day. She posted a crew meeting far enough in the future that she knew she couldn't sleep that long, no matter what, and nodded to Petris.

"Dinner first?" he asked. Heris yawned and shook her head.

"If you're hungry, go ahead—I'm more tired than anything."

"Umm. Perhaps my suggestion was premature?"

"No. I've missed you. It's amazing how few times we've managed to be together. Something always happens. I'm beginning to feel like the heroine in a farce."

"Don't say that." He made a mock-angry face at her. "You'll bring the bad luck down on us."

"Not this time," she said. "The ship's safe, and Sirkin's safe with Meharry in the same section. If the rest of them go wandering, they'll be a match for anything. Besides, they're too tired right now, just like I am. Maybe I'll nap a bit, and then— we'll finally have time to enjoy ourselves."

In the quiet dark of her quarters, she lay against his warm length and felt her muscles unkinking, strand by strand. This was, indeed, better than dinner . . . she dozed off, aware of his hand tracing patterns on her back but unable to stay awake to appreciate them fully. They had time . . . she needed just a little sleep . . .

She was deep in a dream about sunlit fields and people dancing in circles when the insistent voice in the intercom woke her. "Captain Serrano. Captain Serrano. Captain Serrano . . ."

"Here," she said, blinking into the darkness. A sour taste came into her mouth.

"There's an urgent message from downside. It's on a tightlink; you'll have to come to a secure line."

"At once." Petris roused then; she found him looking at her when she turned on a single dim light to dress by. His expression was both rueful and grumpy.

"What happened?"

"I don't know." She didn't, but her heart was racing. It had to be something about Cecelia; the bad feeling she'd had loomed as close as a storm. "It's a tightlink call from downside. Not Cecelia calling, I don't think—they'd have told me—but they said it was urgent."

"I told you not to bring bad luck down on us," he said, but his grin took the sting out of it. "I'll get up; you go on."

"I'll be back soon," she said, and kissed him. Now she was awake, she wanted to leap back into bed with him. Why couldn't she have waked from that dream to the sound of his voice, the feel of his hands, with nothing to do but enjoy herself? With a sigh, she pushed herself away, and went out.

It wasn't really that late, she realized once she was out in the public meeting areas. She found a tightlink booth, and entered it. The ID procedure was almost as complete as for Fleet links, and she had several seconds to wait before the screen cleared from the warning message. She put the headset on.

"Captain Serrano?" It was Ronnie, and he sounded as if he'd been crying.

"What's wrong?" she asked. "Is your aunt—?"

"She's—she may die, they said." His voice broke, then

steadied. "She—she just fell down. And she was breathing oddly, and the doctors think she's had a massive stroke."

Heris found it hard to think. She had anticipated some trouble, but not this. "Where is she? Where are you?"

"She's at St. Cyril's, and I'm at home—at my parents' house. That's where it happened. Mother's at the hospital; she said to stay here and out of the way." He paused, cleared his throat, and continued. "She didn't tell me to tell you, but I thought you should know."

"Thank you. You're right that I needed to know." Heris tried to think who else would need to know. The redecorators? Probably, although they already had the guarantee on the job. The crew, certainly. She wondered whether Cecelia had told Ronnie about the attack on Yrilan and Sirkin . . . was there any possibility that this was a covert action by the Compassionate Hand? "Did you see it?" she asked.

"No. I was there, but in the next room, talking to my father. We didn't hear her fall, but we heard Mother scream. We called emergency medical help, of course . . ."

"Was anyone else there? Any visitors?"

"Well, yes. It was a reception for the Young Artists' League—Mother's a sponsor—and she had a time convincing Aunt Cecelia to come. Why?"

How much to tell him, even on a tightline. She had to risk it. "Ronnie—did your aunt mention the attack on Sirkin?"

"Something happened to Sirkin? What?"

"She was attacked, with her lover, by the Compassionate Hand—a criminal organization—"

"I know about them," Ronnie said, affronted.

"Fine. Her lover was killed, and Sirkin's alive because Oblo and Meharry came into the fight. But think—is there any chance, any chance at all that your aunt's collapse could have been an attack? I don't know how—you were there—but could it have been?"

"You mean—they'd get after her? Like . . . er . . . poison?"

"They might. Ronnie, listen: you must not, absolutely must

not, talk about this to anyone. Anyone. We don't know if it happened, but if it did happen the worst thing you could do is talk about it. Something should give you a clue later on . . . something will happen, or be said . . . but you're the only one available to interpret it. You have to stay alive, well, and free. Is that clear?"

"It's really serious." It was not a question. "You really think— yes. All right. I will keep it quiet, but how do I talk to—wait a minute, someone's here—" The open line hummed gently, rhythmically, with the scrambling effect. She could hear nothing from the far end—she wasn't supposed to. Finally Ronnie came back on, slightly breathless. "Sorry—my father's back. Aunt Cecelia's in a coma; they don't know if she'll come out of it. He thinks not. I—I'll get back to you when I can."

Heris waited for the triple click of the line closing, then the ending sequence on her console. Alongside the shock and fear she felt was a trickle of amusement—once again, something had interrupted her night with Petris. Once again it had been something she couldn't anticipate. She shook her head, and emerged from the booth to find Petris watching her.

"Lady Cecelia?" he asked.

"Yes," she said. "Let's go back—you need to hear about it."

In the little room, both of them glanced at the rumpled bed and away from it again. Heris settled in the chair; Petris pulled the covers back across the bed and sat on its edge.

"She's alive," Heris said. "But I don't know for how long. According to Ronnie, she collapsed suddenly and the doctors are saying it's a stroke."

"She's old," Petris said, answering her doubt, not her words. "And she hasn't had rejuv, has she?"

"No. She told me once she disapproved of it; she had healthy genes, she said, and when her time was up it was only fair to give someone else a chance."

"Silly attitude." Petris scowled. "In a universe this big, there's room for everyone. Besides, she was rich."

"She might have reconsidered—I think she made that

decision when she was unhappy, and stuck to it out of stubbornness. I had been seeing signs of change in her."

"But still—in her eighties, even now, without rejuv. It could be a natural stroke." He cocked his head at her. "But you don't think so, do you?"

"It would be a damned convenient stroke, Petris. Coming so soon after the attack on Sirkin and Yrilan, combined with her . . . er . . . revelations to the Royals about Mr. Smith—" Heris didn't want to be any more specific in quarters that might easily be under surveillance.

"And you said she was in a foul temper about something just a few days ago—some family business. Perhaps there's someone else with a reason to put her out of action. Although temper—isn't that a cause of strokes?"

Heris laughed, and surprised herself. "If it were, no Serrano would have survived to take rejuv. I'm one of the mild ones."

"But it *could* have been a stroke, no enemy action."

"Could have been. There's no way we can tell from here. I just worry—"

"Wouldn't the doctors figure out if it's not a real stroke?"

"I don't know. And if they do think someone did something, that doesn't mean they can fix it. At least they can't blame *us*—we're up here, and she's been down there for days."

"Well. Nothing we can do right now, is there?"

"No, but I—"

"You're not in the mood, I understand that, but do you think you could sleep?"

By this time, Heris wasn't sleepy anymore; she and Petris finally went out for an early breakfast, and came back to tell the rest of the crew. Heris wasn't sure what to do about them. She really wanted to take a shuttle downside and see for herself how Cecelia was. But that would leave the crew with nothing to do but fret. As for the future, if Cecelia died, or stayed in a coma, she wouldn't need a yacht and crew . . . at some point Heris would have to look for another job, and hope a few of her crew could find work on the same ship. Not likely, but . . .

she scolded herself for thinking of her own convenience, her own desires, when a friend lay comatose. Conflicting loyalties tugged at her.

The crew took the news quietly at first. Sirkin still looked shocky from her own loss and her injuries; she sat pale and silent, not meeting anyone's eyes. The others glanced back and forth and deferred their questions. Heris, knowing them so well, knew they had questions, and would come to her individually.

By the time she thought of sleep again, she and Petris both had little interest in pleasure. He pleaded a headache—"Non-traditional as it is, my love, it's boring a hole in my skull and frying my brain"—and went to his own quarters; she slept badly, waking often to think she'd heard the intercom calling.

The next call finally came from the family legal firm two days later. They had no interest in answering her questions, and had plenty of their own. What was the status of Lady Cecelia's yacht? Heris explained about the redecorating. Couldn't it be halted? She had anticipated this question, and had already contacted the redecorators. No—the ship's existing finishes were already being stripped. They could delay applying the new carpeting and wallcoverings, but they couldn't replace those already removed—not without a surcharge. Heris pointed out that Cecelia had loathed the color scheme, and it would make no sense to replace the same one.

"But her *sister* selected it," said the lawyer, in an outraged tone.

Heris wondered whether to mention who was paying for the new one, and decided better not.

"Lady Cecelia preferred something else," she said. "She was quite firm about it."

"I don't doubt," he said sourly. "The point is, if she is, as seems likely, permanently incapacitated, she will have no need for the yacht and a new color scheme hardly seems worth the price. If it's for sale—"

"Perhaps simply having the decorators delay installing the new—that way, any potential buyer could choose his or her own scheme—"

"Perhaps. Now, about the crew payroll—"

"Lady Cecelia had given me permission to authorize payment from the yacht expenses account. I can transmit all the recent transactions, if you'd like."

"Yes, thank you." He seemed a bit surprised. Heris wondered if he'd expected her to try something dishonest.

"And I would like some idea of when a determination will be made about the yacht, since the crew will need the usual warning before being asked to find new positions." That should convince him she wasn't trying to get them on the family payroll forever.

"Oh. Quite. Well, er . . . no hurry, I should think. In case she recovers, though that seems unlikely . . . there's always the chance . . . and anyway, some legal action would have to be taken to transfer control of the yacht to her heirs. Certainly that won't happen for . . . oh . . . sixty days or more."

Heris chose her words carefully. "You mean, I am authorized to maintain and pay an idle crew for sixty days?"

"Well . . . er . . . yes . . . I suppose so . . ." Unspoken conflicts between parsimony and habit cluttered his words.

"I would prefer to have that in writing," Heris said briskly, with no sympathy for his problems. "It's possible that either Lady Cecelia's bankers or Station personnel could have questions."

"Oh, certainly. I'll see that you get that, and I'll speak to her bankers." Faced with an assignment, his voice picked up energy. This was simply business, a routine he was used to. "Of course, that's limited to . . . er . . . the usual schedule of payments."

"Of course. I'm sure Lady Cecelia's records already contain a pay scale and the account activity, but I'll send those along."

Spacenhance were not pleased to have the redecorating halted midway, but maintained a polite, if frosty, demeanor about it. They could, they admitted, simply leave the ship "bare" for a week or so. Even longer, if no other business came in, though if they needed the dock space the yacht would have to be moved to another site. Heris pointed out that she would have to have legal authorization to move it, since Lady Cecelia's affairs were now in the hands of her legal staff, and might soon be a matter of court decision. They subsided so quickly that Heris was sure another player had made the same point more forcibly. The king? Certainly the Crown could command a berth there as long as it wanted.

After another three days of waiting, she tried to contact Cecelia's sister or brother-in-law. A frosty servant informed her that neither was home, that no family member was home, and that inquiries from employees should be made to the family legal representative. She couldn't tell, from the tone, if that was aimed at her, specifically, or at any low-level employee. She realized she didn't even know what other employees Cecelia might have onplanet, besides her maid Myrtis.

The news media had had nothing to say about it, of course, though it showed up on the hospital admissions list. Heris thought of having Oblo insinuate himself into the hospital datanet, but that could have serious repercussions. The hospital census let her know that Cecelia was alive still.

Ronnie called her a day after she'd tried to reach the family.

"She's alive, still in a coma," he said. "They're talking about moving her to a different facility, which prepares people for long-term care."

"Have you seen her yourself?" Heris asked.

"Only through glass. She's hooked up to so many tubes . . . they say that's temporary, until they've got implanted monitors in her. So far she's breathing on her own—"

"No response?"

"None I can see. Of course, she could be sedated. There's no way for me to tell, but I know the family's very concerned. They've had outside consultants already." He sounded as if he wanted to burst into tears.

"What happens now?" Heris asked. "Who decides what to do?"

"My mother's her nearest relative on this planet. Aunt Cecelia had filed all the . . . er . . . directives old people are supposed to file, and my mother agrees with them, so she's the one to sign the papers."

"When will they move her? Do you know?"

"Not exactly. She's out of the first unit, and into something they call the Stabilization Unit. As I understand it, they'll implant the first sensors and something so they can plug feeding tubes and things in. Then they'll send her to this other place. If she comes out of the coma, fine—they can just take the implants out. If she doesn't, there's some other surgery—I don't know it all yet—and they'll send her somewhere for long-term care."

"For the rest of her life," Heris said, trying to take it in.

"That's what they said." Ronnie sounded uncertain. "They said she might live out her normal life span, even." Heris tried to think what that would be for a woman Cecelia's age. "Oh—" Ronnie broke into her thoughts. "Do you know if she was taking any kind of medicine?"

"Your aunt? Not that I know of. She told me she didn't take anything unless she had an injury."

"That's what I told them when they asked, but I thought—if you knew—maybe it would help."

"I can't even look in her quarters," Heris reminded him. "Everything's in storage for refitting. Have you asked Myrtis?"

"Yes, but she didn't know of any. There's another thing—"

"Yes?"

"I'm not sure why, but my parents are really upset with you. They seem to think you've been a bad influence on Aunt Cecelia. I told them about how you shot that admiral, and all, but they have something against you."

Heris frowned. "I wonder what. Did your aunt talk about me?"

"Yes—she thought you were great, but I would've thought

it just bored them—excuse me, but you know what I mean."

"Perhaps she said too much about me; if it bored them, they could decide not to like the boring topic." She said it lightly, but it worried her. Were Cecelia's relatives really that silly?

Several days later, Ronnie called again. "I found out what was upsetting them," he said. "And you need to know."

"What?"

"Aunt Cecelia left you the yacht in her will."

"She *what*? She couldn't have."

"I thought you didn't know," he said, sounding smug. "They think you did. It was one of the first things she did when she got here, apparently. Went to her attorney and had her will changed."

"But she shouldn't have—there's no reason—"

"Well, her attorney argued about it, but she insisted; you know her. And when the doctors said the stroke might have been caused by a drug of some kind, the attorney thought of you, because you would benefit."

"But she's not dead." That popped out; the rest of her mind snagged on "might have been caused by a drug" and hung there, unable to think further.

"She could have died. Besides, you know the law—if she's not competent in law for long enough—I forget how long it is—they open her will and distribute her assets under court guardianship."

"You mean someone can inherit before she's dead?" Heris found she could deal with the lesser curiosity while the greater dread sank deeper into her mind. She had never heard of such a possibility.

"Yes, but with some controls, so if she's suddenly competent again she can regain control." From Ronnie's tone, this was something most people knew about. Most people as rich as his family, at least.

"But—I'm not the sole beneficiary, am I?"

"No, but you're the only one outside family or long-term business associates. She left her forty-seven percent interest in her breeding and training stables to the woman who's owned the other fifty-three percent for the past twenty years, for instance. But that's been expected. The yacht wasn't. And for some reason Mother's really annoyed about it. I think she's still upset with Aunt Cecelia for not liking the decorator she chose. Besides, we don't have a yacht, and Mother's always wanted one."

"You don't?" Keep him talking. Maybe then she could process that dire possibility, figure out what to do.

"No . . . my father always said it made more sense to travel on commercial liners, and if you really needed off-schedule travel you could always charter. We've done that. Of course we have shuttles." To Heris, private deep-space ships made more sense than shuttles, and she said so. Ronnie explained. "If you have your own shuttle, you're never stuck onplanet. And no one knows for sure if you're traveling yourself, which they would in a public shuttle. Aunt Cecelia didn't agree; she'd take the public shuttles as often as not, even if my father offered her the use of ours. Now Bunny's family keeps shuttles on several worlds *and* a yacht. That's the most convenient, but my father says it's far too expensive." Heris gathered her scattered wits and came up with one idea.

"Ronnie, is his daughter—Brun—back here now? Or could you find out?"

"Brun? Oh, Bubbles's new name. Yes, she's here . . . why?"

"Does her father know about Lady Cecelia?"

"Yes, and Bubbles—Brun—says he's upset. Of course he would be; they've been friends all their lives."

"Ask her to call me, will you? I'd like to see her, if possible."

"Of course, but why?"

Heris herself wasn't sure, but something glimmered at the back of her mind, something that might help Cecelia. "We had a long talk before we left Sirialis. I'd just like to chat with her."

"Oh." She could tell from his expression that he thought this was a silly side issue, that she should stick to the problem of Cecelia's coma and the irate family. "Well . . . I'll tell her. Do you want her to come up there?"

"If possible."

Heris wanted to suggest that Brun take some precautions, but she was afraid Ronnie would waste time asking why. And after all, the girl wanted to be an adventurer—give her a chance to show any native talent.

Brun called on an open line, direct to the desk at Heris's hostel. She sounded just like the petulant girl Heris had first met. "Captain Serrano!" Her upper-class accent speared through the conversation in the lounge. Heris sensed others listening to the overspill from the speaker. So much for talent. Brun went on. "Have you seen my blue jewel case?"

"I beg your pardon." It was all Heris could think of, a reflex that meant nothing but bought a few seconds.

"This is Bubbles, Bunny's daughter," the voice went on. "When we were on Lady Cecelia's yacht, I had my blue jewel case and now I can't find it. It's not at Sirialis, and it's not here—it must be on the yacht. Would you please look in the stateroom I was using, and send it to me?"

For a moment Heris wondered if Brun had gone mad. Or if she'd given up the change of name and gone back to being a fluffhead. How could she be worrying about a jewel case with Cecelia in the hospital, in a coma? She could hear the annoyance in her own voice when she answered. "I'm sorry—Lady Cecelia's yacht is empty—everything was removed to storage because the yacht was to be redecorated, but now—"

"But I *need* it!" Brun's voice whined. "I *always* wear that necklace at the family reunion, and it's next week, and if I don't wear it, Mother will want to know why, and—"

"I'm sorry," Heris said. A glimmer of understanding broke through her irritation . . . if Brun was really that devious, she might indeed have talent. "You'd have to get into the storage facility, and I don't know . . ." She let her voice trail away.

"I'll come up there," Brun said, suddenly decisive. "They'll have to let me in—you can introduce me; it's not like I'm a criminal or anything. I just want my own blue jewel case, and I know just where I must have left it, in the second drawer from the bottom in that bedside chest . . ."

"But I'm not sure," Heris said, shaking her head for the benefit of the listeners in the hostel lounge. "I don't think they'll let anyone but Lady Cecelia's agent—"

"But you *are* her agent," Brun said. "You can do it—I know you can. I'll be up there in—let's see—late tonight. I'll call." She broke the connection. Heris looked around and sighed dramatically.

"The rich are different from you and me," said the clerk, with sympathy. Heris shrugged.

"They think they are. Can you believe? She thinks she left something aboard Lady Cecelia's yacht months ago, and expected me to retrieve it. Of course everything's in sealed storage. Of course they aren't going to let her into it."

"Who is she?" the man asked.

"Lord Thornbuckle's youngest daughter. They call her Bubbles."

"Ah—I've heard of her. They *will* let her in, bet you they do. Likely her father owns the company that owns the company that owns them. Might as well cooperate with that kind."

In person, Brun had indeed reverted to the fluffhead Bubbles. Her blonde hair, brushed into a wild aureole, had been tinted pink at the ends. She wore an outfit of pink and lime green which Heris assumed was an extreme of fashion; bright clattering bracelets covered both arms to the elbow.

"Captain Serrano!" Her greeting almost went too far; Heris recognized the tension around the eyes that didn't fit the wide smile. "I'm simply devastated . . . I have to have that necklace."

"Nice to see you again, miss." Heris couldn't bring herself

to call the girl Bubbles, but "Brun" would break the fluffhead cover. "I've checked with the storage company; they will meet with you Mainshift tomorrow. Perhaps you could give me a few more details? They thought the chests in that stateroom had all been empty."

"Oh, of course. Let's go eat somewhere—I'm starved. I'm sure the food's better at my hotel." And Brun turned away, clearly someone who expected flunkies to do as they were told. Heris saw the amused glances of the others in the lounge, and gave them a wry grin as she followed Brun out into the concourse.

✧ Chapter Seven

Cecelia's first sensory impression was smell: not a pleasant scent, but a sharp, penetrating stink she associated with fear and pain. After a timeless rummage through the back shelves of memory, her mind decided it was medicinal, and that probably meant she was in a doctor's office. Gradually, over time she could not guess, she became aware of pressure. She lay on her back; she could feel the contact between a firm surface and her shoulders and her buttocks. She was less sure of her arms and legs . . . and in trying to feel their position realized in one stab of panic that she could not move.

She did feel the leap her heart gave then, and she heard, as if from a great distance, the voices that chattered above her. Her mind rattled around the vast dark space it sensed, and reminded her of other unpleasant wakenings. The eighteenth fence at Wherrin, that bad drop that she'd misjudged in the mud. The time a new prospect had gone completely berserk under a roofed jump, and nearly killed her. She wondered what it had been this time . . . she couldn't quite remember. An event? Training? Foxhunting? Oddly, she couldn't even remember the horse—even any horse she'd worked recently.

The voices above gave her no clue. No one asked her name or what had happened; no one spoke to her at all. A bad sign, that: she knew it from times she'd sat waiting outside for a hurt friend. A few of the technical terms sounded familiar, BP and cardiac function and perfusion. If she didn't know what they meant, she knew they meant something. But others . . . her mind tried to grasp the unfamiliar syllables, but they slipped away. Demyel-something and something about selective pathways and neuromuscular dis-something. The drug names she didn't expect to know, but she knew the voices discussed things to be put in this line or that. A harder pressure against her arm—at least she knew now that her arm was up there, not down here—might be an injection.

It didn't hurt. Nothing hurt, and that scared her. If you didn't hurt, something really big was wrong. The longer it didn't hurt, the worse it was. If it was really bad—her mind shied away from the idea of spinal cord injury, brain injury—you would never hurt again, but that was worst. Sometimes even regeneration tanks wouldn't work on central nervous system injuries.

If she could move something . . . she struggled, first to decide what to move, and then to move. An eyelid. She felt no movement, and the darkness did not lift.

"A bit of excess activity there," someone said. Had she managed a movement she did not feel? She tried again. "Another tenth cc of motor inhibition," she heard. "And increase the primary decoupler one cc an hour." Inhibition? Decoupler? Just as the additional drugs pushed her beneath the surface of thought again, her mind made all the connections and nearly exploded in panic. No accident at all . . . someone had done this to her. On purpose. And she had no way to summon help. Damn, she thought. I was stupid. Heris was right. Hope she figures it out . . .

She woke again, to the same medical-ward smells, the same darkness, the same inability to move or speak.

"Hopeless, I'm afraid," she heard. She didn't recognize the voice. "There's been no change at all, nothing in the brain scans . . . look, here's the first. Massive intracranial bleed, typical cerebral accident. Probably all those years of riding, with repeated small concussions, caused significant weakening in the vascular attachments here and here—"

Someone else was here, not a medical person. Someone who wanted to know if she was going to get well. Someone who cared. If she could only make a sound, a small movement, anything.

"You can see the monitors yourself," the voice said, nearer now. "If we use a strong aversive stimulus—" Acrid fumes stung her nose; her brain screamed danger/poison/run. "—you see a very slight reaction in the brainstem, there. The fourth line. But she doesn't move. I can open an eye—" She felt the pressure on her eyelid, felt the movement across the eye itself, but saw nothing. "No change in pupil size, no response here. Cortical blindness. There's no evidence of auditory response, no indication of higher cortical functions."

"Couldn't you have operated on the bleed?" The voice was male, used to authority, but Cecelia didn't recognize it. Certainly it wasn't her brother-in-law. "With all your facilities—"

"Too diffuse, I'm sorry. We think branches of both cerebral arteries failed at once. As if she'd been repeatedly bludgeoned, but of course that wasn't the cause. I still think the years of riding had something to do with it, but I can't prove it. I've sent for her scans after the previous accidents."

"Could it have been . . . a result of poisoning?" YES! Cecelia thought. Good man. Smart man. Of course it was poisoning.

"I doubt it," the other voice said. "There are neurotoxins, of course, that mimic natural strokes. But the evidence from her scans is clear: this is bleeding." She heard a finger tap on something—a display, perhaps.

"I didn't mean that it wasn't bleeding," the skeptical voice said. "I wondered if someone had induced the bleeding with a poison, perhaps a blood thinner or something of that sort."

"Ah." The professional voice sounded more relaxed now. Of course it would. "According to her records, she wasn't taking any medication of that sort . . . and I don't know if they analyzed her blood for that in the hospital that first night. They should have, of course; I just presumed that if it were a drug it would be in the records when she was transferred here."

So she had been somewhere else and was now who knew where? She wondered where she'd been when she first woke up. Was that the original hospital? Had it been the big down-town one, or the upper-class clinic near her sister's house?

"The thing is," the skeptical voice said, "the family are con-cerned that she might have been under . . . er . . . undue influ-ence, as it were, of someone. Until the formal proceedings, we cannot be sure, but the date of her last testamentary revi-sion suggests that something happened recently. If there should be an unforeseen bequest, and if that individual had exerted undue influence, then there would have been . . . er . . ."

"Motivation to cause her harm. I see, precisely."

Damn. The fool. The utter, incompetent fool. Now who-ever had done this would have a chance to blame it on the one person it couldn't be, and this stupid lawyer—she was sure it was a lawyer—had given them all they needed.

"But that's another problem, and what we really need from you, doctor, is your assessment of prognosis. Is Lady Cecelia going to recover competency, or not? And if so, when? We have petitions of incompetency . . ."

"As I said originally, we cannot hold out much hope of recovery. I would hate to be hasty, but . . . my professional opinion is that irreversible brain damage has occurred, and I would be willing to present the evidence to a court. Although I see no reason for haste—"

"The statutes prescribe the waiting periods, doctor. It has been thirty days—" Thirty days. Thirty *days*. She had to scream, but she couldn't; she forced rage and panic down and listened. "—and petitions may be presented, although of course no final action will be taken just yet." A pause, during which she *felt* someone's gaze across her face, painful in its lack of caring. "It is curious, isn't it, that with so much damage she requires no life support?"

"Unusual, but quite easily explained," said the doctor. She wanted to know his name, wanted to have some name to curse in the darkness. "See here—on this shot—the bleeds stopped short of areas regulating breathing, for instance. It's quite likely that she will live out her normal span."

"Without rejuvenation treatments."

"Oh, certainly. We couldn't recommend rejuvenation for someone in her condition. No, indeed."

Normal span. Her mind calculated . . . at least another ten years, maybe twenty. If she didn't get pneumonia, if she didn't catch a virus. If whoever had done this didn't simply kill her.

And why hadn't they killed her? Why this? Did someone know she was still alive, aware, inside, and was that person gloating over her suffering? If Heris's wicked admiral had been alive, she could have believed that of him.

"I thought I saw a movement, a tremor," said the skeptical voice.

"It's nothing," the doctor said. "Random discharges in peripheral nerves—she's due to be turned again, to prevent pressure sores. Even in these special beds . . . and they do have tremors sometimes. Breakdown products, perhaps, of the damage."

"I see." She heard the footsteps, fading away, and the sigh and thud of a door opening, shutting again.

She had heard and understood. If their damned scans were any good, they'd know she could hear and understand. Had they bothered to look lately? Or were they lying, and displaying fake scans for anyone who visited? Thirty days . . . she'd been here for thirty days? Where was Heris? What had happened to the prince?

Time had no meaning. She slept, she supposed, and woke again; it seemed like a moment of inattention rather than normal sleep. Sometimes she heard voices around her, and sometimes they talked about her; more often they talked of other things. She came to know one woman's voice, and built from her gossipy chatter a picture of someone with bright, avid eyes and a pursed mouth. Then another, who never added to the gossip, but had a satisfied chuckle, as if she were glad to hear bad things about others. The doctor who had talked to the lawyer came infrequently, but she always knew him.

Scents merged with sounds, with pressures. She knew the

smell of her own body and its output; she hated the wet warmth that turned cold too often before someone came to change her. She hated the hands that turned and moved her as if she were a slab of meat . . . she came to hate with special fervor a flowery perfume one pair of hands wore, hands colder and less deft than the others, belonging to a sharp, whining voice that complained of her incontinence.

Hate blurred thought; she fought it back. She could not afford that, any more than she could afford to go insane from the darkness and immobility. Instead, she scrabbled at her memories, struggling to rip another minute detail from the black fog. Gradually she assembled them in order, like torn scraps of a picture laid out on black velvet. That first awakening, with the terrifying talk about drugs to inhibit, to decouple. It had come after whatever happened, but before—and in another place. Then only the odd glimmer, not even clear memories, until the doctor/lawyer conference. A string of clearer memories, then another lapse, after which she no longer felt the wetness of incontinence. From what she overheard, she had had surgery to implant "controllable sphincters"— however that worked. Since then, more and clearer memories, but still no return of function. She could not move; she could not see; she could not talk.

Her mind slid inexorably sideways to the memory of riders she'd known with broken necks or head injuries. But those were injuries, trauma . . . this was something else. She was still thinking, and if she'd had her head crushed against a tree, she wouldn't be.

Thirty days plus. How many plus? Or was it how much plus? For a moment her mind chased that grammatical hare into a thicket of forgotten rules. She yanked it back out, and slapped its nose. Only one thing mattered . . . and it certainly wasn't a point of grammar. She had to find a way out, a way to make some connection to the world—and yet she had to be sure it was the right connection. Whoever had done this would be watching, she was sure, for any untoward behaviors, any return of speech or movement. And how could she tell who was safe, when she couldn't communicate?

Someone had to know. Unless doctors had never known what they were doing, someone had to know she was still alive inside, still capable of thinking . . . still thinking, in fact. Either someone wanted to torment her—and she couldn't think of a good reason, since apparently she didn't even twitch in ways that would amuse a sadist—or someone was concealing her remaining capacity.

She liked that idea better. She had an ally, somewhere, faking brain scans and whatever other tests the medical system used to determine that her brain wasn't working. It would have been easy to kill her, easy to do the damage that was supposed to have been done . . . easy to do that still. But—they hadn't. She had an ally. If she could stay sane, maybe—just maybe—that someone would figure out a way to rescue her and undo the damage.

"You're sure she's aware?" Lorenza had to ask again; she could not hear the answer too often.

"Yes, ma'am. And like I said, the way it's set up, there's a blind feed on her cables; it'll never show up on her scans now that she's got the implants."

Perfect. A delicious shiver fluttered inside her. Cecelia helpless, motionless, blind . . . and knowing it. The only thing that would be better would be a very personal and private way to communicate, to let her know who was responsible. Unfortunately, that wasn't possible, and the original drug would have wiped out her memory of the reception.

"You'll find your investment in Sultan Realty has paid unexpected dividends," Lorenza said to her medical contact. "It will be very profitable, I think you'll agree."

"Yes, ma'am." He cleared his throat. "But I just want to be sure you really understand the maintenance requirements. Because you wanted her aware, she's going to need regular maintenance doses—"

"Are you saying it's reversible? I told you it must not be—"

"It's not reversible, no. Not the main brain damage. But the dose wasn't as massive—it takes tinkering to keep her neuromuscular status where we want it, with normal maintenance at the nursing home feeding her other drugs . . . that's all." He sounded scared, as well he should be. If he crossed her, he knew what to expect.

"Very well." She didn't understand the medical details, and didn't intend to learn. The important thing, all that mattered, was the thought of Cecelia—arrogant, athletic, triumphant Cecelia—reduced to a flaccid blind body that anyone could manipulate. She didn't even have to visit the place herself; it was enough to know that Cecelia inhabited a dark, friendless place where she was utterly helpless, and from which there was no escape. "Your payments will arrive quarterly; that's the normal schedule for dividend payout from Sultan Realty. When it's time for you to invest in another company, your broker will inform you." She cut off the call, and sat poised in her tapestry chair, looking around her exquisite sitting room. All the lovely colors Cecelia would never see again, all the sensual pleasures of silken clothing, savory food and drink, fresh flower-scented air, favorite music, sex . . .

Her brother, the Crown Minister, found her pensive in the firelight, hand pressed to her cheek, and tea cold in the cup beside her on the table.

"What's the matter?" he asked. "Are you ill?"

"It's that poor woman," she said, in a voice that she let tremble a bit. It would seem like regret. "That poor, poor woman, stricken like that . . . I just can't stop thinking about poor dear Cecelia."

Heris faced Brun over the dining table in her suite at the fanciest hotel the Station offered. One waiter hovered, serving expensive food Heris didn't want, but had to pretend to eat. Brun, still playing the spoiled rich girl, gobbled eagerly.

Finally she chose the most elaborate of the dessert pastries offered, and waved the cart and waiter away. "We'll ring when we're through, thanks," she said. As they left, she picked up the pastry and bit into it, showering flakes in all directions. When the door closed, she took a small gray wand out of her pocket and handed it to Heris with a grin.

Heris picked it up, and scanned the room. Apparently clean of recorders, spyeyes, and such, and this wand, activated, made as good a privacy shield as civilian life afforded. She turned it on its side and placed it between them.

"So—you've taken my advice in that direction?"

"Of course. I told you I was serious." Brun put her pastry down, wiped her mouth, and leaned forward. "Ronnie said you wanted to see me about his Aunt Cecelia; I thought I should make it easy to explain."

"Good for you."

"You know what they're saying about you?"

"Ronnie told me some of it."

"Ronnie only knows what his parents tell him. His mother's telling all her friends that you're the most dangerous woman since that charlatan that bilked the Kooslin sisters out of their fortune by pretending to contact their dead lovers . . . and then killed them to cover up when their nephew found out about it. She nearly killed him, too."

"I never heard of that."

"No, you wouldn't have. But the thing is, Berenice is telling everyone that you must have had that kind of influence on Lady Cecelia. She even thinks that stuff on the island didn't really happen—that you hypnotized Aunt Cecelia into thinking it happened. Dad's not here, or he'd set her straight about that. She's hinting that you even did something—no one will say what—to cause the stroke. Ronnie thinks his mother's upset about the redecorating, but I know it's more than that. I'm not sure just what."

"I had thought of going down to see her, of course—"

Brun shook her head. "Better not. I don't think Berenice'd

let you see her; you're not family, and she's got a right to decide who else can visit."

"What about you?"

"Me?" Brun looked startled, then thoughtful. "I'm not family, or one of Cecelia's friends, but . . . I suppose . . . I could be Dad's representative, sort of."

"Exactly what I thought," Heris said. She hesitated a moment, then decided to trust the girl. "Did Ronnie tell you about the will?"

"Will?"

"I presume he didn't, then; it will come out later, if there's a competency hearing, or if Lady Cecelia dies. Apparently, she changed her will almost as soon as she arrived, and she left me a . . . er . . . substantial legacy. The yacht."

Brun's eyes widened. "So *that's* what—"

"That may be part of it. She didn't tell me she was doing this, or I'd have talked her out of it, of course. But the point is, that if there's a chance the stroke was caused by a drug or something, then I'm the obvious suspect. It's understandable that her family would resent the bequest, and that it would make them suspicious of me and my motives. They're not going to listen to anything I say. But I hope you will."

"What else?"

Quickly, Heris outlined the attack on Sirkin and Yrilan, and what she had found out about its background, including the dishonesty of Cecelia's former captain and the loot found aboard the yacht at Takomin Roads. "So you see, I worry that if her stroke was drug-induced—the guilty parties are working for the Compassionate Hand—in retaliation for having their comfortable little smuggling ring disrupted."

"Oh my." Brun's face shifted from one expression to another, fluffhead to practical young woman, as she thought about this. "Is that what Ronnie meant when he said his aunt had been to see the king? Was she complaining to him about the Regular Space Service, perhaps—it wasn't stopping smugglers, but it had dumped you and promoted that horrible admiral?"

"Perhaps," Heris said. She didn't want to mention the prince if it could be avoided. That was another motive for an attack, but one that she had no way of investigating. "My thought was this: it's not unknown for the Compassionate Hand to suborn medical professionals. There was a case in the Chisholm system where doctors certified that someone was paralyzed when he was only drugged. It was meant to terrorize business associates, which it did, and of course it was also terrifying for the victim." Who had died before he could be rescued, but the evidence had been clear enough; the R.S.S. had found the cube records of the drugging and the results. "If you can visit Lady Cecelia, without arousing suspicions—and without it seeming to be my suggestion— perhaps you can ascertain if she is really brain damaged or not. We can set up a discreet way to keep in touch."

"I see." Brun nibbled on the pastry again. "I suppose you don't have any outrageously handsome young men in your crew, do you, that I could pretend to have fallen for on the voyage?"

"No . . . in fact, all those people quit. The only crew member from the voyage you were on is my navigator, Brigdis Sirkin. And she just suffered a loss herself; her lover was killed in that brawl."

Brun's eyes lit up. "Oh, yes. I remember you telling me about her. I think—I think I'd like to meet her. It would be in my character, even as Bubbles, to be wildly sympathetic."

Heris felt immediately protective of Sirkin. "She's not expendable, Brun. I don't want her hurt."

Brun glared back. "I won't hurt her; I'm not that stupid. I'm sorry she lost someone she cared about—that's true. And I will be careful. But I can call her, or meet her, even though she's your crew, if there's a good reason for me to be interested otherwise."

"Just be careful. She's a good person." Heris forced herself to calm down. "And I'll have to ask her." Not even for Cecelia would she expose Sirkin's pain without her permission. "Let's see. Why not have her escort you to the storage company tomorrow—assuming you really should carry out that errand—and I'll have briefed her on the situation. Then it's up to the two of you to make it understandable that you'd keep in touch."

"It's always understandable when rich young people and not-so-rich young people start spending time together," Brun said.

Brun modified her fluffhead persona just slightly the next Mainshift; she appeared at the crew hostel without the pink-tipped spiky hairstyle, opting for a swept-back pouf instead, all the pink ends hidden under an elaborate ribbon arrangement. She wore a more conservative outfit, something she might have worn a year ago in like circumstance. Her heart was pounding; she hoped that she'd find young Sirkin in the hostel lounge, and not Captain Serrano. She liked Captain Serrano, but it was a strain trying to impress her, knowing she wasn't going to succeed, having to try anyway.

Sirkin and another crew member, a blonde woman with sleepy green eyes, waited at the desk. Brun barely remembered Sirkin; the slender dark-haired figure was only vaguely familiar. The other she didn't know at all.

"Captain Serrano had other things to do this morning," the blonde woman said. "I'm Methlin Meharry, and this is Brig Sirkin. Captain said we should escort you to the storage company."

"Yes—well—" She had planned to ask Sirkin to call her Brun, but what about this Meharry? She didn't feel like using her title, and she was getting very tired of Bubbles. The older woman's sleepy green eyes seemed to wake, like a cat's.

"It's all right," she said. "I have the paperwork."

Brun shrugged. "Fine, then. Let's go." If you couldn't figure out what else to do, you could always be rude. On the way, she said to Sirkin, "Captain Serrano told me you had been hurt in a brawl, and your friend was killed—I'm sorry."

"Thank you." Sirkin's voice was low; her eyes clouded. Brun felt like an idiot, a cruel one. This was much harder with Meharry along. She glared at Meharry. Meharry gave her a lazy smile.

"She was damn near killed herself. Don't suppose you rich girls ever have to worry about things like that. Always got protection."

Brun couldn't think what to say—was this Heris's idea of briefing?—but Sirkin spoke up. "That's not fair, Methlin! She was nearly killed in that mess at Sirialis—" Sirkin looked at Brun, who suddenly realized Heris had used her own trick on her. Of course they had set up this quarrel on purpose. Now, what was she supposed to say? Methlin had already given the next line, in a contemptuous drawl.

"Nonsense—it was her Dad's place—how much danger could she be in?"

"Quite enough, thank you." Brun put as much contempt into her own voice. "Sirkin was there; she knows."

"An' you call her like a servant, 'Sir-kin.' She has a name, you know, Miss Priss."

"Methlin!" Was Sirkin really shocked, or was that part of the game? Brun warmed to it.

"It would be impolite of me to use her first name without her permission," she said. "And I don't think much of you, either."

"Captain said I was to come; you can't make me leave," said Meharry, in a dangerous whine that got attention from others on the slideway.

"I'm not trying to make you leave," Brun said. "I'm merely trying to make you observe the rudiments of polite behavior." She hoped Meharry realized she, too, was playing the role; the woman scared her.

"Damned snob," muttered Meharry. Brun pretended not to hear it; she smiled unctuously at Sirkin.

"I'm so sorry, truly. It must have been terrible for you. Captain Serrano always praised you so highly."

"It was . . . she . . . she jumped in front of me." Genuine grief and guilt; Brun felt another pang of guilt. All too clearly she remembered how she and Raffa had felt each other's peril as well as their own. She tried to put that into words.

"When . . . when my friend and I were being shot at, we were as scared for each other . . . once she had to shoot the man who had me at gunpoint, and she was afraid she'd hit me . . ."

Sirkin blinked back tears; Brun wanted to hug her. "You do understand. But your friend lived—was that George?"

"George! No, not George, Raffa. She was the dark-haired one, like you." It suddenly occurred to her that Sirkin might misunderstand something here, but it was not the time to clarify the order of events and feelings.

"Our stop's next," Meharry said loudly. Brun looked up, and led the way out into the concourse and then into the storage company's main office. For the next couple of hours, as the bored and contemptuous storage company workers located and unpacked half a dozen boxes from Lady Cecelia's yacht, to no avail, Meharry made sarcastic remarks about the aristocracy, and Sirkin became Brun's natural ally. Finally, Brun agreed that she must have been mistaken. She cheerfully handed over a credit chip to cover the extra work done on her behalf and murmured to Sirkin that she'd really like to take her to lunch if Meharry would let her come.

By then it seemed natural that Meharry, with a few last caustic comments about the aristocracy, would head back to the crew quarters alone. Brun, alone with Sirkin, said "You know, if you want to talk about it, I really am a safe person to tell. I'm not quite the fluffhead I seem . . ."

"I know," Sirkin said. "Captain Serrano said you had to be pretty tough to survive on the island."

"But if you don't want to, that's fine, too. What's your favorite food?"

After a luxurious lunch, they spent the afternoon showing why not-so-rich girls liked to spend time with rich ones. Brun found it more fun than she expected to take Sirkin to one shop after another, buying her more gifts than she could carry. She had long quit calling her Sirkin: Brig and Brun, they were to each other. Neither mentioned Lady Cecelia that afternoon; neither needed to.

Wakening after wakening . . . time lost all meaning, in the dark, with only ears and nose to accept sensory data and offer meat for Cecelia's thoughts. And the only smells around were artificial, soaps and perfumes and medicines, nothing evocative of her old life. She had read about such things, but never imagined herself so cut off . . . she, who had been a sensualist all her life. She tried to tell herself that at least she felt no pain . . . but she would have traded pain for that nothingness that threatened her mind.

She would not go insane. She would not give whomever had done this the satisfaction. She told herself she was lucky to be old, that the old had more memories to process, more experiences to relive. She worked her way through her own life, trying to be methodical. It was hard; she would like to have spent more time in the good years, on the winning rides, when the jumps flowed by under the flashing hooves. But even in her extraordinary life, those moments were brief compared to the whole. Instead, she tried to concentrate on the duller bits. Just how many tons of hay had she ordered that first winter in Hamley? How many tons of oats, of barley? Which horse had required flaxseed to improve its hooves? What was the name of that farrier who had been found slipping information to the Cosgroves? Had the third groom's name been Alicia or Devra?

Not even the horses were enough. She made herself catalog her wardrobe—not only every garment she owned now, but every garment in every closet since childhood. Had that blue velvet robe been a gift for the Summerfair or Winterfest, and was it Aunt Clarisse or Aunt Jalora? When and where had she bought the raw-silk shirt with the embroidered capelet?

What had finally happened to the uzik-skin boots, or the beaded belt from Tallik? She tried to remember every room she'd walked in, placing the furniture and every ornament. She considered every investment, from the first shares of bank stock she'd bought herself (with a Winterfest gift from her grandfather—he had forbidden her to spend the money on horses, or she would have bought a new Kindleflex saddle) to the most recent argument with her proxy.

Visitors came regularly, in this unnamed place. Berenice, first teary and chattery (reminded by the staff that she should not get hysterical, that she could not bring flowers or food), and her husband Gustav (stiff, ponderous, but gentle when he touched her hand), and even young Ronnie. They talked to her, in a way.

"I don't know if you can hear me, but—"

Berenice talked of their childhood. Sometimes she mentioned things Cecelia had forgotten, things she could then use in the empty hours between visits. This birthday party, that incident at school, a long-forgotten playmate or servant. And she explained, at excruciating length, why she thought Cecelia had been a fool to waste all that time on horses instead of getting married or at least working in the family. She had accepted the idea that years of small head injuries from riding had led to a massive stroke.

Gustav talked of business and politics, but not in a way she could use. He would tell her which stocks were up or down, and who had been elected, as if he were reading a list from a fairly dimwitted periodical—with none of the meat behind the facts. What did she care if Ciskan Pharmaceuticals was up 1/8 point, and Barhyde Royal was down 3/4? Or if the Conservative Social Democrats had won two more seats in the lower house while the Liberal Royalists had gained a critical appointment in the Bureau of Education? Of course, Gustav had never been known for lively repartee, but even he might have realized that someone in a coma is hardly likely to understand the nuances of a field they never mastered while awake.

Ronnie spent the first visit saying what she had hoped to hear: he could not believe that his vital, strong, healthy aunt had been stricken like this; he was sure she was alert inside, listening to him, understanding him. He would never believe Captain Serrano had done this—how could she?—and it would all come right in the end. But she could not communicate anything to him, could not confirm his guess, and gradually he settled into what she thought of as useless small talk. He was no longer in exile, of course; the prince was offplanet somewhere; Raffaele had gone to visit her family before he had actually talked to her about marriage; the Royals seemed rather slack after his adventures on Sirialis. George was back to being odious in the regiment, but came out of it when alone with Ronnie.

This was better than Gustav, but it didn't give her much to work with when he'd gone. And none of them thought to tell her the date, the weather, or even where she was, the things that might have kept her oriented.

It wasn't enough. Still she woke into blankness, helpless and afraid, and at times could not force her mind to work through another memory. The brilliant colors of blood bay and golden chestnut, of the sunlight on a cobbled yard, or a red coat against dark woods, began to gray. She had heard of that—the deep blindness that follows blinding, when the memory of color fades. She could still think yellow and red and blue and green, but the images that came were paler, almost transparent.

Worst were the nightmares when she seemed to wake to a soft voice she could never quite recognize, a voice that whispered "*I did it*," and a hand cold and smooth as porcelain laid along her cheek. Who, she wondered. Who could be so cruel?

✧ Chapter Eight

Meharry had returned to the crew quarters spitting fire against Brun for the benefit of anyone in the public lounge. When Sirkin went to lunch with Brun again the next day, and then to a concert, Meharry took it up with Heris in public.

"That spoiled kid is making a fool out of Sirkin—taking her out, buying her expensive presents. And poor Sirkin—she's not over Amalie yet!"

"I know," Heris said. "I don't like her any better than you do, but we have no right to interfere. If it gets Sirkin's mind off her grief, maybe—"

"It's not healthy," growled Meharry. "It's not as if they could have a real relationship—not someone like that, daughter of some guy too rich to know how many planets he owns."

"Now, wait a minute," Heris said, conscious of all the listening ears. "That's not fair; I met Lord Thornbuckle. He's a friend of Lady Cecelia's, our employer, you may recall. I'll admit, this youngest daughter is something of a . . . problem . . . but she may grow out of it."

"Might," Meharry said, and subsided. "Does Sirkin talk to you about it?" she asked in a milder tone.

"No," Heris admitted, "and I wish she did. You're right; she could get in over her head; she's had no experience with that sort of wealth and privilege. But I can't stop her. Her free time is her own."

Finally, after a whirlwind week, Brun went back downplanet. To Meharry's expressed surprise, she kept up almost daily calls or correspondence with Sirkin.

"Could really be love," said one of the men in the lounge

123

one afternoon. He had heard more than he wanted of Meharry's complaints about Brun, and thought he understood the reason behind them. "Maybe you're just jealous."

"The rich don't love," Meharry said. "They buy. 'Course I'm not jealous; I'm too old for her and besides she's not my type. I just don't want to see her get hurt. She's setting up for it."

Sirkin had walked in on that—they had set up this conversation before but had no takers—and now she said, "I wish you'd mind your own business, Meharry. Just because you were nice to me after Amalie died doesn't mean you own me now!" The man gave a satisfied grin as Sirkin stalked on out the door; Meharry cursed and returned to her quarters.

After several weeks, Heris got the first piece of solid news through her pipeline. Brun had permission to visit Cecelia, but it had taken a request from her father, back on Sirialis, to get it. Right now, Cecelia was being prepared for long-term care, which meant a series of small surgeries; she could not visit until Cecelia had been placed in the permanent care facility her family had chosen.

In the meantime, Cecelia's family had begun the first moves against Heris herself. At the hearing to petition for an Order of Guardianship, Cecelia's will had been formally read . . . and the bequest to Heris noted with dismay by those who hadn't already heard. The first notice she got was a call from a court officer, who informed her that she was now the official owner of the *Sweet Delight*, and court documents to that effect were on the way. Scarcely two hours later, a Station militia officer (not the captain she knew from the murder investigation) showed up to question her about "circumstances pursuant to Lady Cecelia's stroke."

"I don't know anything about it except what Ronnie told me—"

"You weren't there?" He peered at a printout she couldn't read upside down and backwards.

"No; I haven't been downplanet since we came back to

Rockhouse. Lady Cecelia has been back up only once, some days before her stroke. She seemed fine then."

"Tell me about it."

Heris explained about the redecoration of the yacht, about Cecelia's ability to make quick, firm decisions on matters of color and style, about her cheerful mood.

"You don't think having her yacht redone so soon—and in a style so different from what's in fashion—reveals, perhaps, that her mind was already going?" Heris bit back a sharp retort. A stroke was not "a mind going" but a direct physical insult to the brain, with resulting cognitive problems.

"Not at all. Lady Cecelia was not your average old lady, but she seemed every bit as competent and alert as she was when she first hired me. She had never liked the colors her sister chose before; she'd decided to redo the yacht her way. She could afford it—why not?"

"Was she on any medication?"

"Not that I know of."

"You don't think her . . . er . . . euphoric mood might have been the result of some drug?"

"Hardly. It wasn't euphoric, just happy. She didn't use drugs for mood control; she felt that she was a happy, fit, healthy individual who didn't need them."

"She had refused rejuvenation," the man said, as if that proved insanity. Heris explained Cecelia's position.

"She told me that she thought people went into rejuvenation from either fear of death or vanity; she wasn't afraid of death, and she thought vanity was a silly vice." No need to mention that she didn't agree about rejuvenation; it wouldn't convince the man of her innocence or Cecelia's wit.

His voice was disapproving. "She seems to have told you a lot; you hadn't been working for her that long."

"True, I hadn't. But living alone on that yacht, as she did, perhaps she found another woman, younger but not juvenile, a comfortable companion. So it seemed."

"I see. There's been questions asked, I might as well tell

you. Someone down there is setting up to make trouble for you. I hope you know what you're doing."

If there had been the least scrap of evidence that she had had any physical contact with Cecelia in the days before her stroke, or any way to get drugs to her, she would have been arrested for attempted murder. That became clear in the next few days, when the militia asked for repeated interviews, and Cecelia's family's lawyers and the court officers descended. Luckily, the medical evidence suggested that if (it could not be proven) Cecelia's stroke had resulted from poison, the poison would have to have been administered shortly before her collapse. Repeated questioning of her maid and her sister revealed nothing into which Heris could have put such a drug—no medicines taken regularly, no foodstuffs brought down from the ship. Records at the Royal Docks access showed that Lady Cecelia had not even been to her ship on her last visit to the space station; Heris remembered her protest and wondered if Cecelia had had some sort of intuitive knowledge.

Against the animosity of Cecelia's sister and the rest of the family, however, evidence meant little. They had petitioned the court at once to set aside the bequest to Heris on the grounds of undue influence. Perhaps they couldn't prove an assault, but they were sure of the undue influence. Ronnie sent word through Brun that he dared not call Heris directly; they were already recommending treatment for him on the grounds that he, too, might have been under her supposed spell.

It would have been funny, in a story about someone else. Heris found it infuriating and painful. How could anyone think she would hurt Cecelia? She had begun to love the old woman as if she were her own aunt. No—as a friend. She felt hollow inside at the thought of losing her forever. She tried to explain to Petris.

"They think I did this to her," Heris said, looking up from

the cube reader with the latest communication from the family's legal staff. "To get the ship. They think I influenced her to change her will—I didn't even *know* she'd changed her will!"

"I know that. Don't bristle at me."

"They think that I did it all for the ship. Which is why they're insisting that I can't have it."

"Well . . . screw the ship. We can go back to the Service—"

"I'm not so sure. We refused their kind invitation; they may not be willing to have us now. And to find a berth, all of us, somewhere else—" Heris shook her head. It had all seemed to be coming together, a new direction not only possible but rewarding, and now—!

"Well, we're still Lady Cecelia's employees," Oblo put in. He was demonstrating one of his less social abilities with a sharp knife. "As long as we're her employees, we have a right to work on her ship, eh?"

"That's another thing." Heris thumped the hardcopy on her desk. "Since she's believed to be permanently impaired, they say there's no reason to maintain an expensive and useless ship crew. When the yacht's ownership has been determined in court, then it can be crewed with whomever the new owner wants. We're supposed to get out and stay out."

"But you're the designated owner, aren't you?"

"Were you listening, Oblo? The family's petitioned the court to have that part of the will thrown out; Cecelia's own attorney, who drew up the new will, argues that it is an unreasonable bequest to an employee so recent. Apparently all of them think I did something—what, they don't say—to influence the bequest, and some of them think I then did whatever it was that's happened to her."

"Which we aren't sure about," murmured Petris, his gaze sombre.

"Which *I* am sure isn't just a stroke," Heris agreed. "I *told* her she was going into danger . . . but that's beside the point. This letter says we'll be paid through the end of that sixty days they first promised—be glad I got that in writing—and then we're no longer her employees. They're cancelling the redecoration, permanently. They want the ship in deep storage until final disposition. I'm supposed to present my own petition to the court, at my own expense, of course, if I want to contest the petition. They think I'll walk away . . ."

"What else can you do?" Oblo said, eyeing her. "You don't have the money for an attorney. We've been depending on your lady . . ."

"It will split us up," Petris said. "That's what they want—we'll have to ship out separately, because no one hires readymade crews, especially not us. I don't like this."

"It's not fair," Sirkin put in. Everyone looked at her.

"Fair?" Oblo raised one scarred eyebrow. "You're a grownup now, Sirkin. Another voyage, and you'll be almost family."

"Except there isn't going to be another voyage." Heris felt her mind slumping even as she held her body erect. "We don't have the resources. The family's offered me a settlement, not to contest . . . . it's enough for a couple of months living on Rockhouse Minor, but not for all of us. Not nearly enough for a ship."

"For tickets away?"

"Yes, but where? Besides, I don't want to leave Cecelia down there until I know what happened. Maybe even more if I did know what happened." She took another breath. "I have savings, of course. Investments. Maybe enough to contest it, but not if they bring criminal charges for whatever it was that happened to her. They're powerful enough they might be able to do it even without evidence. Since she didn't tell me about the bequest, I wasn't prepared—I don't even know why she did it." She paused. "But I do have legal help. Remember that young man George?"

"Kevil Mahoney's taking your case?" Petris asked, eyes wide.

"No, not himself, but he's recommended someone, and the fee's not as bad as it could be. The problem is, he thinks the settlement might be reasonable. And in any case, he says we must comply with the court order to vacate. I asked about that old 'Possession is nine points—' you always hear about, and he says it has never applied to space vessels. And of course we're not actually in the yacht; she's sitting over there in Spacenhance, empty." With Spacenhance grumbling almost daily about having one of their slots tied up uselessly. If it hadn't been for the Royal connection, they'd have insisted on having the ship moved long before.

"And it'll cost us to live . . ."

"If we can't get other work."

"Like what? Dockside work on Rockhouse Major's simply not available for ship-certified. They don't want crews spending time here, for political reasons. Downside—who wants to work on a dirtball anyway?"

"You're not looking at this as a tactical problem," Arkady said. "Think of Lady Cecelia. We have to stay mobile if we're to help her at all. If we're trapped, whether it's broke, or working for someone else, or in custody, we can't help her."

"You mean get her out?" Sirkin's eyes sparkled. "I like that. We could get a shuttle, and—" Petris put a hand on hers, and she subsided. Heris shook her head, and explained.

"We don't know for certain that she's a prisoner . . . if she's really had a massive stroke, if she's really comatose, we can't just snatch her away from medical care. But if she's not—"

"If she's been . . . disabled . . . ?"

"Yes. Then she needs allies who aren't bound by . . . er . . . the usual considerations."

"Rules," Oblo said with satisfaction. "Laws. Even traditions . . ."

"We need a ship," Petris said. Heris felt the challenge in his gaze. She grinned back at him.

"We have a ship." She took a deep breath. "It is highly illegal, and we will be fugitive criminals, the lawful prey of every R.S.S. ship, every planetary militia . . . but we have a ship."

"Not quite," Oblo pointed out. "You haven't forgotten she's

over in refitting, with all her pretty carpets and plush walls gutted?"

"And all her new weaponry aboard," Heris said. "What do we care what the decks and bulkheads look like?"

"You're actually going to do it," Petris said. She had, she realized, surprised him. "You, Heris Serrano, are actually going to steal a yacht and set off to rescue a friend in peril . . . Do you realize how theatrical this is?"

"It will be even more theatrical when the shooting starts," Heris said. "And we can't just leap into it. We need to know exactly what her condition is. *Sweet Delight*'s not a planetary shuttle; we can't use it to snatch her, even if it's safe to do so. We'll have to find someone with a shuttle first."

She remembered Ronnie saying that both his family and Lord Thornbuckle had private shuttles onplanet, but didn't mention it to the crew. Not yet. She would have Sirkin check with Brun at their next encounter.

It's not working, Cecelia thought in the worst moments. No one will ever come; no one will ever figure it out. If they were going to, they'd have gotten me out by now. And I can't go on like this for years and years; it would be better to go mad and not know any more. She fought herself on that, in the motionless silence, screaming curses at her fears as she had never allowed herself to scream in real life. For a short time the discovery that she had remembered so many expletives that ladies were not supposed to notice amused her. A fine talent for curses, she thought. But it was useless. No one could hear them. She forced herself back to the dry bones of accounting (tons of hay, price of oats and bran, the cost of bits and saddles) as her hope dwindled. How long?

Then one wakening she found herself flooded with emotion. Not the usual fear, but joy so strong she could hardly believe she did not leap from the bed. What—? A smell, a rich, natural scent, overlay the room's usual sterility. Leather, conditioning oil—not quite the smell of a saddle, but certainly one associated with riding. Horse and dog. Cautiously, afraid to respond now because someone might withdraw that aroma, Cecelia sniffed.

"It's so sad to see her this way," said a voice. A voice she knew from before; she struggled to put a name to it. Young, female, not family—who was this? "She loved the out-of-doors so—"

One of the voices she heard often. "I'm sure they did everything they could."

"Oh, of course." A pressure against her cheek, and the scent grew stronger. Her mind drank it in gratefully. Leather, oil, horse, dog, sweat: a hand that had been outdoors? No, a hand alone wouldn't carry that scent. A glove would, she thought. A young woman wearing gloves? Why? Gloves weren't in fashion, unless she'd been mired here so long that fashion had changed again. "But I don't understand why I couldn't bring flowers. She always loved flowers, especially the aromatic ones. It smells so—so sterile in here."

"Strong scents interfere with the room monitoring," the attendant said.

"Oh, dear." The young woman's voice sounded mischievous. "And here I came straight from the track. Should I have showered?"

"No, because you're just visiting. The blowers will clear it out shortly. Now I'll leave you—just a half hour, please, and check at the main desk on your way out."

"Thank you." As Cecelia listened to the familiar soft noises of the doors, the hand never left her cheek. Then, at the final distant click of the outer door, it did. Into her right ear, the same voice, softened to a murmur. "Cecelia, it's Brun. Bunny's daughter. Dad wanted me to visit you; he couldn't believe what happened."

Bubbles. Brun. For a moment her mind tangled the two names, then she remembered, with utter clarity, their last conversation.

"If you have anything left at all, it's olfactory. I saw your nose flare with this—" The smell came back, and Cecelia rejoiced. "I'm going to try some things—smells—and see if you can respond. That was my glove—I rubbed it all over two horses and the stable dog today—"

I knew that, Cecelia thought. She could hardly focus on what Brun was saying; she wanted to cry, scream, and laugh all at once. The familiar beloved scents faded, replaced now by a fruity tang.

"Apple," Brun said. "I'm not supposed to have food in here, I think it's because they don't want you to smell it. I think they know you can." Cecelia struggled to move something, anything, and felt a firm pressure on her arm. "You twitched an eyelid," Brun said. "If you can do it again, I'll take that as a 'Yes.'" Cecelia tried; she could not feel if she succeeded, but Brun gave her another squeeze. "Good. Now I'm going to pretend you can hear me, because my aunt said sometimes people in comas could hear—"

Of course I can hear, Cecelia thought angrily. I just did what you asked me to do! Then she realized that Brun might be dealing with another kind of monitoring. She had to make this look like an innocent visit.

"So," Brun went on, "I'm going to tell you about the last hunt, after you left. You know, I've always wondered what it would be like to be the fox—" A sharp stink of fox entered Cecelia's brain like a knife, clearing away the fog of anger. "Foxes are so cunning," Brun continued. "Clever beasts—I'll bet ours are smarter than Old Earth foxes ever were. But it must be scary. Down there in the dark holes, hearing the hounds coming out the gate—" This time a smell of dog, and another squeeze.

Cecelia struggled to comprehend. Brun was trying to tell her something, something important, but she was too old, too tired, too confused. Foxes? Hounds? Foxes in dark holes . . . like I am, she thought suddenly. With the hounds up there somewhere . . . she could almost feel her mind coming alive now, and hoped that no brainwave monitor was on her at this moment.

"Anyway, there was this kid who decided that the hunt was unfair to foxes. Too easy for us, too hard for them. His first season; he's one of the Delstandon cousins, I think. So he decided to help the fox. He understood that hounds followed the scent, so he figured if he made a false trail, we'd waste our time and the foxes would have a day off." The alternation of fox and dog scent fit with this story; Cecelia wondered where it would lead. "But to get the fox scent, he had to find foxes himself—a den—and you can imagine what happened when Dad's huntsman found him lurking around a den."

Cecelia couldn't, but she concentrated on breaking Brun's code. The huntsman had been signalled with the glove again; she recognized that particular mix now, as well as the constituent scents.

"I thought it was kind of funny, protecting the foxes from someone who wanted to protect them—" Again the stink of fox. "But I guess that happens sometimes." Now a different smell, woodsy and soothing. Change of topic? "I was thinking back to the island—"

Yes. Change of topic indeed. Cecelia found her memory of the island fragmented; she hoped Brun wouldn't depend on something no longer there.

"It was such fun camping there when I was a child. Now I don't know if I'll ever feel the same way about it." This time the smell was oily, dangerous yet attractive. Not leather: metallic plus oil plus some chemical. Abruptly she recognized it. How had Brun smuggled a weapon in here? Or was it just a cloth saturated with the smell of gun oil and ammunition? It meant danger, she was sure of that.

As she realized that, she heard the door opening. "I wish I knew if she even heard me," Brun said, in a different tone, almost petulant. "My aunt says sometimes they can, but she doesn't *do* anything."

"I need to check the monitors," the attendant said. This was the one who liked to gossip.

"Do you think she hears anyone?" Brun asked.

"No, miss. The scans don't show anything; the doctors think she's completely comatose. I just need to check this—" Cecelia felt pressure on her head, then a sparkle ran through her brain, bringing up a vivid picture of her own gloved hands clasped on her knee. Someone was whistling "Showers of Orchids," a song she had not heard or thought of in decades. Then it was gone, and the voice overhead said, "That's all right then. The supervisor thought I'd better check."

"What?" asked Brun.

"Well . . . I suspect it is all that smell of horse you brought in. It seems to have clogged the monitors or something."

"Sorry," said Brun, not at all contritely. "Mum said to come today, and I almost forgot. Didn't have time to clean up first or anything."

"You're another horsewoman?"

"Not like her. To tell the truth, I'm fonder of the jockeys than the horses." The attendant chortled. "But I always pat the horses; the trainers like that."

"Well, your time's almost up," the attendant said. Cecelia wondered if he'd leave again, but he didn't.

"I know," Brun said. "I don't suppose it matters, really. If she can't hear me—and she certainly doesn't respond—why should I stay the whole time anyway? Is her family visiting?"

"Yes, miss. Her sister and brother-in-law and nephew, every week. Each has a special day. If you're going to visit regularly, you should put yourself on the weekly schedule—that way the receptionist will have your tag ready, and the gate guard will have you on the list—"

"Oh, I don't think so." Brun sounded casual. "I've known her all my life, of course, but she's not my aunt. I mean, I care, but it's not like—you know."

"Yes, miss." The satisfaction in the attendant's voice was unmistakable.

"I mean, I might come again before we go back to Sirialis—
I suppose I should—but not every week or anything."

The wonderful smell of horse and dog and leather came
back, as Brun laid her hand on Cecelia's cheek again.
"Goodbye, Lady Cecelia. I'm so sorry—but your friends
haven't forgotten you. You'll always have a place in the hunt."
Cecelia felt Brun's warm lips on her face—a goodbye kiss—
and then she heard her footsteps leaving the room.

Someone knew, at last. Someone believed. Someone outside, someone free, knew she was still alive inside and would
do something about it. What, she could not imagine, or how
or when . . . but something. Cecelia wanted to laugh, to cry, to
leap and shout for joy. Her immobility hurt worse then than it
had for a long time. But hope always hurt, she remembered.
Hope gave the chance of failure, as well as the chance of
success.

She clung to that hope in the timeless dark that followed, as
she replayed her memories again and again. Somewhere, sometime, someone would come and take her away from this, into
the smell of horse and dog and fox, the real world.

Brun invited Sirkin to dinner; Sirkin wore—to Meharry's
voluble disapproval—an expensive outfit Brun had bought her.
Heris paced in her own small room, waiting for Sirkin to return
with some word of Cecelia's condition.

"She'll be late," Petris said, lounging as usual on her bed.
"We could improve the shining hour."

"And be interrupted again? No, thank you. Afterward . . ."

Afterward didn't happen; Sirkin didn't come back until next
Mainshift, arms laden with packages bearing the logos of
expensive stores, and her expression clearly that of someone
whose needs had been satisfied. Brun came with her, wearing
matching earrings, and a smug look.

"Sirkin, you were supposed to be back last midshift," Heris
said. She'd begun to wonder if something had happened to
them, and she felt almost as irritated as she sounded.

"It's my fault," Brun said airily. "I just—it was easier for her to spend the night, and then we overslept—"

"I see, miss." Very formal, for all the ears and eyes. "Sirkin, if you could get yourself into uniform, we are having crew training this shift."

"Yes, Captain." Sirkin accepted a last squeeze from Brun, and went off to her quarters with the load of presents. Brun waved an irreverent goodbye to Heris.

"I hope," Heris said, "you haven't made promises you aren't prepared to keep."

"Not me," Brun said over her shoulder. "I never make promises at all."

Sirkin handed Heris the scrawled note later. *Yes, she's there. They won't let you near her; I'll work something out. Don't worry. Brun.*

Don't worry? How could she not worry? Yet . . . if she herself couldn't rescue Cecelia—and she had not been able to come up with a viable plan for getting her out of the nursing home and away from the planet—she would bet on Brun. They'd just have to figure out a way to have the ship where Brun needed it . . . if that meant stealing it and hiding out somewhere in the meantime.

The Crown summons arrived "by hand"—the hand being a member of the Household, in a formal uniform that no one could overlook. Heris took the summons warily—old-fashioned, imprinted paper, the strokes of a real pen having scored the thick, textured paper with black letters—and wondered what now.

Not that it mattered. A Crown summons had the force of law, although no legislation supported it—it was simply inconceivable that someone invited to an audience would refuse. She noted the time, and the clothing required. A shuttle awaited her. She could not help but think of Cecelia riding a royal shuttle down . . . and where Cecelia was now. She suspected she was meant to think of that.

The messenger waited in the private meeting room while she changed into her formal uniform . . . not as formal as the dress uniform of Fleet, but it would have to do . . . and told Petris where she was going and why. His brow furrowed.

"You might be going into trouble. One of us should come."

"If there's trouble that direction, one wouldn't help. No, you stay free. Here's the authorization codes for the bank, the lockboxes . . ." For every power she held that she could transfer that fast. "Take care of them," she said as she left, and his hand lifted in the old salute. *Make no promises you can't keep. Keep the ones you make.* The old words ran through her mind as she walked beside the messenger, and saw how passersby reacted.

"We have a problem," the king said. He looked much like his son Gerel, only older. Was he as foolish? Heris could not let herself think so. If the king had also been damaged, she could see no hope for any but the conspirators who had done it. He paused, and she wasn't sure if it was for her response, or a decision. "You have already, with Lady Cecelia, been of service to the Crown." Considering that her entire adult life had been spent as a Fleet officer, this was, Heris thought, an understatement. "You know Gerel," the king went on. "Both as himself and as Mr. Smith. You know the . . . er . . . problem he has developed."

"Yes, sir," Heris said. It was all she could say, really. She was glad that the Familias had never taken up the full formality of address of past historical periods.

"You are in a position to do the Crown, and the Familias Regnant, a great service, if you will."

"Of course, sir; it would be a privilege." Provided it didn't take too long or take her away from Lady Cecelia. She was still determined to find a way to help.

"It is a very delicate matter, possibly quite dangerous. I would not consider asking you, were it not for your military background, your proven courage and discretion." Which meant it

was not just delicate and dangerous, but impossible. Others
had been asked and refused, most likely. "And I will understand if you feel you cannot jeopardize your crew, or if the . . .
er . . . legal difficulties you face require your immediate presence and participation."

"Perhaps if you could tell me a bit more," Heris murmured.
She did not miss the flutter of his eyelid, the outward and
visible sign of an inward and secretive nature.

"Let me be frank, Captain Serrano." Which meant he
would divulge as little as possible, she thought sourly. Politi-
cians! "I know, of course, your situation vis-a-vis the
Bellinveau-Barraclough family. Lady Cecelia left you her
yacht in her will; her relatives contest her mental fitness at
the time of the bequest, and have charged you with undue
influence. They have sufficient standing that the court has
agreed to deny you access to the ship while the matter is
under adjudication. You turned out to have unexpected
resources—though they should have realized that officers
of your rank are rarely penniless spendthrifts—and unex-
pectedly good legal advice, thanks to the debt Kevil Mahoney
owes you for the life of his son. You may win in the end, but
in the meantime you will have, unless you find other
employment, no income—nor will your crew." All this,
though Heris knew it, sounded grimmer from his mouth
than she'd allowed herself to think.

"They think you're a greedy, sly woman capable of insinuat-
ing yourself into the affections of an elderly spinster—and
possibly capable of doing her actual harm, by precipitating a
stroke." He stared at her a long moment, then held up his
hand when she opened her mouth. "No—don't answer that. I
disagree with them, in part because I've known Cece all my
life, and when she came to talk to me about Gerel I got an
earful about you as well. I've known Cece, as I said, and she's
never been taken in by anyone charming since she was sixteen
or so. She's a superb, if acerbic, judge of character; she's located
and remarked on all *my* failings. Cece thought you were a

rare find, and I abide by her judgment. That's another reason
for my request."

Heris tried not to shift about in her chair. She was glad to
know the king trusted Cecelia's judgment, but she wished he
would get to the *point*. She distrusted easy compliments and
indirection.

"Now—without going into all the historical tangles—we've
got a mess, the entire Familias Regnant. You saw Gerel's problem—" Heris wished she dared interrupt to say *You mean his
stupidity?* but simply waited. "It's not innate," the king said.
"I'm sure you know that many prominent people have
doubles."

That startled her, and she tried not to show it. "I . . . had
heard of that, sir." And what did that have to do with it?

"No one knows how many of the heads and heirs of prominent families have them, of course. In the military, except for
covert operations, regulations prohibit them for any but flag
officers in major military actions . . . otherwise, we'd be stumbling all over extra Lieutenants Smith and Brown whenever
the real ones wanted to spend an extra thirty days on home
leave. You can understand, I hope, that the royal family is well-
supplied with doubles, both for convenience and security. In
fact, that's how Admiral Lepescu got Gerel away from Naverrn
without anyone noticing. One of his doubles was there; we're
claiming that it was one of his doubles who went to Sirialis,
although I'm afraid Bunny won't believe it."

"I . . . see." Heris wondered for a moment if the foolish
young man could have been the prince's double. She didn't
know the prince, after all. And the Crown would have had to
respond as if he were, even if he weren't. In that case, maybe
only the double was stupid. If the king was telling the truth. It
shocked her to realize how she doubted him.

The king sighed, and steepled his hands. "Captain Serrano,
I must admit—in confidence—that the person you met as
Mr. Smith was in fact the prince. The real prince. He is now
back on Naverrn, and his double is safely back in hiding. That's

not the problem. As I said, his infirmity is not natural—not inborn—and it was induced in much the same way as I think Cece's stroke was induced. I knew about it, of course, from the beginning. It was the threat. They'd killed Jared, his oldest brother—" Heris remembered that, the assassination of the eldest prince, when she was serving aboard the *Stella Maris*. The whole Fleet had gone on alert, expecting some kind of rebellion, but nothing happened. "Until then I hadn't used doubles much; certainly not for the children. After that—with Gerel—we switched him around quite a bit. They were proving they could still find him—and hurt him—without the public scandal of another death."

"Do you know who?" Heris asked. The king shook his head.

"We have three or four major possibilities. You're not a political fool; you can probably figure them out for yourself."

"What do you want me to do?" asked Heris. She wasn't about to speculate about politics; it wasn't her field. Moreover, it was obvious that the king himself, or his faction, must be among the possibilities. Who else would have more opportunity, both for the act and its later concealment? Despite her distaste for the exercise, motives sprouted in her mind: fear, greed, lust for power.

"I daren't trust any medical facility in the Familias," the king said. "But beyond the Compassionate Hand, there's the Guerni Republic. They have the best medical facilities in known space; they trade in biomedical knowledge and skill. I want you to take Gerel there, and see if his condition can be treated or reversed without killing him. I have his entire medical file—the people responsible actually gave me some of the details, to prove they'd done it. Our specialists say they can't do anything without causing permanent damage, even death. I need you, because I dare not send him by Fleet or commercial vessel. Not only would his condition become known, but those responsible would surely intervene. I had planned to ask Cece if she'd be willing to do it, but then she had her stroke . . . if it was a stroke."

Was that openness a sign that the king hadn't done whatever was done to Cecelia? Or just an attempt to convince her? Heris chose her words with care. "You want me to steal the yacht out from under the noses of the family, against all law and regulation, and go to Naverrn and take the prince from there to the Guerni Republic—which is some dozen worlds around two or three stars, if I recall—to attempt a treatment you know nothing about? Begging your pardon, but that seems a . . . very strange proposal."

"Of course it does," the king said. "It *is* a strange proposal. Dangerous—"

"Suicidal," Heris said. "We'll be outlaws here, for having taken the ship when it was under legal dispute, and since we've taken it out of the system, the R.S.S. will be after us as well. It is essential for your plan that we not be known as your agents—and thus you cannot keep the wolves off our track. We can circumvent the Compassionate Hand—it just takes longer—but how are we supposed to pick up the prince when every ship will know we're fugitives already?" Actually, that wasn't such a problem; Oblo had already set up an alternate identity for the *Sweet Delight*. But the king needn't know that. "As for the Guerni Republic . . . exactly where did you expect us to deliver the prince? And how long might the treatment take? And suppose it doesn't work? What will happen then?" Before the king could answer any of this, Heris said "And beyond all that, there's Lady Cecelia. Why should I leave her in peril, among those I cannot trust?"

The king grimaced. "Your oath of service, I could have said once—but I see you do not feel bound at all by that anymore." That stung; Heris felt her teeth grating, but said nothing. She had not broken that oath; others had broken their trust, had failed her. "If I swore to see that Lady Cecelia was protected? That no further harm came to her—assuming that harm has been done?"

"With all due respect, since I do not know what happened, I do not know whom to blame." That came close to accusing the king. At his angry scowl, she added, "I'm sure you intended no harm in the first place, and yet it happened."

"I see." Heris could almost see the ideas shuffling through his head like a pack of cards. She wanted to tell him not to bother coming up with a good story, but one did not interrupt a monarch. It was an impossible mission, and she would be crazy to accept it—except what choice did she have? If she refused it and stayed here, the family would put the yacht in deep storage and her own savings would go to support her and as many of the crew as wanted to stay. She might get other employment, but not with her people, and rumors that she was responsible for Lady Cecelia's condition might keep her unemployed the rest of her life. Without a shuttle—and not even Oblo had found a way to obtain a shuttle secretly—she couldn't get Cecelia offplanet. A ship and a mission—even this mission—was better than nothing.

"You do realize that you cannot help Lady Cecelia yourself," the king said. It was as much threat as bare statement of fact. "She is well-guarded against you in particular. If she has a chance for recovery, it would be with someone else." Heris nodded, dry-mouthed. "If you were gone, perhaps the level of suspicion would drop. Not that that would help her physical condition, but like you I hate to think of her living the rest of her time in what must seem like confinement." The look he gave her then had years of manipulation behind it: was she cowed enough? Had she taken the bait of that implied promise? Heris stared back at him, almost regretting those years of loyal service. But no: it meant something to her, something she still treasured. "I will give you letters patent," the king said finally. "I believe I can trust you not to reveal them except in direst need." When, thought Heris, they wouldn't be worth the elegant old-fashioned paper they were written on, no matter its cost. She could just imagine a Compassionate Hand pirate-merchant holding its fire because of a piece of pressed slush-fiber with writing on it. This, like his assurance that he would protect Cecelia, could not be trusted. But her doubts would do her no good. She made herself smile at the king.

"Sir, I accept your mission." At least it meant a ship, a chance, another short space of freedom. And she might—she *would* find some way to help Cecelia. Perhaps, as the king implied, if she were gone, the family would let down their guard . . . the first glimmer of an idea came to her, but she forced it back. She didn't want anything to show in her face.

The king sat alone with his uncertainties. He would have liked to confide in that captain, explain all the knots in the tangled mess that had led to Gerel's situation, and Cecelia's. He had never meant it to turn out like this. It hadn't been his idea anyway, not the clones or the drugs; he had only wanted to avert another disaster after the deaths of his two older sons. But it was far too late for easy honesty.

✧ Chapter Nine

Heris explained the Crown mission with as little expression in her voice as possible. She had assembled the crew in a private lounge of a respectable hotel, as she'd done at weekly intervals all along, and Oblo had turned on one of his gadgets before she started to speak. Sirkin opened her mouth twice, but subsided. The rest of the crew stared at her without expression.

"You realize the whole thing is a trap." Petris sounded almost angry. She wished he wouldn't. Anger with him was next door to passion, and she had no time for that now.

"Of course," she said. She could feel the additional tension. "But we don't have to walk into the trap."

"I thought we just did." Oblo was giving her his look, the one which made ensigns pale and civilians switch to the other side of streets and slideways.

"So does the Crown," Heris said, grinning. "Safer that way— what do you think they'd do if I refused the bait? Kill us off one by one, like Sirkin's friend, and certainly finish Lady Cecelia. I don't like that solution, but we're vulnerable as long as we're tied to a ship in dock, and weak if we separate. No, we're going to take their bait—then we're going to pick up the whole trap and walk off with it."

"How?" Trust Oblo to get to the sticky bit and say it aloud. Petris, shaking his head, grinned at her.

"I don't know yet. But that's the plan."

"All strategy, no tactics," Petris said. Not an angry voice, but behind the neutrality was doubt. "Unless just staying out of whatever trap they've set is tactics."

144

"I'll work on it," Heris said tartly. "And here's what I need. You each have your list." She handed out the handwritten notes. She sat back and watched their expressions. Oblo's brows rose, and he looked up to give her a short nod. Yes. He'd figured it out.

"But the Crown gave us permission . . . why this?"

"It was indicated to me that they'd rather we looked like outlaws. I have . . . assurance . . . that it will be cleared up later."

"Anything worthwhile?" asked Petris.

"Yes. And not going with us, though they don't know that. I was given letters patent, empowering us to act as one of His Majesty's Fleet in certain matters. To be presented to certain . . . ah . . . personages we are unlikely to find where I was told to meet them."

"Because—?" began Sirkin. Petris gave her his best "civilians are idiots" look. Heris glared at him. Sirkin was their weak point—young, inexperienced, and emotionally vulnerable after Amalie's death. She didn't need any more pressure from any of them. Petris answered Sirkin in a very different tone than his first expression had promised.

"Because either they aren't there, or the captain expects we won't be, or both. And she's not telling us now, because we shouldn't know too much."

"Those letters are staying behind, in what I devoutly hope are secure locations, which I will not divulge even to my crew," Heris said. Kevil Starbridge Mahoney owed her favors; he could jolly well put some unopened documents in his own security files for her.

"Suppose . . . we actually find out who's putting the pressure on the king, and take it off?" That was Sirkin again. Heris was glad Petris hadn't yet squashed her initiative; the girl was young, but she had promise, and her unmilitary background gave her something the others didn't share.

"Fine, if we can do it without having the same pressure land on us," Heris said. "But it's like maneuvers—getting the fire off someone else doesn't make us safe. Our first priority is staying alive, uncaught by the trap we know about and any others."

"And Lady Cecelia?" Sirkin asked. "I thought maybe we could . . ." Her voice trailed away as the others looked at her.

"We can't help her," Heris said firmly. "We're the ones anyone would expect to do something, and for that very reason we can't."

"But someone has to—"

"Sirkin, we have enough to worry about as it is. Keeping the ship free, and whole, and ourselves alive, in the first place." Heris signalled the others with her eyes. Time to leave, before Sirkin asked more questions Heris didn't want to answer, especially since she could. They stood, and Sirkin followed, still looking stubborn. "That's all . . . see you here next week as usual." The weekly dinner meeting, which she hoped the watchers had given up worrying about. Oblo turned off his gadget, with a wink, and Heris went on without a pause. "The court's agreed to hear the case, at least, which I—" She stopped suddenly, as if realizing the gadget was off. "Well, see you next week, if that stinking lawyer doesn't come up with something to drag me downside."

On her way out, she reserved the same room for the same time the following week, as she had from the beginning.

Sirkin agreed to pass along to Brun a message which made no sense to her, but would, Heris hoped, make sense to that inventive young lady. Brun's answer, relayed through Sirkin, showed she had done her homework. She had also had her visit with Cecelia, and she believed Cecelia's coma was not as deep as the medical records indicated.

"How did she get hold of the medical records?" Heris asked, then shook her head. "Never mind. If she says Lady Cecelia is still alive inside, I'll believe it. And if she thinks she can arrange a rescue, we'll get out of her way and let her at it."

"But it's dangerous." Sirkin was looking better these days, and her sparkle had begun to come back. Heris wondered momentarily if it was just time, or if Brun had anything to do with it. She had to admit the two of them seemed to hit it off well. "If they catch her—" That meant Brun, of course.

"If they catch her, she's young, rich, titled, and will have Kevil Mahoney on her side. I'd bet on her not to get caught, though. You didn't see her on the island. I was impressed."

"I wish I had," Sirkin said. Admiration. And Brun wished she knew as much about ships. Heris wondered what would come of this—she hoped it wouldn't cause them any trouble more serious than young people usually had.

Next, Heris went to find Oblo. "I've got our slot," Heris said, with no preamble. "The family's requested that the yacht be put in deep storage. The court agreed. Spacenhance doesn't want the responsibility of moving it, and I've refused to allow a ferry crew, under provisions of my employment contract with Lady Cecelia *and* my rights as possible heir. The court agreed to that, too. Suspicious, but they did agree. So we're to move her."

"But what about stores? If you're planning to go outsystem at once—"

"Are you telling me that the best thief I ever knew can't manage to get a few cargo cubes aboard a yacht guarded by an interior decorator?"

"Well . . . no. But it won't be easy. Those people are strange."

"Oh? You've been checking?"

"Of course." Oblo looked up at the ceiling. "You said get ready for a quick departure, so I thought I'd . . . ease things. Turns out they have an almighty sticky AI on their dockgate."

"But you can do it."

"Unless you're planning to run a year without stopping anywhere, she's fit." He didn't look at her directly, but she knew his face too well to be fooled. He had begun shifting provisions into the yacht long before. It had probably started simply to prove he could bugger the AI.

"Now?"

"I'd like another three shifts, to sort of finish things off. But we could go now, and not be much shorter."

"Good. You can have three shifts, but not a second more, and you'd better not get caught." Oblo looked insulted at that, as well he might.

"And that includes weaponry."

"No problem." By the tone, he'd installed that first. He would.

"Right, then. We file a flight plan for eight shifts from now—" Oblo scowled, and Heris pointed at him. "Think about it. You're going to be sure they are as stupid as you think. If you've been doing something every shift or so, five blanks will make them show themselves, especially with a plan filed. I'll have reserved our space in Rockhouse Minor's deep storage, and tickets back here on the ferry. Show up in uniform; we're Lady Cecelia's employees, and not a gang of toughs who might go larking off somewhere in her ship. Very formal, very sad. Look as grim as you like—you're miserable about this, and you don't mind saying so. But not in the bars yet, not until the last night."

Heris had no trouble looking grim as she filed the flight plan. Everyone knew about the legal dispute; this would make it clear who was winning.

"Tough luck, Captain," said the Traffic head clerk. He had been on Rockhouse for years; she had filed Fleet plans with him. "It's disgusting the way they've messed up what the old lady intended."

"Lady Cecelia is—was—a fine woman," Heris said. "And I only hope they don't scour the tubes when they shut the main drive down over there."

"Oh—you're not going to Duibly's?"

"No. Lady Cecelia's family insists that it's not cost effective, since they don't foresee the ship being used for several local years—and possibly sold away. As you see, they specified Harrigan's." The clerk would know what that meant, in credits and in skill. Harrigan's was a fine deep-storage yard, if you were planning to send a ship or sell it to someone who would be doing a major overhaul anyway. Duibly's, far more expensive, boasted it could power and air up a ship from deep storage in less than 50 hours.

"A shame. A lovely ship, I've heard."

"It is." He wanted to know more; she could tell. "You know, she had just had it redone when I first took command, and she was having it redone again." His eyes widened; he wanted even more details. "Real wood paneling," Heris said. "Furnishings brought up from the family estate. And it was impressive before."

"I know," he said. "Spacenhance has been using the interiors in their advertising. That was their top designer; I wonder why she wanted to change it."

Heris shrugged. "She could, I suppose. Perhaps it didn't have the effect she expected. But you see what I mean."

The clerk nodded as if that had meant something, and sealed the flight plan with a coded magnetic strip.

On the way back from the Traffic Control office, a short brown-haired young woman stopped her at a slideway entrance.

"Captain Serrano?" Her face and voice were slightly familiar. Heris paused, wary.

"Yes?"

"I don't expect you remember me—I was just a very junior ESR-12." Military: environmental systems technician, enlisted. With the specialty and rank, the name came back to her.

"Yes . . . Vivi Skoterin." Another reminder of her earlier failure, though Skoterin might have been junior enough to escape the courts-martial that devastated the officers and NCOs of her former crew. "How have you been? Did you—?"

"They didn't send me to prison, no ma'am. But—but I didn't re-up." No wonder, Heris thought. The young woman looked thin and depressed; what had she been doing?

"Find a job all right?"

"Well, ma'am . . . I just got in . . . been working on a bulk transport, independent carrier, Oslin Brothers. Maybe you know of them?"

Oslin Brothers meant nothing to Heris, but independent carriers of bulk cargo were marginal profit concerns. She shook her head, and Skoterin went on.

"I . . . was hoping for something better. Scuttlebutt around Station is you have your own ship and are hiring some of your former crew . . . and I was wondering . . ." Damn. Heris didn't need this, not now. But responsibilities didn't come when you needed them. At least she could get this woman a square meal and perhaps a little money to help her find a better berth.

"Scuttlebutt's got it slightly wrong, as usual, but come on—at least have lunch with us. You remember Sergeant Meharry and Oblo?" Something flickered in Skoterin's eyes, but Heris dismissed it as recognition. "They'll be glad to see you. Come on, now." Skoterin climbed onto the slideway with her, and Heris spent the trip back to the hostel thinking furiously. What would she do now? She owed Skoterin, as she owed all her former crew . . . and they were short an environmental tech, as Haidar had reminded her only that week. The others were willing to do the work, but in an emergency, they'd have their own stations to keep.

Haidar remembered Skoterin at once, which relieved Heris: what if the woman had been planted on them somehow? While she went off to freshen up for lunch, he said "You will bring her along, won't you, Captain? We really need another tech—I could use two more, in fact."

"You're sure of her?"

"Oh, yes. That's Vivi. Kind of dull, except for her work: she's absolutely reliable. She got top reports from Lieutenant Ganaba—" Lieutenant Ganaba, who had been killed on the island even before the hunt started; Heris had heard the story from Petris. The admiral had not liked to leave officers alive as effective leaders. And Ganaba had been tough; if he approved of Skoterin, then she was good.

"Seems a good solution to me," Heris said. "But if we ask

her, she has to say yes . . . we can't leave her behind to tell the tale."

"Just tell her we're ferrying the yacht, and not the rest of it."

"But that's like hijacking her—"

"Hell, Captain, we're going to kidnap a prince—why not an environmental tech? Besides, she wants a berth."

And Skoterin, offered a short-time job ferrying the yacht, with "maybe a longer job later" agreed at once. Haidar took her off to lunch himself, waving away Heris's offer of funds.

With the flight plan filed, and the *Sweet Delight* entered into the undock sequencer, time seemed to compress. Heris had her own list to complete. Check out of the hostel, with reservations for herself at another, lower-priced hostel for the end of the week. Consigning the letters patent to Kevil Mahoney's office downside; she sweated out the hours until he called to confirm receipt. The messenger service was supposed to be secure, but one never knew.

She had avoided telling Spacenhance about the new orders, lest they send someone aboard to do something and find what Oblo had stashed. So at the last reasonable time, when she was due aboard to begin the undocking procedures, she stopped by the Spacenhance office and showed her official authorization.

"But you can't—" said the decorative person in the front office.

"Court orders it," Heris said. "Long-term storage has been arranged at Harrigan's, Bay 85; I'm due aboard to begin undock in ten minutes."

"But—"

"I don't see the problem," Heris said. "You had the cease-work order more than 40 days ago; surely the ship's just sitting there empty—isn't it?"

"Well, yes, but—I'll have to check with a manager." Not *the* manager, Heris noted, but *a* manager. Soon the woman Heris had seen before came out of the back rooms.

"Captain Serrano! How nice. Mil tells me you're moving Lady Cecelia's yacht into deep storage . . . does this mean the court has ruled against you?"

"Not yet, just until the case is heard and finally settled. Her family petitioned the court, and the court agreed."

"Well, that's too bad. Such a lovely ship. We can have her ready for you in . . . oh . . . another twenty-four hours. How's that?"

"Sorry. I've got undock starting in eight minutes; we're on the sequencer, and we have a flight plan. The Harrigan's berth is time-logged, and we have passage back to Major on Triamnos. If you'll just give me the access codes—"

"But Captain! The ship isn't—it's not ready. You know we had to stop in the middle—"

Heris shrugged. She had expected Spacenhance to try some kind of delay but this seemed silly. "As I told your assistant, you had the cease-work order weeks ago; surely your people aren't using the ship . . ."

"Well, no, it's not that . . . it's just such a mess. We don't like to let even an unfinished job go out of here in that state—"

"Sorry, but this time you must." Heris stared her down; the woman seemed uncommonly flustered, and Heris wondered if Spacenhance was involved in some kind of smuggling, and had been using the yacht as a storage bay. If so, they were about to be in real trouble. All of them.

"Well. I suppose if you're on the sequencer—" Traffic Control had a reputation for shredding anyone who fouled up the system, including Stationside companies whose failure to comply with ships' orders caused the delay. Heris had never liked Traffic Control's tyranny, but this time she blessed it.

"I'll just come with you," the woman said. Heris didn't argue. Six minutes was cutting it close, even for her.

The crew waited, looking as solemn and grim as Heris could have hoped, in formal dark blue. But the Spacenhance woman hardly glanced at them, opening the gates and hatches one after another. Heris hardly had time to glance at the status board, and see that it was safely green, before the woman opened the access hatch itself and started into it.

"Excuse me," Heris said firmly. "We really don't have much time before undock starts—if you could just get back to the dock—"

"Oh . . . right." The woman still looked nervous; Heris's suspicions went up another notch. She smiled anyway, and led the way past the Spacenhance manager, trusting Oblo to make sure she didn't stay aboard.

The ship smelled funny. She had expected a new smell, cleaning solutions or solvents or something like that, but this was a strange, yeasty odor. Perhaps that's what bothered Spacenhance—maybe whatever they used to strip the carpets and wall coverings smelled bad, and they didn't want clients to know. The bridge still looked too tiny, especially with the new screens crammed into every spare corner. Before, it had looked like a toy . . . now, it looked like some electronic hobbyist's workbench.

Heris took her seat and called Traffic Control. She could hear the crew moving into position; in her mind's eye she followed them all to their stations.

"*Sweet Delight*, Heris Serrano commanding, initiating undocking procedures."

"Confirm your flight plan to Rockhouse Minor, Harrigan's Long-Term Storage; please accept course burst."

"Accepting." Heris shunted the course to Sirkin's board, and went on with the interminable formalities of undocking from Rockhouse Major. Registration, ownership, insurance, ship's beacon profiles, accounting details. Even though they weren't going outsystem (as far as Traffic Control knew) the rules required long minutes of voice confirmation of details already on file. The cost of pursuing legal remedies against ships who left Stations owing money meant that it was much easier to insist on clear accounts before they left. If so much as a single glass of ale were outstanding, the ship could lose her place in the sequence and be assessed a hefty fine, to boot.

After the formalities came the systems checks, which she watched carefully. The ship had been aired up the entire time, but something might still be wrong. At least she now had crew she trusted. All boards were green except the newest: those would stay dark, untouched, until they had cleared the Station. Those, if detected, could get them in trouble.

"Tug approaching," said Traffic Control. "Channel 186."

"Thanks." Heris switched to the tug's channel. She would have preferred a hot start, but no civilian ship left Rockhouse Major under its own power. She checked to see that the yacht's bustle had been deployed; Petris gave her a thumb's up. With no pilot (a rating not used on the Fleet vessels) he had taken over some of those functions.

"Captain Serrano, *Sweet Delight,*" she said on the tug's channel. The memory of the first time she'd said that, undocking here long months before, came to her. She felt very differently now.

"Station Tug 16," came the reply. "Permission to grapple." She was glad it wasn't the same tug; that would have been a bit too much coincidence.

"Permission to grapple." She felt the jar; Tug 16 was a lot clumsier than the earlier one. The status lights switched through the color sequence, and ended green.

"All fast," the tug captain said. "Your port bustle coupling is a bit stretchy, though." Excuses. He had come in too fast. "On your signal."

She called Traffic Control on their channel. "Captain Serrano of *Sweet Delight*: permission to undock, on your signal."

"All clear on Station. Confirm all clear aboard?"

Nothing but green on any of the boards; her crew nodded. "All clear aboard." Twenty seconds. She, the Stationmaster on watch in Traffic Control, and the tug captain all counted together, but the computer actually broke the connection to the Station. She watched the display as the tug dragged them slowly away from the crowded traffic near Rockhouse Major. This would be a shorter tug, because they were headed for

Minor, on an insystem route. In fact, the tug could give them the correct vector and let them ride that trajectory most of the way to Minor, but Heris had chosen the more common option of powering up and "hopping" it.

When the tug released them, she called for the insystem drive.

"Insystem drive, sir." Petris, that was. "Normal powerup." The lights flicked once, as the internal power switched from the storage units to the generators working off the drive.

"Engage." Now the artificial gravity shivered momentarily, then steadied, as the insystem drive pushed them along the course handed out by Traffic Control. Not that they would stay on it long. "Turn on the new scanners." Oblo reached up and did so. Now she had almost as much data on traffic in near space as Traffic Control.

Insystem space had no blind corners, no places where the sudden change in acceleration of a yacht would go unnoticed. As soon as they started their move away from assigned course, Traffic Control would be all over them. So might any fast-moving patrol craft, though none showed on the scans. It felt very strange. She had never, in her entire life, done anything intentionally wrong. Even as a child, she had always asked permission, always followed the rules . . . well, most of the rules. She had cut herself off from the Fleet for a good cause, she thought; now she was cut off from all lawful society. She hoped the cause was good enough. She *really* hoped her mathematics was good enough.

What they had was the advantage of small mass and initiative. The longer she waited, the less initiative . . .

Petris reached back and caught her hand. "You don't have to do this, just to impress me," he said. "If you think it's wrong—"

"I think it's all wrong," Heris said. "But this is the least wrong part of it. No. We'll go and scandalize the Fleet, and then get blown away by a smuggler or something—"

"You don't really think that . . ."

"No, not without a fight." *Do it*, she told herself fiercely. And as always, cementing the responsibility, she made the move herself. Flat down on the board: the main drives answered smoothly, and the *Sweet Delight*, bouncing like a leaf in a rapid, skipped out of her plotted course. They needed another 10,000 kilometers . . . She sweated, watching the plots. It should take a few seconds to register; someone should be tapping the screens, wondering what had happened to the plots. Then it would take time to transmit the message. No one had the right firing angle for missiles; no one could intercept with tractors before they got their critical distance. Optical weapons would fry them—no civilian vessel carried shields—but the overrun could be tricky. She knew there was traffic beyond them, bound on other routes. She had counted on that.

Seconds ticked by. They still had the civilian beacon on; no use to play games with it in a system where their ID was known.

"There," Oblo said, with grim satisfaction, as one of his lights blinked red, then returned to green. "Stripped it, even though they should've known who we were."

"Wondering," Petris said. "They're wondering what happened."

"Not for long," Heris said. Even as she spoke, the Traffic Control blared at them.

Course error! Course error! Contact Traffic Control Officer at once.

Automatically, Heris's finger found the button, but she stopped it before the channel opened. When she glanced around, they were watching her. She pulled her hand back, and shrugged. "Nothing to say. We'll wait it out." At the edge of her vision, in front of Oblo, the counter ran down the long chain of numbers.

General warning! Vessel off course in sector Red Alpha Two! All traffic alert! Do not change course without direct orders! Stand by for Traffic Control override! The words crawled across the navigation near-scan screen, and bellowed from the speakers. The new scanners showed the reaction in color changes, as other traffic dumped velocity or changed course. Heris had counted on that, too. Everyone believed in Traffic Control until something went wrong, at which point at least twenty percent of the captains would use their own judgment. Time after time that had proven deadly, but it happened anyway. Now Traffic Control had more to worry about than one yacht off course, as each panicky ship caused problems for others.

A tight beam obliterated Traffic Control's blare, and the near-scan screen showed a face in Fleet gray, with the insignia of an admiral on his shoulders. Maartens, it must be; he had just taken command of Fleet at Rockhouse Major. He had served with Lepescu, though she didn't know if they'd been friends. "Damn you, Serrano," the man said. Heris stared back, impassive. Of course they knew, but she wasn't going to give him her visual. "I never thought even you would cripple an old woman just to get a free ride. We'll find you." A threat she trusted, as she trusted a knife to be sharp. But it bit deep anyway; she made herself stare into those angry eyes until the beam cut off. Then she cut the link to Traffic Control herself. She didn't need that nonsense blaring at her. They weren't going to impede anyone's course more than another few seconds.

"We're clear in theory," Oblo said. She gave him a tight smile.

"Then let's surprise them." With the new control systems, she had only one button to push; she wished she could have heard the comments from Traffic Control when their abrupt skip into FTL left an unstable bubble in the local space for others to avoid.

They were still alive. She didn't think she'd ever heard of anyone using FTL drive that close to a planet, and she hadn't entirely trusted the theory that said it was possible for something of their mass. But they were alive, the *Sweet Delight* as solid as ever, and presumably they hadn't destroyed anything vital back there. She had gotten as far from the main stations as she could, although there were too many satellites up to avoid them all.

"And now," Oblo said, with his crooked leer, "for a life of piracy and plunder, eh? Gold, girls, adventure—"

"Shut up," Petris said, so that she didn't have to comment. "First we have to find a quiet place to do a little cosmetic work on our friend here."

Heris tried to relax. Nothing could have followed them; not even the escorts could have gone into FTL so close. Pursuit would have hours of boost to get out far enough, by which time they would have nothing to follow. They had slipped their leash. She looked around at her crew. They looked busy and outwardly calm, but she suspected more than one felt the same internal tremors she did. They had not set out in life to become criminals. Those who had been through the disastrous court-martial would be more hardened, but Sirkin— she glanced again at the young navigator. Sirkin had had a promising career before her, and no military background. Now she had lost her lover and her career . . . but the latter had been her own choice. Still she must feel strange, the youngest and the only one without military experience, without years of working with Heris.

But her face, when she turned to face Heris, seemed calm enough. "Captain, the new equipment's working well. It's—I really can pick up navigation points even here." *Here* being that indefinable location into which FTL drives projected. Heris grinned at her.

"Just remember that the apparent motion you'll see isn't right. When we drop out, we won't be where you would expect, but where the charts say." Sirkin looked confused, and Heris didn't blame her. The military navigational gear which Oblo had liberated had counterintuitive properties which Sirkin would learn best by experience. The point of it was not to steer by the detected navigation nodes, but to detect other vessels in FTL state.

They passed two more jump points safely, with no pursuit detected. Heris didn't fool herself that this meant no pursuit—it meant only successful, and very temporary, evasion. Finally they returned to normal space in a region with no known maintenance stations. As Petris had said, they needed to do a bit of work on the yacht.

Better Luck had been built at the same yards, within a year of *Sweet Delight*, the utility version of the same hull. She'd been modified for carrying very low temperature cargo, then rebuilt to handle rough landings, then rebuilt again to return her to a deep-space freighter, reclaiming the cargo space lost to the landing gear. She had been lost to the finance company, which chose to scrap her rather than pay for refitting (the last cargo had rotted when the low-temp compartments failed, and the stench had gone into the deck tiling.) Oblo had her registration number, and her papers—or a reasonable facsimile—and the overall hull design matched. Now he was making sure the beacon matched, too . . . and the little tramp freighter had never operated in this region of space.

"I wonder how Lady Cecelia is," Sirkin said one day. "If Brun's been able to do anything . . ."

"We all wonder," Heris said. She knew someone would have let Cecelia know she'd run off with the ship; she hated that, knowing Cecelia would feel betrayed.

Lorenza had listened without interruption to the Crown Minister's version of the theft of the yacht. Now she said, "So—it was that Serrano person after all, eh?"

"I suppose." The Crown Minister seemed more interested in his ham with raisin sauce. "Suppose she got tired of waiting for the court to rule. Silly—it might have ruled in her favor. There are all sorts of precedents for enforcing quite stupid wills."

"Berenice is sure they'd have ruled against her. Even if she didn't poison Cecelia herself, it was clearly a matter of undue influence."

He stopped to put maple-apple-walnut butter on a roll. "You women! I think you were convinced the captain did it just because she's another woman, and one who wears a uniform."

Lorenza raised her eyebrows at him, slowly. "Now, Piercy, you know that's not fair. I have nothing against military women; I have the highest admiration for their courage and their dedication. But this woman was no longer military; she left under a cloud—"

"She was cleared," the Crown Minister said. Lorenza wondered why he was being stubborn. Did he know something she should know?

"I understand that her own family—her own well-known family—didn't stand behind her. That tells me something. Even if she was cleared, they may know something that never came out in court. It wouldn't be the first time."

"True." He was retreating; he had turned his attack to the ham, and then to the rice pilaf.

"Berenice says Bunny's daughter Bubbles started acting odd after spending time with her on Sirialis. Wanted to change her name, or something."

"Bubbles has been acting like a fool since she hit puberty," the Crown Minister said, and took a long swallow of his wine. "It wouldn't take a yacht captain to send her off on another tack." That struck him as funny, and he laughed aloud. Lorenza didn't smile, and he ran down finally. "Sorry—a nautical joke."

"My point is that it's now perfectly clear she did something underhanded to influence poor Cecelia. And now she's stolen the yacht. Just what you'd expect."

"Do you ever visit Cecelia?" the Crown Minister asked. She almost smiled at his transparent attempt to change the subject and make her feel guilty.

"Yes, occasionally. I'm going tomorrow, in fact." She had not been able to resist, after all. Twice now she had sat beside the bed, her soft hand on Cecelia's unresisting cheek, and murmured into her ear. *I did it. I did it.* That was all: no name, only the whisper. It excited her so she could hardly conceal it all the way home. And now she could be the one to tell Cecelia that her precious yacht captain had stolen her yacht . . . that she had been abandoned once more. If she had had any hope left, that should finish it. Lorenza let herself imagine the depths of that despair . . . what it must be like to have one's last hope snuffed out by a voice in the darkness. She was very glad she had specified that Cecelia's auditory mechanisms should be left intact.

✧ Chapter Ten

"This is the craziest idea I ever heard." Ronnie glared at Brun. "You want to take a sick, paralyzed old lady up in a hot-air balloon, then bang around in a shuttle, then—and what are you going to do when you get to Rockhouse Major?"

"I'm not going to Rockhouse Major." Brun glared back. "Dad's yacht is at Minor; that's all you need to know."

"A balloon—dammit, you can't fly a balloon like a plane. They just drift. How can you possibly be sure you'll even get there—or do you expect me to chase you across country on foot with Aunt Cecelia over my shoulder?"

"No, of course not. And yes, I can aim a balloon—there are ways. They're clumsier than planes, but quieter and much more difficult to find on scans designed for planes and shuttles. I can be there within fifteen minutes of a set time, and close enough that you won't have to run any races."

"So what do you want me to do?"

"You visit her—you have a regular pass."

"Yeah, but they're still watching me." Less warily since Serrano had run off with his aunt's yacht, but still watching.

"That's fine. They can watch you all they want. What's your regular visiting day?"

"Saturday, of course, when I have a half-day off. You know this already—"

"Yes, but I'm checking my own plans. Your mother visits on Tuesdays, and your father on Thursdays, and you on Saturdays—and you almost never miss—"

"I liked her," Ronnie said. He noticed the past tense, and wished he had said "like" even though it wasn't true. No one

162

could like that limp, unresponsive body in the bed. And he had only Brun's conviction, formed in that one visit, that Cecelia-the-person still lived inside her inert shell, to give him hope.

"So while they watch you, and her, it's just routine. They expect you."

"I still can't walk out with her—"

"You won't have to. All you have to do is get her unhooked from the bed, and outside. Like this—" Brun flipped open her notecomp and showed him the plan. She had it all down, all the medical background, sketches of wires and tubes and things he didn't want to look at. What to do in which order, what he would have to take with him. Suggestions for making sure the bothersome attendants didn't interrupt—he thought of another way himself, and realized he was being drawn in. It still looked ridiculous, but Ronnie didn't argue. He didn't have anything better to offer. He didn't have anything at all. And the longer they left Aunt Cecelia trapped in her helplessness, the worse for her . . . he could hardly believe anyone could stay sane month after month.

"When, then?"

"Festival of the Air, of course." He felt himself flushing. He'd been so miserable he'd forgotten that annual celebration was almost upon them. "Plenty of confusion in the air—for some reason the wilder sorts are thinking of dropping in on the starchier resorts and sanctuaries in the area. Can't think why." She grinned. "And no, it's not traceable to me. Now—let's get busy. You'll have to practice getting a flight suit on me when I'm lying limp."

Oblo had managed to load the yacht with a surprising number of amenities. Toiletries, leisure clothes, entertainment cubes, and a cube reader. Music disks and players. Despite the bare bulkheads and naked decks, the lack of furniture, ample bedding, and bright-colored pillows made comfortable nooks for lounging and sleeping. Heris asked about the pillows—she could not imagine Oblo sneaking through the docks with big puffy orange and puce and turquoise pillows under his arms—and he gave her his best innocent glare.

"Bare decks get cold, Captain. You know that." Then a sheepish grin. "And besides, these pillows . . . they were sort of . . . lying about somewhere . . ."

"Somewhere?" She could feel her eyebrows rising.

Now he stared at the overhead. "To tell you the truth—" which meant it would be his fiction. "They belonged to someone Meharry and I kind of blame for that girl Amalie's death." Possibilities ran through Heris's mind, and she settled on the obvious.

"That therapist?"

He grinned as if he was glad she'd figured it out. "Yeah. Had this big room with lots of pillows in it. Needed cleaning, they did. Cleaners picked them up, delivered them. We sort of . . . liberated them on the way back." As a specimen of Oblo's vengeance, this was mild. Heris decided to let it go.

"You know it was wrong," she said.

"So was getting Amalie killed and Sirkin hurt," he said, with no remorse. "Captain, it was the *least* we could do." About what she'd expected; she managed not to laugh until he was out of her office.

So far the voyage was going well. Skoterin had not protested when she realized they were not, in fact, ferrying the yacht a short distance. She had been glad of a longer job, she said, and she trusted the captain. Heris found that amazing, but then so were the others trusting her. She got along well with the others, though she was younger by some years than anyone but Sirkin. Heris wondered if that would turn into anything. She couldn't remember what Skoterin's preferences had been—if she'd ever known. Not that it mattered, really. As long as they both did their work. Sirkin she saw on the bridge; she was happily absorbing all Oblo and Guar could teach her about the new navigational equipment. Haidar reported that Skoterin was as efficient as he remembered. All she had to worry about was the mission itself.

❖   ❖   ❖

"I wish there were a way to be sure the Crown offer was faked," Heris grumbled. "Then we wouldn't have to bother with this ridiculous rendezvous. What if the prince doesn't show up?" She had never enjoyed covert ops, and didn't now. Petris ignored that, and kept rubbing her shoulders. Oblo had the bridge, with Arkady Ginese to second him; nothing would get by those two. She and Petris had retired to her cabin, where they turned up the thermostat and lowered the lights so that they could enjoy the rest of the shift out of uniform. Surely this time nothing could interrupt them, not in FTL space.

"What kind of job do you think we can get as cover if we need it?" he asked. His hands slid lower; she wondered if he really meant to continue a serious conversation or if this was just another form of teasing. She was almost afraid to try the response she was eager to make; the obstacles to their pleasure had gone far beyond a joke. What would happen *this* time if they started something? She felt she would die of frustration if they didn't.

"Soft side of legal, I expect." Heris did not meet his eyes, and leaned back against him. Maybe he would take the hint and continue without talking about it. Petris shifted her in his arms, and she quit thinking about future problems. Present pleasure was enough for now. Apparently he thought so too; he quit asking silly questions. And nothing interrupted them, though she didn't think of that for some time.

But afterwards, they came back to it. A small tramp cargo ship couldn't simply idle along from place to place; it had to have cargo, and destinations. Otherwise, as they knew well, the authorities would have questions, backed up with force.

"It would be simpler if we had two ships," Heris said finally. She rolled over and stretched. "We could transfer cargo from one to the other, as if—*what is that*?" Her convulsive lurch upset Petris, who had been curled over watching her stretch; they collided, and then Heris was out of the bed, clutching the sheet, and pointing at the bulkhead above him.

"What?" Petris glared first at her, then at the bulkhead. Then his gaze sharpened. "I—don't have any idea." He edged away from the bulkhead, and got off the bed.

"It's alive," Heris said. She was aware that her voice had squeaked, and still hadn't returned to normal. The thing was just lighter than the bulkhead, a dull creamy white, as long as her hand. It had long antennae; she could just see them wiggling.

"And there's more than one of them," Petris said. He pointed. Out of the crack between bulkhead and bunk, two more of the things crept.

Heris had wrapped the sheet tightly around herself; now she leaned closer. "Six legs . . . antennae . . . you know what it looks like? It looks like an albino—" Something skittered down her leg, from under the sheet, and tickled her toes as it ran over them. "COCKROACH!" She was out of the sheet before she knew it, and across the room. Shuddering, she looked back. Petris, on one foot, looked around like someone who had forgotten what the other leg was for. Neither of them had anything handy for whapping a cockroach, because ships didn't have cockroaches. Ships were routinely cleaned out before and after each trip; everyone feared vermin.

"Albino cockroaches?" Petris said, still on one leg like some kind of exotic bird. "Do they . . . I mean, what do they eat?"

Heris headed for the shower. "I don't know, but they're filthy. It's disgusting. On my ship!" She strode into the shower and bounced back out. "They're in there, too!"

"They like warmth, I recall," Petris said. He was back on two feet, but looked anxious. "We turned up the heat in here—"

"And what if they're all over the ship?" Heris asked. She had a nightmare vision of a full-bore inspection arriving to find her and her first officer and lover stark naked amid swarming albino cockroaches. Could she claim they'd eaten her uniform? And would they?

"They probably are," Petris said gloomily. He shook out his

shirt before putting it on. "And they probably breed. Where could they have come from? None of us had been out of Station quarantine."

"*That's* why the redecorators didn't want us on the ship," Heris said. She remembered the frightened look on the woman's face. It made sense if she was afraid of being caught with illegal biologicals. "They put them here."

"But why?"

"I . . . don't know. But we had best find out. Perhaps they're used in some stage of the process."

"It can't be legal." Petris shook out his shoes, one by one, before putting them on. "It's against all the regulations I ever heard of to have biologicals on a Station or a ship. Except for the registered ones, like you told me Lady Cecelia had."

"I wonder." Heris checked her own clothes carefully before getting back into them. "At least we now have a cargo."

"These? They're not cargo—they're a reason to quarantine us." He sounded horrified at the thought. Heris felt the same way but struggled to think past her revulsion.

"Yes, but . . . let's assume the decorators keep them, and put them here. That means they're valuable to the decorators. That might mean they're valuable to another firm doing the same work somewhere else."

He looked dubious. "I don't see how. First we'd have to catch them, confine them somewhere, take care of them. We don't even know what they're *for.*"

"Can you catch one?" Heris asked, pointing to the cluster that still clung to the bulkhead over the bunk.

"Me?" He looked at her. She looked back, pointedly. "Oh, all right. If they're poisonous or something, though, you had better figure out how to save my life, or I'll haunt you."

"I should figure out first what to keep it in . . . let me think—something in the galley should hold it. And we'll turn the temperature down, in case they're more active in warmth. If I remember, most insects are."

Once clothed, she found the pale cockroaches just as

disgusting, but less frightening. If they attacked, they'd hit her clothes and not her skin. She shuddered, remembering the touch of those legs. With the thermostat down, she had an excuse for shivering.

"I suppose you want me to stay here while you fetch a cage?" Petris didn't sound happy about that.

"I can stay," Heris said. "Get a food container with a tight lid—except we'll have to ventilate it somehow—I wonder what size holes these things can crawl through."

He came back with a canister whose top had a dozen perforations; Heris wondered why, then it occurred to her it looked like a giant salt shaker. Perhaps that was how Cecelia's cook had covered pastry with powdered sugar.

"We had similar things back home," Petris said, as he smacked the open end of the canister down over the nearest cockroach and carefully slid a flat piece of metal under it to trap it. "Farmers hate 'em too—those ate crops, clothing, pillows, rugs—"

"Rugs?" Heris stared at him. "Like—the carpet that used to be here?"

"We didn't have real carpet; we had rugs woven of plant fiber and animal hair. Some handwoven, and some factory-produced. But yes, they ate holes in rugs. And upholstery. Old-fashioned books, too, especially the bindings. My uncle said it was the glue. And they'd make a mess of data cubes left lying around, even though they couldn't eat them. They'd leave their . . . mess . . . on them, which glopped up the cube readers. Why?"

"Because . . . that may be why the decorators have them. I hadn't really thought about it but . . . the stuff the decorators take out of a ship—all the wall coverings and carpet and upholstery—has to go somewhere. They'd pay to have it processed in the Station recycler, and then they'd have to pay to replace that with new material. Imported or fabricated, either one. Let me run the figures . . ."

This was something she could work out, once she thought

of it. And the specifications were in the contract she'd brought along. She called them up. "Look—here's an estimate of square meters, times minimum thickness of carpet, of wall covering, of upholstery. Which comes to—" She looked at the volume result. "—And they're required to give chemical composition—organics—so in case anything's volatile, what kind of outgassing the ship's environmentals will have to handle. Interesting."

"What?"

"If they're honest, given the density and composition, the volume of material they'd have to have processed onstation or transport would cost them—" She called in the financial subroutines. "Too much. Plus replacement. I'll figure that both ways, local processing and importation. No, three ways—from planetary sources and importation from more distant sources." The result exceeded the bid on Cecelia's job.

"Can't be," Petris said. "You've made a mistake somewhere."

"I might have," Heris said. "But if I didn't, and if these disgusting insects were put here for a reason—and if they eat rugs and pillows and upholstery—"

"They eat them," Petris said, with distaste. "They certainly don't manufacture their replacements. It might be cheaper to have them gobble up the client's old stuff, but unless they can be cooked into delicious banquet meals, I don't see how that helps." Then his face changed expression. "Unless, of course, they're cooked into something else—the new furnishings."

"That's sick," Heris said. "Besides, how could you get them all back out?"

"It would explain why they risk breaking the vermin laws, if it did work."

"And it gives us something to sell," Heris said. "Both the information and the . . . er . . . samples."

"It certainly establishes us as outlaws," Petris said. "Selling vermin—carrying them loose on a spaceship?"

"Not loose if we can capture them," Heris said. "I don't want any more surprises."

Capturing the clots of pale cockroaches in Heris's cabin turned out to be easy, but everyone soon knew that those had not been the only ones aboard. Although their pale color made them hard to spot in some locations, they were obvious in the galley when someone flipped the lights on and they scuttered for dark corners. They swarmed to every food spill, and for a while food spills were more common. Even Heris, who had convinced herself they were harmless, dropped a mug of soup when one ran up her arm. Eventually the crew learned to tolerate the sight of them—or at least not drop things—but no one liked it.

"What's this thing?" asked Nasiru Haidar one day, carrying the tiny object gingerly between thumb and forefinger. "And I already know it's not a dropping—I've learned to recognize those."

Petris peered at it. "Egg case, and it's already hatched. Or they have. So they're fertile."

"How fast do they reproduce?" Nasiru asked.

Petris shrugged. "I have no idea. Where I grew up, the entire life cycle of some insects was only 20 planetary days— and our days were close to Old Earth days, they said."

"And these insects were mature when introduced—possibly more than ten days before we undocked. So they could have laid eggs immediately they came aboard—"

"It's possible that we undocked with only egg cases," Petris said, "and all the cockroaches on the ship are those who came with us as eggs."

"So I couldn't have seen them," muttered Oblo. Everyone had pointed out that he'd been aboard the ship, stashing supplies. He'd insisted there were no cockroaches then.

"Possible." Heris grimaced. "What doesn't seem possible is getting them all. I wish we knew how long ago that had hatched. Are the ones we see now first or second generation? Or worse?"

Haidar and Skoterin, with their specialty in environmental systems, seemed the logical ones to devise living quarters for the captured cockroaches, and ways of eliminating those still loose. Heris hoped Cecelia would never need to know that she had had cockroaches running loose all over her ship.

✦   ✦   ✦

Brun waved at her friends as her balloon tugged on the mooring lines. Dozens of other balloons obscured her view of the hills. She signalled her handler, who released the line; she kept a steady burn as the balloon rose. A few were already high above her, bright colors hardly visible; a dozen released within a second of her release, and still more waited for a last passenger. The Festival of the Air . . . she remembered how she'd gasped the first time she saw all the balloons and kites and gliders and parasails. She'd had to learn to pretend disdain, even while learning to pilot a balloon; she'd claimed her father made her do it. But she'd always loved it.

Surface winds pushed her back over the taller hills, away from her goal. She didn't hurry to rise above them. Half a dozen balloons she knew well were drifting as she was, toward the course marker on the highest hill ten kilometers away.

"Racing, are you?" called a Kentworth, from a yellow balloon striped with purple. "I thought you declared non-competitive this year."

"Declarations are secret; the wind doesn't lie!" she yelled back. Every year some people pretended not to be racing until the race itself; it was one of the things she'd counted on. She let the balloon sag as it approached the next ridge of hills; with the wind behind her, she'd gain altitude here anyway, and she didn't want to be pushed into the contrary winds aloft. Not yet.

She was still a couple of kilometers short of the first marker when she turned on the burner. She had let herself sag below most of the competitors, but that was her style. Now the burner's roar drowned out the sound of others, and the hooting and cheering of watchers below. Slowly at first her balloon steadied, then lifted . . . then surged upward, as if yanked by a string.

"Damn!" she yelled. The nearest balloon might or might not hear her over the burner, but anyone watching or recording her on cube could see her mouth moving. "Burner's stuck on; I'm going to lose my wind—" She hauled herself up onto the basket rim, and banged noisily at the burner with a wrench as the balloon surged upward. Her stomach protested; she ignored it. It was no worse than a fast elevator ride. Around her, then below, the others receded to multicolored blobs. When she felt the wind shift, she whacked the burner control in the right place, which she'd been studiously missing, and turned it off. In the silence, she heard laughter from below, and one bellow asking if she needed help. "No," she yelled back down. "Fine now." The balloon kept rising; it had plenty of heat in it, and the air at this level was cooler.

She leaned out, watching all the other craft in the air. She knew what the winds aloft had been when she launched, but winds changed . . . she was drifting back now, away from the course marker, back past the launch site where balloons just launching looked like overstuffed sofa pillows. Half a dozen balloons were higher and ahead, well on their second race leg, having passed the first course marker before gaining altitude to ride the other wind direction.

The morning's mist had cleared, and now the remnants thickened into clouds defining the boundaries of different air masses. She pulled the burner control and sent the balloon up another several hundred feet. Up here somewhere she should find a current angling in from the approaching low pressure . . . over there where the clouds thickened into murk.

Ronnie craned his head to look over the guardhouse at the first of the balloons. Of course it wasn't time for Brun's yet . . . He looked at the guard, who smirked at him.

"Festival of the Air . . . you like it, sir?"

Ronnie allowed himself to look abashed. He had practiced the expression for two days now. "I know it's childish, but—it's always been my favorite seasonal festival. If I hadn't had to come visiting today, I could've been up there too . . . not that I don't love my Aunt Cecelia, of course." He put on what he hoped was a contrite but haughty look. The man nodded.

"A bit dull, visiting elderly relatives. They tell you all about their childhoods—"

"Well . . . not my aunt," Ronnie said. He was sure the man knew already; he had to assume that. "She . . . she can't speak, actually. She had a stroke."

"Ah." The man nodded again. "Sorry to hear that, sir. Makes it harder to visit, I expect. Although perhaps she can hear you, give some sign that she knows you're there?"

Ronnie felt cold. He wanted to smash the man's head on the ground. Instead, he shook his own head. "No . . . they say not. She's just a vegetable, just lying there. But Mother says . . . I mean, I would come anyway, she's my aunt, but . . ."

"But not today, if you didn't have to? No shame in that, sir; at least you came. It speaks well of your family."

Ronnie nodded without speaking as the man held out a stamped visitor's pass. He could feel the man's eyes watching his back as he walked up the beautifully landscaped lawn. Could the man tell that he had something under his clothes? In his pockets? He glanced up, and walked on with his head thrown back as if he could not resist watching the balloonists.

As required, he checked in at the main desk, where he was told his aunt's room number—the same as always, he was relieved to note. Her condition was unchanged, the receptionist said; he would please observe the rules of the facility, including . . . His mind tuned the voice out. He could have recited them by heart. No smoking, no alcohol, no eating in the room, no tampering with equipment or medication. He was free to use the toilet, or drink from the water fountain; if he required something else, he could ring for an attendant. He could stay two hours, but he would have to leave immediately if his aunt required active medical treatment. He nodded, as always, and exchanged his entrance pass for a unit pass that gave him access only to his aunt's treatment unit. The receptionist, safe behind her counter, hardly looked at him except for a quick glance at his face.

"And no flowers," the receptionist said to his departing back.

Sometimes they offered an escort; if they were busy, they didn't. This time no staff member came to check on him, and he strode along a neat stone pathway edged with flowers, free to think without interruption.

If they failed, his aunt would die. He was sure of that—either they made a clean getaway, or whoever had done this would kill her. Or you, his mind said suddenly, forcing on him an image of himself in Cecelia's state. He shuddered; sweat ran cold down his back. He saw, without registering them, other people walking on other paths: family members of other patients, staff in the cheerful, bright coveralls they wore. The treatment units, low stone-faced buildings scattered among trees and lawns and flowerbeds, looked like expensive apartments. The path led him around one, then another. He saw a terrace outside one, with someone in a hoverchair talking to two people in normal clothes. Off to one side, on a smooth stretch of lawn, a patient struggled to walk from a hoverchair to a picnic table spread with food.

At last he came to the final row of buildings, to Cecelia's treatment unit. Like the others, it was stone-faced and low, with a covered terrace on this side. The terrace on the far side had no roof; that should make it easier. He put his card in the door, which slid open. Inside, the expected staff member, this time the gray-haired man in yellow, who checked his pass, his ID, and reminded him again of the rules.

"She's having a good day," the man said with a wide smile. "And I've just finished toileting and bathing her; she's all fresh and sweet for you." Ronnie wanted to gag, but managed to thank the man. "If she could see," the man went on, "she'd have a perfect view of the Festival . . . at least you can enjoy it."

Ronnie wondered whether a fake sulk or a pretense of boredom would be better. "I wish I could," he said, letting his anger edge that. "If I hadn't—I mean—my regiment's got a contestant up."

"Ah—balloon or glider?"

"Both, of course." Ronnie pulled himself up and tried for pompous. It had been easy last year, when he still thought the regiment's place in the air races mattered.

"Well, you can see them through her window . . . or, if you wish, open the sliding door onto the west terrace. It won't bother her." Again, that faint cynical edge.

Ronnie shook his head. "I'd better not. If Mother found out I was neglecting Aunt Cecelia to look at the Festival, she'd skin me."

The man laughed. "I won't tell. Go ahead."

"I think she gets the tapes or something; she knew last week when I read for half an hour." He had read for half an hour, setting up this situation; his mother hadn't mentioned it, but he was sure tapes were being made, and someone at this level shouldn't know how many people got copies.

Now the man looked uneasy. "Oh . . . ah . . . that's easy to arrange. I can put it on a loop, for . . ."

Ronnie took the bait. "Would you? I'd be terribly grateful. It can't matter to Aunt Cecelia; you're all very tactful about it, but the doctor said her brain was gone. And if I have to spend all today cooped up in here, just looking at her and pretending to talk to her—" He held out his credit chip. "I'd like to buy a fruit punch, too . . ." The man fed the chip into the unit reader, flicking the buttons, and handed it back to Ronnie when it popped free. The cash—how much Ronnie couldn't tell—never actually changed hands.

"What you do," the man said, "is go in there and act normal for about ten minutes. Don't just sit still: pour some water, touch her hand, sit down, stand up, talk to her softly. Then come out, and go to the toilet; I'll loop the tape at that point and only an expert will know you're just repeating things for the rest of your visit. See this button? Push it when you leave, and it'll put the tape back to realtime."

"Thanks," Ronnie said. He had no idea if the man was honest, or honestly dishonest, but it was worth a try.

He went in and for ten minutes that felt like ten years acted like a bumbling, nervous, miserable nephew . . . as near as he could, the same he'd acted in all his visits. The bed's automatic movements still made him nervous; it looked and sounded as if some animal were rolling and twisting under the covers. He stroked Cecelia's cool, dry brow, and her thin, wrinkled, flaccid hands; he murmured to her, then turned away to wipe his eyes and pour himself a glass of water. Finally he left, and went into the toilet in the outer room. When he came out, the man in yellow stood by the outside door, gave him a final thumbs-up, and left.

Ronnie went back to Cecelia and sat there a little longer before letting himself look outside. Behind Cecelia's unit, the clinic land ran down to the river, a meadow mowed just too high for comfortable walking. He could see four or five balloons from inside the room, one quite low . . . but it was the wrong color. A parasail slid across, a long low glide that ended with a landing at the far end of the meadow. Ronnie gave Cecelia a kiss on the brow, and then walked over and opened the glass door to the terrace.

Balloons crowded above him, the whoosh of the burners much louder now. The air smelled fresh, the scent of mown grass mingling with a faint tang of smoke from the burners. He heard laughter, shouts, shrill cries of excitement or dismay. People hung over the edges of baskets and waved; he waved back. Some balloonists could indeed steer, he saw: not all used the same method, but he saw balloons wallowing across the wind with the aid of propellers, compressed-air jets, and even oddly-shaped "rudders." All in brilliant colors, in stripes and stars and plaids . . . he took a quick look at his watch, then tried to peer upwind. She ought to be here soon.

And he had to unhook his aunt from her monitors, praying that the attendant had been honest, that the tape was on a loop, that the loop included her monitors. He ducked back inside, and put on the thin surgical gloves he'd brought. Inside his own shirt and slacks were clothes for her—pants and shirt, socks, soft slippers. Folded flat between his jacket and its lining was a thin balloonist's coverall with garish stripes. Bubbles was supposed to bring something to cover Cecelia's hair.

Quickly, with a murmured apology, he threw back the covers. The sight of her thin white legs, her feet strapped into braces "to prevent contractures" nearly broke his concentration. As gently as he could, he unstrapped them, and struggled to put her socks on. He had never dressed even a child; he had no idea how hard it was to put socks on without cooperation. Then he lifted her legs and worked each foot into one leg of the slacks. She seemed so much heavier than she looked; he was having to tug and yank at her. He hoped it didn't hurt.

Bubbles had warned him what he might find next. The tubes, the bags . . . he didn't want to think about it, let alone look at it or touch it—but he had to. He glanced, feeling the blood rush to his face even though he was alone with an unconscious woman. Nothing. His breath came out in a gasp. She must have had—his mind, avoiding the present, struggled for the phrases—that surgery which implanted a programmable sphincter control. Without really looking, he wrestled the slacks up to her hips, and with a skillful lift he'd practiced on Bubbles, all the way up to her waist. He wouldn't have made it without that practice; he should have practiced all the dressing, but he'd assumed it would be easier. Perhaps the attendants who cared for her did more than guard against intruders.

His eyes registered the scars on her belly, but he refused to stop and stare at them. Now for the rest. He risked another quick glance outside, and saw the rose and silver balloon in the distance. He ducked back inside; he had to work quickly.

The bed sighed and gurgled, arching against his knee. He wished he knew how to turn it off. Of course it had saved Cecelia from pressure sores, but he couldn't lean against it without his skin crawling. Trying not to feel anything at the sight, he pulled open the front of the clinic gown. He had to find the ports through which she was fed, suctioned, medicated. A flat, peach-colored plastic oval on her upper chest must be one; three little caps stuck up like grotesque nipples, one blue, one green, one yellow. Behind her right ear, another plastic oval, this one with a silver nipple.

If the monitors don't use external wires—and most don't these days—they'll have built-in transmitters to either the bed, with relays to a nursing station, or direct to the nursing station. He remembered that, the quiet voice of the specialist. *Either sort can transmit up to thirty meters.* Which meant that nothing should show on the monitors—even if they were being watched—until Cecelia was more than ten meters from the bed. He had that much time to get well away from the unit, before the alarms went off.

No external wires today, and nothing connected to the ports. It should have been simple, but the feel of his aunt's flaccid body, as he pulled her forward, pulled off the gown, and worked her arms into the shirt, made it difficult. Now the coverall . . . this was quicker, since it had been designed to fit loosely over clothes, and since he had practiced how to put it on Brun. Of course, she wasn't as limp, even when she tried to lie still. He rolled Cecelia up on one side, fighting the wavelike motion of the bed, and got foot and hand into the loose sleeves. He worked the coverall close under her, then rolled her back over, tugged—and fitted the second arm and leg in. Then the pressure seals . . . and now she looked like a fallen balloonist, a normal person, a real person.

It must have taken hours; Bubbles would have drifted past. He was vaguely aware of sounds from outside, hoots and cries and angry voices back toward the main buildings, laughter and shouts from the meadow. He picked his aunt up, again surprised at how heavy she was, and moved near the door. The rose and silver balloon blocked his view upwind; he looked up to see Bubbles's white face staring back at him. The balloon sagged heavily, the basket scraping through the ornamental hedge between the next unit and this; it tilted half-over before breaking free. Then it dragged along the ground, and bumped the edge of the terrace.

"Now!" Bubbles said. "I can't stop it—"

Ronnie lunged outside, clumsy with the weight in his arms. He staggered into the side of the basket; Bubbles grabbed his aunt by the shoulders and pulled. Together, they got her over the basket's rim and in, although she landed heavily almost on her head.

"Straighten her out!" Ronnie said urgently, as the balloon pulled the basket along. "Get her head up—"

"Get back inside!" Bubbles snarled. He wanted to protest, but her hand was already on the burner control, and the roaring flame drowned out anything he could say. He looked around. Bubbles's balloon had blocked his view of the meadow and the air overhead; he hoped it had blocked others' view of the basket for that critical few moments. Now that it was past, he could see that the meadow roiled with balloons, parasails, even two gliders being hastily dewinged for transport.

When he went back into the empty room, the open bed seemed to stab his heart; his eyes filled. Forcing himself to be calm, he checked the IV pump and stripped off the medicine label—it might or might not help, but it was worth a try. Then he pulled the covers up and went into the unit's front room. He badly wanted to use the toilet, but didn't dare take the time. Now he had to get out—to be seen leaving, with nothing in his hands, and no aunt slung over his shoulder. He reached for the outer door, and remembered that he still had on those gloves. He was supposed to have put them in the basket for Bubbles to take away. Instead, he'd have to have them in his pocket, along with the medicine label.

On the east terrace, he could see more of the confusion wrought by the Festival of the Air participants. Someone's balloon had caught its basket solidly in a large tree, and attendants and balloonist were having a loud argument about it. Several other balloons had apparently dropped baskets of confetti and party toys, which littered lawns and walkways.

"We're just having a picnic!" he heard someone say—someone over his head, in the tree-trapped basket. "And we thought your old geezers might like to see a little color and life—"

"It's trespass," said a dark-coated man that Ronnie recognized as an administrator.

"Hi, Ronnie!" called a girl in the same basket. He peered up; the administrator, he knew, was watching him. "Come to our picnic."

He made himself laugh. "Picnic? In a tree? What are you idiots doing this time?"

"We're headed down to the shore, but Corey had a bet with George on who could drop a marker square in the middle of the administration building—"

"Why?" Ronnie asked, amused in spite of himself. It was the sort of thing George would think of. All they had told him was that they needed lots of balloons hanging around the nursing home on some ridiculous pretext.

"I don't know." The girl, whom he vaguely remembered from last Season, had dyed her hair in streaks of green and blue, and wore a tan coverall with one blue and one green arm. "Somebody said this would be a good place. Cheer up the patients who couldn't come to the Festival. Anyway, why not climb up and come along?"

"Because you're not going anywhere," Ronnie pointed out. "Not until you get out of that tree. Besides, your balloon is deflating—haven't you noticed?"

"Oh." The girl looked and shrugged, then turned on the young man. "I told you you were too low, Corey. We'll be stuck here for hours, and the others will have all the fun."

"You could ride with me," Ronnie offered. "It's not as much fun as flying there, but more fun than hanging in a tree like an ornament."

"No!" The administrator looked angrier than ever. "Unauthorized persons cannot just wander around unsupervised. You—" He turned on Ronnie. "Where's your pass?"

"Here." Ronnie held it out. "I'm on my way out; couldn't I escort Andalance? It's not her fault."

"She's an intruder. A trespasser—"

"Oh, come on. It's the *Festival*—" Corey sounded both angry and slightly drunk. "She's my date—"

"She didn't trespass intentionally," Ronnie said. The longer he stood here arguing, the more obvious it was that he didn't have his aunt hidden on his person. He told himself that the gloves in his pocket didn't really glow bright yellow, either. "And it would get her out of your tree. Or I could help free the basket—it looks like you've got other problems, too."

"No," the man said again, handing Ronnie's pass back. "It would be most helpful if you would simply check out now. If we clear the property of legitimate guests it will be easier to deal with these—" He glared upward. Corey made a rude noise.

"Well—if that's what you want—" Ronnie shrugged, and turned away, looking he hoped like someone reluctant to leave. He gave a last glance up to the trapped basket. "I'll take your place, shall I, Corey? Sing by the bonfire and all?"

"You can't go; you aren't flying," Corey yelled back.

"I can pick up a parasail at home—there's still enough daylight. Enjoy your treehouse." Ronnie walked on, ignoring the jeers behind him. He made himself walk slowly, looking up when a balloon's burner whooshed overhead, grinning and shaking his head when a shower of glittery confetti covered him in blue and turquoise. At the main desk, a crowd of visitors clustered, complaining about the noise and confusion, about being forced to leave early. Ronnie handed his pass to the harried receptionist with a shrug and smile, and accepted the gate pass she gave him.

Someone tapped his shoulder and said, "Isn't your aunt in that last row?"

"Yes, why?" Ronnie said without flinching.

"All that noise—and I saw one balloon land almost on top of that row, dragging the basket along—"

"Must have been after I left," Ronnie said. "It won't bother her, I'm sorry to say."

"Oh?" The avid curiosity of the other man annoyed Ronnie, but he knew he must answer.

"She's in a coma," he said. "Has been for months."

"Oh, well, that's not so bad. But still. My father nearly had another stroke, when he saw someone fall out of a basket and have to climb back in."

"It's just the Festival," Ronnie said vaguely and turned away. He had to get out of here. He made it out the door, down the long walk to the gatehouse, in a clump of departing visitors. Another low-flying balloon nearly scalped him—someone behind yelled a warning—and the guard at the gatehouse was shaking his head when he collected the gate passes.

"Every year or so they get wild like this. No, madam, I don't know why. The administration sends warnings out to all the Families and the Clubs, but ever so often they take it into their heads to ignore the rules. Can't explain it. I don't think it's so bad myself; patients might enjoy a bit more color and excitement, but I can see why it riles the staff. Like this young gentleman here, with that blue confetti—what fell on the ground, someone's got to clean up."

He had made it to his own vehicle; he had started it up. Others crowded the exits; he glanced behind, half-expecting to see someone running to stop him. But nothing. He was on the road home; no one signalled him, no pursuit appeared. At home he faced the tricky part. While his parents had agreed that "something must be done" it had been clear that whatever was done must be done secretly. None of them ever discussed possibilities. For all he knew, they had their own plans to rescue Cecelia, and he had just ruined them. Then again, maybe they'd given up. But they certainly had no idea what he'd been part of. Suddenly the casual self-invitation to the beach party sounded like just the thing.

He left a message on the house board, and went to get his parasail out of storage.

✧ Chapter Eleven

Brun crouched as the burner roared, and pulled the blanket she'd brought along over Cecelia's crumpled form. Finally—it always seemed to take too long—the balloon rose with a jerk, and the basket hung straight beneath it. "Sorry!" Brun yelled down at someone who had had to dive away from the basket on the terrace behind another unit. "Bad currents." She watched ahead: there. She could continue to ascend between that balloon and the other—and there was just room to use the directional thruster as well. Carefully, while tossing sackfuls of confetti out with one hand, she set the thruster controls and pumped the burner.

The idea had been to rise directly above Cecelia's unit, in hopes of not triggering any alarms when her monitor-transmitters went out of range, and then catch a strong wind home. But the surface breeze, twisting between the units and deflected as well by so many jostling balloons, didn't cooperate. She was already more than thirty meters from the room where Cecelia's bed had been; she needed to gain altitude and start running *now*.

Her balloon rose; she felt the pressure in her boots. Now she could see over the last row of units. Was that Ronnie, walking toward the administration building? Someone had caught a basket in a tree; that balloon, deflating, draped itself over the tree like a discarded party dress. She didn't envy the owner. If they got it out at all, there'd be plenty of rips to repair. A vast green-and-silver surface blocked her view as it slid by, someone else's balloon. Out the other side, she saw yellow striped with light blue. Above, her own balloon blocked

183

her view. She had to hope that she didn't bump into someone from below.

Now she was higher than most of the others—than anyone near. Behind and below, balloons obscured her view of the nursing home and its meadow. Most were still aflight, but some were on the ground, surrounded by clumps of people. Ahead and higher were other balloons headed for the shore, but no one was near her. That in itself was dangerous . . . anyone might notice the color of a balloon that lifted too suddenly from the nursing home. She looked back again, glad to see that five or six others were rising as fast now. They would block a clear view of hers from the ground.

She let go the burner controls. In the sudden silence, she checked her gauges. Still rising, slowly. She knelt beside the crumpled shape, and as gently as she could tugged Cecelia to a half-sitting position. The older woman's skin was cold, but she had a strong regular pulse and she seemed to be breathing normally. Brun stuffed a pillow under her head.

"It's Brun, Lady Cecelia. If you can hear me—we've got you out. Here, smell this." She tugged out her riding gloves, and laid them against Cecelia's face. A nostril fluttered. "That's it. Horse and dog and out-of-doors. I can't talk more—we're in the air."

She stood up again. Behind, the other balloons were gaining altitude on her; the nursing home was now a blur of dark trees and bright meadow, the units scarcely visible. With any luck, the attendants were still too busy with the chaos to be watching her.

From here, at this altitude, the wind would take her straight to the picnic site on the shore. Above, the northbound current of air should be shifting as the front neared, and the southbound current above that would sweep her past the shore, on across the bay to the peninsula where her landing crew waited. She eyed the clouds to the west.

❖   ❖   ❖

The residual sense of where her body was jolted Cecelia into wakefulness. Something was wrong. Pressures in the wrong place, strange noises—yelling voices in the distance, harsh roars—and then she felt herself falling, and cramped into a position she could not change. She smelled a fuel gas, and something that reminded her of flower baskets without the flowers. And, in great gusts, the fresh green smell of spring she had been kept from. Mown grass, oak trees, the bitter tang of willow. Outside? She was outside?

It must be the rescue she had prayed for. Overhead, the roaring went on and on; she felt a vague nausea. Then the roaring ceased. In the silence, she heard distant roars, distant voices, and the nearby creaking of . . . baskets again? She felt herself being moved. Then the scent of horse and dog and leather, and the girl's voice, reassuring her.

She wanted to cry for joy; she wished she could move a finger, at least. But it was enough, just to be out of that place.

"There's a chance of surveillance," Brun said above her. "I can't talk to you all the time—but don't be afraid."

She wasn't afraid now. She wasn't afraid for the first time since the hospital. If the balloon—she had put together her memories of the roaring burner, the smell of gas, the sound of wicker—fell out of the sky and killed them both, she would not be afraid. Not now.

She busied her mind with interpretation of the smells that rose from below through the basket. That made it easier to ignore the lurch in her stomach every time the burner roared and the balloon lifted abruptly. At some point they flew near enough to a bakery to sail through a gust of aroma from new bread, and she tried to guess which city. She recognized the damp-rot smell of the shore, and wanted desperately to ask which shore . . . because she began to feel she almost knew where they were.

"Heading southeast," Brun said, as if she'd heard the question. "Out over water, and into a little weather. Now that we're farther from shore, I'll put the rain cover on you."

She heard the rustle of it, and later the spat of raindrops. The air smelled rich and clean, heady. She wanted to breathe in, and only in, forever. She would have been glad to have the rain on her face. Her skin felt starved for the moisture, the changing pressures.

The landing, when it came, produced a jolt she could feel. Then the disorienting sensation of being put in all the wrong positions. Hauled out like a sack of grain, she thought. I certainly can't help. Brun said little, only brief phrases to the others—how many others?—who were handling her. Then a familiar position, flat on her back on some surface, but a vibration rumbling the entire surface.

The scents of a spring night still enchanted her. They must be in a vehicle with open windows: she could smell the new grass, a fruit orchard in bloom, all the good smells of open country. No one talked; all she could hear was the windrush outside. When the vehicle stopped, she felt movement again, as her surface (bed? stretcher?) was lifted out and rolled somewhere. She sniffed again. This smelled mechanical, almost industrial. Metal, plastics, pavement . . . something that sounded like a very large door on rollers, with metallic echoes beyond. A warehouse? A factory?

Another lift, and she was in a different set of smells. Almost all plastics and fine oils, like a . . . like a . . . shuttle. A shuttle—she was being shipped offplanet? Still no conversation, just the faint sounds of feet on the floor, and the snick of buckles fastening. If I were making this up, Cecelia thought, I would figure out some way for my heroine to communicate. It's entirely too boring to lie here knowing nothing.

Footsteps moved away, and something went *chunk* with the finality normally associated with hatches closing. She could feel no more vibration—no, there it was, the slightest rhythmic thump that must be tires passing over seams on the runway.

Her mind ran through the private shuttleports, and decided they were at Bunny's Crown residence. She felt the firm

pressure of acceleration on her body, and the rhythmic bumps
came closer together . . . then ceased. Wherever they were
going, they were on the way. Wherever they were going, it
had to be better than where she'd been.

"I'm sorry I couldn't talk to you earlier," Brun said. Her
hand, smelling of soap lightly pine scented, lay along Cecelia's
cheek. "Those who helped me could not know who you
were." She chuckled, and went on. "They think you're a
drunken friend of mine, who's going to wake up on Station
as the result of a Festival wager. You're wearing balloonist
gear, and it's fortunate you don't look your age. You probably wonder why we took the risk of taking you offplanet
right away."

Cecelia hadn't yet wondered that, but now she did. Why
not simply hide her somewhere until she recovered?

"We expect a solid search effort," Brun went on. "We weren't
sure if they'd implanted a locator of some kind, and we wanted
you out of range of detectors. And they might start checking
private shuttle flights after tonight. Luckily, with the Festival,
there's sure to be more than one private shuttle up. And . . .
we don't know how long your recovery will take."

Behind that, Cecelia caught a concern that it might not
come. She wanted to signal, to convince Brun that she was
alive inside, but nothing worked.

"We need to get you to good medical care—someone we
know is safe, and not part of the plot—in a place where it
won't be interrupted."

The questions she could not ask whirled through Cecelia's
mind. What about Ronnie? Where were they going? What
had happened to her own yacht? And Heris? What kind of
medical care, and how did Brun know the doctors were safe,
and how long was it going to take to get her life back? She
didn't even know exactly how long she'd been like this—
months, at least, because the Festival was in spring, but she
couldn't remember exactly when *it* had happened. She did

remember that rehabilitation took longer the longer someone was down.

"It's going to seem disjointed, I know." Brun's voice had the edge that came from trying to stay calm when it wasn't easy. "First yanking you out of that bed and into the balloon basket, and then into the shuttle—and the transfer at Rockhouse Minor is going to be tricky, too—and we've got a priority undock already filed. We couldn't get most of the equipment Dad's neurologist said we needed onto the yacht, so some things will have to wait until we get where we're going."

Which she still hadn't said. Cecelia wondered if Brun knew, or if she had a reason not to say it aloud. She'd already said enough to make any surveillance tapes dangerous.

"Actually we're still arguing about that." Again, it was as if Brun had read her thoughts. "The specialists want you at a major medical facility, but Dad says that's too dangerous; whoever did this is bound to be checking the best-known facilities. He wanted you back home, but your Captain Serrano said the same argument applied to that. She thinks you ought to be somewhere with horses, somewhere obscure. There's a couple of possibilities—Dad's been checking them out, and once we get to the yacht, I'll have his latest advice. But there's the medical problem."

The medical problem. Whatever had been done to her, whatever might be undone. She wanted to argue her own case, demand the risks of the top specialists, explain who might have done this, and why. But that would have to wait until she could talk—if she ever could.

Cecelia surprised herself by falling asleep in the shuttle. Real sleep, deep comfortable sleep. She felt safe, with Brun's hand on her cheek, safer than she had felt in months.

When she woke, the voices overhead sounded medical again, and for a moment she panicked. But the medicinal smells interwove with more pleasant ones, and Brun's voice made up part of the conversation.

"—better strip the programming on those sphincters."

A woman's voice; she sounded as if she were scowling. "We'll want to keep her hydrated, but we don't want any distension."

"But let's check the drug port—they may have an implanted delivery system, and there might still be residuals."

"Just remember that she can hear you," Brun said, from a little distance. "Talk to her, not just about her." Then, taking her own advice, she spoke to Cecelia. "You're on the yacht now; I think you went to sleep for a while, though it's hard to tell. You've got Dr. Czerda and Dr. Illik with you, right now."

"I'm Czerda," the woman's voice said. "I'm a geriatric neurologist, with special interest in pharmacological insults. I'm checking the ports on your chest: cardiac monitor, venous access, feeding tube. There's a . . . yes . . . a set of three miniature pumps in the venous access. I'm going to have to take these out very carefully . . ." Cecelia could just feel a faint tug, disconcerting but not painful. "Brun—if you'll take these over to the bench there—"

"Can you tell what the drugs are?" Brun asked.

"Probably. At least we can tell the class, and if it's referenced we can identify it precisely. If not . . . it may take a while. What the drugs do is my specialty, but identifying them isn't. We can get it done, though. Now . . . I'm going to leave the rest of this in; we'll want the cardiac monitor and the venous access, although I hope we can get her—you, sorry—off the feeding tube and back on oral."

"I've got the signals on the implants," the man's voice said. "Standard Zynnis model fives, and we have the manuals." His voice came toward Cecelia's head. "Brun says you're hearing us; I know that's possible. I'm Dr. Illik; you met me at Sirialis when young Ronnie was in the hospital there. I was the tall skinny bald one." Cecelia remembered a pleasant, homely face and jug ears. "We're going to give you the same kind of care that you had, except that we'll be triggering your bladder implant more often. Right now you need that again; it's been over twelve hours." He sounded embarrassed; Cecelia had long given up embarrassment. It wasn't her fault someone else had to operate her once-private functions. She could tell when they changed her body position, although she wasn't sure how much, and she could hear the result when the implant opened. It did feel better, although she'd hardly known what the vague discomfort was.

"We're not going to mess with your cranial access right now," Czerda said. "There's a small chance they put in a lockout circuit that could hurt you if we didn't key in correctly. I want a full readout of everything else first, and we're going to try to get your cranial implant to talk to our monitors. So far it's not. But I would like to see if you can swallow. We did that ultrasound when you first came aboard, and I don't think they bothered to do an esophageal pinch."

Cecelia had no idea what an esophageal pinch was, but assumed it had something to do with whether or not she could eat. The thought of actually tasting food again thrilled her. Her mouth filled with saliva. Surely she had to be able to swallow, or she'd have choked before now.

"Now . . . what I'm going to put at your lips is a soft plastic nipple, on a water bottle. When you feel it, try to suck."

She felt nothing, then a dull bump as something hit a tooth. She tried to suck, but wasn't sure she remembered how. She had not had anything in her mouth in a long time.

"Serious loss of sensation," Czerda said. "Let's see . . ."

A cool wetness tasting faintly of lemon filled her mouth. Cecelia swallowed without thinking; her tongue felt ungainly and misshapen, but she didn't choke.

"Very good," Czerda said. "That time I squeezed some out; I'd like you to do it this time."

Cecelia struggled with a recalcitrant tongue and cheek muscles that no longer worked willingly. A tiny drip rewarded her, then a trickle.

"That's too much," Illik said. "Look at the cardiac monitor—she's straining."

"But it's something." Czerda sounded angry. "Even a tiny,

weak suck, and we know she's still got that. Let's see about something else—"

This time it was cold, and sweet, and smooth . . . a chilled custard, perhaps. The flavor developed in Cecelia's mouth, from the initial sweetness to a rich, fruity taste . . . and she was able to swallow the spoonful, savoring the feel of it all the way down her throat. Date-caramel custard, with a touch of almond essence, she thought.

"Oh, very good," Czerda said. "Brun, do you happen to know what foods she liked best?"

"She had one of the best cooks anywhere," Brun said. "She liked good food, all kinds." Not *all kinds*, Cecelia thought. Prustocean cuisine is ghastly, and there's no way anyone can cook Abrolc cephalopods so they don't taste like oily rubber. Surely Brun could remember her favorite spices, at least.

"Great. If she can eat custards now, she'll be able to eat solids very soon. I'm glad I insisted on including a dietician in the primary team." Dietician! Cecelia wanted to glare. Dieticians thought more of nutrition than flavor; she imagined herself with a mouthful of pureed halobeets, unmitigated by spices. "We'll leave the feeding tube access in, just in case, but the sooner she's on an oral diet, the sooner we can get her an oral communication system."

"You mean talking?"

"No, not at first." Cecelia hoped she was wrong about the undertone that suggested *Maybe never*. "Her inability to talk could be all neuromuscular—loss of control of voluntary muscles of speech—or it could also involve central language problems. I suspect the latter. But if she can swallow, that means she can control her tongue and breath—and that means she can learn to suck and blow, and that means she can use a mechanical system to signal. Yes and no, at least, and probably a lot more."

"But if she can swallow, then why can't she move her jaw?"

"Good question. It could be a local paralysis, either from an injection into the nerve, or maintained by the drugs we found in that packet. Or, in a woman her age, it could be simple arthritis of the temperomandibular joint. If they kept her jaw immobilized for long enough, muscle atrophy and arthritis together could produce what seemed to be paralysis. At any rate, until she has control of her jaw, she can't chew. We can open and close it—and we will—but that's not really chewing."

Cecelia knew exactly whom she'd bite if she had the chance, these long-winded idiots who blathered on as if she weren't there.

Lorenza grimaced when the light flashed on her deskcomp. Someone wanted her badly enough to override the recorded message explaining that she wasn't available. She hated being interrupted after dinner. It had better be a real emergency. She picked up an impressive-looking pile of documents before flicking the screen on. That way whoever it was would know she had been interrupted in the midst of real work.

On the screen, Berenice's distorted face looked much older, as if her rejuv were failing all at once, and her words at first made no sense. "She's gone! She's gone!"

"Who?" A maid, a cook, even a pregnant cow, thought Lorenza idly. Why did people think she was a mind reader?

"Cecelia!" Berenice said, too loudly. "She disappeared from the home sometime today. After Ronnie's visit, in fact; he says she was certainly there when he was. The attendant who let him in remembers that—"

"Maybe Ronnie's playing a prank." Lorenza's mind raced. Crazy young men did such things. Cecelia gone? What would it mean? She felt cold, and then excited. "Perhaps he took her out for a joyride or something." Perhaps another enemy had abducted her, raped her, killed her.

"No—there was some kind of mixup with the Festival, lots of balloonists coming down in that meadow, and some getting caught in the trees. Lots of people saw Ronnie leave, and he was alone. Besides, he's as confused as I am—I can tell; I'm his mother. Lori, she's *gone*. She'll *die* without care—I can't bear to think of it—" Berenice, who had quarrelled with Cecelia for years, still actually cared about her. Lorenza thought that was stupid, but knew better than to argue that Cecelia was better off dead. Especially for her own purposes.

"Who do you think—could it be that awful yacht captain?"

"Oh, no. She's been gone for weeks—and she couldn't have come back in the system without being caught. It's just—I can't figure out why anyone would do this!" Lorenza made soothing noises. She could think of several reasons, and after a while produced the one she thought most useful.

"There's always kidnapping for ransom, although in her condition most such people would expect you to abandon her. Perhaps . . . someone, some business associate, wants to do something with her assets. If they produced an imposter, and claimed she'd recovered . . ."

"I hadn't thought of that." Berenice's voice had calmed; she might be overemotional, but she wasn't stupid. Not really. "We've had auditors checking things over to be sure that captain hadn't been embezzling—maybe someone else was."

"Or maybe that captain had an ally," Lorenza said.

"I'll tell Gustav," Berenice said firmly, and cut off what Lorenza was about to say.

Surely it would be all right. Someone had kidnapped a helpless old lady—it would be either for ransom or—the idea made more sense the longer she thought about it—to produce an apparently recovered imposter, whose remaining lapses of memory and function could be laid to the injury. Or Cecelia herself, with an AI unit implanted so that she seemed to speak what someone else had chosen. If they had enough time, whoever had done this, they could even produce a clone-Cecelia. Of course, not even a clone-Cecelia would know what had been done to her, or how, or who.

She was, therefore, unprepared for the second call, from her medical agent.

"What do you mean, trouble?" she asked airily. "It's nothing to do with us; I didn't snatch her."

"Have you forgotten what I told you? She needs maintenance doses—and anyone who scans her now will find those implants. If they're removed, a high-level scan will show brain activity."

"You said it was irreversible." She fought the impulse to scowl at the screen. She never scowled; scowling caused wrinkles.

"Under the circumstances we had, yes. But not in a medical facility I can't get into, or send someone to. Oh, she'll never get up and walk off—at least, I don't think so—but once someone suspects she's still cognating, they'll start looking at her old scans and know they were falsified. And then they'll figure out how, and that leads to who. I want out—I want transportation and a lump sum, enough to live on—"

"Wait a minute—you're running out on me? Won't that make it obvious you did it?"

"Not if you set it up right. Do you know what they do to medical professionals who do something like this? I'll be in therapeutic reassignment the rest of my life. No. I want out. You've got to get me out of here."

"But you say she can't really recover . . ."

"Of course not. Not really. But they don't need *her* testimony to put me at risk, I tell you. And if they catch me, I'll tell them who it was—I've no reason to protect you if I'm going to prison. It's to your advantage to keep me safe."

"I see. Well, then . . . it will take me a day or so . . ." To choose which way to eliminate this unstable and most undesirable of accomplices. To make sure it would not be traced to her. To see if it could possibly be done in person . . . she would miss the visits to Cecelia, the chance to savor that triumph. This one could make up for it.

✧ Chapter Twelve

The transfer station at Naverrn had none of the luxury and elegance of Rockhouse Major. It was as large—it had to be, to handle the transfers of entire troopships—but only in the Exchange did any civilians color and brighten the drab corridors and docksides. The *Better Luck* had come in, with its new identity unchallenged—just another scruffy little tramp freighter and her slipshod crew.

"Recognition's supposed to be easy," Heris said, eyeing the material she'd been given. "The prince has seen me; I've seen him."

"But the double," said Petris. "You might mistake the double for the prince."

"The double doesn't know me. He won't approach. It's true, both of them will be there . . . but only one will come aboard."

Like all but the restricted stations, Naverrn Station had no objection to civilian traffic—in moderation—and civilians could shop at the Exchange, paying higher prices. Heris was claiming a subcontract with Outworld Parcel, one of the independent companies transferring small hardcopy documents and packages for individuals who preferred not to use the government mail service. The Crown had provided such documents, and arranged for her to dump any business received at a nearby Outworld Parcel main depot.

Heris checked in at the Outworld Parcel local office, handing the clerk the little strip of platinum-embossed plastic. The clerk glanced at her as he fed the strip into the reader. "You're new on this run, aren't you? What happened to Sal?"

Heris shrugged. "Have no idea. I don't ask questions—they shift me around wherever there's a gap."

"Oh. Maybe that port drive pod finally went sour, and he's in refitting." The clerk touched a keypad and a sign lighted up: *Outgoing Active.* "How long are you here for? There's only a few letters now, but if you'll be here long enough for a shuttle from below, I can guarantee at least a 50 kilo cargo."

"How long's that?" asked Heris, as if she didn't know the shuttle schedule already.

"Let me check our downside office," the clerk said, and vanished into a back room. A few minutes later he came out. "You're in luck. They can add the downside accumulation to the next shuttle, and that's tomorrow's. It'll be up here by 1800, but it won't unload until 2000, at least."

"I suppose," Heris said, feigning reluctance. "They didn't say I'd have to wait; it was supposed to be a scoop and run . . ."

"Are you time-locked for your next destination?" That would make it a legal requirement to keep the schedule.

"No." As if she'd just decided, Heris gave a quick nod. "Fine—we can wait. Let me know the mass and cubage when the shuttle lifts. You have the codes." He would return the identification strip when she signed for the outgoing mail.

The Exchange was next door; Heris glanced in at rows of displayed merchandise. Once such places had been her territory; she had paid the lower, military price; she had felt at home. Now—she made herself enter, with a quick smile at the security guard by the door.

"New onstation?" he asked.

"Right. The *Better Luck*; we have a subcontract with Outworld Parcel."

"About time," the guard said, grinning. "I'm expecting a package from my parents—"

"Sorry," Heris said. "I was sent on pickup—we didn't bring anything." The guard glowered at her.

"Dammit! It's been twice as long as government mail, and it's supposed to be quicker."

"The guy at the office said maybe Sal had a drive out and had to go to refitting," Heris said. Offering gossip would at least make her seem knowledgeable about it. "We weren't told—but if that's true, another ship will have picked up that load and be bringing it." She only hoped Sal himself wouldn't show up in the next day or so.

"Well, enjoy yourself," said the guard, in a tone that implied no one could do that on this station. "Shop your little heart out."

Heris wandered around, picking up an entertainment cube and a box of sweets, for which she paid an outrageous price. Having heard this complaint often from civilians while she was still in the Fleet, she grumbled at the guard on her way out. "Dammit, the prices go up every trip—you expect us to maintain you in luxury, while hardworking taxpayers go short—" The guard gave her the same bored look she had given others, and she almost giggled.

Naverrn Station, according to its listings, had no housing for transient civilians, and no recreational facilities—not even a gym, and only one place to eat, a vast and gloomy cafeteria clearly meant to feed hordes of troops in a hurry. Heris glanced into it and realized that her crew would much rather eat off of Oblo's stolen supplies aboard than the sort of mush they'd get here. She wondered why anyone would come up to the Station on liberty; Naverrn itself was a pleasant planet, and the training base (she'd seen the holograms) looked far more attractive than this empty, boring station.

When the shuttle arrived, Naverrn Station took on a spurious gaiety. Heris cast a critical eye on the young officers, and almost immediately thought better of Ronnie and George at their worst. The Royal Aerospace Service (known to those in the Regular Space Service as the Royal ASS) attracted the wealthy and highborn into its officer corps; its enlisted personnel were recruited mostly from those just below the Regular Space Service cutoffs. The young officers sported a foppish uniform with an abundance of braid and shiny metal: sky-blue tunics with cream facings over dark-blue trousers, cream and scarlet piping on every seam, tall shiny boots. No wonder they seemed as businesslike and military as a gaggle of debutantes. Most of them quickly shed their colorful uniforms for even more outlandish and expensive civilian clothes. Whatever sense they might have shown at their duties onplanet, they shed as quickly, and Heris saw little sign of supervision or discipline. She was glad she had no responsibility for them.

Naverrn stationers wouldn't put themselves out for a small tramp freighter, which could be assumed to have no spending power, but fifty familiar Royal junior officers were another matter. Heris could hardly believe it was the same service area she'd seen before. Suddenly there were dozens of attractive young men and women (far more than one per officer, she suspected) strolling the corridors, bait for even more colorful fish. A door that had presented only a blank gray metal face before now opened on a cozy bar with a live band playing in one corner. The smell of real food wafted out another door that Heris hadn't seen. Two sleek, dripping, naked figures chased each other out a door just in front of her; she heard splashes and yells from inside that argued for the existence of a swimming pool.

But where was the prince? He should have had a message—they had sent one in the code given them—and he was supposed to make the contact. She would have no excuse to hang about once she'd collected the Outworld Parcels cargo. She needed to find him—or have him find her—now. She strolled back toward the OP office, to check the status of the cargo.

"Another shift, at least, even with no more problems," the clerk told her. He looked harried; a line of impatient young officers had hand-carried mail and packages to check through. "Tarash is out with something she ate, and Jivi sprained an ankle, but the clinic is packed. It always is, with this bunch."

"Fine. Let me know."

That still didn't find the prince, she thought, as she walked on back to the docking area. Where could he be lurking? Why hadn't he contacted her? Back aboard *Better Luck*, she checked on the progress of the cockroach egg hunt. They had cleared the bridge, and the galleys, and were working on the owner's quarters. If the prince found cockroaches aboard, Heris knew the news would spread. She took a look at what had been an elegant guest suite, in which the prince had travelled from Sirialis. Bare decking and bulkheads, just as in crew quarters, with the bed platform's framing all too visible. Oblo had installed a bare-bones communications node, nothing like the handsome system Cecelia had had, with its touchscreens and voice-response. Plenty of bedding, though, and towels, and those colorful pillows. Worst, though, the suite still held a faint odor of cockroach. Heris realized she was wrinkling her nose. That would never do; she'd send someone to buy an olfactory screen.

Gradually, Cecelia began to regain a sense of structure in her existence. Brun and the other attendants spoke to her often, telling her what time it was, what watch, who was in the room, what they had done, and were about to do. She could not see the light level change, or the colors they described on the walls, but she could imagine it all. She began to know, when she woke, what shift to expect, who would be in the room. So she knew it was morning—ship's morning, early in the main dayshift—when the doctors both arrived to explain her situation as they then understood it.

"Lady Cecelia, I'm now sure that you are able to hear—and, I hope, understand—what we're saying. I'm going to explain what tests we've done, what more we can do aboard the yacht, and what we'll be trying to do later. You may know more about what happened to you than we do, although we're ready to make an educated guess. The drugs we found in the venous access reservoirs consisted of a perfectly ordinary array of cardiac drugs—which would have been dispensed automatically at signals from the cardiac monitor—and some very unusual neuroactive drugs, one of them not in the data banks at all. I suspect that these drugs were merely for maintenance, not the ones that caused the initial damage. We cannot tell yet how much function will return just because you no longer have the maintenance drugs in your system, or how long it will take. It depends on how the damage was done, and whether the maintenance drugs were considered essential or just a safeguard against spontaneous recovery.

"I can tell you that the maintenance drugs targeted voluntary muscle innervation, motor and sensory both. Thus I expect you to regain some sensation of touch, and some ability to move. How much is impossible to say. It is unusual for someone with your level of deficit to be able to breathe spontaneously—they did a fine job of sparing respiratory function. It's amazing that you can hear, and yet the few medical records we were able to get indicate that you couldn't—that your auditory cortex was inactive in the presence of both speech and sound. Either someone fiddled with the scans, or . . . I can't imagine what."

Cecelia struggled to remember the early days, what everyone had said. She knew the lawyer had been told she could not hear; she had heard that. She remembered hearing about the scans that were supposed to prove it. That suggested intentional deception. But she had no way to let Dr. Czerda know what she had heard.

Over the next few days, sensation returned slowly, in odd patches. One time Cecelia woke, she felt the side of her face as if it were a patch of harsh cloth laid on her skull. She felt the slight pressure of air against it from the ventilator. The nurse's gentle facewashing felt like being scrubbed with a broom. Still she could not move, could not flinch away. Later that day, she had an uncanny sensation in her left arm, as if something were crawling down it from shoulder to elbow, and from there along the outside of her forearm to her little finger. The feeling grew to a tingle, then an itch, then a painful

throbbing that subsided gradually over far too long a time.
Each time Czerda came in, she touched Cecelia everywhere,
explaining the process over and over. The monitors they had,
crude as they were compared to those in a major neuro ward,
showed Cecelia's response . . . and Czerda was mapping the
return of sensation. The nurses and Brun massaged her,
too . . . and gradually, fitfully, she remapped the feeling of
her own body.

Blank patches remained. Her left upper chest had no sensation: Czerda explained that was where the implanted ports
were. They'd probably destroyed the innervation there. That
was standard practice. She felt nothing on the insides of both
arms . . . where the median nerve should have supplied sensation and controlled movement. One foot regained sensation, in a maddening pins-and-needles form, days before the
other. Her nose itched.

The first movement, the first *real* movement, came when
the nurse's washcloth dripped cold on her shoulder. She
flinched . . . and knew she moved even as the nurse exclaimed.
She tried again.

"Again!" said Czerda, who had come at the nurse's call.
Cecelia twitched again, as proud as if she'd just taken a big
drop jump. "That's great. Now try the other one."

Cecelia tried, but couldn't remember how to move that
shoulder. Someone tickled her, just above the collarbone. Ah.
Yes. She struggled again, and felt her skin move against the
sheet.

"Not as strong, but something. Good progress . . . keep doing
that."

She kept doing that, but it didn't seem to lead anywhere.
She tried to imagine what it looked like, the twitch of a shoulder. Not as communicative as a facial expression. And no matter how she struggled, she couldn't move her hands. Surely
she would have to move her hands to use sign language. Then,
three days later, when Czerda had pulled her lower jaw down,
she snapped it closed so hard her teeth hurt. She couldn't

open it . . . but she could close it when Czerda opened it again. Czerda chuckled.

"Yes—a good response. Now we start your communication training. I know you're an intelligent adult, and I know there's lots you want to say, but we'll start with what we need to know first. We want you to have a yes and a no. Right now your shoulder jerk is your strongest motion: let's try one jerk for yes, and two for no. Understand?"

Cecelia twitched her shoulder with contemptuous ease. She could have done that three days ago—why hadn't they told her? Why hadn't she thought of it?

"Good. Now . . . did you like your breakfast?" Breakfast had been a bland flavor of custard; she had never liked bland anything. She gave two twitches. "Excellent. You may not realize it, but you've just demonstrated that your higher language functions are still intact: you understood both directions and a question form. Did you like lunch?" One twitch. Lunch had been the date-caramel-almond custard, her favorite of the flavors she'd had.

"Now I've got to ask you a lot of boring questions that are standard on neuro-psych exams. And I'm going to record this, on full video, because it may be used in court to establish your competency."

Cecelia hadn't thought of that. Could someone who only twitched one shoulder be considered competent legally? She had thought she couldn't fight that battle until she was well.

"Is your name Cecelia de Marktos?" One twitch. That wasn't her full name, but she used the short form oftener than the long. "Do you know where you are?" Now that was a hopeless question. She knew she was on a yacht, but she had no idea where the yacht was. She shrugged both shoulders, the right more strongly. Apparently that got through; Czerda muttered "Bad question" and changed it to, "Are you in a hospital?" Two twitches. "Are you in a spacecraft?" One twitch. "Are you aware of the nature of your disability?" One twitch. "Was this disability the result of natural causes?" Two twitches. No one was going to believe this, Cecelia thought. It might convince Czerda, or Bunny, but she couldn't see it working in court. Czerda proceeded to questions of reasoning and general knowledge, most of them ridiculously easy: "Is a circle a geometric solid?" No, of course not. "Is a horse a mammal?" Yes, dummy. "Did you name Heris Serrano a beneficiary in your will?" Yes. Cecelia came alert again. "Did Heris Serrano unduly influence you to make her a beneficiary in your will?" No! She made that twitch as big as she could, and then a muscle in her back cramped. She gasped. Czerda stopped the questions, and patiently massaged the cramp out.

"I wish we could give you muscle relaxants," she said. "But I don't want to risk any more dissociation between your nerves and your muscles. Things are bad enough."

Cecelia wondered what that meant. She had thought things were going well. If she could move a shoulder now, if she could answer questions . . . she pushed aside her own doubts and refused to pay attention to the doctor's. Whatever the medical agenda, her own would include figuring out a way to ask for specific foods, things with more flavor and more texture.

Now, with even that meagre amount of communication, the days moved more swiftly. Would she like to try something with more texture? *Yes* . . . and a mouthful of something soft but grainy—still too bland—challenged her ability to move her tongue and swallow it. Would she like music? *Yes*. This music? *No*. Trial and error—more error than success, at first—remapped her choices in flavors and music. As she had feared, the dietician could not be persuaded to offer really tasty food, and there was no way to say *More garlic, you idiot!* with a twitch of the shoulder.

She learned to move her knees, one by one, and wished someone would think of using the twitch of her other shoulder and both knees for other useful signals, but no one did. Yet. In her mind she fashioned her own code: more, less, not yet, hurry up, enough, go away, question. The question signal would have been really helpful; she had more to ask them, she thought, than they had to ask her. But she realized, from their talk, that they were fully engaged already in discovering what had been done to her, and what might be done about it. For the urgency they conveyed, she could forgive a lot.

"Captain—two young . . . gentlemen to see you." Petris's voice carried some message, but she wasn't sure what. This had to be the prince, and presumably some necessary companion. Valet, bodyguard, whatever. Heris made her way quickly to the access tube.

The prince all right, just the same as she'd seen in Sirialis, with that smug little smile on his face. Beside him—she blinked as she focused on the other face. The same face, rather. Side by side, two apparent princes, both with that smug little smile. Both in uniform, for a wonder . . . her mind ran headlong into the logical flaw here.

The prince and his double, of course, but the prince and his double were not to be seen together. Certainly not here, not now. If someone saw them both enter *Better Luck* and only one of them left . . .

"Welcome aboard," Heris said, trying to think this out. "Mr. Smith, I believe?" She offered the same bland smile to both of them, no longer sure which was which. It was very *good* plastic surgery, she told herself.

"Yes," they said. "Mr. Smith." Even their voices sounded alike, which might mean vocal training or surgery there, too. Impressive, but still stupid. If they'd both come up on the shuttle with the others, then everyone on the Station knew.

"We don't have a lot of time for games," she said, trying for a combination of sweet reason and firmness. "We'll be departing as soon as the Outworld Parcel cargo comes aboard, and in the meantime we'll need to ensure that your . . . er . . . double has appropriate cover."

"I just came to tell you I'm not going," one of the young men said. "I don't want to spend more time on this yacht, especially since it's not even carpeted." He looked at the bare deck and bulkheads with contempt.

"But your father planned—" Heris began. The other young man interrupted.

"If my father insists, let my double do it."

"Sir, it's extremely important—" Heris began, but the first one interrupted this time.

"Besides, I'm perfectly healthy; there's nothing wrong with me. My own physician checked me out after we arrived at Rockhouse." His voice was petulant; Heris wondered if it was really higher, more childish, than it had been. His blue eyes were guileless as a child's; his expression mildly annoyed. Nothing quite fit.

"Your father told us to take you," Heris said. She softened her voice, speaking as she would to a younger child. This time the prince didn't interrupt. "He really wanted you to go—he said you would—"

"But I don't want to," the second young man said. In exactly the same voice.

"But he'll be mad at me," Heris said, in almost the same tone, with the same quaver. She'd seen that work once, with a hysterical Senior Minister. It didn't work this time.

"So?" They both glanced around, boredom and contempt plain on their features. Heris wanted to smack their heads together.

"We shouldn't discuss this here," she said. "Come along to the bridge—you never saw it before, did you?—and we can settle things there."

"It won't make any difference," said one of them languidly. "I'm not going."

Heris refrained from comment, simply gave them the regulation smile that so often got her way. They shrugged and followed her into the ship, scuffing their boot heels on the deck and commenting on the yacht's ugliness in this state. At least they didn't comment on any odd smells—perhaps the last of the cockroach odor had adhered to the powdery scavengers in the air circulation. She stopped by her office, to show the prince and his double the official authorization from the king himself.

"I didn't doubt you," the prince said. She hoped this was the prince. "I quite understand that you are who you are, and my father told you to come get me. But I'm not going." *Oh yes you are, you little tick*, thought Heris. Aloud, she said nothing then, leading the way to the bridge.

"Pretty," the prince said, as if she'd given him a toy he didn't want, and he felt it necessary to be polite. He was looking at Sirkin, she realized after a moment, not the bridge layout at all. Ginese gave him a look and Heris began to hope the other one was the prince. She'd forgotten the prince's temporary attraction to Raffaele; perhaps he liked dark-haired girls best, and considered Sirkin an adequate substitute.

"If you had more girls like this," the double said—or was it the prince?— "I might reconsider. But it simply won't do."

"Perhaps you should take a look around," Heris said. "Your suite is a little bare now, but we've funds to provide some. . . . amenities . . . from the Station sources. Let Mr. Ginese show you around—" She gave Ginese another look; he nodded. The prince and his double shrugged.

"It's terribly dull on Station this time—might as well." And they followed Ginese meekly. Heris allowed herself a brief grin.

"Lambs to the slaughter," she said softly. Meharry grinned, but Sirkin looked shocked.

"What are you going to do?" asked Petris.

"I wish you hadn't asked," Heris said. "If we take him by force, that blows the double's cover—and the king said it was important to have the double to cover for him."

"If we don't take him by force, he won't come," Petris said. He had a plug in his ear, listening to the conversation with Ginese somewhere else in the ship. "He's blathering on about the social calendar on the liner where they will have plenty of girls, he says."

"I knew this was a stupid idea," Heris said. "His father should have known he wouldn't want to come. Unless that was the plan. The possibilities for a double cross on this mission are endless." She drummed her fingers on her console. "I'm afraid we're going to have to do it, though. The only way to help Lady Cecelia is to lead the trouble away from her . . . and if we're believed to have kidnapped the prince, everyone in the Familias will be after us."

"How can we be sure we've snatched the right one?"

"Standard ID scan. We've got the data from his father."

"It won't work," said one of the princes, when she put it to them.

"Of course it will," Heris said. "You can't fool a full-ID scan with plastic surgery."

"Fine. Go ahead." He smirked. So did the other prince. Heris wanted to hit both of them, but thought better of it. If she did, she'd be sure to hit the real prince—and that wouldn't do.

The ID scans of both young men took only a few minutes, but the results made no sense. "Both of them are the prince," said Heris. She heard the disbelief in her voice. "Or neither, if they're identical twins—clones—"

"Clone doubles are illegal," Petris said. "Not that that would stop the Crown."

Heris felt like pulling her hair. "It's . . . ridiculous. *Why* didn't the king tell us—"

"If he knew."

"He must have known. This is just like the slowness—he, of all people, cannot *not* know." Heris glared at the scan results. "How am I supposed to know which is which? Dammit—it's like something out of an entertainment cube, a joke or something. And it's not funny."

"So—what do we do?"

"We take them both," Heris said. "And we keep them separate—we'll have to use the original guest suites—and surely there'll be something in the real prince's memories of the affair on Sirialis that will make it clear who is which."

"Umm. And the . . . er . . . reaction?"

Heris found herself grinning in spite of everything. "Well, you know what they say—when you haven't any other place to step, it doesn't matter which foot lands in the shit first."

✧ Chapter Thirteen

Naverrn Station expected ships to arrive and depart on their own power—a fortunate circumstance. With Kulkul and Petris on the boards, the *Better Luck* powerup went smoothly, the displays rising through orange and yellow to the steady green of full insystem power. The FTL drive next—it was only slightly risky to powerup the jump units while docked. Using them was another matter; Heris had no intention of risking another near-planet jump.

"Weapons?" Heris asked. Arkady Ginese flashed her a wicked grin.

"Code Two," he said. "We'll go three once we're outside the near-scans." Bringing their weapons to full readiness might set off the Station's own defensive armament. Too many bloody results had taught Stationmasters to take no chances with ships in dock.

"Nav?"

"Ready, ma'am," Sirkin said. Her voice was steady; she had plotted an unusual course around to the Guerni Republic. They both hoped it would confuse any chance encounter, and avoid any confrontation with ships of the Compassionate Hand.

"Naverrn Station, the *Better Luck* requests permission to undock—" Still formal.

"On the count, *Better Luck* . . ." On the count, the cables and umbilicals detached, some coiling back to the Station and others to the ship. Tiny attitude controls nudged the ship back, away from the rotating Station. With the power on, the ship's own artificial gravity created their internal field; they felt none of the change in acceleration so visible in the external monitors as Heris brought in the main drives and began the long curve out toward the safe jump radius. Naverrn shrank visibly, the terminator creeping along its blue-and-white ball as they swung toward the nightside. An hour passed, then another and another.

"Station scans faded below detection; no other scans detected," Ginese said. He glanced at her, brows raised.

Heris had considered whether to wait until they made the first jump transition to bring the weapons up, but that had its own risk. If they were unlucky, they could come out of jumpspace into trouble. "Weapons to Code Three," she said.

"Sir," said Ginese; now his board had a row of scarlet dots at the top, with green columns below. He grinned. "The tree's lit, Captain."

"Thank you, Mr. Ginese," said Heris formally; she grinned back at him. "Now if we—"

"Oh, *shit.*" No one had to ask what had happened; all the boards showed it. A ship—a *large* ship, armed, its weapons ready, had just dropped into the system and painted them with its scans. And there they were, their own illicit weaponry up and active, as detectable as a searchlight on a dark night. "Douse it?"

"Too late," Heris said. "We'd look even more suspicious if we blanked. We shouldn't be detecting their scans. What is it?" Their scans should be as good—and the other ship wouldn't know they had such accurate scans. She hoped.

"Big—military—armed to the teeth, light cruiser. If we're lucky it's a Royal ASS ship full of rich playboys. Lemme see—"

"Dumping vee like anything," Oblo commented. "They came in really hot, and they don't care who knows it. That turbulence pattern's a lot like—"

"Corsair class. *Not* Royals. Regs. Standard assortment up—" Which meant about half the total armament. Heris felt a pang of longing and pushed it away. She had had the bridge of a

Corsair Class cruiser . . . she knew exactly what that captain would be seeing. And thinking.

"Time to jump status?" she asked.

Sirkin glanced at her. "Emergency, like at Rockhouse?" She didn't wait for an answer; her fingers were flying on her board, calling up the data. "Naverrn's a little more massive, and there's that satellite; we should use their combined center of mass for the calculation . . ." Heris didn't interrupt; she had her eye on the other ship's plot as the data points multiplied.

"She'll have her data coming back from us," Ginese said. "She's still on course for Naverrn."

"The angle isn't wide enough yet," Heris said. "Got a beacon strip?"

"Just—now. Fleet beacon . . . now let me see, what did they say the encryption key was?"

Even in the crisis, that got Heris's attention. "You got the encryption key as well as the other stuff?"

"Wouldn't be near as useful without. Ah. Yes. Regular Space Service, we knew that. Corsair Class light cruiser, we knew that. *Martine Scolare*, we didn't know that, and commanded by Arash Livadhi. Worse luck."

"Too true." Heris stared at the scan, and wished it different. The Livadhi family had as long a history in the Fleet as Serrano's; a Markos Livadhi had commanded through most of the campaign that established the Familias Regnant.

"Arash Livadhi," said Petris. "That means Esteban Koutsoudas as scanner one. We are really in a nest of comets." Koutsoudas was himself a legend, known for building up entire ships from the faintest data.

"Fourteen minutes, seventeen seconds," Sirkin said. "At our present acceleration and course."

To run or not to run. With Livadhi commanding, with Koutsoudas on scan, the Fleet vessel could not miss them and would not ignore them. The Fleet vessel had a considerable excess of vee; it might find maneuver difficult. Or it might not;

a cruiser was by no means as clumsy as a freighter of the same mass.

"Eleven minutes, twenty six seconds at maximum acceleration," Sirkin said, answering the next question Heris would have asked. Good for her, Heris thought. *If we get out of this I'll tell her so.*

If they ran, they'd look guilty. But they looked guilty now— she could easily imagine what Arash Livadhi was thinking, arriving insystem to find an absurdly small freighter lighting up his scans with weapons that belonged on his own cruiser. He'd be asking Naverrn Station about them, and Naverrn Station wouldn't have any answers to satisfy him. His curly red hair would be standing up in peaks already; the incredible Koutsoudas (she remembered coveting Koutsoudas for her own crew) would be checking their signature against his personal memory of tens of thousands of ship signatures. Had he ever scanned Cecelia's ship? If so, he would know who they really were. Or did they already—had they been sent here to intercept?

If they ran, they might reach a safe distance for jump transition before Livadhi's equally trained weapons crews could get them. Especially since he'd have to contact them first. But if they ran, he'd follow. If they didn't run, maybe they could brazen it out.

"They have nothing against us," murmured Petris, not giving advice but stating his knowledge.

They could answer the hail that was surely coming; they could spin out a plausible story long enough to make the jump point . . . maybe. Livadhi had always been one to check every detail; he would want not only code but voice communication; not only voice but visual—and there it would all fall apart. Heris felt cold all over. No mere change of uniform would work with Livadhi: he knew her. They had served together as junior officers on the *Moreno Divide*. Moreover, he knew Petris and Ginese by sight; he had been aboard her ship several times, and they'd both been on the bridge. And if he had followed the courts-martial (or any of his bridge crew had) he would know every face on this ship but Sirkin's. Could Sirkin play the role of captain for the time it would take? No. Heris could not ask that.

"Arash Livadhi knows us," Heris said. She advanced power, pushing the insystem drive to the limit listed for the *Better Luck*. She had another ten gravs of acceleration in reserve, but using them would reveal that the beacon data were false. She saw on every face but Sirkin's the recognition. Then came the hail she expected, as if in response to the change in acceleration, though she knew it had originated before. She sent in reply the standard coded message. Oblo grunted.

"They've stripped our beacon. Took 'em long enough."

"I wish I knew if they'd queried the Station yet." Livadhi tended to do things in order, but he had his own flashes of brilliance. If the delay in stripping their beacon meant he'd tight beamed the Station and waited for a reply, he could have known about the disappearance of the prince and his double . . . although Heris hoped no one had noticed yet. The shuttle to the planet wasn't supposed to leave for another eleven standard hours, and she had expected no real search for him until a few hours before boarding. She'd counted on that delay to get out of reach. But he would have the ship's identity as they'd given it to the station; he would have something to compare that beacon blurt with. Worst case, the station might even have sent visuals of the *Better Luck*'s captain.

Heris stared at the display, which attempted to simplify the complex spatial relationships of both ships and the Station, and the planetary mass. The cruiser decelerating relative to the planet; the *Better Luck* accelerating away; the interlocking rotations of planet and satellite and Station. Once the scan computer had plotted the cruiser's course and decel pattern, it displayed blue; changes would come up highlighted in orange. She hoped to see nothing but blue until they jumped, but she expected at any moment an ominous flare.

"Time?" she asked Sirkin.

"Ten minutes four seconds," Sirkin said. Blast. Livadhi was reacting as quickly as ever. And why was he here, anyway? No R.S.S. presence had been expected; nothing the king had given her showed any planned activity near Naverrn at all. Unless this was the king's double cross. It seemed entirely possible.

There. The blue cone caught fire; the tip burned orange. If she were Livadhi, she'd go ballistic, using the planetary satellite's mass to redevelop velocity and swing around, then push the cruiser's insystem drive to its limit to catch up with the trader. That is, knowing what she wanted him to know; *Better Luck*, as built, could not possibly outrun the cruiser to the standard jump distance. Why stress his ship and waste power, when the easy way would work?

But if he knew all of it—if he knew what ship this really was, and who captained her, and what she'd done leaving Rockhouse Major . . . *I do wish we'd been able to mount really effective screens on a hull this size*, she thought. To Sirkin she said, "Display the remaining time to the closest computed jump distance, and give me thirty-second counts." Then, to Ginese, "I expect pursuit and warning. I prefer not to engage at this time." She preferred not to engage at any time, certainly not with Arash Livadhi's cruiser. By any sensible calculation, he could blow them away easily. The orange-tipped blue cone, she saw, was now leaning drunkenly to one side as the scan computer calculated new possibilities. He wasn't going to do it the easy way; he was wasting considerable power to make the course correction necessary for a direct pursuit. That suggested he knew too much already.

Another hail, this one demanding voice communication. Heris grimaced. "At least he's still calling us *Better Luck*," she said. "There's a chance—"

But there wasn't. The scan display showed a white star where the last fleck of orange had been: a microjump. It lit again to show the cruiser much closer, its vector now approaching theirs. Heris admired the precision and daring of that maneuver, even as she wished his navigator had miscalculated.

"Nine minutes, thirty seconds," Sirkin said.

Heris sent a voiceburst, the reply expected from a ship requested to give voice communication, in a directional beam aimed toward the cruiser's previous course prediction but intersecting the new. Livadhi couldn't know about their new scans; he would expect that. He might pick up the reply, or he might hail again. The seconds crawled past; the displays showed their velocity increasing, the distance to a safe jump point decreasing, and the cruiser coming up behind them with a clear advantage in acceleration. Only five gravs, but enough to cut their margin to the jump point dangerously close. Moreover, he had more in reserve once past the kink of the course change, and onto the flatter curve of their own course.

"Nine minutes," said Sirkin.

If he knew, if he guessed, that the ship he chased was *Sweet Delight*, he'd know she had more acceleration in reserve. He'd account for that. But if he thought he was overhauling a ship already at full power, he might not expect that last burst; she might be able to get into FTL before he got her. Heris weighed possibilities. His aggressive pursuit suggested he knew; his use of their faked identity suggested he didn't . . .

"His communications to the Station should be blurring out," Oblo said. "Screens are up, half-power, and his own turbulence is in the way."

"He got something," Heris said. "Something he didn't like."

"Yes, but they're not shooting at us." The unspoken *yet* rang in her ears.

"There might be another reason for that," Heris said, putting her worst fears out for them all. "If they've missed the prince, onstation . . . and if they told Livadhi . . . he won't blow us away, but he'll be on our track forever."

"So the good news would be a shot across the bows?" asked Ginese. Sirkin gave a sudden twitch, as if she'd only now realized what was going on.

"In a way. Thing is, if he knows who I am, then he knows how I would've reacted—"

"Would have?"

"I've changed," Heris said. "So have we all." The veterans settled; without a word spoken, she knew she had reassured them about something no one could articulate. Sirkin glanced at the display.

"Eight minutes, thirty seconds."

Another request for voice communications, as if he had not received the first; he might not have, if his shields distorted the angled beam. Heris checked. If she had the standard civilian-quality scans, would she have had time to notice the new position? Yes. She sent the same packaged burst. It didn't sound much like her, she thought, though a comparison to her own voiceprint would show that it was. At the least, the accent suggested someone with years of spacer experience, commercial or military. Heris wondered how long it would take him to react to this. Several seconds to arrive, several seconds to decompress and play—she had made the message longer than strictly necessary. A few seconds for the return . . . any additional time off the clock was his reaction time.

"His optical weapons are just within range," Ginese reported. "They still have active scans on us, and theirs are hot, but I'm not detecting the targeting bursts I'd expect."

Would he wait until he could deliver more firepower, or would he act now? It was harder to deliver a warning shot from behind but easier to blow someone away . . . was he wondering which to do? He would need to be much closer to deliver a warning in front of them; he had to be sure it went off far enough in front. The seconds ran on.

"Eight minutes," said Sirkin.

This time it was a voiceburst hail; Oblo had it running almost as Heris saw the communications board flicker.

"F.R.C.S. *Better Luck*," came the voice. "This is the Familias Regular Space Service frigate *Skyfarer*. You are suspected of carrying contraband. Heave to for inspection." An old term,

and not what they would do if they were going to comply . . .
and . . . *frigate*? Named the *Skyfarer*? Heris stared across the
bridge at Oblo, who shook his head.

"No, sir—ma'am—that's no frigate. But look at the old
scan."

On the original scan board, which they'd left in because it
was the standard required, the R.S.S. ship's profile did indeed
resemble a frigate—half the mass of a cruiser. That made no
sense. Why would a captain misrepresent his ship that way?
Did he expect her to willingly engage a frigate? Surely in
attempting to stop a civilian vessel, it was better to claim all
the ship size you had . . . she'd always done so.

"Our weapons profile should look to him about even, if he
were a frigate," Ginese pointed out. "If we engaged, then he'd
be legally in his rights—"

"To blow us away," Heris said. "I do remember that much.
But if that's his game, he can't know the prince is aboard." *Or
can he?* she wondered. If the king—or anyone else—wanted
to get rid of the inconveniently stupid prince, this would be a
way . . . a tragedy of course, but one to be blamed on the
unstable Captain Serrano. And perhaps on her employer or
the employer's family.

"You're going to tell him?" Petris's eyebrows rose.

"Of course not. We're not supposed to have tight beam
capability; it would be telling him and everyone else in this
system."

On the tight beam, Livadhi's familiar face had an earnest
expression that sat oddly with the rumpled red curls she
remembered. Behind his head was the curved wall of the
communications booth, which meant he hoped his crew wasn't
spiking into this conversation.

"Captain Serrano, it is imperative that we keep this as short
as possible." His stubby hands raked his hair again, so that one
lock stuck straight up. "You have . . . er . . . the wrong person
aboard your ship."

"Four minutes," Sirkin said.

"I know you can make jump inside the usual radius; you did it before. But don't do it now. Please."

Fleet captains rarely said "please" to civilian captains they had already ordered to heave to.

"I don't want to have to fire on you," Livadhi said. "But under the circumstances, it would be necessary. I say again, you have the wrong person aboard. You must not complete your mission."

Great. He knew about the mission and the prince, which meant he'd been sent here to intercept her. So much for the honor of kings, Heris thought, and wondered if he knew the actual radius at which she *would* risk jump. They had the data from her earlier jump, but . . . would that give them the same figures Sirkin was using?

And she had no tight beam for response. Anything she sent would be available to other listeners in time.

Carefully, weighing each word, she composed her response. "All persons aboard this ship have His Majesty's permission to be here."

"Captain Serrano—Heris—you know me!" Livadhi was sweating. And since he could be a coldhearted bastard when he wanted to—he had not been sweating when they'd stood before old Admiral Connaught to answer his questions about the alleged massacre of civilians on Chisholm Station—something about this bothered him. "You have the wrong . . . er . . . individual; it's not Mr. Smith, but a . . . er . . ."

"I have two individuals," Heris said. "Both carry legal identification which matches their descriptions; neither is a fugitive." Captive, yes, but not fugitives. And of course they both fit the description of the same person, but that was another problem, not his. Would he realize from what she said that she meant the prince and his double?

"You have two clones," Livadhi said. "I have the real prince, and we need to get him aboard your ship. Without anyone noticing, although the way you've been behaving, anyone would . . ."

"Captain Livadhi—" Had she ever called him Arash? Had she ever really run her fingers through those rumpled red curls, and felt a thrill? If so, it was the thrill of being noticed by someone slightly senior, the thrill of ambition realized, not the thrill of passion. She could remember *that* bit well enough. "We received departure clearance from Naverrn Station; our course since then has been in accordance with the filed plan. We took on only a single bin of cargo, the Outworld Parcel shipment, for which we hold a legitimate subcontract. All personnel aboard have been identified by legal methods and none is a fugitive from justice." More than that she could not say. Would not say.

"Three minutes," said Sirkin.

"We cannot let you continue with clones in place of the prince," Livadhi said. "It would embarrass the Crown—"

It would more than embarrass the Crown; the illegality of using unmarked clones as royal doubles would throw a political bombshell. Heris could not begin to imagine what would be destroyed.

"They're in easy range now," Ginese put in. "Not just the OR weaponry, but the overboosted missiles, too. Either boost us out of here, or we're dinner on the table."

"Heris, you have to trust me," Livadhi said. "I know it's hard; I know about the . . . er . . . problem you had, but you have to ignore that. You know I wasn't part of that." But did she? Ambitious, hard-driving: how could she know that Livadhi hadn't been part of Lepescu's clique?

"We have to talk," Livadhi said. "Face-to-face—or I'm sorry, but—"

"Meet you at the Tank," Heris said. Would he remember, and understand, that reference? It was worth a try. To her relief, his face relaxed.

"Deep or shallow?" he asked.

"The orange bucket," she said, hoping for the best.

"Two minutes, thirty seconds," Sirkin said.

Livadhi's face constricted in a mass of wrinkles, as he seemed to pry the memory out of some corner of his brain. Then he grinned. "Your honor, Heris?"

"Absolutely." With the word, she called in the last acceleration in reserve, and the *Better Luck* aka *Sweet Delight* skipped forward, momentarily outranging the cruiser. Livadhi's tight beam lost its lock, and before he could reestablish contact, they had reached the jump threshold. Heris held her hand up, waiting precious seconds, until the beam found them, only then chopping a signal to Sirkin. The ship flipped into FTL space.

Petris let out a whoosh of breath. "You cut that fine," he said.

"Should I give them more accurate data?" Heris asked, with relief now that it was over. "He'll assume I jumped as soon as I could—why else accelerate like that? And that's our safe margin now—what I just made for us."

"But how'd you know he'd try to talk again and not shoot?" asked Sirkin.

Heris shrugged. "It was worth a try. Either we have the prince, or just clones, as he said. If we have the prince, I doubt he'd fire *on* us without fire *from* us. That would create a lot of records to be faked. If we don't—if the prince is somewhere else—that's another set of problems. Suppose Livadhi has the prince aboard . . . he must look out for his welfare . . . he will not invite attack. He was in our range by the time we broke the link. If he doesn't have the prince, there's still the clones . . . I would imagine he'd like to bring them back where they came from."

"What's that business about meeting at a tank?" asked Petris.

"Well . . ." Heris rubbed her nose absently. "It's true, in a way. I did promise to meet him, and I do feel bound by that promise, but it should work out all right."

"Care to explain?"

"Don't look down your nose at me. You know perfectly well it's officers' slang; you're about to find out what it means." She put the Reference Quads up on the secondary screen. "In every sector, there's a mapped set of coordinates called the Tank. If one wants to meet somewhere discreet, for any reason, that's where one goes . . ."

"And every Fleet officer knows it, so it's about as secret as how many royals it takes to screw in a lightbulb?"

"Not quite that bad. Not just one set of coordinates, actually, but one for each combination of officers. It starts in training; each class has its own definition. Then once you're out in the Fleet, it's a matter of relationships. If you become friends with someone, you may choose to share your definition of Tank. For one sector, or several, or all. In fact, it's always shifting, because we use it even within a single ship, or on a Station. Lazy people might give the same set to everyone, but neither Livadhi nor I were lazy—not that way. *Orange bucket*, to him, means a particular set of coordinates—" She highlighted them. "In this sector, and not a difficult jump away. Nor out of the way to where we want to go."

"Weapons?" asked Ginese.

"Oh, live of course. Just in case he's got someone with him, or we hit bad luck again. Sirkin—what's our onboard time going to look like to reach those coordinates?"

"Thirty hours, give or take—what insert velocity?"

"I'd like to come in slow, minimal turbulence. We'll be on a similar vector, unless he double-jumps, which will give us even more time. Work out the details." She pushed herself to her feet. "And now, if you'll join me, Petris, we'll have a word with our passengers."

The first passenger had improved the shining hours since they left Naverrn by going to sleep. He snored, curled on his side in the sleepsack. Heris listened awhile, and decided the snore was genuine, not faked. No one could create all those little gurgles for punctuation on purpose, not without giggling.

"Let him complete his slumbers," she said. "We'll have a word with the other one."

The other one glowered at them from the sleepsack he had

folded into a seating pad. "This is unconscionable. Not even a bed."

"I know," Heris said. "It's so sad that both of you must suffer. But your father expects you will understand."

"My father!" That with a snarl. "Easy enough for him to send me off without even my servants."

"If either you or your . . . double . . . had been cooperative, we might have been able to improve matters," Heris pointed out. "Now that we're under way, suppose you tell us which you are."

"Which?"

Heris wished she dared smack him. "Whether you are the prince, or he's the fellow down the corridor," she said.

"Oh." He appeared to ponder that much longer than necessary. "I . . . don't think either of us is the prince," he said.

"You don't think," Heris said. Was he trying to be cute, or could he possibly not know?

"No . . . I'm not entirely sure. I mean, I know *I'm* not the prince. But we switch around so much, you know, that I rather lose track."

"All clones?" Heris asked. "All *his* clones?"

"I suppose so," the young man said. "I never really thought."

"And do you have a name? When you aren't using the prince's, I mean?"

"Mr. Smith," he said, with a grin. "Gerald Smith. It's all I've ever been called. We all use it—his name is Gerel, so ours had to be close enough that his would be familiar, and yet not the same. My middle initial's B, and I'm the second one."

Heris wanted to ask him if they were all as stupid as the prince himself, but thought better of it. More important at the moment was the size of her problem. "How many of you clones are there?"

"Three, at least," he said promptly. "I went through the first stages of training with two others; our fourth had a metabolic problem and died early. But we might not have been the only cluster. On the other hand, we're almost never all together, so if one of us died in the line of duty, the others wouldn't know."

If there were three clones—or more—then the putative prince Livadhi had might not be the prince at all. "Why so many? I thought clones were expensive, and the confusion must have been difficult—"

He shrugged. "We're also prone to losses in the early embryonic stages, just as nonclones are. Given the expense, they don't take chances; they bring a cluster along together. If it's absolutely necessary to have a clone in place—as it is here—it's much safer to have a spare or two."

"Or three," Heris said. Where was the prince himself? With Livadhi? Somewhere else? "By any chance, was another clone on Naverrn? Or the prince himself?"

"No—I was primary, this trip, and Gerald C. was secondary. At least, I think that's Gerald C. you've got in the other room. I don't know where Gerald A. or Gerel Prime is."

"Gerel Prime being your code name for the prince?" The clone nodded. Heris could not see any difference between him and the prince she had transported from Sirialis. If that had been the prince—she had a sudden chilling suspicion that maybe her passenger had been one of the other clones, and the prince himself not involved in any of that mess. Yet the king clearly thought that had been the real one.

"How are you briefed about the prince's activities?" Heris asked. A minor matter now, but it might provide useful information. "Surely all of you must be kept up-to-date on his recent actions—and he on yours. Who monitors your . . . ah . . . personal interactions, and your personality profile?"

"We all carry implanted recorders," the clone said. She had trouble thinking of him as Gerald B., but she made herself repeat it silently. This was Gerald B., an individual, though genetically identical . . . "They're harvested regularly, by a Crown-certified technician, and we're retaped with the others at the same time. Usually takes a couple of hours. I've been told the prince is also equipped for retaping."

"Like training tapes?" Heris asked.

The clone—Gerald B., she reminded herself again—frowned. "I've been told it's like the military training tapes, the ones used before simulator training."

"Ah." With the right drug induction, those were powerful—one could almost believe one had already been through the simulators.

"As for the personality profile, we're evaluated on that at every retaping, as we are for physical parameters." Heris noted that Gerald B. seemed a lot more cooperative now than he had been, and wondered why. Did he have some conditioned response to a phrase she'd used, or was the admission of his clone identity a releaser for more cooperation? "That's why I'm not sure about the others," he went on. "We're not encouraged to concern ourselves with the actual identity of the person presenting himself as the prince. Nor are we encouraged to form independent relationships with each other. We're just doubles; our value lies in being mistaken for the prince, not each other."

What a sad life, Heris thought. But as if he'd read her mind, Gerald B. grinned at her. "Don't pity me," he said. "I see so many singletons trying to be mistaken for a parent, a mentor, a patron . . . they, who could be themselves wholly and freely, choose to copy another almost as closely as I must. So it can't be that bad. Besides—my prime is a wealthy, privileged young man. I enjoy those advantages even when I'm not on."

True, but such a philosophical outlook was nothing like the prince as Heris had known him. Were they as bright as the prince should have been? And if so, how did they feign stupidity? Did they know it was stupidity they were feigning? "Have you been retaped on what happened at Sirialis?" she asked.

"Oh, yes. A courier brought both physician and tapes . . . it was an emergency, such a dramatic break. Actually there was some concern that Gerald A., who had been first doubling right then, should have broken his role to inform the authorities when the prince left, but it was decided once more that our role should be confined to doubling, not surveillance."

Curiouser and curiouser. Gerald B. began to sound more and more intelligent and mature. That alone made it likely he wasn't the prince; he could feign stupidity more easily than a stupid person could feign intelligence. But—again she wondered if the real prince had been the one drugged.

"So . . . you would not know from seeing someone on a ship-to-ship video if it were the prince or another clone?"

"Nor just from seeing him. Only if he broke role, and revealed himself."

Livadhi arrived at the rendezvous an hour after Heris, weapons dark to her scan. A good sign, if he hadn't managed to fox her scans. Nor did his weapons light, though he must have known hers were hot. Slowly, they brought the ships close, cutting the delay in communication so it was hardly noticeable.

"You don't entirely trust me," Livadhi said.

"No—should I?" Heris gestured around her. "You know these people—members of my crew, court-martialed with false evidence, imprisoned. Too many of them died. Where were you, Livadhi? When I needed friends in the Fleet, when I needed someone to testify at my own hearing?"

His eyes fell. "I was . . . convinced you had done what they said. Sorry, Heris, but that's the truth. Your own cousin Marlon—your uncle Sabado—I thought if they spoke against you, with such sorrow and regret, it must be true."

"Yet you had known me." She wasn't as angry as she'd expected to be. His lack of support hurt, but it had melted into the general pain that none of her friends at Fleet had come to her aid. She shrugged, putting aside that aspect of the situation. "You wonder why I don't trust you now? That's the smallest part of it. You've heard about Lepescu?"

"Only that he died, and rumor said discreditably." His eyes glittered; she could almost see the questions struggling for precedence in his head.

"He was involved in a group that hunted humans for sport,"

Heris said. His eyes widened; even with what he knew of Lepescu that shocked him. "He was killed, and the surviving victims freed. More than that I should not say."

"You—were there?" A transparent attempt to be indirect. Heris could not contain her laughter. He scowled.

"I was there," she said. "I witnessed it." Let him wonder if she was one of the hunted, or there in some other role. Right now he did not deserve to know more. "He's definitely dead," she went on. "And so are his associates on that trip, while records have been found listing those who accompanied him other times." Livadhi stirred. Heris searched his face, finding nothing certain.

"If you have such experience," she went on, "it's one more reason I should not trust you. Although . . . I myself suspect he sometimes lured officers into it, and then blackmailed them later." Livadhi flushed. Heris simply looked at him until his color returned to normal. So. Now she knew. But what would he do?

"I suppose . . . the Crown knows all about it." His voice was low, hoarse.

"I would imagine so," Heris said carefully. She didn't actually know what the various investigators had turned up, but if Livadhi wanted to think she did, that suited her purpose.

"Nobody said anything—I mean, I haven't heard any rumors."

Heris shrugged. "I suppose the investigations aren't complete, and they're not moving until they are. Besides, why ruin the careers of good officers for one mistake?" That came out a little bitter, and she meant it to. Her one "mistake" had saved lives and won a battle, but still cost her a career.

Livadhi looked at her oddly. "I hope that attitude prevails," he said. "Though I'm surprised to find you so lenient."

"You mistake me," Heris said. "I'm not lenient at all. This is not my fight. Carrying out the king's request is. I will not let any . . . old grievances get in my way."

"I see." Livadhi's face was carefully neutral again. "And you have no interest in rekindling an old friendship? You would prefer that . . . former shipmate?"

"My former shipmates suffered considerably on my behalf," Heris said, ignoring the implication. If Livadhi had heard about Petris, it was still none of his business. "They proved themselves trustworthy. Can you blame me for wanting to put trust where it's been rewarded before?"

"No, I suppose not. Well, then what about the mission?"

"You tell me what your mission was, and I will decide if you're a potential help or hindrance to mine," Heris said. Livadhi's stare took on new respect.

"You've acquired an even keener edge to your blade," he said. "You know the regulations—"

"And the realities," Heris said. "Come, now—if you are loyal to the Crown and the Familias, you know why I have to hear your mission, and before I tell you of mine."

"All right." Livadhi sighed, and Heris sensed that his resistance had ended. "I was told that you were going to Naverrn Station to take the prince to the Guerni Republic, but that by a mix-up, the prince's double was there instead. I was supposed to transport the prince and intercept you, ensuring that you had the right person aboard. I was to do this not while you were onstation, but in deepspace, to avoid detection. We expected you to be there another day or so, and I was going to hang about insystem—as you know, R.S.S. ships do sometimes observe in that system. My . . . er . . . sources told me that one of your crew had obtained, if that's the right word, a tight beam receiver, so I planned to contact you before you left Naverrn Station, so that we could rendezvous at a distance, making it look like a routine inspection."

"Except that there are no routine inspections out here," Heris said. "As you well know."

"It was all I could think of," Livadhi said.

Heris would like to have made a sharp comeback, but she couldn't think of a better plan herself, not off the top of her head.

"What were you supposed to do with the double I had?"

"Take him to Xavier, where he's booked on a commercial liner, and put him aboard."

"I see." How much to explain? "You're right: we were supposed to impersonate a small independent cargo vessel, and transport the prince to the Guerni Republic." She was not about to explain for what purpose. "I was told his double would take over on Naverrn."

"But you snatched his double—"

"But only because he was refusing to come, and I could not distinguish them . . . since they were clones."

"That should have told you they were fakes, neither of them the prince."

"Not . . . necessarily. After all, they matched the prince's ID specs."

Livadhi looked startled. "They can't. They're clones of each other, not of the prince."

"Let's check that out," Heris said. She spread out the hardcopy of the identification specs in front of the scanner. "Is this what you got?"

Livadhi peered at it. "Yes . . . close, at least. I'll need to check mine." He touched one of his screens, and pointed a wand at the input screen from Heris. After a moment, he blanked his screen. "The same, our computer says. And our man matches. That means—"

"Three clones. One of them the prince."

"Maybe," Livadhi said. "And maybe not."

"There's only one thing to do," Heris said. "Get all three of them where we were supposed to take the prince and let the medical personnel sort it out."

"But that will risk detection," Livadhi said.

"So would taking in a vat-grown clone as the prince," Heris replied. "Do you think they couldn't tell? The clones tell me that there is a technique, not part of the identification scan, but something to do with leftover markers of accelerated growth."

"But I can't take my ship off to the Guerni Republic. I have another assignment."

"Then send your putative prince over here, and I'll take all three of them."

"But—alone?"

"You said it yourself. If you show up there in a Familias R.S.S. cruiser, it'll be an Incident with a capital I. It's safe enough for me; I've never been there, and neither has this ship."

"I don't like it," Livadhi muttered. "But I can't think what else to do. I suppose you have a shuttle lock on that thing?"

"Yes," Heris said. She nodded to Petris and Kulkul, who picked up their weapons and left the bridge. "You can send your pinnace over and swim him through the tube."

"By the way," Livadhi said a few minutes later, when the pinnace was on its way. "I am authorized to tell you that a certain Lady Cecelia disappeared from an extended care medical facility a few weeks after you left Rockhouse Major. Would you like to explain that to me?"

"No," Heris said shortly. "I would not." But that wouldn't do; Livadhi would pursue the mystery eagerly, just to annoy her. "She was my former employer," she said. "You may have heard—she had a stroke, and her family blamed me. That's why the king thought my leaving with the yacht wouldn't be connected to any plan of his." That far she could go.

"But why was I told to tell you?"

Heris shrugged. "I can't imagine. I can't say I think much of her family, keeping her in a place with no better surveillance than that. I hope she's in good hands." What could she say to change direction? The obvious topic came to her. "Who's your new admiral?"

Livadhi grimaced. "Silipu, remember her?" His comments on the changes in command since Lepescu's death filled all the time it took to unload the prince and retrieve the pinnace. When he signed off, she wondered just how much she'd fooled him.

✧ Chapter Fourteen

"We're almost there," Brun said. Cecelia had come to prefer her hands to others; she had no professional skill, but a very human affection to convey. Amazing how different she was from the girl who had thrown up in the lounge of Cecelia's yacht. It was hard to believe she had ever seemed a shrill-voiced selfish fluffhead. Was it the adventure she'd had on the island, or just normal maturation? She had helped dress Cecelia, this time in clothes Cecelia could feel—soft pants and shirt, a soft tunic, low soft boots. She had helped lift Cecelia into the hoverchair; the inflated supports held Cecelia's head steady and gave her, she hoped, the look of someone disabled but alert. For now, the hoverchair was locked down . . . Cecelia felt a moment's panic, but Brun's hand stroking her hair calmed her. She hated herself for that panic; she could not get used to being helpless, blind, vulnerable. She wanted to be brave and calm. "It's all right," Brun was saying. "You are brave. It's just—no one could be, every single minute."

If this was what children could be like, she should have had children. Ronnie, whom she'd despised, and this girl, whom she had once dismissed as a fluffhead, had rescued her when adults her own age either didn't care or couldn't think what to do. She would have to revise her ideas about young people. Of course, when she herself was young she'd known young people had sense. But looking back at her own idiocies later, she'd forgotten the generosity, the courage . . .

Pressure pushed her back into the chair. They were close, then, to the landing site. A thud, a rumble that rattled her bones. Landing, rolling along a landing field. Her stomach argued; without sight, she felt nausea and swallowed it nervously.

The chair, unlocked, floated at Brun's push through air that stank of fuels and hot metals and plastics, then into a smell of leather and dust. She heard the clicks that meant the chair was being locked down again. She heard the rustle of clothes, the thump of cases being loaded. A vehicle, filling with people and luggage. Then a jerk and swerve, and more movement she could not see.

A cool current of air blew the hair off her face. Soon it smelled of morning in the country, though a different country than she'd left. A pungent herb tickled her nose, teasing her with a vagrant memory. She should know that smell, and these others that crowded in: pines, dew-wet grass under the sun, plowed fields, horses, cattle, goats. Cecelia breathed it in. Only a few weeks ago, she'd been trapped in the sterile room without even the scent of flowers. Now . . . she could eat, and move a few muscles on her own, and live in a place that smelled good.

Finally it all came together, the sharp smell of the purple-flowered herb, the broader, roasting scent of tall yellow flowers edging the road, the squatty resinous pines of the dry hills and the lush grass of valleys. She knew which planet, of all the planets she'd visited, and she began to suspect the exact place.

She knew when the vehicle turned where she had come. Her body had felt that sequence of swerves and bounces too often to forget it. Into her mind sprang the picture she had had so long on the screen of her study . . . the stable yard, with its rows of stalls . . . the cats sprawled in the sun after a night chasing mice . . . the long house with its high-ceilinged rooms that were cool even in midsummer.

She felt the hot tears running down her face. "Do you know where you are now?" asked Brun. Her shoulder came up, emphatic *yes*. I'm home, she wanted to say. I'm where I should never have left. Home on Rotterdam, at the stable I left to Meredith. The vehicle they were in—the old farm van?—

rolled to a bumpy stop. Had no one ever fixed that wet spot in the driveway? She knew within ten centimeters where they were, just far enough past the mud puddle that someone stepping out wouldn't land in it, pulled to one side to let the hay trucks get to the gate.

A horse whickered, down the row, and another answered. Near feeding time, she thought. She heard a door open, heard the clatter of pails, and someone in boots scuffing out of the feed room. She smelled hay, and oats, and molasses, and horses, and leather . . .

But it was going to be worse, in a way. To be here, among horses and the people who cared for them, and be unable to move, to see, to talk, to ride. Pain and longing contended in her mind. Another horse whickered. She recognized that it was not the same as either of the others; at least she had not lost her ear for horse voices. Though what good it would do . . . she argued back at herself. At least it was going to be better than that sterile nursing home. And they thought she had a chance of recovery, at least partial recovery.

She felt the coolness when the hoverchair reached the shadow of the entrance. Up three steps and across the porch. The house smelled different. Someone here had cooked foods she didn't particularly like, and the downstairs hall didn't have the pleasant aroma of leather, but a more formal scent—something floral but artificial. But she recognized the soft rattle of the lift doors, and the machine-oil smell. She had had the lift installed after struggling up the spiral stairs one too many times on crutches . . . that broken ankle, the third one. She wouldn't buy a hoverchair then; only old people used them. Brun pushed her hoverchair into the lift, and slid the doors closed.

The lift jerked, and whined, and they were on their way upstairs. She wished she could see the upstairs passage, with the arched windows on either end, and the shining wood floor—or was it still shining? She could hear Brun's shoes on the floor, and it sounded polished.

"You'll be in your own room," Brun said. "It's not the same, of course. The furnishings—do you want me to describe them?" She waited while Cecelia thought about that. She had such vivid memories of this room, every detail of fabric, every ornament on the shelf above the window. She wanted to sink back into that . . . and yet, the room sounded different, and smelled different. She'd have that discord between the visual memory and the auditory reality if she clung to the past.

Her shoulder jerked *yes*, and Brun squeezed it a moment. "I'll bet you remember everything, and wish you could keep it that way. But here's what it looks like to me. The walls are dark cream—" They'd aged, Cecelia thought. They needed a new coat of paint every few years to keep the precise tone Cecelia had chosen. "—there's a medbed in place of yours; you'll be on monitoring awhile longer. But the cover is one of those Rekkian handwoven blankets in green and gold and tan, with flecks of orange in the gold. The pattern's more an irregular stripe than anything else. The bed has its head against the far wall; the window over the yard will be on your left as you lie in bed. Is that right?" Cecelia signalled *yes* again. "Good. We didn't put anything on the windows. There's a wooden chest, painted oxblood red, against the wall opposite the bed, and a tall bookcase/chest on the wall to the right, next to that window. A couple of reproduction Derrian side chairs we picked up in the city, and no rug in here at all."

Cecelia wanted to ask about the pictures on the wall. She had taken her Piucci originals, the portraits of her top horses, but had left behind the old hunting scenes. But Brun said nothing about that. She heard other footsteps in the passage, and waited.

"Here are your clothes," Dr. Czerda said. "Your new clothes, I should say. Your friends thought of trying to get your own, clothes you knew by feel and smell, but decided it was too risky. Brun gave us a shopping list, and you're now equipped with the basics, in colors she remembers you wearing. Including riding attire."

Riding attire? She couldn't ride—might never ride again.

For all she knew, she was bloated up to the size of Brun's hot air balloon, and no horse could hold her up. She jerked her shoulder *No* and hoped it carried the exclamation point she intended.

"Yes," Brun said. "You've got breeches and boots and helmet for the very good reason that you're going to ride again. You *are!*" In that was the fierceness of the young, who thought wanting something enough made it happen. Cecelia had heard that tone in her own voice, when she'd insisted she would ride again, after this or that accident. Then she had believed it. Now . . . she wasn't sure.

"You're facing a time limit," the doctor said. "One formal—the legal requirement to show competency before your estate is finally distributed—and one informal—before whoever did this to you finds you. So we aren't going to waste any time: you will have a full schedule of rehab work, every day, no vacations."

Cecelia thought about that, and her immediate wish to stretch out on that unseen medbed, and jerked her shoulder *Yes* with as much emphasis as the earlier *No*. She was tired, but better to be tired than forever lost in this helplessness.

"Except tonight," the doctor said. "Most of your therapists are still in transit. We didn't want to make it obvious where you were if someone is keeping track of them, so they've had to take roundabout routes. So tonight you can just rest."

Until that moment, she hadn't thought of pursuit—Brun had mentioned it, but reality itself seemed hardly real. Now, with the familiar smells and sounds around her, the thought of being recaptured, returned to a blank prison existence, terrified her. It was the wrong place; it was the obvious place. Anyone would know where she was. What fools!

Brun recognized her panic somehow. "It's all right," she kept saying. "It's not as obvious as you think."

Why not? she wanted to say. Brun went on to explain. Rotterdam had horses, but no advanced medical facilities. It was far from the logical place for someone in her condition. Moreover, her lifelong investments in Rotterdam—not only money, but time and friendship—meant that few mouths would talk. And even if they did, Rotterdam lay far off the usual networks of transport and communication.

"They'll figure out it was Dad's yacht, eventually. They'll think of Sirialis, and then Corhulm, where most of our pharmaceutical research is done. They may send a query about Rotterdam, but—I'm assured nothing will come of it. At least for months."

Cecelia hoped Brun was right. She would much rather die than go back to that nonlife.

Her earlier experiences in recovering from more minor injuries helped only a little. It had been twenty years since her last broken bone—well, *large* broken bone—and longer than that since the near-fatal headlong crash in the Trials. She had forgotten how infuriating it was to struggle, panting, for what seemed like hours, in order to twitch something slightly—and then have the physical therapist's bright, cheerful voice say "Pretty good, hon, now do it again." And again and again, until she was a quivering wreck. She had forgotten how much weakened muscles and ligaments hurt when forced to work again; she had forgotten how even the best therapists talked over patients' heads, as if they weren't really there. "There's a spike on that adductus longius" and "Yeah, and isn't that a twitch in the flexor radialis?" and "If she doesn't get something going on these extensors we're going to have to start splinting; the tone's up on the flexors." She hated that; she wanted them to remind her what they were talking about, and what it meant.

And she was tired. Bone-tired, sore, short of sleep—because she woke in a panic, night after night, afraid she was back in the nursing home. With so limited a communication system, she couldn't tell them that, and they'd decided she would sleep better alone. She was too old for this; she didn't have the resilience, the sheer energy, that she had had two decades before. She had not believed she was old—not the woman who could still ride to hounds—but now she believed it. If she had been able to talk, she would have said it; she would have argued, out of exhaustion and despair, that they were wasting their time. She couldn't talk; she could only endure.

But twice a day, between sessions with physical therapists and occupational therapists and massage therapists and tests and all the rest, Brun took her out to the stable yard. That was her reward for a good morning, incentive for a good afternoon. She learned each horse's voice, and the voices of the stablehands only a few days later. Brun poured handfuls of sweet feed into her passive hand, and she felt the soft velvet horse lips mumbling over her palm. Brun lifted her hands, and laid them against satiny necks and shoulders. The first time her fingers really moved, it was along a horse's shoulder; her first strong grasp was of a horse's mane.

And yet she hated the obviousness of it. She did not want her love of horses to be so utilitarian, so selfish. They deserved her love for themselves, not because it could help her therapy. She would have sulked, except how could she sulk when she couldn't talk at all? How could she rage, when her movements were slow and awkward, and she couldn't scream?

Cecelia free. Heris held that thought in mind as she laid out the roundabout safe course from their present location to the Guerni Republic. It had to be Brun's plan; she told herself that the villains in this piece had no reason to abscond with Cecelia. Only her friends did; only Brun could have put together the resources to do it. She imagined Cecelia in Sirialis; it was easy to imagine her in rooms Heris had seen, around horses and people she knew. Obvious, of course, to the king and anyone else, but—she put it out of her mind. Brun had acted; the first part had gone well. She could do nothing herself until she'd delivered these clones and the prince (if he was one of them.) Then, she promised herself, then she would find Cecelia.

Somewhat to Heris's surprise, the rest of the trip to the Guerni Republic went peacefully, jump point after jump point, day after day after day. The three clones, each of whom insisted he was not the prince, were less trouble than Ronnie and George had been at first. They agreed to wear nametags to help the crew avoid the confusion of offering a meal to a clone who had already eaten. This helped, although it occurred to Heris that they might switch the nametags for a lark. Heris could not assess their intelligence, not with the possibility— no, likelihood—that they would not cooperate and perform at their best. Yet they seemed to have more common sense than she'd expected.

"There's no use our pretending, with all three of us here," A. said when she asked. "Our cover's blown, totally, as far as you and the others aboard this ship are concerned. You know we're clones of the prince; you know what that means legally. It wouldn't matter if one of us were the prince; the damage has already been done."

Heris didn't like the sound of that. Cold tickles ran down her spine, as if a frozen cockroach were rousing there. "You mean we're now a danger to the prince, or to the Crown?"

"No—we are." That one wore Gerald B.'s tag. "After all, that cruiser captain knows; some of his crew either know or suspect. There's no way to be sure the secret's safe even if they silenced you. They'll probably dump us."

"Kill you?" asked Petris, putting down his fork.

"No, there are other ways. They can do plastic surgery to make us no longer doubles, and there's some kind of way to mark our genomes more prominently."

"Look through the microscope and the chromosomes spell CLONE," said one of the others. He sounded perfectly calm about it; Heris wondered if that was part of their act.

"But what will you do?" Petris asked. "Have you had any . . ." He paused, struggling for a tactful way to say it.

"Job training?" asked the one with the C. tag. "No, we just laze around acting like silly-ass rich boys." One of the others snorted, and Heris realized it was supposed to be a joke.

"Some," said the one who had snorted. "Lots of courses in all sorts of things he's supposed to know. Of course, we didn't attend formal classes, or get degrees, but I'm sure they'll cobble up some sort of resume for us."

They seemed remarkably unconcerned, but they were, Heris reminded herself, twenty or more years younger than she. People that age had more confidence than their lack of experience warranted.

Except for Sirkin. Something was wrong, and Heris couldn't quite figure it out. Of course, she would still be grieving for Amalie—that might be it. She had seen violent death up close for the first time in her life, and the victim was someone she loved. But Heris had seen other young people deal with their first serious losses. Usually, they came back to normal in fits and spurts, but with an upward trend. Sirkin had seemed to be recovering normally, but then took a downward turn. Heris didn't expect her to be lively, happy, or full of the sparkle that had first convinced her the girl was a good prospect, but she did expect consistent good work at her job. And that's where Sirkin had begun to fail.

Only little things so far—a missing log entry after a course change, a data cube left out on the counter rather than filed in its case. Heris had been tactful at first, murmuring reminders when she found the data cube, noticed the missing entry. Sirkin had looked appropriately remorseful and made quick corrections. But it went on. The other crew had noticed, and Heris arrived on the bridge one day to find Oblo giving Sirkin a serious scolding.

"I don't care what your problem is, bright eyes, but if you don't shape up, the captain'll kick your tail off this ship the next port we come to. It's not like you can't do better—we know you can. And don't tell me it's grieving over Yrilan, because we could tell you were really falling for Brun." Heris paused, just out of sight. Perhaps Oblo could do better at unkinking Sirkin than she had so far.

"But I tell you, I *did* log the jump coordinates. I entered them shift before last—" Sirkin sounded more defensive than apologetic.

"They're not here. And Issi was on just after you—are you telling me he wiped your log entry?"

"No! I don't know—I know I made that entry; I went over it twice because I know I've been making mistakes somehow . . . it was there, I swear—"

"Don't bother; you don't know how." Oblo in that mood was dangerous; Heris could feel the hostility oozing out of him from here. "See here, girl: you have only two possibilities. Either you didn't enter anything, or someone wiped it. I know damn well Issi wouldn't wipe it, nor would I, nor would the captain. Who are you accusing? You think one of those clones sneaked in here?"

"I don't know!" Sirkin's voice trembled; Heris heard her take a deep breath that was almost a sob. "I don't know what's happening . . . I was so careful . . . and then it's gone . . ."

"I've got to tell the captain; you know that. I can't pretend not to notice something like that. It could kill us all later."

"I know that," Sirkin said. "I—I can't explain it." Heris shook her head, and went on in. Sirkin looked tired and unkempt—that was new. She had always been neatly groomed and bright-eyed. What could be wrong with the girl?

"Ms. Sirkin . . . I'll see you in my office, please." She did not miss the desperate look Sirkin threw at Oblo, who gave her no encouragement at all.

Sirkin's explanation, if one could call it that, made little sense. She was trying to be careful; she didn't understand how these mistakes happened; she was sure she'd logged the course changes and jump points, and had no idea how they had vanished from the log. Her hands trembled, and her eyes were bloodshot.

"Are you taking anything?" Heris asked. Drugs seemed likely, given the combination of physical appearance and absentmindedness. Sirkin hadn't used before, that she knew of, but in the stress of Yrilan's death perhaps the girl had started.

"No, ma'am. Not even the pills the doctor gave me after . . . after Amalie . . ." Her voice broke. "Things are just coming undone," she said, tears beginning to slide down her cheeks. "And . . . and that makes me sound like Amalie. She used to say things like that . . . I wonder if she felt like this, trying and trying and nothing seems to work . . ."

Heris had no intention of getting off into that blind alley. Amalie Yrilan's excuses were no longer anyone's problem. "Sirkin, we both know you're capable of better. You were doing extremely well up until we left Rockhouse Major. You must have some idea what's gone wrong. Is someone . . . bothering you?" She was sure she could trust her former crew not to harass a young civilian, but it was only fair to ask. Skoterin, the newest? She'd have expected one of the others to notice and straighten out the offender, or tell her. No, more likely one of the clones, assuming a royal right to any pretty face and body. She wouldn't put it past them to bring drugs aboard, either.

"No, ma'am. Nobody's bothered me. I know I . . . still miss Amalie, but I honestly don't think it's that. It's just—I do something, or think I do something, and then later it's not done. I don't understand it. Maybe I'm going crazy." She looked up with an expression Heris had seen too many times on youngsters who had somehow gotten out of their depth and hoped an elder had a magic solution. "Going crazy" had been a favorite hypothesis in one ship, because there were medicines for going crazy. Simple inattention and laziness had no cure.

"I don't think you're going crazy," Heris said. She tried to sound both calm and firm. "But I do think you can pull yourself together—and you must. Tell you what. Let's let another bridge officer sign off on your log entries for a few days. If *those* entries disappear, we'll know it's not your fault . . . and you'll have a witness to having made them. How's that?" It was an insult, but Sirkin took the suggestion as gratefully as if it had been praise. "Now—take the rest of this shift off—we've no jump points coming up—and put yourself to bed. You look exhausted."

"Yes, ma'am."

As Heris expected, Sirkin's log entries didn't disappear when someone else countersigned them. So . . . logically . . . Sirkin had never made the earlier entries. It wasn't a computer glitch; it was the far more common human error. Sirkin seemed to be making fewer of them now, in all categories—another data point on the plot of carelessness. Her appearance improved; she looked almost normal, if not the bright-eyed girl she had been. Oblo and Issi reported that she seemed alert, careful, everything she should be.

Just to be sure, Heris asked about conflicts with the crew; as she'd expected, they all insisted they liked the girl. None of them reported conflict with anyone else. And a discreet surveillance indicated that she wasn't sneaking off to one of the clones (or any of them to her) when she was off-duty.

Yet . . . what had made Sirkin suddenly careless? Even in the aftermath of Amalie's death, she had done tedious jobs with her former precision. Why now? Heris worried, unsatisfied. She sensed something wrong and promised herself to pursue it once the clones had been delivered safely for medical attention.

One morning Cecelia lay in her bed and did her best to hate herself to death. She was too old to rage at simple unfairness, but the unfairness of her situation went beyond anything she could accept. When Brun came to dress her and take her to breakfast, she did not respond to the usual morning sallies. The smell of hot bread and sage honey roused no response. She wasn't hungry, and she wouldn't eat. After the necessary rituals of personal care, she waited for her first workout, numb and passive.

"We've got someone new," Dr. Czerda said. Czerda had begun to sound increasingly apologetic; it grated on Cecelia. "A specialist who might help. We had to wait, because she's so well-known—just the person they might be watching."

"Hi," a woman's voice said. "I'm Carly, your new therapist."

Another new therapist. Cecelia needed that like she needed a fluorescent bathing suit. She was glad she couldn't say what first came to mind: such a string of obscenity would alienate all of them. "You're very angry," Carly said, in a voice that offered neither blame nor apology. "Did you know you could show that without words?"

Cecelia did not bother to twitch her answer. It was a lucky guess, that was all, or the infuriating certainty that she was in a predicted stage. They couldn't tell; they'd been nagging her because she didn't have control of her facial muscles, so it couldn't be the scowl she would like to have worn.

A warm hand lay on her arm; it radiated comfort. "Here," Carly said. "Anger tenses certain muscle groups, and fear tenses different ones. You're tense in all the anger groups. I don't think the others saw that, because of the overall weakness. Does it make you even more angry that I know you're angry?"

Cecelia thought about it, drawn into the intellectual puzzle despite herself. If it was an observation of her, of her real self, she didn't mind. It was being put into a category that made her want to scream.

"You're not as angry now," Carly said. Her hand moved slowly along Cecelia's arm. "Perhaps because I paid real attention to you, and not a theory?" Her voice, almost as warm as her hand, conveyed honest curiosity, real interest.

Cecelia could feel herself calming, the prickly rage receding. "You've had good therapists, but they're young," Carly said. "And the enthusiasms of younglings can drive anyone mature to tears or screams. Besides, they've worked you too hard. I think you're tired, more than they've believed. Would you like to sleep?"

Cecelia twitched *yes*, and then shrugged both shoulders.

"You would, but what's the use? Or, you would but then this session is wasted?" Carly waited. Cecelia wondered how she was supposed to answer that with a yes or no, and in the silence—a peaceful, accepting silence—wondered if she could move anything else enough to communicate. She had clamped onto a horse's mane, first with her right hand, and then with both. If the first alternative was one hand, the second could be both. She tried to visualize her hands moving, and felt the fabric under her fingers slide across her fingertips.

"Both hands," Carly said, with approval. "That would be the second choice, I expect. Can you confirm with your shoulder?"

Yes.

"Then I would say this session is not a waste, even if you sleep the rest of it. You're tense, and angry, and very tired. I'm going to make you comfortable."

Carly's warm hands, steady and firm, kneaded sore muscles and ligaments. Not the massages that Cecelia remembered, but something deeper and more serious. Soon she was drifting, not quite in contact with her aging body, but not in the sensory limbo of the drugs. She felt warm, contented, relaxed, and very sleepy.

When she woke, she felt completely adrift. Someone's hands steadied her back; she was leaning against—over?—something.

"It's all right," Carly said. "You slept well, and now you're resting on a large padded ball. If your arms feel funny, it's because they're hanging free, not at your sides."

It felt worse than funny; it felt ridiculous. Yet it also felt good, and she was rested and comfortable.

"Can you wiggle your hands again?" Carly asked. Something about her voice, her mature, calm voice, maintained the relaxation. Cecelia tried. With her arms resting against the curve of the ball, almost dangling, she could move her fingers. She could feel them shift across the fabric one by one. "Excellent," Carly said. "Some of the things they worried about aren't so. You don't have real spasticity in your fingers; the weakness and the tension in your arms have made it seem so. In this position, when you're rested, you might even tap a keyboard."

A keyboard. A keyboard meant letters, meant words, meant language, meant—she had been told this—a speech synthesizer. Real communication, not just twitches and jerks. She wanted to cry and laugh at once; she felt her shoulders seize, cramping. Carly rubbed the cramps out.

"Right now, the biochemical responses of your limbic system are working against you. Like anyone else, you'll do best when you're relaxed and happy. That's my job."

Why hadn't the others thought of this? Cecelia felt the difference in Carly's hands, as they responded to her muscles rather than trying to overpower them. Her arms twitched, trembled, then finally hung relaxed and heavy. Comfortable. It had been so long since she'd been really comfortable.

"It's been known for a very long time," Carly said. "But it's tricky to do, and a lot of people don't think it's important. If a regen tank will work, if the rehab is expected to be short, they say why bother? I think it's always worth it, for the patient's comfort if nothing else. And in cases like this, it's essential."

Cecelia felt mildly alert, rested, ready to try again. That afternoon, the relentless work with weights seemed less impossible. She was sweating, gasping, sore—but it made sense again. Afterwards, Carly gave her another massage, easing the pains of the exercises, and she slept well that night, waking rested and eager to go on.

Day by day, Carly suggested modifications to the various therapists—a tactile guide that let her get a bit of food to her own mouth, a communication system that used every movement she could make to signal meaning. After that came a communication board, with tactile clues for its segments; Carly promised that work on that would give her the strength and precision to use a real keyboard later. Cecelia began to believe again that she could make it out of this mess, that she would not be a helpless blind victim forever. Now her anger rose from impatience, not despair; she wanted her life back, and she wanted it now.

The Guerni Republic traded widely with a dozen different political entities. On one side, the Compassionate Hand and the Familias Regnant beyond. On the other, Aethar's World

and its allies (a confederation so loose it refused the name).
On yet another, some solo worlds so scattered that political
union had so far been impractical. Like Italy's central protru-
sion into the Mediterranean on old Earth (back when that
body of water was known as Mare Nostrum), the Guerni
Republic enjoyed a location both handy for trade and easy to
defend.

Astrophysicists had argued the unlikelihood of six stars
of the right type, with assorted habitable planets, arriving at such a configuration by chance, but the unanswer-
able counterargument was that everything—even the
taste of chocolate—was inherently unlikely, difficult as
it may be to imagine a universe without chocolate in it.
The Guernesi preferred to believe their situation had
been created for them by a beneficent deity, and
shrugged off contrary theories as the envy of those God
chose not to favor. In case that envy went further than
bad-mannered carping, the Guernesi maintained an alert
and quietly competent military, as the Compassionate
Hand had found. As practical in its way as the Guerni
Republic, the Benignity declared the Guernesi off-limits
to Compassionate Hand activity—at least as long as delicate probes of the defenses showed them to be still alert
and effective.

As a result of their location and the resulting trade, the
Guernesi had developed efficient and relatively painless
entrance protocols. But efficient, painless, and swift did not
mean careless.

"While it's no concern of ours, are you aware that your broad-
cast ID and your ship do not agree?" asked the bright-faced
young woman in blue.

"I beg your pardon?"

"According to our database, the *Better Luck* was scrapped
over in Jim-dandy eight years ago. I know the Familias records
aren't kept that long, but if you bought this ship as the *Better
Luck* we could provide the data to sustain a claim of fraud."

For a price, of course. The Guernesi, polite and willing to help, did nothing for nothing.

"Uh ... I don't think that will be necessary." Heris had trouble not looking at Oblo. He would be embarrassed.

"On the other hand, if you reprogrammed the beacon, your tech did an excellent job—even got the warble in the 92 band exactly right. We have people who would pay a bonus for that kind of work, if that individual is here and wants to immigrate—" Another thing about the Guernesi, they were always looking for a profit.

"Now, I notice you have major ship weapons aboard ..." And how had they figured that out? With the weapons locked down, no scan should have detected them. "Since you've come in past Compassionate Hand space, I'm afraid we'll have to visually inspect and seal them ... I don't want to insult you, but the Benignity tries our borders at intervals."

"How—!" Oblo couldn't contain himself. "Your scans are—are they for sale?"

The young woman dimpled at him. "Of course, sir. I can give your captain a list of suppliers certified by the government. We have no restrictions on the foreign purchase of military-grade materials."

"Mr. Ginese will accompany you on your inspection of the weapons," Heris said. "What about small arms?"

"May not be taken off the ship; the penalty is death, and destruction of the ship that brought you." That was clear enough. "If you want to shoot yourselves aboard your own ship, that's your business." She spoke into a communicator hooked to her uniform collar; the language was unfamiliar. "I'm just asking our weapons inspection team to step aboard ... if your Mr. Ginese will meet them at the access hatch?" Of course. Heris was already impressed. She had never been here—R.S.S. vessels visited only on ambassadorial duty—and the rumors she'd heard didn't begin to match the reality.

"You do not have to state your business here," the young woman went on, "but if you do, it would be my pleasure to advise you on the easiest way to accomplish your purposes."

"Medical technology," Heris said. "I understand that you have superb research and clinical facilities—"

"Yes—can you mention a specialty?"

"Neurology, specifically the treatment of neurochemically induced cognitive dysfunction." That had been in the papers the king had given her.

"Ah, yes." The inspector spoke into her collar mic again, and waited a moment. "According to the current listings, I'd recommend Music—"

"Music?" Heris knew she must have looked and sounded as confused as she felt. The younger woman smiled, but not in mockery.

"Sorry, Captain. It's this translator. All the planets of Guerni's fifth star are named for the artes liberales: music, mathematics, history, and so on. Music is the planet with the largest medical complex devoted to neurology. From here, it's a very short jump, and about two weeks on insystem drive—we do ask, by the way, that you do not jump except at the designated jump points: we have a lot of traffic. By the time you arrive, Music Station will have a list of contacts for you. Do you wish to append any patient data at this time?"

"No," said Heris, feeling slightly overwhelmed. "No, thank you."

"Our pleasure. As soon as my team reports your weapons sealed, you're free to go. By the way, while I'm sure you wouldn't think of doing any such thing, I should warn you that unsealing your weapons will be a cause for retaliation, even should you manage to frustrate the automatic detonators on the seals which are designed to blow a ship of the size that usually carries these weapons. Good day!"

Heris had worried about getting three identical young men named Smith through the Customs Inspection at Music Station. She had imagined every possible complication, but when she brought up the problem, all three laughed.

"We're used to this," Gerald A. said. "If we don't wear the same clothes, or stand together, or go through the same intake booth too close together, no one will notice. All the machines care about is whether our physical features match our formal ID. And of course they do, from blood type and retinal scan to DNA analysis."

"We can do costuming," Gerald B. said. "But it's not really necessary here." Heris wondered. She still didn't trust their judgment; she still suspected that one of them actually was the prince, concealed by a shell-game with the nametags. But when they showed up at her office, without the nametags and in different outfits, she had to admit they no longer looked so identical. One wore a scruffy set of spacer coveralls he must have gotten from a crew member; he slouched against the wall looking sullen and grubby. Another displayed himself with the peacock air of a young man of fashion, and the third had the earnest, slightly harried look of a businessman late for a conference. They looked different enough, but how lax were the Guernesi?

Heris continued to worry until she was through Customs herself, with her royal letters to the physicians, and found the three Smiths grinning at her from the shuttle waiting lounge.

✧ Chapter Fifteen

Carly's influence on the treatment team extended into the stable as well. Maris Magerston had been Cecelia's hippotherapist from the beginning, when she had been slung over the horse's back like a stuffed doll . . . she knew that wasn't a fair description, but that's what it had felt like to her. Although Maris had patiently explained *why* she was sprawled on a broad pad, facing backwards, she still hated it. In her mind she had composed one furious argument after another, shutting out Maris's description of this and that muscle group doing important things. She didn't want to be this way, an inert load on the horse's back; she felt ridiculous, ugly, flabby, useless, old. She wanted to *ride*, and that meant sitting up and facing forward.

She arrived one day for her session to find an argument going on between Carly and Maris; Brun, pushing her hoverchair, guided it into the tackroom out of sight and let her listen. Maris sounded angry and defensive; Carly, as usual, sounded calm and cheerful, as she said she thought Cecelia was ready to ride properly.

"We start all our clients that way," Maris said. "I've read those articles, thank you—" Carly must have handed her something. "We're not quite as ignorant out here as you seem to think. But it's dangerous to rush clients . . . and she's over eighty . . ."

Carly took her up on the oblique attack. "Are you upset that I've been called in to supervise?"

"Oh, no!" Definite bitterness; Cecelia could imagine Maris's expression. "We're not *bitter*. We're just local therapists on a

249

backwoods planet, all so grateful for a chance to learn from the *great* Dr. Callum-Wolff."

"You sound pretty upset to me . . . I probably would be, too. You've been doing a good job for a lot of people all your career here; you do what you've been taught, and people get better . . . and I come along telling you to change. Is that about it?" Carly's voice held no anger and no defensiveness.

"Well . . ." Maris sounded much calmer. Then she actually chuckled. "Actually, I have your training cubes, up through three years ago. I'd have come to your presentations, if you'd ever come here before." A long pause. "The thing is . . . Lady Cecelia's really special on this planet, to a lot of people. And we were all trained as strict structuralists, Spinvirians. 'When you know the electrochemical scan of a nerve, you know what it can do.' Period. If I let her get hurt—especially doing something new—"

"Ah. Tough choice. I see your problem. Well, I could be bossy and overrule you—that'd give you an out—but I'd rather not. I do wish you'd let us try." That tone restored—at least symbolically—Maris's authority.

"Oh, why not? At worst, she'll just fall off."

Brun pushed her back out, as if they'd just arrived; Cecelia hoped her expression hadn't betrayed a joy she wasn't supposed to feel yet. This time they lifted her up into a proper saddle, facing forward. It felt entirely wrong: her legs were wrong, her back was wrong, her seat was wrong. She couldn't *see*. She felt a warm hand on either leg: Brun, on the right, and the stable girl Driw on the left. They had been to every session; and Brun had told her enough about Driw that she felt she knew the groom well.

"We're going to move, now," said Maris. "Circling to the right." *NO*, she thought, but she didn't move her shoulder. Pride left her that much dignity. She heard Maris cluck; the horse moved under her and she sagged sideways. Brun's firm hands propped her up. She could feel her legs flopping uselessly against the saddle; only the hands of her helpers kept her on the horse.

But she was sitting up, facing forward. Gradually, the saddle beneath her took on a familiar rhythm; she could feel the horse's stride as its barrel bunched and lengthened, swung slightly from side to side. Maris began to talk, again explaining what the horse was doing to enforce movements Cecelia's body must learn to make. Cecelia decided not to listen. Her back began to feel the horse the way it used to; she had no attention left for someone's words.

"Good," Brun murmured. "You're doing better." It didn't feel like balancing better; her spine felt as solid as her luncheon custard. But somewhere between lurches from side to side, she felt for a moment that it was *right* again. Somewhere in each stride, she was riding.

"Think of halting," Maris said. Cecelia tried to let herself sink into the saddle the way she would have, and felt herself slump forward as the horse halted. The helper's hands caught her. "Good for you!" Maris said. "You halted her yourself. Now—think forward."

Cecelia waited a moment, recovering what balance she could from the halt, and tried to remember how. She felt her spine lengthen, the pressure in her seat bones, a rising tension between her and the horse. Then the horse lunged forward into a trot, and for one instant Cecelia's body responded moving with the beat, just as Maris said "Whoa!" The horse slowed, but already Cecelia was off-balance, sliding gracelessly off the outside into Driw's arms. Both of them fell.

"Are you hurt?" Brun sounded terrified. Cecelia quickly signalled *no*. She wasn't hurt at all. She was exultant. She had stopped a horse. She had compelled it forward. Without the use of her arms or legs, blind, unable to speak, she had nonetheless controlled a horse again.

"That'll be enough for today," Maris said, closer. Cecelia jerked her shoulder, *no*. "We'll have to check for damage. I was afraid of this—"

"She said no," Carly said. "She's not upset by a soft fall like that."

"But she's over eighty! And she shouldn't have been able to get this horse to trot. I'll have to switch to another—"

"Cecelia." That was Carly, grasping her hands now. "Cecelia, you did it! You stopped her; you got her into a trot. Are you happy about it?"

Yes! Of course she was happy about it. She tried to remember their other signals; right now she was too excited to think. "More"—that's what she wanted to say. Was she supposed to jerk her right knee, or her left? "Muhhh," she heard herself say softly. "Muhhh . . ." and then the shoulder jerk for *yes*.

"More, yes? You want to ride more?"

YES! Why hadn't she established a signal for "Dammit, you idiot!" Why hadn't she established a signal for "reins?" She flexed her fingers in Carly's, then pulled slightly.

"She wants to hold the reins, don't you, Lady Cecelia?" That was Brun, bless her, who knew more about riding than Carly.

"Maris, I think she needs to try again."

"All right." Maris was resigned, not hostile.

It was going to work. She knew it. This time Cecelia ignored the need for helpers, ignored the internal voice that told her how ridiculous she must look. The saddle felt familiar this time. The nubbly surface of the reins against her fingers felt better than fine silver or silk. By the end of that session she had halted the horse three more times, and started her into a walk, all with no surprises. She felt as if she had regained herself.

Steadily, both her riding and her other therapies made progress. She could grip the special table tools (she did not consider them flatware) and get most solid foods into her mouth. With someone to remind her where they were on the tray, she could choose for herself whether to follow a bite of ham with a bite of toast, or eat all the fruit first. She could sit in a regular chair, if it had a straight back, and with leg braces on could stand supported, leaning against a chest support, to use a keyboard or scrawl with a crayon. She could push the buttons to control her hoverchair; she could, at last, use a keyboard. Bit by bit, her voice came back, though most words defeated her; she began to spell things out, as she did on the keyboard.

Now, for the first time since the dark months in the nursing home, she began worrying at the problem of what had really happened. Who had done this? Why?

She was dozing one afternoon, after the best ride she had yet had. Maris had taken her out into one of the big fields on a lead line, and they had ridden together in the open. The horse had a lovely long flat walk; she had enjoyed the longer stretches of straight movement, the sound of wind in the trees at the edge of the field and the feel of it on her face. A pleasant lunch, a relaxing nap . . .

In one white-light burst, memory returned. She was at Berenice's dressed for that damned reception; she could feel the ivory silk smooth on her shoulders, the weight of her favorite necklace on her chest. Berenice had worn pale green, and the other ladies were much the same, a gaggle of old women in appropriate pastels, she thought sourly. It didn't matter if some of them had had rejuvenation; they were still old. She remembered them as children; they remembered her the same way. She hated this kind of thing. Gabble, gabble, nibble and sip, sit listening to a mediocre string trio, and then make a donation to whatever cause. Simpler just to make the donation and go do what you wanted, but she was trying to get Berenice to come around on the subject of Heris Serrano, so she had agreed to "be good" at the reception.

At her elbow, that insipid twit Lorenza. Amazing that a man like Piercy could have a sister like Lorenza. Lorenza, of course, had gone for rejuvenation, early and often, but she had always cared more for her complexion than anything else. *I am being nice*, Cecelia reminded herself, and smiled at Lorenza. Smooth gold hair, fair skin looking thirty—but those eyes held all of eighty years of malice. It was unnerving, those wicked old eyes in that young face . . . exactly why Cecelia hated the thought of rejuv for herself.

"Dear Cecelia, I haven't seen you for years," Lorenza said. Cecelia shivered. It was a soft voice, insistently gentle; why did it grate so on her ears?

"Well, I run off a lot," Cecelia said. She felt big and coarse next to Lorenza; she always had. As a child, Lorenza had been picture perfect, the quiet, well-behaved, clean and tidy girl to whom Cecelia had been compared when in disgrace. *Why can't you be more like dear Lorenza?* had come from both her mother and Berenice, every time she'd broken something, or come home dirty and disheveled. "I just got back." Her neck felt hot; she always felt she should say more to Lorenza, but she never could think what.

"I understand you took care of dear Ronnie for Berenice," Lorenza said, smiling up at her. There was nothing overtly wrong with that statement, but Cecelia was sweating.

"Yes . . . he's changed a lot. Fine young man." Too late, she realized that admitted he hadn't been. If Berenice heard, she'd be furious. Cecelia wished she were anyplace else—outside, by preference, and hoped she wouldn't trip over her own feet. Dammit! She was over eighty, rich and famous in her own right; she didn't need to feel like this about Lorenza. *I am being good*, she told herself again.

"You look hot, dear," Lorenza said. "Here—have a glass of juice." She produced a glass, snatched no doubt from some passing waiter, and offered it. Cecelia didn't want juice; she wanted out. But she had promised to be good; she tried not to grimace as she sipped the tangy-sweet juice. Interesting flavor—spiced with cinnamon and something else, she decided. She turned to thank Lorenza, and found to her surprise that the other woman had disappeared.

Cecelia gasped. She was shaking, her heart racing, and someone had hold of her hands. She knew, after a wild moment of panic, where she was, and what had happened. Lorenza. Lorenza had poisoned her. And she knew why, or part of why. It made sense now. And she had to tell them, before Lorenza poisoned Ronnie and Berenice and Bunny's family and the Mahoneys . . . and for that matter Heris and the crew and the prince.

"Cecelia! Tell us . . . try . . ."

Struggling, fighting her uncooperative body, she managed to spell it out. L.o.r.e.n.z.a. D.i.d. I.t. They didn't have to ask her what; they understood that much. Brun's voice cut across the others.

"The Crown Minister's sister? *That* Lorenza?"

Yes. Back to the new signal system; it was faster than spelling.

"Why?" Brun asked, and put the keyboard into her hands.

Dared she tell now? What if Lorenza had an agent here? Panic shook her, but she had to try it. If she died, she had to save the others.

Letter by letter, she got it out; no one interrupted. "P.r.i.n.c.e. m.a.d.e. s.t.u.p.i.d. D.r.u.g.s. K.i.n.g. k.n.o.w.s G.e.o.r.g.e. d.e.m.o. L.o.r.e.n.z.a. g.a.v.e. d.r.u.g. R.o.n.n.i.e. n.o.t.i.c.e.d. T.o.l.d. m.e."

"And you told the king—Ronnie said that," Brun broke in then. "He didn't tell me about George . . . but I remember a joke about the term George almost flunked out of school. Was that it?"

Bless her wits. *Yes*.

"Lorenza did it because you know—because you told the king, and he must've told the Crown Minister who told her—and that means she might get the others. Ronnie—!"

Yes.

"His family?"

Yes.

"More?"

Yes. Of course, you idiot! When she finally could, she would give Carly an earful about what nonverbal people really wanted to say.

"Right, let me think." Brun thought aloud, either from habit or courtesy to Cecelia; Cecelia could imagine her intent face. "Anyone Ronnie might've talked to. His family. Me. Maybe my family as well. And George! Of course, and George's father. Heris Serrano, she knew, but I don't know if anyone else knows that."

Yes. The king would figure it out; he would already have told the Crown Minister. And didn't Brun say something about Heris having a mission from the king, that apparent theft of the yacht?

"So what do we do?" That was Brun to the others, and the gabble of voices rose. Cecelia began spelling again; that silenced them for the moment.

"G.o. t.e.l.l. R.o.n.n.i.e. G.o. t.o. R.o.c.k.h.o.u.s.e. w.a.r.n. t.h.e.m."

"Me?" Brun asked

Yes. They would listen to Brun; they wouldn't listen to any of the others. "C.a.r.e.f.u.l." she spelled.

"I'll leave now," Brun said in her ear. "I'll be careful, and I'll make sure no one else gets hurt." With a quick hug, she was gone; Cecelia heard her quick steps on the stairs.

It was all very well to say "I'll leave now," but she could hardly walk to the nearest spaceport carrying her clothes in a sack. Brun rummaged through her drawers, trying to think of twenty things at once. She needed her papers, her credit cubes, enough clothes. How long would it take by commercial carriers? What were their schedules? Why hadn't she kept the yacht here? That was easy—it had to go somewhere else and not be obvious about it. She didn't even know where it was.

"I'll drive you to the port." That was Driw, the groom who helped with the hippotherapy. She had ridden out with Driw, times she wasn't with Cecelia; she liked the tough, competent little woman.

"I don't even know when things leave," Brun said. Driw grinned at her.

"Here—the closest thing we have to a schedule." A battered folder, listing every ship that intended to arrive at the port for a year at a time. Which meant not often. "Are you going to travel in that?" *That* being the shorts and pullover Brun had put on as usual that morning. With a startled look at herself in the mirror, Brun dove into the shower, then into something that wouldn't instantly trigger suspicions. She hoped.

On the bumpy road out, she quit trying to read the schedule and instead tried to remember all the things Captain Serrano had told her. Cautions, things to think of—too many. Driw drove the way Cecelia had ridden in the horse trials: flat out, attacking every obstacle (curves, corners, other traffic) with utter concentration. When they reached the paved road that led to the port, Brun dared to say, "Are there any traffic laws?"

Driw chuckled. She had both legs extended, and one arm hanging out the window of the stable feed truck. "Yes . . . but not much enforcement. As long as I don't kill anybody—" She paused, to swerve around a tractor hauling three huge round bales of hay. "—we shouldn't have any problems. The port's on our side of the city."

Brun could just read the fine print of the schedule now; the truck only lurched occasionally. She had lost track of the date and had to ask Driw, who only knew it in local time: they had thirteen thirty-two day months, with names like Ock and Bir and Urg. For a moment her mind drifted to the possible language of the first settlers, then she dragged it back to the important stuff. If this was 14 Urg, then . . . damn. Nothing due for two days; she might as well have stayed at the stable.

"Except that there's other stuff sometimes," Driw said. "You know—casual, unscheduled stuff. It's faster, I hear. Kareem got to the Wherrin Trials in less than eight days, while the shortest scheduled passenger time was twelve. 'Course, it's kind of rough, he said, but I figured you were in a hurry."

Brun nodded. She could always find a room at the port, she supposed. She didn't remember much about it, actually, landing with Cecelia in the shuttle that one time. It had seemed small and bare, compared to the commercial ports she knew, but busier than the home port on Sirialis. She would just have to figure it out herself. That felt scary, but also exciting.

It was more scary and less exciting three hours later, after Driw had dropped her off at the shabby little shuttle terminal. The status board there showed nothing up at the Station but a bulk hauler headed for Romney—the wrong direction. Her schedule was out of date; the next scheduled passenger ship, also to Romney, wouldn't arrive for four days. Unscheduled was, of course, unscheduled. The shuttle . . . *the* shuttle, she realized, meant there was only one . . . was on its way up, and wouldn't be back until the next day. In the meantime, there was nowhere to sleep, because the people who ran the hostel were on vacation.

Brun put her gear in a locker and wandered outside. The shuttleport was also the regional airport; that terminal lay across a half mile or so of paved runways and scrubby grass. She could see aircraft moving over there, and wondered if any other terminal would do better. Probably not: there was only one Station aloft, and what mattered was its traffic. No wonder they hadn't been found yet.

"Hey—you!" She turned to find the shuttleport clerk leaning out the door. He waved, and she strode back in. "You're that friend of Cecelia de Marktos, aren't you?"

"Yes," Brun said, wondering slightly.

"Where you going?"

Should she tell him? She hadn't planned to tell anyone here, and buy her ticket on the Station. "Back home for a bit," she said. "Rockhouse."

"Mmm. Got money?"

"Some."

"If you're in a hurry—a friend of hers, y'know, is a friend of ours—might be there's a fellow could help you."

"Tell me," Brun said, trying not to sound too eager.

"Private shuttle," the clerk said. "Over at E-bay." He pointed at a wall, beyond which was presumably E-bay. "I'll tell him you're coming," the clerk said. Which assumed she would. But otherwise she'd just have to sleep on the floor waiting for the regular shuttle. Brun smiled her thanks, retrieved her duffle from the locker, and walked out again.

E-bay was neither bay nor hangar, but a large angled parking slot off the shuttle runway. On it was something that looked too small to be a shuttle. It looked, in fact, like one of the training planes Ronnie and George flew in the Royals. Its hatch was propped open, and someone stooped by it, tossing bundles inside. Brun walked closer, more uncertain the closer she got. The locals tended toward casual dress and behavior, but the young man in scuffed coveralls with shabby boots and a dirty scarf around his neck looked worse than Cecelia's grooms. He glanced up as she came nearer.

"You're that girl's been over at the lady's—you brought her, right?"

"Yes." No use denying what eager gossips had spread.

"She better?" He had bright black eyes, and rumpled black hair.

"Much better," Brun said.

"She sent you?" The eyes had intelligence, and some real concern for Cecelia. Brun wondered why.

"Uh . . . sort of, yes."

"I'm going up. Then on to Caskar, if that's any use." Brun wasn't sure, and she'd left the schedule in the truck. Her helplessness must have showed, because he sighed and explained. "Caskar—eight days—gets you a bigger port. Should be something going through each way within a few days. Here most everything's going to Romney."

"I noticed," she said, but couldn't help a doubtful look at the shuttle. Travel in *that* for eight days. He interpreted that look correctly.

"She's little, but she's stout. Get us there safely. If you don't mind it being a bit rough."

"No—no, that's fine. How much?"

"Well . . . say . . . eight hundred?" That was ridiculously low; she started to say something and he was already talking. "I hate to say that, but see, I can't afford the fuel myself. Not right now. I know it's for the lady, but . . ."

"No, that's fine," Brun said. "I thought it would be more. Look—why not a round thousand?" He wouldn't take more than the eight hundred, and had her insert the cube herself.

"That way you know I didn't cheat you. Now—they'll release the fuel . . ."

In the end she had to help him drag the fuel hoses over and start the pumps. The little ship held an astonishing load of fuel; Brun wondered if it would get off the ground once it started. Inside, she hardly had room to turn around.

"You fly?" the young man asked.

"A little." Her Rockhouse and Sirialis licenses would be no good here; each world regulated its own pilots since the differences in atmospheres, gravity, and weather made specific knowledge necessary.

"Just sit there, then, and keep an eye out." The copilot's seat, up in the needle nose of the shuttle, gave her a great view of the ground going past as they trundled along the runway. It seemed they had gone a mile or more, and she was wondering if they'd ever get airspeed, when the vibration of the gear died away and they were airborne. With a suddenness she did not expect from the long run, the young man tipped up the nose, did something to the controls, and the craft acted like a real shuttle, shoving her back in her seat for long minutes as the sky darkened from light blue to royal to midnight.

"No . . . traffic control?" Brun asked, aware that she had asked this question in another context only a few hours before.

"Nah . . . not enough traffic." The shuttle had minimal scans, she noticed. Minimal everything. "Do you really need to stop at the Station?" he went on. "I'd just as soon go straight on over—save us a few hours."

"Fine." Brun looked out the little port to see stars beginning to show as they reached the fringes of atmosphere. She could hardly believe she was riding in something like this, with someone whose name she didn't even know yet, to go into deep space and spend eight days . . . she was terrified. She was blissfully happy.

"I'm Brun, by the way." That seemed to have been right; he turned to grin at her and held out a calloused hand.

"I'm Cory. Stefan Orinder's son. The lady helped my dad out a lot when he arrived. Just let me set up the course, here, and get the autopilot locked in . . ."

Eight days later, Brun debarked at Caskar Station in the same outfit she'd started in. Cory's ship had no shower, although it did have a functioning toilet. Mostly functioning. She had had plenty of food (sandwiches, soup, tinned stew) and half as much sleep as she needed, because she stood watch with Cory. She knew all about Cory's family, three generations backwards and out to third cousins by marriage, and why his family would do anything for Lady Cecelia, including forget that she herself had ever existed and taken a ride on Cory's ship. She knew it would be an insult to tuck an extra two hundred credits into one of the cabinets, but she promised to tell Cecelia who had helped her.

Her first stop on Caskar Station was a public restroom, where she paid for a hot shower and sudsed herself thoroughly. She dumped her clothes in a washer and called up the status board on the restroom screen. Ah. A passenger ship headed for Greenland (which she knew from Cory's tutoring was more-or-less the way she wanted to go) would be in the next day. She called up its schedule. Twelve days to Greenland, six more to Okkerland, ten to Baskome. At Baskome she could get direct service to Rockhouse Major, no stops, on a major carrier. That looked good, except that the ship from here got there one day late, and the next Rockhouse connection wasn't for sixteen days. Damn.

Here she couldn't use Cecelia's influence . . . but—she looked at herself in the restroom mirror—maybe she could use her own. Or her wits. After all, even after these months, they might be looking for Lord Thornbuckle's daughter. She didn't want to lead them to Lady Cecelia. Not yet, not until she'd had another competency hearing, and regained her legal identity. Wits, then.

The status board showed five ships at this much busier Station. None were scheduled passenger ships, but Cory had explained that many freighters, scheduled and unscheduled, carried a few passengers. The big shipping firms had the better accommodations, but were pickier about who they took; the smaller firms—or owner-operator tramp freighters—would take anyone but an obvious criminal, especially if he or she were willing to do some of the less favored chores aboard.

Ten hours later, Brun was aboard the *Bucclos Success*, shoveling manure. Though most livestock was shipped as frozen embryos, some travelled "whole," in its mature state. Such a ship was known to crews as a "shit shoveler" for obvious reasons. The oversized environmental system had been built to handle the bulk and nitrogen load, but someone had to get the stuff from the animal pens into the system. A human and a shovel worked as efficiently as anything else, especially when valuable animals had to be coddled. Brun's stable experience got her the job—and a free berth.

A third of the cargo was horses, heavy drafters. Another third was hybrid cattlopes, their long straight horns cut short and tipped with bulky foam knobs for shipment. The rest were mixed medium and small: eight pens of dairy goats, seven of does and one of bucks; sixteen pens of sheep; fifty-eight cages of pedigreed rabbits, some of them carrying embryos of other species; sixty cages of small fowl and thirty cages of large. Brun had expected to be put to work with the horses, but as casual labor she was assigned wherever there was need. She learned to mix feed for goats and sheep, hose down the cattlope pens, change waterers and feeders for rabbits and birds. For sixteen days, she spent twelve-hour shifts caring for noisy demanding smelly critters, and eight hours of her shift off sound asleep in her surprisingly comfortable bunk.

"With all that methane production, we have plenty of onboard power generation," one of the others explained. "And we have to carry extra water anyway." Plenty of hot water for showers, an exercise room used mostly by bridge officers (everyone else got plenty of exercise caring for the animals), even a small swimming pool. And in sixteen days, Brun left the ship at Baskome Station. They would have taken her farther—she was hardworking and stayed out of quarrels and she wasn't afraid of the larger animals—but they weren't going where she wanted to go. She got actual pay—less than her private allowance for the same period, but the first money she had ever earned in her life. She turned in the credit strip the ship's paymaster handed her at the first bankstation she saw, and got back a cube representing her present balance in a newly opened Baskome Station account. It did not escape her notice that if she didn't have to spend more than that in her time here, she would not have to touch her own accounts, which might be under surveillance.

Baskome Station looked like real civilization. Besides the bankstation, which had both automated booths and a couple of windows with live tellers, the first concourse she came to had logos of all the standard travellers' organizations and credit services. She had her cards, of course, but if she used them . . . no. It would be a challenge, as well as prudent, to make it to Rockhouse without alerting any watchers. She wouldn't try to use a fake identity, but "Brunnhilde Charlotte Meager" without her usual wild clothes and credit cubes might be anyone. She didn't think anyone would be looking for her in the hold of a livestock hauler, for instance.

So she bypassed the expensive sectors of Baskome Station, the luxury hotel, the fine restaurants, and got a room at a hostel for transient crew—people who lived on such jobs as shoveling manure and running forklifts in warehouses. She ate at the little cafe two doors down, and washed her clothes in a smelly little laundry where the washing machines overflowed at least once a shift.

The transient crew hostel had its own version of the status board, with listings of crew openings and comments by those who had worked for different ships. Brun discovered she had a reputation which had preceded her (how, she couldn't figure out)—someone on the *Bucclos Success* had spread the word that she was a hard worker and trouble-free, so she had offers posted to her mail slot by the time she thought to check it. The rest of her reputation she didn't know about until later.

She picked what seemed like the fastest way to Rockhouse Major, a bulk hauler carrying fish protein meal. Two shifts out of Baskome Station, she discovered that "nice kid" was not the label to carry among people who thought "nice" meant "naive and helpless." And while she wasn't all that helpless, in proving it she broke the wrist and nose of the permanent crewman who tried to rape her. In a dispute between permanent and transient crew, transients are always wrong. Brun found herself facing an angry captain, while the first mate pored over her identification and other belongings.

"I suppose you can explain why someone named Brun Meager, if that is your real name, would have credit cubes and strips that belong to the Carvineau family? Brunnhilde Charlotte Meager-Carvineau, which according to my database is Lord Thornbuckle's youngest daughter. Or do you want to try to tell me you *are* Lord Thornbuckle's youngest daughter? The one who appears in society papers as Bubbles Carvineau . . . admittedly she is blonde, and so are you, but that hardly seems adequate . . . did you kill her for her papers, or is she wandering around someplace trying to convince a thickheaded planetary militia that she's not some farmer's daughter?"

None of the answers that came first seemed likely to help the situation. Brun wondered what Captain Serrano would have done if (as seemed most unlikely) she'd ever been in a similar fix. One thing, she wouldn't make any jokes, such as that her father *was* a farmer, among other things. A family saying she'd heard since childhood—*When in doubt, tell the truth*—came to mind. It might work.

"Those are my papers, sir," she said. *Respect costs nothing, and pays a high dividend,* she had heard from her grandmother. She hadn't believed it then, but she had never been at the mercy of someone as angry as the captain looked.

"So you *are* claiming to be this . . . uh . . . Lord Thornbuckle's daughter?"

"Yes, sir."

"Care to explain why you're traveling on a freighter carrying fishmeal and working your passage when you could buy the whole damn freighter, according to your credit rating?" Blast. If they'd done a credit check, then anyone watching might pick up where she was. Nothing to do about it now; she had more urgent problems. The first mate's expression was as forbidding as the captain's, and she'd already heard about his propensities from the relief cook.

The truth, but not the whole truth. "Sir, I . . . I wanted to prove I wasn't just a fluffhead like they said."

A snort, not amused. "The way you broke Slim's wrist—" The nose, it seemed, wasn't worth mentioning— "I wouldn't think anyone would call you a fluffhead. Hothead, maybe. How'd you get a reputation as trouble-free on the *Winter*? I thought Jos Haskins was a better judge of character than that."

Brun felt her ears heating up. "Nobody on that ship tried to drag me into a bunk and rape me."

"What's so bad about Slim? Does he have bad breath, or what?" That was the mate; the captain quelled him with a look.

"The point is, I have trouble believing Lord Thornbuckle would let his daughter go off working transient crew jobs halfway across Familias space. Does he know where you are?"

"Well . . . no, sir." He would have found out from the yacht's crew where she had been, with Lady Cecelia; he had expected her to stay there. She suspected he wouldn't be entirely pleased to know where she was now . . . and as for her mother . . .

"My mother would have a cat," she said, thinking aloud. This time the captain's snort was amusement. She eyed him, wondering if she could take advantage of that momentary lapse in his anger. Probably not.

"Tell you what," the captain said. "We can't afford legal trouble, of any type. I don't really care who you are, but if you're who these papers say, you've no business pretending to be a commoner, and if you're not—" He looked down his nose to read the full thing, "—Brunnhilde Charlotte Meager-Carvineau, then her family needs to know someone else is using her papers. This is something for law enforcement to sort out. I'm confiscating your ID and your credit cubes until we arrive at Rockhouse; I'll turn them over to the Station militia. Do you happen to know the balances of the accounts?"

She hadn't looked at them in some time. "Not really, sir. Why?" That admission, she saw, shook his conviction that she was an imposter.

"Because you and I and my mate are going to certify the balances as of this date, so you can be sure—or the real Brunnhilde Charlotte's family can be sure—that I haven't run off with some of it. And if you're the real Brunnhilde Charlotte, I will allow you to send a message to your family, if you wish. Charged as an advance on your salary."

Did she wish? She tried to think what the date would be on Rockhouse—the local date, not Universal. Her father might be there for the biennial Council meeting—Uncle Serval would be, anyway—and even Buttons might be there. But what could she say? Could she phrase a warning so they would understand it, and not get themselves into worse danger? And she really did not want the Crown Minister or his sister Lorenza to know she was on her way.

She came down finally on the side of caution—both kinds. Caution with the captain (perhaps he'd see that an imposter would hardly send a message to a home that wasn't hers) and with her family (so they couldn't reveal information they didn't have).

"I'd like to send a message, but I don't want to tell them when I'm arriving. As you said, my parents would not approve of my . . . er . . . choice of conveyance."

"I'm not prepared to lie for you, young woman."

"No, sir. Could you send: 'You were right; I'm on my way home,' and then 'Love, Brun'?"

"Tell me one thing—why do the society papers say your name is Carvineau when your papers say it's Meager?"

"My mother's name is Meager; all the children use the maternal last name on identification until we're twenty-five. It's supposed to be safer."

"Ah. Well, Ms. Meager, consider yourself warned against any further brawling; you are confined to quarters except when on duty in the galley—I'm taking you off general duty and making you the cook's assistant—and as I said, your identification and other materials will be turned over to Station militia when we reach Rockhouse. Do you have anything further to say?"

"No, sir."

"Right then. Get to work."

She had plenty of time locked in her tiny cubicle with its blank walls and hard bunk to realize how close she had come to complete disaster. And how close it still was . . . suppose the mate decided to come after her, too? He didn't, but she slept badly the rest of the trip.

✧ Chapter Sixteen

Brun discovered that Rockhouse Major turned a different face to transient crew suspected of impersonating rich girls. Her captain had contacted Station militia, and she found herself and her papers in a dingy, cluttered office, watched by a bored but obviously capable young person of doubtful gender with a sidearm.

"If I could just make a call," she kept saying. No one answered. People in uniform wandered in and out; voices spoke at a distance that blurred the words but not the emotion: boredom, hostility, defiance, fear.

Finally, a tired-eyed older man appeared, looked at her, shook his head, and said "Come on." He led her to a proper ID booth, where in only a few minutes her retinal scan, fingerprints, and other data confirmed her papers. He shook his head again. "You really *are* Lord Thornbuckle's daughter. Would you mind explaining what you were doing hiring on as transient crew?"

"It was an adventure," Brun said. She realized now just how silly that sounded, and she didn't seem able to find the insouciant tone she had cultivated in years past. He just stared at her, a tired man who clearly wished spoiled rich kids wouldn't waste his time.

"Do you need anything?" he asked finally.

"No . . . if I can have my things."

"Yes—just sign here." Her credit cubes and strips, itemized, lay on the sheet he pointed to. She started to sign and he pointed, making it clear he wanted no mistakes. She checked then, and found nothing missing. Her battered little duffle, with its few changes of clothes, seemed full enough, and if it wasn't she could buy replacements. "The captain said if you were legal, he'd deposit your pay, less a fine for brawling. What'd you do, if you don't mind my asking?"

Brun shrugged. "Another crewman tried to jump me; I broke his nose and wrist. Stupid—I should've seen it coming."

"I don't know what it is you kids are looking for," the man said, shaking his head yet again. "You've got everything . . . why look for trouble?"

Brun smiled at him. "I'm sorry—I was stupid, and I'm going home to admit it—is that all right?"

This time he really looked at her, and his eyes warmed. "I'm glad you weren't hurt," he said. "We see enough kids getting hurt."

Out in the concourse, she was still a scruffy transient spacer to look at, dirty and shabby, with an ordinary scuffed duffle over her shoulder. She ambled along, relaxing a bit in this familiar territory. First she would get something to eat, then a shower—no, a shower first, then call Ronnie—no, call the estate downside and get someone to send the shuttle up—she slowed, as she came to a bank of public communications booths. She put her duffle on the shelf of an empty booth and started to close the door. Someone leaned across from another, a big bulky man who looked both frustrated and dangerous.

"Hey—you just came out of that militia station, didn't you?"

"Yeah." No sense arguing, if she'd been seen.

"Seen a rich-bitch youngster in there, the kind that throws their weight around?"

Her belly tightened. "No," she said shortly. "All I saw was this fat cop tryin' to make out I was somebody else."

"Dammit." His strong fingers tapped the partition. "I'm supposed to find this girl—loudmouth blonde, they said, real stylish, some mucky-muck lord's daughter. Sure you haven't seen her?"

"Not me. Is that the only militia station?"

"No, worse luck. Where you in from?" His eyes were intent, measuring. "You permcrew or transient?"

"Transient now." Brun tried for a sullen tone. She held up her well-calloused hand. "Signed onto a shit shoveler as cook's assistant, and they had me down in the stalls three shifts out of four. I didn't leave home to be some cow's personal assistant."

His eyes lost interest after a long look at her hand. "Yeah, well, I guess you didn't meet any daughters of the aristocracy shoveling manure." He moved away, toward the militia station entrance. Brun could not move. She had to move. If he went in, if he talked to that man, he would know . . .

She picked up the headpiece, put it back as if uncertain, and moved on down the concourse. How could someone like that be looking for her already? Had something happened? She lengthened her stride, almost ran into someone pausing to look in a display window, and told herself not to spook. The captain had queried ahead about her . . . anyone who watched the militia regularly might have overheard. As long as she got off Rockhouse Major before that dangerous man could find her, she should be safe.

She took a slideway, then a tram, putting a sector and two levels between her and the militia office before she dared stop at another combooth cluster. This was higher-income territory, though her scruffy clothes weren't that unusual. No used-clothing stores here, but also none of the high-priced places that expected you to know their names. Display windows showed the latest style; she'd been gone long enough for them to change. Thigh boots? Laced socks? Tunics were longer, dresses shorter, and someone had decided to ignore the waistline again. They'd done that when she was twelve, too—but then the top colors had been muted moss greens and browns. Now the fashion seemed to be icy pastels. She stared at a long tunic patterned with zigzags of pale pink on pale green over pink slacks as she waited for her connection to go through. She had decided to start by warning Ronnie.

"Yes?" It sounded like Ronnie's voice, but a very cautious

Ronnie. Brun hoped it was; Ronnie she might influence, but anyone else in his family would lecture first and listen afterwards, if then.

"Ronnie?"

"Yes, who is this?"

"It's me. Brun . . . Bubbles . . . you know." Then, as she heard him take a deep breath that would no doubt end in a loud outcry, she went on quickly. "Don't say my name! Don't! I'm up at Rockhouse Major and you're in great danger and so is your family. Don't say anything—pretend I'm someone else. George, maybe."

"I was expecting a call from him—er—from Gerry, that is. I don't really have time to chat right now . . ." He must have done something to the privacy shield; behind him now she could hear high voices chattering, glasses clinking. What was local time down there? She'd completely forgotten to check. "Listen, George," he went on. "Why don't you call me back later?"

"Shield again," Brun said. When the background sound disappeared again, she continued. "Ronnie, you must listen. It's critical—I'm being followed. Your aunt has remembered who did it to her."

"Then she's—" With an abrupt change of voice, "—she's not *pregnant!* I don't believe it. And if she is, it's certainly not *mine*. Who does she think she is?"

Brun grinned. Ronnie had an unexpected gift for this. "Lorenza. You know, the fluffy one with the soft voice, with the important brother . . ."

"Oh, I say. Surely not—harmless as a—and besides, she's here."

"Now?" Brun broke off, appalled at the squeak in her voice. More quietly, she went on. "Ronnie, believe me. Poison. Don't take anything she offers—get out of there, now. Get George—he's in danger, too. I'll explain when I get down—" Though how she was going to do that without using her ID and thus triggering pursuit, she didn't know.

"Well, of course we'll come," Ronnie said brightly, as if agreeing to a party invitation. "Short notice no bother. Anything for the Royals, what?"

"Don't overdo it," Brun said. "Assuming she's listening."

"Read my lips," Ronnie said, in the same bright tone. "It's no problem. We'll be there. Pick a number."

That old game. Now, what were the shuttleslot codes for this Station? The booth had local datanet access; she punched up the information she needed.

"E-19 or 21."

"Be there soonest."

Brun put down the headset. Soonest gave no real idea of how long it would take Ronnie to extricate himself from his house, find George, get to the family shuttle, file flight plans, and get here. Right that moment she wanted him here instantly, someone she knew, someone she could trust. She was getting very, very tired of adventure.

Ronnie closed the satellite circuits carefully and clicked off the privacy shield. It wouldn't have been hard for someone to tap into that unscrambled call, if they'd had a mind to. Had anyone? He'd better assume the worst.

"Ronnie, dear, who was that?" His mother, in her long lace gown, stood at the door of a room full of older women, all similarly dressed. They were talking and eating all at once, stocking up for an evening at the theater.

"Fellow at the Regiment," he said. "Sorry—seems something has come up."

"Oh, no! I was counting on you, dear. Why can't they get George or someone else?"

"I'm supposed to pick George up on the way, actually. Sorry, Mother, it's rather urgent." Curiosity lit her eyes.

"What, dear?"

"Now Mother, you know I'm not supposed to talk about Regimental business." Her face clouded; she opened her mouth. He gave her the old smile, the one that always melted her. "But I will tell you, because I know you won't gossip, that some fellow's gotten in a bit of trouble about this girl—claims she's pregnant, claims she can prove whose . . . you know."

"Ah." Her face cleared. "But you have the implant—and the law doesn't—"

"There's law, and there's family," Ronnie said. "All of us who . . . er . . . knew her, as it were, must confer with the Regimental legal staff. Terribly confidential; you won't tell any of your old cats, will you?"

"It wasn't you!? You and Raffa . . . ?"

"Nothing to do with me and Raffa. A wild party a while back; I know I didn't reverse my implant, or even know the girl, but there could be a claim if I don't go in and have it checked out. And they've got the gene militia or whatever they are standing by. Oh—remember I told you George and a few of us were taking the shuttle up after the opera? I think we'll just go on after this—it's too much trouble to stop back by—" He was appalled at his own invention; the story seemed to be sprouting branches and luxuriant foliage in all directions. He could almost see the young woman he had supposedly partied with, although her motivations wavered: was she trying to claw her way up the social ladder from a not-quite-important family, or was she a muckraking journalist out to expose the foibles of the rich and notorious? She had a sister in entertainment; she had worn purple that night that had never happened; she had a fake diamond collar . . .

"Be careful, Ronnie—"

"Of course, Mother." In ways she would never know, he intended to be very careful. He was already in evening clothes, and he didn't have time to change. As he went toward the door, he heard Lorenza calling to his mother, and shivered in spite of himself. How could he leave her there, in peril? But Brun's was worse, he told himself.

George, dressing for the same evening's entertainment— he had also been snagged as an acceptable young male escort for the party of mothers and aunts attending the theater—was glad enough to hear he wouldn't be seeing a revival of Darwinian grand opera.

"But Lorenza!" he said, buttoning the soft shirt he had grabbed to replace the dress shirt he hadn't fastened yet. "Are you sure?"

"Brun is sure that my aunt is sure. That's enough for me, at least until we talk more to Brun. And she's being hunted, she says."

"Lorenza. Dad needs to know this. He's at the office—"

"Call from the shuttle—we've got to go. I told Mother an incredible lie about a pregnant girl accusing half the Regiment, and all of us having to have genetic scans, and if she calls—even though I told her it was all being kept quiet—"

"The colonel will have cats, and then have us for breakfast. Right. I'm ready." He looked at Ronnie. "But you—you'll stick out like anything, up there." He dug into his closet and bundled up another shirt and pair of casual slacks. "We'll take these along—you can change on the shuttle while I call."

Ronnie reflected that George was a good deal less odious lately. Of course he had been through that mess on Sirialis, and being shot in the gut was, according to the redoubtable Captain Serrano, a specific for youthful idiocy, but still. George had been odious for years; he had not so much turned over a new leaf as uprooted an entire forest.

On the shuttle trip to Rockhouse Major, Ronnie told George all he knew or suspected and had kept from him before. "Brun said if anyone else knew my aunt was conscious inside, her life would be in danger. I couldn't talk to anyone . . . I thought it was because she'd gone to see the king about Gerel—"

"About the prince? Why? Just because he showed up on Sirialis?"

"No . . . because on the trip home I noticed something." Even now he was reluctant to tell George—but if the worst happened, someone had to know. And he had begun to think George was involved, had been from the beginning. "Do you remember that term when you nearly flunked all your subjects?"

George grimaced. "Not as clearly as I should, but I've heard about it often enough. My father insists it proves the need of diligent application—that's his term—that even the brightest boy can't skate by forever on native brilliance. The masters— well, you remember. As far as they were concerned I was a typically lazy, careless, spoiled young brat. I thought I was working harder than I ever had, but nothing came of it—I suppose they were right, and I was fooling myself thinking I was working. Daydreaming, maybe."

"I think you were right, George, and they didn't recognize it. At thirteen, they expect boys to slack off, daydream, hang around making mischief with others. So when your grades dropped, that's what they said. But I think it was something else."

"What, then? Hormones?"

"No—at least not your native hormones . . . George, this is *very* secret."

"Right. I nearly flunk all my courses and it's on my permanent records, and it's now a great secret. Nobody knows except you and every other boy I was at school with, all the masters, my family—" George's talent for being odious had not, Ronnie realized, vanished; it had merely been in hiding.

"Shut up, George," he said cheerfully. He actually felt better knowing George was not abandoning a lifelong habit. "I think someone made you stupid for a while. On purpose."

"Made me stupid! Why?" Then that handsome face changed, became more like his father's. "Oh . . . and you said something about the prince . . . and he changed schools . . ."

"And got a reputation for silly-ass idiocy. Like that quarrel with me—" Ronnie reflected that his own end of that quarrel didn't argue for any great intelligence either, and flushed, but George didn't take that up.

"The prince is stupid. The prince is—he can't be, Ron, someone would've noticed. Someone would have told the king."

"Aunt Cecelia did just that, after we got back. On her usual high horse about it, too."

"And *then* she has that stroke you say wasn't a real stroke. Like my term of being stupid wasn't real stupidity. Like the prince—" George stopped and looked at Ronnie with dawning comprehension.

"Isn't really stupid. Not on his own."

"But mine went away. Why didn't the prince's?" Then he answered his own question. "Because someone wanted him to stay that way. And it had to be—" They stared at each other and said in unison, "The king."

"Oh . . . dear." Ronnie remembered that he had planned to change and began pulling the studs from his dress shirt. "Oh . . . my. We are in trouble."

George, with nothing to occupy his mind but the problem at hand, leaned back in his seat. "If your aunt claims Lorenza poisoned her, and if that's why Lorenza poisoned her, then Lorenza may have done it to the prince."

Ronnie paused, his shirt half-undone. "Remember that scandal a few years ago about the Graham-Scolaris?"

"Of course. Dad defended the old man."

"What if . . . what if Lorenza supplies all sorts of useful poisons—chemicals—not just to the Crown but to others?"

"What, a medieval poisoner in our midst? That's awfully dramatic, Ronnie."

"So is a stupid prince kept that way for years. So was my aunt's collapse."

"Point taken." George frowned at him, and Ronnie remembered he hadn't finished changing. He tore off the dress shirt and shrugged into George's casual one. A bit tight across the shoulders, but not enough to matter. He buttoned it slowly, still thinking.

"Something else I just thought of . . . remember when Gerel's older brothers died? That assassination, and then the duel?"

"Yes—do you think they were stupid, too?"

"No—I remember, though, that was when we were what? Twelve, thirteen, along in there. Before your bad term, anyway. And Jared was almost thirty; there was talk of having the Grand Council Familias agree to his succession in advance."

Now George frowned. "I don't—yes, just a minute. I think they actually did, and then rescinded it after he died, so it wouldn't interfere with Nadrel's or Gerel's succession later."

"I remember Gerel getting lots of visits from his brothers right before that. Picnics and so on. Remember? He'd wanted to ask us along, and his brothers said no, and he was annoyed with them. Then afterwards, he was all excited about something he wouldn't tell us . . ."

"I don't remember any of that." George tossed Ronnie a tie. "Here—put on this anachronism. That shirt needs a reason to look tight across the shoulders."

"But—" Ronnie stretched his neck, and worked the tie into position. "But I remember—and you and he were thick as anything for a week or so—you were grinning all over your face, and wouldn't tell me—"

"Was that the time you tried to get it out of me by twisting my arm?"

"No—we already knew that wouldn't work. No, we tried bribery—an entire box of chocolate. You scarfed the lot and refused to divulge. You don't remember?"

"No . . . only it was next term I had trouble. You don't suppose someone really did drug me, and it took the memory, too?"

"I know Gerel avoided you that term—you'd gotten involved with those Hampton Reef boys."

George shuddered. "I do remember them. Nasty beasts, and then the next year I couldn't scrape them away. Thank heavens they transferred at midterm."

The shuttle intercom chimed, and the pilot spoke. "We're in the Rockhouse Major approach now, gentlemen. If you'd take your seats, please, and prepare for docking . . ."

❖   ❖   ❖

Brun wanted a shower, food, and sleep, in that order, but ahead of everything else in her personal queue was safety. She changed levels and sectors again, finally choosing a spacers' hostel down the row from the one Heris had used before she left. She didn't dare use that one, in case someone was watching it, or the clerk recognized her—unlikely as that seemed. Cleanliness felt wonderful—better than food, and she'd just as soon sleep, she decided, stretching out on the comfortable bunk. Ronnie couldn't possibly get here for several hours, probably six or seven. She could sleep safely at least two of them.

The buzzing timer woke her from the kind of vaguely unpleasant dream that isn't a nightmare but leaves a dull, foreboding feeling behind the eyes. Another shower cleared most of it from her head. Now she was really hungry. She checked the time. If he really had left home right away, if he had gone straight to the family's shuttle, and if they'd gotten priority clearance, Ronnie might be arriving within the hour. She would head for the shuttle deck and get something to eat there.

The timer informed her it was partway into second shift—aftermain, some called it. Both names were on the timer's dial. That meant the Station equivalent of nightlife, including the nightcrawlers. Brun dug through her duffle for possible outfits that wouldn't be too visible and wouldn't say the wrong things. She didn't want to be transient crew anymore, and she certainly didn't want to stick out as Lord Thornbuckle's daughter out being adventurous. She just hadn't brought the right clothes . . . but she had brought enough makeup.

Down the way, she found a clothing store for people with no imagination. Not the pastels she'd seen before, but good old boring classic beiges and browns and grays and dull blues. Clerks' clothes, maybe. Brun found that even so she was drawn to the most striking outfits in the shop; she kept picking up accessories that screamed "Look at me!" No. Buy what she automatically disdained. The blue slacks, the beige top, the brown belt—not the braided one, not the one with sequins, just plain brown. Sensible brown shoes. In the mirror she looked like a low-income copy of her mother . . . if you were born with those bones, plain looked classic. What could look just plain . . . plain? A different blouse, blue and rose flowers scattered loosely on beige, and a bit too tight. Beige shoes with little gold doodads on them. That helped; they made her feet hurt, so she walked differently. She could do the rest with makeup.

When she reached the shuttle deck, the status boards showed three private shuttles on approach, identified only by registration number. Great. She had never known the registration number of Ronnie's family's shuttle. Then one of the other numbers sank in. That was *her* family's shuttle, the same one she'd taken Cecelia up in. Had Ronnie been crazy enough to borrow that one? The watchers would be looking for it.

Brun ducked quickly into one of the fast-food outlets that opened onto the concourse. She ordered the first thing she saw, and took it to a windowseat. Between bites of something greasy and meaty coated with something doughy, she scanned the area for the man who had spoken to her before. Of course he wouldn't have been alone—and she had no idea what other watchers might look like. The food helped; her stomach gurgled its contentment, and she felt her courage returning. She was clean, and fed, and didn't look anything like her earlier self—either of them.

"Sorry we're having to wait a bit," the shuttle pilot said. "There's quite a crowd of arrivals just now."

"Private shuttles?" Ronnie asked.

"Yes—Lord Thornbuckle's is just ahead of us."

George and Ronnie stared at each other. "Why would she call me, if she was going to call the family shuttle?" Ronnie asked. "Or did I misunderstand—we were trying to talk in a sort of instant code—"

"I suppose it could be another family member, though that's

quite a coincidence. And they usually bring the family yacht in over at Minor, to avoid the traffic."

"The yacht's not operational," Ronnie said. "Don't you remember? Some kind of harebrained terrorist attack or something."

"So it could be one of the others, come by commercial passenger service." George peered out the tiny window. Ronnie, looking past his head, could make nothing of the strings of lights. Finally—not that long by the clock on the forward bulkhead—he felt the slight bump of docking. When the status lights turned green, he led George out the access tube to the reception lounge. Across from the access tube was the door into the public corridor that led to the concourse. A status screen above it showed that Lord Thornbuckle's shuttle was docked to their right.

Ronnie headed that way, receiving a polite nod from the man at the door to that lounge. He didn't see Brun anywhere.

Brun saw Ronnie and her brother at the same moment. Buttons, looking happy and relaxed, with his fiancée Sarah on his arm, strolled along the concourse from the commercial gates toward the entrance to the private shuttle bays. Ronnie was just coming out, looking around.

Brun had just had time to notice Sarah's outfit—flowing rose silk, a corsage of fresh white roses—when Sarah staggered, and the corsage blew apart, leaving a single red rose. Buttons threw himself on top of her; the tough-looking man who had spoken to Brun rushed at them, weapon in hand. People in the concourse screamed; some dove for the floor. Brun pushed away from the table and tried to get to her brother, but the people in the doorway were backing away. She pushed and shoved, using elbows and sharp kicks to move them.

Over their heads, she could see Ronnie turn toward the trouble, and then make a flying tackle on the armed man. George erupted from the corridor behind him; the two of them were on the attacker by the time Brun got free of the tangle and staggered across the concourse, cursing her new shoes. In the distance, whistles blew; she hoped someone had had the sense to call Station militia. And medical help.

"Help me!" Buttons was saying. "She's bleeding—!" Brun fell on her knees beside him and unzipped her duffle, pulling out her last clean shirt.

"Here," she said, stuffing it in the wound. The months she'd spent with therapists and doctors gave her more knowledge than she wanted of what lay behind the blood. But Sarah had a pulse, and was breathing. Buttons looked at her and his eyes widened.

"What are *you* doing here?"

"Saving Sarah," Brun said. Sarah opened her eyes.

"That really hurts," she said, and closed them again. Typical of Sarah, Brun thought. No wasted words, no unnecessary fuss.

"It's my fault," Brun said to Buttons. "He thought I was Sarah—I mean, the other way around."

"Who?" But he had already turned toward the continuing tussle between Ronnie and George and the attacker, who had acquired allies from points unknown. Just as it looked like spreading into a wholesale brawl, the militia arrived.

The same tired-eyed man Brun had met before took their statements after Sarah had been taken to the Station clinic. His gaze sharpened when he recognized Brun and the blood on her clothes.

"Did you expect to meet your sister here?" he asked Buttons. "Was that your purpose?"

"No—Sarah and I had legal business to transact before our wedding. Brun's been out of touch quite a while; I frankly didn't know where she was."

"Ah. And you . . . gentlemen . . ." Ronnie and George were attempting to look innocent and noble through their bruises. "You . . . were coming up to meet this young gentleman, perhaps?"

"No . . . actually . . ." Ronnie's eyes slid toward Brun's. She nodded. "We had come up to meet Brun. She called me."

"I see. You are also . . ." He was clearly groping for the word. Brun spoke up.

"We aren't engaged, but we've been friends a long time. I didn't want to call our people until I'd had a chance to clean up and change—"

"Yes," drawled Buttons, looking her up and down. She recognized that tone; he was going to back her, but have his own fun. "I can see why. Mother would have had a fit. Where have you been, anyway?"

"Working as transient crew," Brun said, holding up her calloused hand for him to see. "I was hoping to get my hair done and so on before she knew I was anywhere around. Besides, there was a little trouble when I arrived."

"Do you have any idea why someone shot your fiancée?" The militia officer interrupted.

"No," Buttons said. Brun wondered a moment about that flat negative, but she didn't challenge him. Instead, she answered.

"I do. I think he meant to shoot me, and didn't have a good description." The man's eyebrows went up. Brun explained. "A man stopped me after I left the militia station earlier and asked if I'd seen a rich young woman in there. He knew my name, and a rough description, but the way I was dressed then, he didn't recognize me. It scared me; it's one reason I called Ronnie."

"Well, then, miss, do you know why someone might want to shoot you?"

"No—but it's clear someone did, and since Sarah and I are both blonde, and about the same height, he probably figured someone heading for our shuttle, with my brother, was the right person."

"I see. If you'll thumbsign this report, then—" With a sideways glance at Buttons, Brun pressed her thumb to the pad, and the man nodded. "That's it for now—I presume you'll be available downside if we need you?"

"Yes, of course."

"I'm staying up here," Buttons said. "Until Sarah's released. I don't know how long it will take—if they'll do the regen here, or ship her down. Brun, since Ronnie's here with their shuttle, could you ride with him?"

"Of course." Something in his voice suggested he needed to talk with her alone. "Do you mind if we come with you to the clinic?"

"No . . . that's fine . . ." He stood, and looked about uncertainly. The militia had dispersed the crowd and the four of them stood alone. Then he looked down at Brun. "The thing is, I'm still worried about you. Did you know Lady Cecelia had filed for reinstatement of competency?"

"What? I thought she'd wait until—"

"She didn't wait; it was on the nets four days ago. There's been an uproar you wouldn't believe in the press and among the Families. Dad's afraid she's in danger—and you, of course. We didn't put a query on your ID because we didn't want to call attention to it, so we haven't known where you were—"

"But somebody did," Brun said. "Or at least they were watching for any word of me."

"Yes. Dad's convinced now that you were right—he's had his doubts—but that means whoever did it will be moving. You and Ronnie are both prime targets. Frankly I think you'd better get in that shuttle and go—and then stay on the estate. Don't go into town; we don't know just how hard whoever it is will come after you."

"But you and Sarah?" Should she tell him about Lorenza now? Or would it make it more dangerous for him? She was too tired to think.

"We should be safe now that they know she's not you."

"Buttons, there's something we need to tell you—" Ronnie had lowered his voice. "It's really important. George and I think we know—"

"Not here. Take Brun, get down to our place, and *stay there*. I'll be along as soon as Sarah can travel. They'll probably send her down for regen treatment when she's stabilized. Dad's on his way, too."

Buttons turned away with a little wave; Brun suddenly felt the weight of fear and exhaustion settle back on her shoulders. Her feet hurt.

"He's right," she said. "Let's go home."

✧ Chapter Seventeen

The grounds of the Institute of Neuroscience had lush green lawns and flowering shrubs. A few low domes protruded through the greenery, and a stubby blocklike building rose from a grove of trees in the distance. Heris rode a silent electric car hardly big enough for her and the driver from the public transit stop to the entrance, and wondered aloud at the spaciousness.

"A bomb attack thirty years ago," the driver said, over his shoulder. "The Benignity, of course. They thought they were getting a manufacturing complex . . . we rebuilt underground, even though that's no real protection against modern munitions. But it was all ugly and crowded before; this way we have something pretty to look at."

At the front desk, Heris handed over her official documents, with the Royal Seal of the Familias Regnant. She had noticed three nondescript men in the waiting room . . . Geralds all, scattered among the other patients.

"Ah—are you the patient, Captain?"

"No. But I would prefer not to explain here."

"Of course. Perhaps you and . . . is the patient here?" The clerk managed, heroically Heris thought, not to peer into the waiting room.

"Yes."

"Then perhaps you and the patient would come this way." Heris gave the hand signal the Geralds had taught her, and one by one they ambled up to the desk, leaned over, and took the colored card the clerk held up. Her eyes widened but she said nothing.

❖   ❖   ❖

Doctors Koshinsky and Velun. Male and female, short and tall, thick and thin, dark and fair. Koshinsky's dark beard was only slightly darker than his skin, and he came up to Velun's elegant silk-clad shoulder. Heris wondered what they thought of her and the clones. The clones had shed their disguises, and now wore identical coveralls; they looked like a frieze of tall blond princes, to which she was a short dark punctuation. Or, in the metaphor of music (she still thought it was strange to name a planet Music), "da-da-da-dum."

"Can you describe the problem any more precisely, Captain?" asked Dr. Velun. Height, blonde hair, a glacial beauty . . . she could be mother or aunt to those princes.

"I thought that was in the king's letter."

"Unfortunately not. What it says is that he was given a demonstration of a drug to inhibit higher cognitive processes, and its reversibility, in a person of his son's age. Then that same drug—he thinks—was administered to his son, causing a relative inability to learn and perform cognitive tasks at the level his innate abilities warranted—" She broke off and gave Heris a hostile look. "Quite frankly, Captain Serrano, we would regard such a use of any method of lowering intelligence to be quite unethical. In our culture, intelligence is respected."

"If I understand correctly," Heris said, "the king was given a choice of having his son partially and temporarily incapacitated or assassinated; his older sons had both died, one by assassination and one in . . . er . . . dubious circumstances. It was not an easy choice."

"Even so," Dr. Velun said. "And now, I understand, he wants to see if the effect can be reversed by someone other than the . . . mmm . . . perpetrator?"

"That's right. I should also mention that the use of clone doubles is not only unethical but illegal in our society."

"Not here," Dr. Koshinsky said. "We grow clones all the time; we've nothing against clones. They have full legal identity."

"The problem is, these clones have been trained to be the prince's doubles. Now each of them claims he is not the prince, that the prince is somewhere else. I was twice informed that the person I was taking aboard was the prince, only . . ." Heris nodded at the three. "Only I have no way of telling the difference. And I think it likely that they are somehow programmed or conditioned not to reveal the prince's identity."

"Were the clones also treated to inhibit their intelligence?"

"I don't know. I wasn't even told there were clones."

"Hmm. Then, the first step is to examine these young men—with their permission of course—"

"Certainly," said the three princes, or clones, or Geralds. And, still in unison, "You won't be able to distinguish us from one another." Heris had her doubts. Anyone who could scan weapons an R.S.S. ship would miss might well have new and better ways to tell a prime from its clone.

Two days later, Dr. Velun called Heris in for another conference. She had a stack of data cubes and a cube player already set up.

"Let me tell you what we've found out so far . . . do you have a medical background, by any chance?"

"No, sorry."

"Well—I'll do my best. Do ask questions when they occur, will you? Now. We know that the prince is a Registered Embryo. Now in the Familias Regnant, that means an embryo guaranteed to carry the genetic markers of the certified biological parents. All known flaws eliminated, and enhancements included—"

"Enhancements?"

The doctor was glad to explain. "Legally, all the genes—whole genes—must come from either the certified mother or the certified father. Given a sufficiency of sperm and ova, from almost anyone, it's possible to select desirable—even outstanding—gene fragments. Humans are superbly heterozygous; it's only a question of knowing which sequences correlate with which desired trait. But there are practical limits on the quantity of genetic material . . . time constraints, for instance. By the time you've located the single recessive gene you want, in one of the fifty million sperm you examined, the ovum may be overripe. If it's not to be a gamble, much like the original, you use enhancements."

"And those are?"

"Gene *fragments*, not whole genes, which means they can be substituted—with the usual techniques—" Heris had no idea what the usual techniques were and didn't really care. "For instance, intelligence. Everyone has known since Old Earth times that intelligence is not a single entity, a single faculty. There are modules, specialized clumps of neurons which preferentially work with certain inputs." That made Heris think of the yacht's scanning computers—this one for detecting one kind of input and interpreting it, and that one for another. She said that and Dr. Velun looked pained. "Not really. Or rather, in a way, but not completely. The human brain has developmental preferences, but it's also remarkably plastic: it responds to experience, so that the more experience in a cognitive domain, the more likely that function is to work well. But more important, to this patient, is what happens when things go wrong."

Heris nodded. She found it hard to concentrate, even though she needed to be able to explain to the king later. What had gone wrong was the prince got stupid: simple, and—if not reparable—the end of the king's hopes. The doctor talked on and on, and Heris felt herself falling more and more behind. What was a dedicated neuron? What did Dr. Velun mean by saying that some of them were supposed to die off?

Dr. Velun began to talk about drugs that might have caused the prince's problem. "One thing that would work is a protein that blocks the production of a given neurotransmitter by tying up the RNA on which the protein would be constructed—I presume you do know something about biochemistry—?"

She must have recognized Heris's glazed incomprehension

at last. "Sorry," Heris said. "My specialty lies elsewhere. I know what DNA is—" Sort of, she thought to herself. A spiral molecule of genetic material, that was about it. "But the function of different kinds of RNA—that's beyond me."

Dr. Velun looked pained, started with a chemical description, stopped short, glared at her, and finally shrugged. "You won't get it, not in the time we have."

Perversely, Heris was now determined to understand. "Look—if you'll give me time to read something—even a child's version—I'm sure I can learn. It's just that it's so far from my own background—"

Velun's face contracted in a scowl. "Right. Warfare. I suppose you know how to kill people."

This sort of hostility was familiar; Heris smiled at her. "Well, yes, but so do you. Any medical researcher knows as many lethal tricks as I do. No, my expertise is in the equipment and the personnel—to take just one system, knowing how the environmental system aboard each class of ship works, where the pipes are, how many technicians are needed to service it, and what to look for to be sure it's working correctly. I must know the interactions of all shipboard systems, so that if the electrical system goes down for any reason, I can keep the ship's crew alive without the electrically powered pumps and blowers in the environmental system."

"Engineering," the doctor muttered.

Heris let her smile widen. "Yes, it is. So is clinical medicine, to my view: know the systems, recognize when something's wrong, and know what to do about it."

That coaxed a tiny smile. "Well . . . I suppose. We like to think of ourselves as researchers, too."

"I'm sure you are. So are some of us—spacefleet officers, I mean. A friend of mine solved a century-old problem in oxygen exchange systems. That's never been my talent—I can keep on top of existing systems, but I'm not an innovator. But I know and respect those who are."

"Well." Velun seemed to be considering that fairly. "If you

really want to know, then, there's an undergraduate course on cube—I have a copy because my second daughter's going to be taking it next year. Or, if you want a fast take, there's the induction trainer."

The induction trainer gave Heris a headache. Still, it was fast. She agreed.

When she came up from the course, the first thing she thought of was not the prince, but Lady Cecelia. She had a glimmer of what might have been done to her, although she recognized her own inexpertise.

"Could that—the same mechanism—cause a strokelike appearance in an elderly patient?"

This time she talked to Dr. Koshinsky; Dr. Velun was, he said, busily working out sequences . . . and now Heris understood, in principle, what that was and why it was important. Dr. Koshinsky rocked back on his heels, considering her suggestion. "Not by itself, I wouldn't think. It could maintain that appearance, but the onset would be too slow. Why?"

Heris explained all she knew of Cecelia's condition. "One of her visitors described what looked like an implanted delivery system for drugs. That could be the maintenance drug you're talking about."

The doctor's eyebrows went up. "Is this a . . . political person you're speaking of?"

"Heavens no." Heris wondered, even as she said it, if that were completely true. Lady Cecelia did not choose to involve herself in politics much, but she had, after all, pressured the Crown into arranging the pardon and restitution for convicted military personnel. If that wasn't political power, Heris wondered what was. She tried to explain to the puzzled doctor. "She's a very wealthy, very independent elderly lady—my former employer, in fact. In perfect health, so far as anyone knew. She collapsed in what appeared to be a stroke, followed by coma, but we have reason to suspect that's not what really happened. If she was felled by some chemical attack, could you reverse it?"

The doctor pursed his lips. "We'd have to get to her, or her to us. There's no way I'd touch this long distance. Where is she?"

"I have no idea. I can—possibly—get in contact with someone who knows where she is."

"It would be better to intervene as soon as possible. If spontaneous recovery doesn't occur in the absence of the neurotoxins, degeneration cán occur from inhibition of response."

"I—don't know how her recovery has gone."

"Find out. You're sure this was an intentional injury?"

"Reasonably sure. She had made some enemies." Heris paused a moment, then added. "In fact, I was suspected of having done it." If their investigation revealed this, better she had been open about it. "Her family, a very prominent one, was upset because she mentioned me in her will." She paused a moment, and realized there was no real advantage to concealing Cecelia's identity. "Lady Cecelia de Marktos . . ." He was nodding before she finished the full thing; he recognized the name.

"I see. But you want her to recover." It was not quite a question. Heris fought back the automatic anger.

"Yes. Not only is she my employer, she's my friend. She's . . . remarkable." There was no way to describe Cecelia to a stranger. Heris's memory presented an image of Cecelia on that special horse at Bunny's, wind whipping back her short grizzled hair, face alight as they galloped down to a stone wall. "You'd have to know her."

"As a matter of fact, I know a little. My niece is horse crazy, and we gave her the complete set of *Great Riders*. So I've seen Lady Cecelia, at least as she was at her peak." He paused, then went on. "If you don't know where she was taken, may I suggest a possibility? She used to own a stud farm and training facility on Rotterdam . . ."

"She wouldn't be there," Heris said quickly. "It's too obvious. She'd have been taken somewhere less . . ."

"The thing is, you could find out without much trouble. She's known and loved in the world of those who breed and train performance horses. They don't care about politics, on the whole, but they do care about each other. They will know where she is, I'm sure, and while they may not tell you, they'll tell her friends you're looking."

It was a chance, the best one she'd had. "Do you need me here while you work on the prince?"

"Not really."

"Then—I think I'll go find her. Bring her back. You have adequate security here . . . ?"

"We hope so."

"Then I can leave the prince and his clones—or the clones without the prince—and, by the way, haven't you found any way yet to distinguish them?"

"Not yet. They claim they were told it was possible, but none of them knows how it worked. Or so they say. It's a pity; I have to say we find their creation and use as mere doubles very bothersome. As I said before, we consider clones to be fully human, with the same rights as other humans. These young men seem to think they have no right to exist without their so-called prime. It is an ethical problem for us, because we would normally attempt to give them the psychological support they need to become independent, fully-functioning adults . . . yet this is not what your king asked for in his contract, and we suspect he will not approve that service. You are only his agent, I realize, but if you're going back to Familias space, I hope you can convey to him our very grave reservations. We would like to have some guarantee that these young men will be granted some sort of citizenship when they return."

"Do they need all three clones to untangle them?" Petris asked when she reported this conversation.

"I don't know. Why?"

"Because like you I worry about assassination. If those doctors are so convinced the clones should be treated like everyone else, then they aren't going to confine them. After all, they're healthy, full of energy . . . what do you want to bet they'll decide to give them outpatient privileges or something? I agree that we should try to find Lady Cecelia and bring her here if she wants to come—but even though the king lied to us, we still have that obligation." Petris sounded as if he'd been thinking about this for days.

"So, what do you suggest?"

"Take one or two of the clones with us. Openly. Then if someone tries to wipe them out, they'll get only two—or one—whatever."

"Ah. So which should I take?"

"I don't see that it matters; let them choose."

"Get us ready, then. I want to leave as soon as possible."

"I suppose I should warn you that Oblo's made some new friends." But there was a trickle of amusement in Petris's voice.

"What this time?" Heris asked.

"Well, he got a good deal on a new ship identity that he thinks will hold up better than the last one. . . . we're now the *Harper Valley*, in case you want to know."

✧ Chapter Eighteen

"This Court is now ready to record the first session of the competency hearings of Lady Cecelia de Marktos, who is petitioning for the reversal of the Order of Guardianship imposed by the Crown Court after medical certification of irreversible coma. Present in the Court—" Present in the Court were local magistrates, attorneys Bunny had hired on Lady Cecelia's behalf, her medical staff, and attorneys representing those who had originally instituted the Order of Guardianship: her family. Later, if this Court ruled in her favor, she would have to do the same things again, in another court, but for now Bunny thought it should be enough.

First her medical team instructed the Court in her signal system. The shoulder jerks, the knee movements, the hand clasps. They demonstrated the lapcomp she would use, and everyone present got to try it out. Thus her testimony couldn't be programmed into the machine—not overtly, anyway. The synthesized voice had been shaped to sound like hers, from old tapes, but her attorneys recommended that she use both the body movements and the lapcomp, to provide additional evidence of her understanding and competency.

The session began with the same sorts of questions Dr. Czerda had asked months before on the yacht. Did she know her name? Was it Lady Cecelia—this time the magistrate asked using the entire formal string. Did she know the date, the place, the circumstances? She answered yes; she was able, with the lapcomp's help, to give the date in both local and Universal calendars. Did she know the date of her injury, and had she been conscious continually since?

That was trickier. Brun had finally told her the date when she was supposed to have collapsed with the stroke: she could give that. But she had lost weeks in the first drug-induced coma. They had anticipated this question, and had decided that her struggle to answer it honestly, within the limits of her equipment, would stand her in good stead.

Her family's attorney, evidently poorly briefed, seemed most determined to prove she was not Lady Cecelia, and then that she had been unduly influenced by Heris Serrano. Her medical team dealt with the first (at least to the satisfaction of that court) by providing the biochemical profile proving her identity. Since such profiles were the standard way of proving identity, the attorney was reduced to arguing that it might have been faked. His argument about Heris was harder to counter. Bunny's attorneys led her through the questions.

No, Heris Serrano had not known about the bequest. No, she did not think leaving a yacht to a yacht captain was peculiar. The yacht represented only a small percentage of her total estate, and no interest in the businesses which provided the bulk of her—and her family's—wealth. No, she did not think Heris Serrano had had anything to do with her accident. Her attorney spoke.

"Since we have established this lady's identity and her mental alertness, despite a terrible ordeal, we ask a summary judgment in her favor, reversing the Order of Guardianship." Cecelia heard the faint rustle as Bunny's lawyer sat back down, the louder stir of others, the creak and rasp of the opposing lawyer standing, most likely to object.

"Just a moment," the presiding magistrate said. Cecelia heard the hollow thock of the gavel. She wished she could see his face. He sounded reasonable, but she was used to judging people by a combination of their expressions and their actions. "All this court need consider is Lady Cecelia's mental status. And on that point, I wish to state that I am now convinced that the individual seated there—" Cecelia assumed he pointed at her. "—and introduced in this court as Lady Cecelia is in fact Lady Cecelia. Clearly, Lady Cecelia is not comatose; she is oriented in time and place, and knows her own identity. But whether that constitutes adequate mental capacity to require that the guardianship be withdrawn, and her affairs returned to her sole control, remains in doubt—"

"Exactly what we said!" interrupted her family's lawyer.

"It is not," Bunny's lawyer interrupted as quickly. "You claimed this wasn't even Lady Cecelia."

"It seemed reasonable to doubt the identity of someone appearing at so great a distance from Lady Cecelia's last known location, when the management of great assets were at stake," said her family's lawyer frostily. "After Lady Cecelia's disappearance, with all the publicity, anyone could have decided to claim to be her. Any lapses of memory could be attributed to the stroke or subsequent medication . . . it would be very hard to prove in the absence of definitive biochemical identification—"

"Which, Ser, was presented. Now, if you don't mind—" Was that a crumb of humor in the magistrate's voice? Cecelia hoped for it.

"Not at all."

"Very well, then. I am going to address some questions to Lady Cecelia, and I wish you legal gentlemen to keep quiet, and not interfere. If I need interpretation of her signal system, I will ask her medical and rehabilitative staff to assist. But I want *her* answers, indicative of *her* understanding, unaffected by your comments. If you do interfere, I will consider that adversely in rendering my judgment. Do I make myself clear?" He had, of course, made himself very clear. Cecelia braced herself. Now it would come.

"Lady Cecelia . . ." The timbre of his voice changed; Cecelia groaned inwardly. A sort of spurious sweetness oozed from it, the tone of an adult who is trying to communicate with a child believed to be slightly dimwitted. "Let me explain the situation." She already knew the situation; her lawyers had explained it in detail. "If you had come before the first competency hearing as you are now, I am certain that no Order of Guardianship would have been issued. However, you did not represent yourself, and no one challenged the presumption that your condition was completely disabling and permanent. Indeed, I cannot find a precedent for this situation in this jurisdiction's records, and the only similar cases in the entire Familias Regnant are not, in fact, that similar."

He paused. Cecelia realized he was planning to drag everyone through the entire legal history of competency hearings, Orders of Guardianship, and so on. How she wished she could say "Get on with it, dammit!"

"Reversing an Order of Guardianship requires some proof that you are capable of managing your affairs—at least choosing and designating an appropriate representative. Is that clear?"

"Yes." Cecelia used the synthetic voice for that one, and she could tell by the indrawn breaths that it surprised more than one in the court.

"I want you to explain, as well as you are able, what you consider your main business interests," the magistrate said. "Can you tell me something about your affairs, enough that I know you understand the extent of your holdings?"

This they had not expected. Cecelia could hear her lawyers shifting on their seats. She hoped they would keep quiet; she knew, if she could only figure out a way to communicate it. First the easy signal, the "yes" for "Yes, I understand." Then—she formed the list in her mind, and began spelling them into the synthesizer input. "B.e.c.o.n.I.n.v.e.s.t.m.e.n.t.s." Pause. "M.e.t.a.l.s a.n.d h.e.a.v.y i.n.d.u.s.t.r.y." Pause. "Forty-seven point six—" the synthesizer handled numbers more easily than spelled words. "p.e.r.c.e.n.t." Pause. "E.q.w.i.n.f.o.u.n.d.a.t.i.o.n." Pause. "Eighty-five p.e.r.c.e.n.t." Pause. Laboriously, she spelled on and on, seeing in her mind's eye the logos and prospectuses and annual reports of the various corporations,

partnerships, limited and unlimited companies, in
which she had once (and should still) have an interest.

"Excuse me, Lady Cecelia," the magistrate interrupted,
when she was halfway through trying to explain that she had
an undivided fifth of an eighth part of the great mining ven-
ture on Castila. She stopped short, suddenly aware that her
back ached, sweat had glued her blouse to her back, and she
had no idea how long she'd been "talking." His voice now held
the respect she hoped for. "That's enough; I can see that
explaining this is a laborious process with the communication
system you now have. Clearly, however, you do know your
holdings; I've no doubt you could complete the list, but there's
no reason to put you through it."

"Objection!" The opposing lawyer's voice sounded more
resigned than hopeful. "She might have been given the list to
memorize; it could even have been programmed in . . ."

"Overruled. This court sees the effort Lady Cecelia is making; this court believes that effort is hers. I have only a few
more questions, ma'am. For the record, I want to ask why you
willed your yacht to your captain of a short time."

"She . . . saved . . . my . . . life." Those words were in the
synthesizer; she had insisted on that phrase, but had chosen to
leave it as separate words which she would have to call out one
by one. "On . . . Sirialis."

"Ah." Under the magistrate's satisfied word she heard a
datacube clattering on the opposition's table. She realized then
that Heris must not have mentioned that little escapade. Some
of her resentment vanished. If they thought it was just a
whim . . . *I have a right to my whims*, she told herself. Still,
whims could mean loss of judgment. With no reason given at
all—and she had not wanted to embarrass her captain by
mentioning the reason in the will—her family had had only
the worst reasons to consider. Ronnie should have told them,
but perhaps they hadn't listened to the family scapegrace. "And
I presume, Lady Cecelia, that you need access to your assets
in part to pay for your rehabilitation and further treatment."

"Yes." And to return to her own life, and to control her world again, though she couldn't say it. Yet.

"If you please—" That was her family's lawyer; she recognized a last-ditch strain in his voice. "I'm sure Lady Cecelia's family would be glad to pay whatever medical expenses she has incurred or may incur—"

"Objection!" Bunny's lawyer. "Her family incarcerated Lady Cecelia in a long term care facility where she was given no effective treatment—"

"They were told there was none!"

"Which turned out to be untrue, as you can see. Lady Cecelia must be free to choose her own treatment, since her choice has already been shown to be better than her family's abuse and neglect."

"Gentlemen!" The magistrate's gavel, twice. "Enough squabbling. It is clear to this court that the individual seated here is in fact Lady Cecelia de Marktos, that she is not comatose, that she is in fact fully oriented as defined by law, that she is aware of her business interests, and capable of communicating her wishes and orders to her chosen agents, and that her medical status is not stable, but evolving toward increasing ability. Moreover, she is capable of giving rational explanations for her actions in the past and present. She is, quite certainly, legally competent. As you all know, in this very unusual circumstance, it is not possible to overturn an Order of Guardianship completely with one hearing. However, as of this date I order that Lady Cecelia's Order be transferred to Court supervision, pending final revocation. Also as of this date, Lady Cecelia regains her access to all her accounts, wherever they are; I order that her family give this Court a complete listing of all such accounts by the end of this business day. Notification of financial institutions will begin immediately. Within thirty days, I expect a complete accounting of the Guardianship to date; at that time I confidently expect that a subsequent hearing will restore Lady Cecelia's status in all respects. From this date, the family is not to make any decisions respecting Lady Cecelia's holdings without her express permission, given through this court. I will expect Lady Cecelia to name a legal representative of her choice to whom she will assign power of attorney for the purpose of transacting business until her condition improves."

Cecelia felt as if she could float out of her chair and up to the ceiling. Around her, rustles and scrapes and carefully muffled mutters indicated the legal actors reacting to the verdict. She pressed the keyboard and the synthesizer said, "Thank you, sir."

"Now," her lawyer said on the way back to the house, "Now you can start living again."

Cecelia let herself sink into the cushioned seat. Living again? This was far better than a few months ago, but she'd hardly call it living.

"Of course there's a lot of busywork stacked up," he went on. She knew what that was—medical and legal bills, that Bunny had guaranteed for her, but that she would now need to authorize. "It won't take too long," he said, in the tone that business people used when they meant less than a week. "As soon as the accounts are accessible again—tomorrow, probably, for the local lines, and within a week for the others. I don't expect the . . . other side . . . to make any trouble about it." From a firm with long experience in dealing with prominent families, he was not about to bad-mouth her relatives, even now. It had all been a matter of business, he had assured her. Nothing personal, just the need to keep the family assets from evaporating in a crisis.

Now, with her credit restored, with the ability to pay her own bills, and choose her own medical care, she was surprised to find herself as angry with her family as ever. She still didn't think it was only a matter of business; there had been some satisfaction at seeing the renegade brought low . . . and while Berenice and Gustav had not actually done the deed, they had consented to the humiliation she'd suffered far too easily.

She longed to stride into Berenice's parlor and tell her sister exactly what she thought.

With that thought, she realized that in restoring her legal competence, the magistrate had unwittingly told her attacker she was alive, dangerous, and—worst of all—where she was. Panic stiffened her; she fought to reach the keyboard which, in the car, was out of her reach.

"What? What's wrong?" He was smart enough to hand it to her, and hit the power switch.

"L.o.r.e.n.z.a. w.i.l.l. k.n.o.w. I.D. w.i.l.l. g.o. a.c.t.i.v.e."

"Oh . . . dear." From the tone of his voice, he understood the problem. He should. "But—it's automatic when legal status is restored. At least she won't know where you are; that's not part of the system . . ." She waited impatiently for him to figure it out. "Except—she knows your sister. No doubt your family told everyone about this hearing." Yes, of course. And worse. She had respected the king's desire for secrecy; she had not told anyone at all what she knew about the prince. She was now sure, though she had no proof, that Lorenza had provided whatever it was that made the prince stupid. If Lorenza panicked, and started picking off Cecelia's relatives on the grounds she might have told them something, she might soon be the only person who knew about the prince.

It was going to be a working day, not a celebration, and she wasn't going to waste time on busywork after all.

Heris approached the Rotterdam Station cautiously. She still didn't think this was where Lady Cecelia had been taken, but just in case she didn't want to blunder into any R.S.S. or law enforcement scrutiny. Oblo insisted that *Sweet Delight's* latest identity would hold up to anyone's checking, but she preferred not to test it if possible.

The Station itself had a scuffed old clunker of a freighter nuzzled into one docking station, and two small chartered passenger vessels spaced around the ring from it. The Stationmaster, who ran Traffic Control herself during mainshift, told Heris to dock four slots down from the freighter.

"That charter's a bunch of high-powered lawyers," she told Heris, while explaining which coupling protocol they used—Rotterdam Station had no tugs. "Couldn't come on the same ship—not them. Ridiculous! Bet it comes out of our taxes, some way."

Two ships full of lawyers? Heris suspected they'd found Cecelia, and so had someone else. Several someones else.

"And now you. We haven't seen so much unexpected traffic in years. I don't suppose you want to declare your business?"

"Bloodstock," said Heris, inspired. After all, Cecelia was supposed to have had a training farm. "We hauled something for Lord Thornbuckle last year—" His children, when Cecelia was aboard, but the Stationmaster didn't need to know that.

"Ah. You're horse people?"

"Well . . . I'd hate to claim that; I've got no land of my own. I ride, of course."

"Over fences?"

"To hounds," Heris said, hoping this would work the miracle the doctor had mentioned.

"Mmm. Better come by my office, Captain."

Heris left everyone aboard when they'd docked, and made her way alone to the Stationmaster's office. There, she found a stout gray-haired woman with only one arm yelling into a vidcom.

"No, you may *not* preempt a scheduled shuttle flight, and I don't care who your employer is! We got people downside depend on that shuttle, people that live here, and you can just wait your turn like anyone else." She glanced at Heris, waved her out of pickup range, and continued the argument. "Or you can charter a plane, fly to the other shuttleport, and see if they've got room for you. Take your pick." She cut off the complainer, and grinned at Heris.

"You know Lady Cecelia. You know Bunny . . . right?"

"Uh . . . yes, Stationmaster."

"Forget that. M'name's Annie. Who told you she was here?"

"Nobody—a doctor over in the Guerni Republic said to start looking here because this was where she'd had the training stable. Frankly, I thought that was too obvious . . ."

"But someone would've heard? Good thinking. Situation now is she just got her legal status back . . . those snobs I was arguing with were her family's lawyers trying to keep her from it. Probably getting fat fees from managing her affairs."

Heris blinked. Cecelia well enough to get a competency hearing and reverse the earlier ruling? Perhaps she didn't need any more medical treatment . . . but surely she'd need her own transportation.

"By the way," the Stationmaster said, "you might want to avoid those lawyers. First thing they did when they arrived is show a holo of you all over this Station asking if anyone had seen you." She grinned. "Of course we hadn't, and we haven't now. You didn't tell me your name was Heris Serrano, and that ship out there isn't the *Sweet Delight*, or even that other name—what was it?—*Better Luck*. Where'd you get the new beacon, Miskrei Refitters over at Golan?"

Heris had to laugh. "Annie, you'd make a good match for one of my crew. Any way I can get transport down without running into those lawyers coming up?"

"Why do you think I told them they couldn't charter a special run of the shuttle? Down shuttle leaves in half an hour; they've found out its return run is fully booked, and with any luck they'll all be on their way over to Suuinen to catch the other one."

"Is there a young woman named Brun with Lady Cecelia?" She hoped so; maybe Brun could figure out what was going wrong with Sirkin.

"That blonde girl? Bunny's daughter, isn't she? No, she took off for Rockhouse a while back with Cory—well, you don't know him."

Heris wondered what that was about, but she had a shuttle to catch. "My second-in-command's Kennvinard Petris, and the other seniors . . ." She gave the Stationmaster the names. She almost named Oblo instead of Sirkin, but that would insult the girl, and besides she had an awful vision of what Oblo and the Stationmaster could do in the way of mischief if they put their heads together. She would not be responsible for that—not until she needed it. "None of my people should come onto the Station except Skoterin; the others were known to be part of my crew back at Rockhouse Major. I'll tell them, too." She called the ship, and explained quickly. Skoterin, and only Skoterin, could leave the ship for anything the others wanted or needed.

The down shuttle had only two other passengers, both obviously Station personnel on regular business. Heris tried to relax—the shuttle's battered interior did nothing to promote its passengers' confidence—and endured the rough ride silently. Sure enough, the shuttle station onplanet was almost empty; the clerk ignored her request for a communications console, and simply led her out the door. A big green truck huffed clouds of smelly exhaust at her, and a thin dark-haired girl leaned out the window. "You for the stable? The . . . uh . . . captain?"

"Right." If the girl didn't say her name, she wouldn't, though she could see no watchers. The girl pushed open the other door, and Heris climbed up. Amazing. She had seen no sign of customs checks. Did they let anyone on and off the planet without even checking identification?

"Lady Cecelia's *really* glad you're here," the girl said, as the truck lurched off in a series of slightly controlled leaps. "Sorry about that—Cory was supposed to have fixed the transmission. It's the road, really. It shakes everything loose." She was already driving at a speed that made Heris nervous, ignoring the warning signs as she approached the road beyond the shuttleport. The truck leaped forward, into a gap between another truck loaded with square bales of hay, and one hauling livestock. Heris didn't recognize the animals: dark, large, and hairy.

"I'm Driw," the girl continued, as if she hadn't heard the squeal of brakes and tires, the bellows of rage from the other drivers. "I'm one of the grooms, and I always get stuck with the driving." The truck swayed as she put on speed, and overtook the hay truck ahead. Heris found herself staring fixedly out the side window; she didn't want to know about oncoming traffic. "Because I'm safe," Driw said, taking a sharp curve on fewer wheels than the vehicle possessed. Heris could hear its frame protesting. "Everyone else has wrecked the truck at least twice, and Merry—that's Meredith Lunn, Lady Cecelia's partner—said I was to do all the driving." She laughed, the easy laugh of someone who finds it natural, and Heris tried to unclench her own hands from the seat.

"Don't worry," Driw said. "We've got a load of feed back there; it'll keep us on the road."

Heris had a vision of the feedsacks reaching down grainy fingers to grip the road—or perhaps it was molasses in sweet feed—and felt herself relaxing. If she died in a feed truck driven by a crazed groom, it would at least be unique. No Serrano she'd ever heard of had done that. She began to notice the countryside—the gently rolling terrain, the trees edging fields fenced for horses, the horses themselves.

"How is she?" she asked.

"Lady Cecelia? Better . . . when she got here, she couldn't do more than lie in the bed and twitch. Now . . . she can walk a little, with supports. She can spell things out on a keyboard, and there's a voice synthesizer. She's ridden again—"

"Ridden?"

"Well . . . riding therapy, not real riding. On a horse, though. They tried to fit her with some kind of artificial vision things—looked like something out of a monster-adventure entertainment cube, metal contact lenses. She can feed herself, and things like that . . . 'course, I haven't seen all this, it's what I hear. You taking her away?"

"Whatever she wants," Heris said. "If she still needs medical care—"

"She needs to kill the bitch who did it to her," Driw said coldly. Heris was startled. Aside from her driving, she had seemed like such a nice girl, not at all violent. "There we are—see the gates?" Heris didn't pick out the gates, surrounded by a thicker clump of trees, until Driw swerved through them. Heris barely grabbed hold in time, but Driw seemed to think the turn routine.

On the gravelled road, or drive, beyond the gates, Driw slowed down a little and grinned at Heris. "You didn't squeak once—most outsiders do. That girl Brun, for instance."

"Were you testing me, or just being efficient?" Heris asked.

"A little of both," Driw said. "We're very fond of Lady Cecelia. Wanted to know if her friends were tough enough to do her any good. There's the place." The place: brick house and brick-and-stone stable yard. Heris recognized it from the holo in Cecelia's study aboard the yacht. Here, the horses were real, black and bay and chestnut and gray . . . here the stable cat lounged on a pile of saddle pads waiting to be washed; a dog sprawled in the sun. Someone waved to the truck and pointed. Driw swung away from the stable gate to follow a track around one side. "They want the feed in the old barn," she explained. "Won't take but a few minutes. You can walk through to the house."

Heris felt scared, and angry with herself for that. She did not want to see the ruin of the woman she had come to respect and even love. She reminded herself that Cecelia, locked in the dark in a helpless body, must have been more terrified, with more reason.

She felt her hands cramping and tried to unclench them. Cecelia was better; she'd been told Cecelia was better. But that single image she'd seen, of the motionless body, the expressionless face, stayed in her mind's eye. She could imagine nothing between that and Cecelia well . . . and Cecelia was a long way from well.

She walked through the stable yard, the forecourt, up to

the graceful little porch on the big house. She felt she knew it; Cecelia had talked about it enough. But inside, it looked more like a medical center. Parallel bars and weight machines surrounded by colored mats to the right. Massive gray cabinets that might house anything at all to the left. Ahead were the stairs—and coming down, step by careful step, the tall, lean figure she had been afraid to see lying flat, helpless.

Over and under her loose shirt and slacks, Heris could see tubes and wires, the structure and electronic connections that let her walk. One hand clamped to the rail, and the other lay atop a boxlike machine attached to the wide belt around her waist. Her eyes looked odd . . . some kind of contact lenses, Heris decided, though they looked opaque. A headband flickered, red and green. What was that? Beside her, but not touching her, was a competent-looking woman with dark hair in a thick braid. She looked up and smiled at Heris.

"You must be Captain Serrano—we heard Driw's truck go by."

"Yes—I am." For an instant, she didn't know whether to speak to Cecelia or not; manners won out. "I'm glad to see you up again, milady," Heris said. Cecelia smiled. Clearly it was a struggle to smile; the movement of her face was deliberate. Her left hand moved over the top of the box at her waist.

"I'm glad to see you." A synthesized voice, only vaguely like Cecelia's, came from the box. "I heard you driving in."

Heris couldn't think what to say. She wanted to stare, to figure out what each blinking light, tube, and cable were for, but she didn't want to embarrass Cecelia.

"How . . . is . . . my . . . ship?" asked Cecelia. The voice still didn't sound like her, but Heris accepted it as her speech.

"She's . . . a mess, frankly." Heris shook herself. She could certainly talk about the ship. "I don't know how much you've heard . . . we had to yank her out of the decorators, bare naked, and make a run for it." How much to explain? "The king—asked a favor of me. It was hinted that my taking it would ensure your safety."

"And . . . you . . . did . . . it?"

"I'm working on it. Perhaps you'd like to sit down?" That ungainly figure poised on the stairs made her nervous.

"I . . . want . . . to . . . go." Go? Heris scowled, uncertain what Cecelia meant and unwilling to ask. The other woman on the stairs touched Cecelia's arm lightly.

"May I explain? You said it was urgent."

"Yes." Cecelia continued her slow, difficult progress on down the stairs. The other woman moved with her, but spoke to Heris.

"Lady Cecelia's competency hearing ended yesterday. She has recovered her memory of the incident that started all this some weeks ago, including who administered the drug, but she hasn't told the court yet. She didn't want that person to know she had the memory, because it imperiled her family."

"Back on Rockhouse," said Heris. "Where's Brun?"

"She sent Brun, as soon as she recovered the memory, to warn her family—discreetly—against the individual. Anyway, because of the competency hearing, the person who injured her now knows where she is, and because the magistrates ruled in her favor, her ID is now flagged active on the universal datanets. She has to presume the individual knows that, and will take action. None of us feel that Rotterdam is safe for her anymore. Passenger service is infrequent, and in her condition she still needs medical attendants. We had thought of sending her off on the same ship that carried her lawyers, but that ship is known—"

"That's easy," Heris said. "The yacht looks terrible right now, but it's roomy and safe—and we're not using its original ID beacon. How many people will she need along?"

"But if they've seen you—at the spaceport—"

"The Stationmaster saw to it that no one did. The only one of my crew who has permission to leave the ship is a woman who joined us the day we left Rockhouse—they won't associate her with me or Lady Cecelia. Let's get things packed and on the way."

"Lady Cecelia," the other woman said. Cecelia had made it to the bottom stair, and the chair beside it. "How soon could you be ready to leave?"

"Now." The synthesized voice had no tone for humor, but Heris was sure Cecelia intended it. "Go . . . pack. Let . . . me . . . talk . . . to . . . Heris."

"We'll need comfort items," Heris said, as the other woman started away. "We have only minimal bedding—you might want to load that sort of thing."

"She told me her yacht had had a swimming pool—is that operational?"

"Yes, though again the walls in the gym are bare. We had the pool filled in the Golan Republic—and that's what I wanted to tell you, milady. The doctors believe that the neurochemical assault you suffered is very similar to what was done to the prince. If so, it may be reversible. However, they will need a detailed history, and your own tissues to work on. I can take you there, if you want to risk it."

"Yes. I . . . trust . . . you . . ." Cecelia said.

The big sprawling house that had seemed to be dozing in the afternoon sun erupted like a kicked anthill. Heris crouched on the bottom step of the stairs, holding Cecelia's hands in hers, until someone fetched another chair for her. Four or five women in blue tunics bustled in and out, up and down stairs. Boxes and suitcases began to accumulate in the front hall, as the sun slanted farther and farther through the windows into the room.

"I . . . knew . . . you . . . would . . . come . . ." Cecelia said. Her hand squeezed Heris's. "Brun . . . knew . . . you . . . had . . . to . . . leave . . ."

"I'm sorry I couldn't get you out right away," Heris said. "Your family blamed me—and I didn't even know about the bequest."

"No. It's . . . all . . . right . . ."

The lift whirred, and out came two women, a hoverchair, and another stack of boxes. Two men came in from outside and began carrying the growing pile out to the driveway. Heris heard a truck motor grinding up from the stable, and winced at the thought of Cecelia at the mercy of Driw's driving. The lift came down again, this time with what looked like a hospital bed folded up. A woman in a big apron appeared at their side with trays.

"Milady—time for your snack." Heris watched as Cecelia managed to find the food on her plate and get it into her mouth without incident.

"Milady, I'm sorry, but . . . are those artificial eyes?"

"No . . . not . . . exactly. Ask . . . medical." Cecelia went on eating; Heris was suddenly ravenous and found herself engulfing one thick sandwich after another. Where, and how, had Cecelia found another great cook?

"I should see about the shuttle schedule," Heris said finally, around a last bite of fresh bread stuffed with something delicious. She was sure it had celery and herbs and cheese in it, but what else?

"Don't worry about that," said the cheerful woman she had first met on the stairs. "I called Annie, and she'll make sure we've got one. She thinks we should wait until the opposition lawyers have left."

Shadows chased the sun across the driveway, and up the front of the house, leaving the windows clear to a distant blaze of sunset behind trees. Heris stood up to stretch, and walked outside. Fine brushes of cloud high overhead; the sound of buckets and boots and water faucets from the stable yard. A shaggy dog stood up to look at her, then shook itself and wandered away, tail wagging gently. So peaceful here—she wanted to stretch out and sleep the night away.

"Excuse me, ma'am," said someone behind her, and she shifted aside. The folded bed was coming down the front steps, a mattress balanced atop and almost hiding the men carrying it.

❖　　　❖　　　❖

The caravan started for the shuttleport well after dark. Heris, breathing in the fresh damp air, found herself wishing she could stay longer. She rode with Cecelia, two of her medical team, and a lawyer, in a real car; Driw drove the truck with supplies and equipment; another car carried the rest of the medical team. And the cook.

The lawyer had kept Cecelia busy all evening. They could not risk alienating the magistrates with her disappearance; calls and letters had been necessary. Now he was taking notes on her orders for the next few months—who could vote which stock in which company, what to do if Berenice and Gustav tried to interfere further in the recovery of her competent status.

Heris marveled at Cecelia's energy. She looked . . . old, sick, exhausted. But she pushed herself, kept going, stayed alert. Heris dozed, half ashamed of that, but knowing she had a long watch ahead when she must be alert.

✧ Chapter Nineteen

Although it was nighttime, the shuttleport looked dark and almost deserted. Heris wondered what had gone wrong. Then someone came out of the dimly lit terminal and leaned into the driver's side of their car. "Ah—it's you. Just go on out to the runway . . . follow the yellow lights."

In this way, the caravan trundled down a long runway to a dark shape bulked at the end of it. Heris felt she'd fallen into some surrealistic action-adventure. She had never, even in dreams, imagined herself sneaking along a darkened runway toward a clandestine shuttle. And she had a burning curiosity about what Cecelia could possibly have done to generate this level of loyalty on the planet.

She had no time to ask while the truckload of gear was put aboard the shuttle's cargo bay, while she and the medical team carefully eased Cecelia and her attachments into the shuttle's shabby passenger compartment. They were not the only passengers, either. After Cecelia and her party were aboard, half a dozen others climbed up and settled themselves at the back of the passenger space. Perfectly ordinary, the sort of people you'd expect to find taking a shuttle flight up the surface of any planet . . . except, Heris noticed, they all had remarkably similar bulges in their clothes.

At the Station, Heris noticed that one of the chartered passenger ships had gone, and the corridors were almost deserted. Everyone—including the shuttle's other passengers—helped unload the shuttle and move its cargo to the yacht. There Heris found Annie—offduty, as she explained—and Oblo lounging in the loading area.

"I thought I told you to stay aboard," Heris said to Oblo. He gave her his innocent look, and she winced inwardly. What had he been up to?

"I am aboard," he said. "Legally—there's the line." He stretched. "I was chatting with Annie here on the Station com, and we discovered some mutual interests, so when she got offshift, she came over . . ."

"Right. Fine. Now let's get our owner aboard, and her gear installed." Oblo looked hurt, another of his certified expressions, and vanished up the access tube. Annie gave Heris a cheerful grin, intended to disarm.

"Thought you wouldn't mind if I came around and made sure your lady's ship was secure. Just in case those lawyers snooped, although since all our exterior videos seem to be on the blink right now . . ."

Heris found herself smiling in spite of her annoyance. "Amazing how equipment around here seems to behave," she said. "For instance, the shuttle tonight—"

"Had a block in the hydraulic line to the steering of the nosewheel," Annie said promptly. "They couldn't seem to get it to roll into the usual parking slot, and decided it was safer to keep it on the straight runway."

"And yet they felt it was safe enough to fly . . . ?"

Annie shrugged. "It got you here, didn't it? And if any nosy person was looking for unusual activity, all they saw was a dark field." Heris nodded, not bothering to mention that any decent surveillance gear would pierce the darkness like a needle into wax . . . but Annie must know that.

"It was most convenient," Heris said instead. Annie chuckled.

"We hoped so." Then her expression sobered. "By the way, that tech you had running errands for the ship—Skoterin, isn't it?" Heris nodded. "One of those lawyers stopped her and talked to her a few minutes. I'd given her warning they might be coming through, but I guess she was curious or something—"

"I'll talk to her," Heris said. "They'd been briefed, of course; I'm sure she said something appropriate, but I'll check."

"Do that," Annie said. Then, looking past Heris, her eyes lit up. "Milady—it's good to see you again. And you do look so much better."

To Heris, Cecelia looked pale and exhausted . . . but Annie would have seen her the first time she came through, she realized. She must have looked much worse then. Now Cecelia struggled and achieved a smile.

"Thank . . . you . . . Annie . . ."

Behind Cecelia came the trail of people pushing dollies loaded with equipment, luggage, odds and ends. Heris left Cecelia with her medical people and Annie, and went on into the ship to get the crew ready for departure. To Oblo, who had been hovering in the access tube as if afraid he'd miss something, she gave the task of directing traffic.

"Brigdis, we're going to want a fast, but very safe, course back to the Guerni Republic," she said, coming onto the bridge. She was glad to see that Sirkin looked bright-eyed and capable again; she had done much better on the trip from Guerni, and Heris hoped whatever had been wrong was now over and done with. "We don't want to take any chances with the Benignity, not with our decoy clone and Lady Cecelia aboard." Not ever, but especially not now. "Methlin—" Arkady was offwatch at the moment, "—I want our weapons ready, but not lit. If we do run into trouble, I want to be able to surprise them. Make sure standby mode is really standby."

"I've got this course plotted already, Captain," Sirkin said. She sounded a bit tentative, but presumably her confidence would return in time. Heris looked at the string of numbers, and the display. She realized she was too tired to follow through all the calculations.

"Did you check this with Oblo?"

"No, ma'am, not yet . . . he's not been back to the bridge this watch. Vivi got me the latest data from the Stationmaster's nav file—I thought if she went for it, instead of calling in, nobody could tap the line . . ."

"Good idea." For an instant, Heris wondered why Annie hadn't mentioned that when she was talking about Skoterin . . . but Annie was offwatch now, and might have been when Sirkin requested the data. It didn't really matter. The outside communications board blinked, and Heris reached for it.

"Captain Serrano, this is Stationmaster Tadeuz." His voice sounded as friendly as Annie's. "If Annie's still over there, would you ask her to step 'round the office? I've got a question for her."

"Of course," Heris said, wondering why he hadn't used the Station paging system.

"Sort of a confidential thing," Tadeuz said in her ear. "Nothing to worry you, though. More like a filing problem."

"I'll tell her right away," Heris said. "What about clearance for departure?"

"I'd like five minutes, just to make sure nobody's coming up for a shift change, ten if you can give it to me, otherwise you're cleared." Just like that. Heris had never heard of anything so casual, anywhere.

"I'll tell Annie," she said again, and went off shaking her head.

Annie was still chatting with Cecelia; the tail end of the equipment train was just about to enter the access tube.

"Stationmaster Tadeuz asked me to tell you he'd like to see you in the office," Heris said to Annie.

"Then why didn't he—oh. Sorry, milady, but I'd better scoot. Hope to see you again soon, in even better health. Bye, Captain . . ." And Annie took off down the corridor much faster than her looks suggested.

"I've got to go back aboard, milady," Heris said to Cecelia. "We'll be able to depart once everything is aboard and stowed."

"And how long will that be?" asked the woman with her.

"I'm not sure," Heris said. "I'd guess less than an hour; Lady

Cecelia can come aboard now, but there's no place to sit, really. No furniture except what's just come aboard."

"Better . . . there . . . than . . . here . . ." Cecelia's hands moved on the hoverchair controls and the chair lifted, swaying slightly.

"Good idea," Heris said. She felt stupid not to have realized that Cecelia didn't need any other chair to sit on.

Inside, the ship was still in chaos. The woman with Cecelia locked down the hoverchair in the lounge, and went to help the others arrange Cecelia's suite. Heris saw the clone looking out of his quarters and beckoned. "Here—why don't you keep Lady Cecelia company until we're ready to leave. Lady Cecelia, this is Gerald B. Smith, one of the prince's doubles." She didn't want to explain the clone business now. "Mr. Smith, Lady Cecelia de Marktos."

"Yes, ma'am." Gerald B. smiled at her, and gathered some bright colored pillows to make himself a soft seat on the bare decking. "Lady Cecelia, I'm delighted to meet you again. We've met, though I was at the time impersonating my prime, the prince."

"I . . . shall . . . call . . . you . . . Mr. . . . Smith . . ." Cecelia said. Heris decided they'd do well enough alone, and went back to her own work. Petris had the engineering figures ready for her; Haidar had computed the new load on the environmental system (well within its capabilities) and had a projection for the supplies that would be needed at Guerni. Meharry and Ginese were discussing the exact amount of power necessary to keep the weapons just below scannable levels.

"Not Guerni scans, of course," Meharry said. "We know about *them* now. I think they'd know if the toothpick in your pocket was intended for offensive use . . . maybe they read minds, do you think?"

"I don't think. Mind reading is a myth. I just wish we had their capability," Heris said. "But you think our stuff isn't scannable by normal means?"

"We could ask the Stationmaster to look us over," Meharry said.

"No . . ." Heris thought about it a moment longer, then shook her head. "So far I've seen no sign that anyone on this Station—or this planet—wishes Lady Cecelia ill, but why take chances? I'll trust your judgment."

She reminded herself that she wanted to speak to Skoterin, but Skoterin was busy in the guts of the ship, resetting flow rates to accommodate the larger load on the environmental system. Haidar, on his way to help her, said he'd give her the word once all the chores were finished. No hurry, Heris thought. In fact, it was a duty so low in priority that she didn't put it into her deskcomp for a reminder request.

Getting the *Sweet Delight* back into deepspace and a jump or so away from Rotterdam was all that really concerned her. She did a final walk-through inspection after the last loaders left and Lady Cecelia was settled in her bed in her own suite. Everything looked as it should, her crew alert and at their stations, and nothing lying around where it shouldn't be. Undock had none of the ceremony she was used to . . . no financial records to clear, no lists of regulations to follow . . . she wondered what would happen if any sort of government inspection ventured this far from the center of Familias space. Did they ever? Could Annie or Tadeuz adhere to rules (what rules?) if they found it necessary?

But with the yacht in insystem drive, and the Station receding in the distance, she put that out of her mind. However it was run, by whatever gang of independents, that Station wouldn't be there without some kind of discipline. Its air had been good, its water plentiful, its power supply and gravity controls steady. The docking collars had held pressure—so what was she fretting about? Heris grinned as she realized what it was . . . she had spent so many years putting up with boring, routine double and triple checks, because she had believed them necessary. Without them, stations would fall out of the sky, air would fail, spacecraft would go boom. And here was someone ignoring—or at least seeming to ignore—the usual precautions, and doing very well anyway. She resented the time she'd wasted.

She also resented the return of Sirkin's mysterious problem. Nothing happened on her first shift, but as they were approaching the first jump point, Oblo reported that Sirkin had left an open circuit in the communications control mechanism. Not a fatal error—yet—but a sign of carelessness. Heris was furious when he called her about it. Enough was enough. She'd replace Sirkin when they got to Guerni. She flung off the covers and dressed, thinking how to say it, and how to explain to Lady Cecelia. It was simply too bad to have to bother her now, in her condition.

When she was dressed, she went to the bridge, where the tension needed no words to express. Ginese nodded at her, and Kulkul handed her the log, with Oblo's entry. All three of them looked as upset as she felt. Heris read it, and looked at the circuits herself. Anger and sorrow both—she hated to see someone with potential go bad, but that's what Sirkin was doing.

"Have Sirkin report to my office," she said to Kulkul, the watch officer.

The Sirkin who appeared seemed to be the bright-eyed, alert Sirkin she had first worked with, the young woman who should have had a successful career ahead of her.

"Yes, ma'am?" She was even smiling, and nothing in voice or manner suggested any concern about her own duties. Heris handed her the log.

"Can you explain that entry, Ms. Sirkin?" The formality wiped the smile from Sirkin's face; she reached for the log with the first signs of uncertainty. As she read it, her face flushed.

"But I—it can't be!"

"I assure you, Ms. Sirkin, that Mr. Vissisuan neither lies nor makes elementary mistakes. You signed off your shift; he found the open circuit. Those are facts; I asked for an explanation."

Now Sirkin looked as miserable as she should. "I—I don't . . .

know how it happened, Captain. I didn't—I swear I didn't leave any circuits open, but I know Oblo wouldn't . . . wouldn't make it up. I—I don't know—"

Heris picked up the log Sirkin had dropped. "Ms. Sirkin, my patience has run out. Whatever your problems, I don't want them on my ship. You will be released from contract when we arrive at Golan. Until then, Mr. Vissisuan will serve as Nav First; you will perform such duties as Mr. Vissisuan and Mr. Guar can oversee. You can expect to have your work checked very carefully, and any more lapses will be reflected in my statements to any future employer. You have done good work in the past; I hate to handicap you with a bad reference, but I'm not going to risk lives . . . do you understand?"

Sirkin had gone so pale Heris was afraid she might faint. "Yes, ma'am," she said in a voice empty of all emotion.

"You may go," Heris said. "You're offshift now; see if you can pull yourself together in time to be of some help to Issi Guar next shift."

"Yes, ma'am." Sirkin left with the gait of someone who has just taken a bad wound and hasn't felt it yet. Heris wanted to clobber the girl and cradle her at the same time. What a waste of talent! If she could only clear her head . . . but she'd learned early in her career that you could spend only so much time trying to rehabilitate losers. Get rid of them, and get on with the job—which, right now, meant getting Lady Cecelia and Mr. Smith safely to the Golan Republic.

She went back to the bridge. "Oblo, you're now Nav First and Issi's your second. I don't want Sirkin standing any watches alone; she's to back up Issi during the jumps next watch, and do any other routine work you and Issi can check."

"Yes, Captain." He looked angry, but she knew it was more with circumstances than either Sirkin or herself. He had liked Sirkin—they all had—and they all felt betrayed by her failures. Padoc Kulkul, who rarely said anything at all, spoke up.

"Good idea, Captain. I know you and Petris both liked her and I had nothing against her before . . . but we can't risk anything now."

"Meharry's really mad," Ginese said without turning around. "She thought a lot of the girl."

"So did I. Now, with Sirkin off any solo watches, Nav's going to be as short as the rest of you—" A general chuckle. Navigation/Communication had had three to the other sections' two, but no one had minded. "If you need help up here, grab Skoterin from Haidar. She's capable of watching a board for a few minutes."

"And she's Fleet," Ginese said, this time looking at Heris. "We know we can trust Fleet—at least our old crew."

"Right. Now—I think whatever's wrong with Sirkin is psychological, personal, but there's the smallest chance it's not. We know her lover was killed by Compassionate Hand bravos. We know her lover may have been recruited by that woman you saw, Oblo—"

"That counselor—"

"Right. It's just barely conceivable that Sirkin was recruited too—then or later, perhaps terrorized after Yrilan's death—and if so, she could be working for the Benignity. I don't want her near the communications—they'll have a hard time finding one little yacht bouncing around jump after jump, but not if someone's got us lighted up for them."

"What about that course she laid out?" Oblo asked. "What if it's wrong—takes us into C.H. space or something?"

"Check it. She said . . . let me think . . . that Skoterin brought her up-to-date chart data from the Stationmaster's office. Let's ask Skoterin."

Skoterin, roused from her offshift sleep, arrived on the bridge looking only mildly puffy around the eyes, and answered Heris's questions readily.

"Yes, ma'am; I did go over to the Stationmaster's office for Ms. Sirkin. Made sense to me we didn't want to use the Station voicecom without knowing if anyone could listen in. That other shuttle had come with the lawyers from Lady Cecelia's competency hearing."

"Ah—yes. Annie mentioned that you'd talked to one of them. What happened?"

Skoterin grinned. "One of 'em stopped me, and wanted to know what ship I was off of. Guess they'd noticed the Station employees' uniform on the way down or something. I told 'em just what you had said was our story. 'We're the *Harper Valley*,' I said, and told 'em we were an independent freighter picking up a load of frozen equine sperm and embryos. Wanted to know where we were bound next, and I said 'Wherever the captain wants, I reckon. I'm just a mole.' They didn't know what that meant, and I told 'em environmental tech, and they said what was our captain's name, and I said he was a sorry sonuvabitch named Livadhi, which was all I could think of at the time. They said did we work for Lord Thornbuckle, and I said I wished! and they said oh never mind, she doesn't know anything we want to know, and I thought to myself, *little you know*, and they went off and so did I."

"I wonder why they asked about Lord Thornbuckle," Heris said. "Unless they've figured out that it was Brun who brought Lady Cecelia here. Good job, Vivi; they may find out that Livadhi is an R.S.S. captain but it won't do them much good. Now—about the charts and things you picked up—"

"Yes, ma'am. Got those from the Stationmaster, and came back without running into any more of those people, and gave the data to Ms. Sirkin." Heris noted that the formality in referring to Sirkin came easily to Skoterin.

"Is this what you gave her?" Heris asked, pointing to the data cube and hardcopy on Oblo's desk.

Skoterin looked. "Yes, ma'am. 'Course, I don't know what it means. Jump points and stuff, but not what."

"That's fine, then. Go on back to bed." When Skoterin had left the bridge, Heris turned to Oblo.

"Check the course Sirkin laid in against those sheets, and make sure she actually used the current data. I don't want us stumbling into Benignity space because of Sirkin's carelessness."

"Yes, ma'am." Oblo went to work. Heris sat there, wishing she were back in bed with Petris, but knowing it was too late. It seemed their jinx had returned. Besides, something nagged at her. Skoterin's story had been plausible—and Skoterin wasn't the problem anyway—so what could Sirkin have been up to, besides getting current data? Had she known the lawyers were aboard the Station just then? Had she wanted Skoterin to be seen and questioned? If—somehow—she had managed to let them know that the ship in dock was Cecelia's yacht, then getting Skoterin out there to be seen was one way of giving the enemy a complete crew list. They already knew about the others; she had counted on Skoterin going unrecognized—and now they knew about Skoterin, too.

That didn't satisfy her either, but she could not reconcile the two Sirkins, the two possible explanations for sending Skoterin out.

Next mainshift, Cecelia sent for her. Heris came into Cecelia's suite to find her sitting up in the hoverchair, an attendant with her.

"We didn't have time to explain all Lady Cecelia's signal system to you," the attendant said, before Heris could even greet her employer.

"Lady Cecelia," Heris said pointedly, "Always good to see you."

"Bev . . . will . . . help . . . you," Cecelia said.

"Fine; I'll be glad to learn whatever I can. Are you interested in what's been happening with your ship?" Cecelia's shoulder jerked. Was that a response?

"That is Lady Cecelia's easiest way to say 'yes,' " the attendant explained. "Lady Cecelia, show her 'no.' " That was the other shoulder. Heris realized that what she had taken for uncontrollable twitching in the shuttle on the way up had been Cecelia "talking."

"Right shoulder for 'yes' and left shoulder for 'no'?" Heris asked. Cecelia gave a quick jerk of her right shoulder. "I got that. What next?"

What next took longer to learn, but an hour later, Heris was a good bit more comfortable with twitches, jerks, hand clenches, and the timbre of the synthesized voice. Cecelia had even allowed her to hear her own voice—distorted, uneven in volume and pitch, but her biological voice.

"I'm amazed," Heris said. "I confess I hadn't imagined anything like this. It's so different from—" From the inert helplessness she'd been told of, or the full recovery of a feisty, healthy woman that she'd hoped for.

"We didn't dare try a regen tank," the attendant said. "Use of regen tanks with neurological problems is tricky at best. You sometimes get good responses, but more often the deficit 'hardens,' as it were. Much safer not to try it until neurochemical repair's been done. Then it's fine for dealing with residual physical deficits."

"I . . . see." Heris remembered that she had more information on the techniques the Guerni Republic doctors had suggested. "I'm going to download everything I got in the Guerni Republic to your deskcomp . . . or . . . ?"

Yes. A firm response. Heris wondered if the visual prosthesis allowed her to read displays, or could be hooked to a computer output, but she didn't like to ask. The attendant seemed to recognize her discomfort.

"I can read it to Lady Cecelia; her visual capacity is fairly blunt at this time."

"Mr. Smith . . . is . . . prince?" Cecelia interrupted. Heris was surprised.

"No . . . he's the prince's double. Didn't I say that? I'm not sure where the prince is."

"Not . . . double. He . . . is . . . prince."

"Lady Cecelia . . ." Even though several dozens of people now knew about the clones, Heris was reluctant to discuss them in front of an attendant she didn't know. She picked her words with care. "Even though I admit he looks like the prince, and sounds like the prince, I have been informed by . . . er . . . reliable sources that he is not the prince."

"C.l.o.n.e.?" That came out spelled, letter by letter, in the synthesized voice; evidently no one had thought she needed the whole word.

"Er . . . milady, clone doubles are, as I'm sure you know, illegal."

"Not . . . my . . . question . . ." Whatever her employer had lost, none of it had been intelligence points. Or the determination to find out what she wanted to find out. Heris mentally threw up her hands and answered.

"Yes, milady, he's a clone. Moreover there are several clone doubles." Quickly, as clearly as she could, she explained the king's mission, her problem with the clones on Naverrn, and the discovery that Livadhi's ship had yet another one. "And we don't know which, if any, is the prime—the prince. They call him their prime. They all have the same memories: they're given deep-conditioning tapes after each separation, so that they're up to date."

"If . . . all . . . alike . . . doesn't . . . matter." Heris had privately thought this for some time; why not just declare one of the capable clones the prince, and quietly retire the damaged prince? The answer, of course, was that someone might have planned just that, and the apparently capable clone could be someone's pawn. So might the prince.

"We left two of them at Guerni, and brought one along as a decoy, for the safety of those in the medical center. If Sirkin hasn't botched our course, we'll have them all back together and then let the doctors sort it out. If they can."

Cecelia scowled, as difficult an operation as her smile. "That . . . nice . . . Sirkin? What . . . is . . . wrong?"

"I don't know. You remember her lover was killed—well, I made allowances for that. She seemed to be coming out of it, doing better, until after we'd left Naverrn. Then she started making careless mistakes, doing sloppy work." Heris paused.

She still couldn't reconcile the Sirkin who did the calculations for those emergency jumps with someone who would forget to make necessary log entries, leave switches on the wrong settings and so forth. She took a deep breath. "I'm cancelling her contract when we get to Guerin. I won't risk your life—or mine, for that matter—on someone like that."

No. No mistaking that answer.

"Lady Cecelia, I must. I liked her too; you know I did. But a navigator's error can kill the whole crew. I've talked to her, Oblo's talked to her—we've all tried to help her. She made another serious mistake after we left Rotterdam. I can't take the chance."

No. "Wrong . . . you . . . are . . . wrong." Lady Cecelia's synthesizer had little expression, but there was no way to miss the strong emphasis of that shoulder jerk.

"I wish I were," Heris said. She debated telling Cecelia of her other suspicions about Sirkin and decided against it. If the girl merely had personal problems, she would not want to have planted other ideas. Time would tell. Besides, Cecelia was a fine one to give warnings—she had ignored Heris's warnings, and look what happened. She glanced at the wall display. "I'm sorry, but I need to get back to the bridge. We can discuss Sirkin later. We're coming into a series of critical jumps to circumnavigate Compassionate Hand territory."

When she returned to the bridge, Skoterin smiled at her from the secondary Nav board, and Sirkin was nowhere to be seen. Fine. If Issi and Oblo felt more comfortable with an old crewmate there instead of an unstable civilian, she'd accept that.

The first three jumps went without incident. Here the Benignity had thrust a long arm into former Familias space, but since there were no habitable worlds in the area no response had been made. It was easy enough to jump over the Compassionate Hand corridor; in fact, it set up a nice series of jumps to avoid the rest of the Benignity. The only tricky bit was a rotating gravitational anomaly in the neighborhood of the fourth jump point. After bouncing through the first three jumps, it was necessary to drop into normal space and time the next jump to avoid the rapid G changes of the anomaly's active arm. Current charts—such as those Skoterin had picked up from Rotterdam Station— gave ships the best chance to get through that fourth jump with the least wasted time. A mistake in timing could send a ship directly into the Benignity—and the Benignity was known to take advantage of any such lapses.

Heris reviewed the charts several times before that critical fourth jump to make sure their course would not take them too close to the Benignity. Even if it did, they should be safe: they were small, fast, and it would be sheer bad luck if anyone were patrolling the area where they might emerge. She had Oblo check and recheck the course too, both against the charts and against older references.

"The new one's a bit closer, but the border shifts over there, with the anomaly and all. I'd say this was fine."

"Very well." They dropped back into normal space on the mark; Oblo pulled up scan data at once, and began cursing. Heris didn't have to ask. Something—and she wouldn't wager it was sheer bad luck—had gone wrong.

"We're off course—*way* off course." He threw the display up on the main screen. "We should be there—" A green circle, fairly near the red dashed line that represented the border of the Benignity. "And instead we're *here*." Another green circle, this one not so close to the red dashed line, on the opposite side. "And we're entirely too near a gas giant to play games with jumps out. We'll have to crawl it."

"Just what system are we in?" Heris asked.

"Nothing we want to be in." Oblo was scrolling past entries in the reference library, looking for a chart with more detail. "Ah. Not good. Not good at all. The Benignity has bases on the larger moons of this big lump of gravity we're too close to, and the way we dropped out of jumpspace on their doorstep, they could hardly miss us."

"It can hardly be an accident," Ginese said. Neither he nor Meharry turned from their boards. "Coming out right on top of a Benignity base . . . it has to be . . ."

"I know," Heris said. She swatted down the last of her regrets, and touched the control that would lock Sirkin in her quarters, for all the good that would do now. At least she couldn't cause any more mischief. Then she opened the ship's intercom and explained, as briefly as she could, what had gone wrong. "I want Mr. Smith and Lady Cecelia protected, while we have any options at all." There weren't any options, if the Compassionate Hand responded. She would ask Lady Cecelia, out of courtesy, but was sure she'd prefer death to being a Compassionate Hand captive. As for Mr. Smith, he could not be allowed to fall alive into their hands.

"Captain—" That was Ginese. "Ships are on us, and their weapons are hot."

"How many?" she asked.

"Only two," he said, sounding surprised. So was she. If she'd been that base commander, if she'd known (and he must have known) such a prize was coming, she'd have had a net of every available craft, just in case.

✧ Chapter Twenty

Sirkin, slumped in dull misery on her bunk, heard first the delicate snick of the door lock going home, and then the intercom. She clenched her hands in her quilted coverlet. It was impossible. She had checked and rechecked that course; she had paid attention to every warning in the charts . . . she could *not* have made such an error. But here they were, and of course—she had to admit the logic of it—the captain had decided she was responsible. She was the traitor.

I am not! She wanted to scream that aloud, but what good would it do? No one would believe her. All the miseries of the past months landed on her again. Amalie's weakness and Amalie's betrayal . . . and then Amalie's death, the way that mutilated face and body looked in the morgue. Hot tears rolled down Sirkin's face; she didn't notice. And she had tried, tried so hard to work her way out of it. She had acted cheerful; she had gone on working. She had even enjoyed (and felt guilty for enjoying) those visits with Lord Thornbuckle's daughter. Her hand strayed to the locket Brun had bought her; inside was the lock of Amalie's hair Meharry had snipped. Brun—if Brun were here, *she* wouldn't believe it was Sirkin's fault.

Except it had to be. She knew Oblo and the others couldn't be doing it; they were too loyal to Captain Serrano. Besides, why would they start playing tricks now, when everything had gone so well on the way back from Sirialis? It made no sense. She knew she was no traitor; she knew she had done her work carefully. Yet the work she did came undone somehow, between one watch and the next, and if it wasn't Oblo or Issi Guar, who could it be? Was she going crazy? Was she losing her memory? Had someone planted some kind of mind-control in her? The thought terrified her. She sank into a daze of misery, staring at the opposite bulkhead.

When her door lock clicked again, she thought someone had come to kill her. She didn't really care anymore, she told herself, but her gut churned with fear and she felt icy cold. She watched the door slide open with sick dread.

"I . . . know . . . you . . . didn't . . . do . . . that . . ." Lower than she was looking, in the hoverchair, Lady Cecelia. She had not seen Lady Cecelia since she came aboard, and the shock brought her out of herself. She rolled off the bunk and stood up, instantly dizzy from time she'd spent motionless.

"Sit . . . down . . . don't . . . faint."

Sirkin struggled with her dizziness and finally did what she was told, slumping back to the bunk. Lady Cecelia carried a set of keying wands, and looked as smug as her condition allowed.

"You shouldn't—the captain will be really angry—"

"Let . . . her."

"But she's right—something is wrong, and it must have been my fault, because I know Oblo wouldn't—" She was babbling, and couldn't stop; she wanted to cry and fought not to.

"She . . . is . . . wrong . . . I . . . told . . . her . . ."

"Did she say you could let me out?" Hope rose—maybe the captain had found out what really happened; maybe it wasn't her fault after all. Lady Cecelia's face contorted with what she wanted to say, and couldn't.

"Not . . . that. . . . Earlier . . ." Lady Cecelia guided the hoverchair into the cubicle, crowding the bunk, and closed the door behind her. "She . . . doesn't . . . know . . . I . . . came . . . here. . . . She . . . is . . . wrong . . . about . . . you."

"How do you know?" Rude, she realized a moment later, but she had to know.

"Age . . ." Lady Cecelia said, and grinned a death's head grin. "You . . . are . . . not . . . that . . . kind . . . of . . . girl." She held up her hand, a clear signal for Sirkin to listen without interrupting. "Who . . . joined . . ." Pause. "Ship . . . last?"

That had to mean crew, Sirkin thought. "Vivi Skoterin, just before we left Rockhouse. She's from the ship Captain Serrano had in the R.S.S. She's an environmental tech."

"Where . . . now?"

"On the bridge, I expect. Oblo asked her to stand in for me as navigation second during the jumps."

"No . . . Mistake . . ."

"Well, she's not trained as a navigator, but all she has to do is check the numbers as Oblo enters them."

"No . . . that . . . is . . . the . . . mistake."

She wasn't getting all that Lady Cecelia meant.

"She . . . is . . . problem . . ."

Sirkin stared at the old lady, shocked.

"Skoterin? But she's—she's one of *them*. She served with them before. They trust her—" Even as she said it, she saw the flaw in that. They trusted her; it didn't make her trust- worthy. "She couldn't have . . ." she breathed, even as she realized that Skoterin might very well have been able to make Sirkin look incompetent. "She . . . she *brought* me those charts—the ones I used to set up the course . . . the *wrong* course." Inside, a great joyous shout in her head: *Not my fault. It's not my fault. I'm not crazy.*

Lady Cecelia nodded. "She . . . made . . . you . . . look . . . bad . . ." Long pause. "Captain . . . did . . . not . . . look . . . fur- ther . . . mistake."

Sirkin's relief rebounded to fear. "It's too late, though. We're going to be attacked—captured—"

"Not . . . captured . . ." Lady Cecelia's head jerked through a slow shake. "It . . . is . . . too . . . convenient . . . if . . . we . . . disappear. Prince . . . me . . . and . . . all."

"We do have weapons; we might fight free," Sirkin said hopefully. "That is, if Vivi hasn't—"

"She . . . would . . . have . . ." Lady Cecelia said. "But . . . prince . . . help . . ." She turned the hoverchair, opened the door again, and started out as Sirkin stood up uncertainly. "Come . . . with . . . me . . ."

Once the enemy ships began their stalk, Heris gave no further thought to her passengers. At the end, if capture seemed likely, she'd make sure they didn't suffer, but now she had a battle to fight. Maybe.

"How far do we have to go before we can jump?" she asked Oblo.

"A long way . . . my first approximation is over seven hours. Thing's got moons as massive as your average planet—we don't want to be wrong . . ."

"Fine—keep an eye on it. Arkady, what are we facing?"

"Right now just two, but of course our scans are skewed at this relative velocity. Looks like they knew what vector to expect for our insertion but not how much vee we'd have on us. They're running parallel and catching up. And no, we can't outrun them, not if they're the usual C.H. cruiser-weight." He paused, and transferred his scan data to her display. "You can see the weaponry—all hot and ready to fire. Want me to bring them up? I don't think it's enough to scare them off, but—"

"No. We can't bluff, but maybe we can surprise them when it counts." Heris glanced over at his boards, where the status lights showed ships' weapons as strings of green lights, each column tipped with one yellow. "I wonder why they didn't take us when we dropped out," she asked, not expecting an answer. "The logical thing for them to do is blow us away—no one knew we would be inside Benignity space—and if they did know, they'd shrug and go 'Oops.' If we quietly disappear, it solves a lot of problems for some powerful people."

"I'd be glad to quietly disappear if I could figure out how," Oblo said, scowling at his board. "Vivi, pull up this section in Shirmer's Atlas, will you? Maybe they've got something—"

"Yessir." Heris watched as Skoterin picked her way around the backup navigation board, punching first one key then another. Slow—of course, she didn't know the board well; it wasn't her specialty. If only Sirkin—the good Sirkin—had been there . . . but no use wishing. Suddenly Ginese and Meharry both cursed and started tapping at their boards.

"What?" Heris asked, though she could see from here that the weapons boards had changed color. Green lights had gone orange; the yellow lights at the top had gone to blue; the system was locked down, nonfunctional.

"Damn her!" Petris turned to glare at Heris. "What do you want to bet she had a control tap to her quarters?"

"No bet. Go down there and—" And what? Kill her? Heris couldn't give that order, not yet. "Get it fixed," she said. "Call Mr. Guar to the bridge, Oblo; you need more experienced help. Skoterin, get back to Mr. Haidar, and tell him to unlock the small arms. Bring us each a weapon, and start stacking the excess in the corridor. Here's the key wand for the weapons locker."

"Yes, Captain." Skoterin hurried away; Petris grabbed a toolkit off the bulkhead and followed her.

"They stripped our beacon," Oblo said. "Maybe they wanted to be sure they had the right ship . . ."

"Maybe." Seconds ticked away.

"Heris, Sirkin isn't in her quarters." Petris, on the open intercom. "And I can't find any control tap. She might have been somewhere else when you locked the doors—" He sounded both angry and uncertain. Heris tried to remember if she'd actually checked the personal monitors to confirm Sirkin's location . . . she didn't know.

"Or she might have gotten out. If she's been planning this, she might have key wands—"

"I'm not finding a hard tap," Ginese said, from the deck under his control boards. "Not one single thread that shouldn't be here. Of course, a directed magnetic pulse could do that, but it would have to be close."

"A control override would work, anywhere between here

and the weapons themselves," Meharry said. She, too, was half under her console, prodding at things.

"But not on this ship—it's not like a ship designed for fighting. We had no regional alternative nodes. Remember how we had to route the cables all over the place? To knock the whole board down like that, it'd have to be intercepting signals pretty high up . . . which ought to show as an additional cable . . . or be a pulse signal from somewhere on the bridge." Arkady's voice sounded muffled as he disappeared completely from view. "And I don't see . . ."

Meharry's face popped up from beneath her console. "Mine's clean. I see what you mean, Arkady. We put in that shielding—if it's pulse, it has to be on the bridge somewhere."

Heris said, "What about a secondary? Something exterior to signal a controller on the bridge, through the regular optical cables, and set off a pulse signal?"

"Might be. Complicated, though. Doesn't always work even on *our* ships." Our ships clearly meant R.S.S. ships. "What's Sirkin's secondary training?"

"She could do it," Heris said, answering the real question. "I had her crawling through all the computer controls on the first voyage—she knows as much about this ship's electrical and electronic layout as I do. The only thing she might not know is the weapons systems you installed when she wasn't aboard."

"INTRUDER. FAMILIAS SHIP *HARPER VALLEY*." That was on the broad band, in their own language—heavily accented, but quite understandable.

"Just in case we didn't know who we were," Oblo said with a shrug. "Now what, Captain?"

"Well, they didn't blow us away straight off," Heris said. "Let's see what they do with this." She thought a moment, then said "Send them a voiceburst, just as we did with Livadhi." That might buy a few seconds—but they needed hours. She got back on the intercom. "Petris—better link with Skoterin and get yourself a weapon. Wherever Sirkin is, she might be dangerous."

"Right." He had left Sirkin's quarters, she saw on the personnel monitor, and headed toward the main service corridor. She couldn't find Sirkin now, but that made sense; she'd have taken off the tagger, and probably done something to keep the automatic sensors from recognizing her. Heris hadn't yet entered the data for all Cecelia's medical team, so she didn't know who made up that cluster of dots outside Mr. Smith's quarters, the cluster now moving along a corridor toward the service area.

"Lady Cecelia," Heris said over the intercom. "Please stay in your quarters, and get your medical team with you. It is not safe to wander around right now."

"INTRUDER SHIP *HARPER VALLEY* CEASE MANEUVERS OR WE WILL FIRE ON YOU."

"So tactful," Ginese said.

"I've got the last squirt out of her," Oblo said. "Trying to get in the shadow of that moon—"

"Which you hope no one is hiding behind," Heris murmured. "I would be."

"Swing out, then?"

"Costs us vee, gains us space. I hate the feeling we're being driven into a preset trap."

"Fine." He made adjustments on his board. Meharry straightened.

"That's odd."

"What?"

"You touched your board, and mine flickered. Do something on the other one."

Issigai Guar, on the secondary, shrugged, and fed in a query.

"Aha." Meharry reached for her own toolkit and fiddled with it. "So that's—it's controlled from your board, Issi. Let me get at it." He pushed back willingly, and Meharry ran her instruments over it. "She must have set this up with a time delay, so anyone touching the board after a certain time would set off a signal locking up weapons control. Clever. If she'd been better at the patches, my board wouldn't have flickered and we'd never have found it. Glad she was careless about this, too."

"They're targeting," Ginese said. Meaning, *Shut up and fix it*.

"I'm not wasting time," Meharry said. She plucked the overlay off the top of the secondary board and prodded something underneath with delicacy. "This little beauty—I don't want to blow anything if it's wired that way—can just now slip . . . *out*." She slipped the tiny object into her pocket.

Heris saw, before Ginese could speak, his board come live. One by one, the orange lights turned green, one column after another as the weapons ran through self-checks and warmed.

"Code Three as soon as you can, Mr. Ginese," Heris said. Meharry's board began to green up, far slower than Heris wanted. Guar was reassembling his console; Oblo wore an expression of limpid unconcern that Heris knew from earlier battles.

"LAST WARNING. INTRUDER SHIP CEASE MANEUVERING IN TEN SECONDS OR WE WILL FIRE ON YOU." Nicely calculated, that. The transmission lag was down to eight seconds, but the whole—

"Here it goes—" said Ginese. On the large screen, the tracks of the other ships, the analysis of their weaponry, the first white-hot arcs as two missiles lofted toward where they would be, one from each pursuer. His board was almost completely green, the yellow dots lit now halfway across the top.

And in the corridors of the yacht, small-arms fire erupted, short and disastrous. Then silence. Meharry shifted her board's controls to Ginese, and moved to stand by the bridge hatch.

"Lockdown, Captain?"

"No—we've got loyal crew out there . . ."

Oblo was up, too. "Issi, your control. I can go out—"

"No . . . there's only one to worry about, and with any luck she's dead." And with enough luck there's no hole in the hull, and no one else was hit, and Lady Cecelia and Mr. Smith are still safe for the brief length of this uneven fight. All that ran through Heris's mind as she watched on the screen the enemy's missiles coming nearer. On Ginese's board, the yellow dots turned red as the weapons came operational.

"Let's just see . . ." Ginese said. His finger stabbed at the board and the two missiles seemed to stagger in their course, then swerve aside. "Yeah. Still works fine."

Heris let out the breath she had taken. "If they could all be that easy," she said. That hadn't even required their offensive weaponry. Ginese chuckled, a sound to strike any sensible person cold.

"Then I couldn't play with my other little darlings." His shoulders tensed, watching his displays, and he murmured, "Oh, you would . . . idiots."

Heris didn't interrupt with questions. The second wave of missiles had been launched before the enemy would have had time to get scan data back from the yacht's activated weapons. Four, this time, bracketing their expected course. These Arkady dispatched with contemptuous ease. What mattered now was what else they would use . . . their scans revealed optical and ballistic possibilities.

"Response, Captain?" They could of course launch a counterattack—no one was there to remind her it was a bad idea to get into a slugfest with two larger ships.

"Let's try to dodge their bullets and help them run low on ammunition," Heris said. "Why change what's working?" She kept an eye on Oblo's scanning screens . . . if that moon had held a trap, and if the pursuers had realized they weren't going into it, a third ship might come dashing out right about . . . *there*. But they had trusted too much to their trap; the third ship had low relative vee, and though boosting frantically, was caught deep in the well with little maneuverability.

"There's a target, Mr. Ginese, if you just want something to shoot at."

"A bit chancy," he said. "I'd rather save what we've got for these two."

"Just don't forget that third one; if it launches something at us, it could still hurt us."

"Right, Captain." In the tone of teach-your-grandmother-to-suck-eggs. In that long pause, while the enemy realized they had an armed ship and not a helpless victim to subdue, while the enemy commander—Heris imagined—cursed and chose an alternate plan—she had time to wonder why it was so *quiet*. Someone should have reported back by now.

She called up the personnel monitor again, and saw the cluster of green dots in exactly the wrong place, down in the service corridor near the weapons locker. What if Sirkin had attacked Lady Cecelia—shot the clone—was holding Lady Cecelia hostage?

"Meharry."

"Yes, Captain."

Heris pointed to the layout with the little green dots. "Get down there and find out what's going on—and break it up. First priority, secure the ship; next, Lady Cecelia; next, Mr. Smith."

"Yes, sir!" Meharry's sleepy green eyes were wide awake now, and eager. Oblo moved forward but Heris waved him back.

"No—we've got a battle up here, too, and you can do either nav or weapons. Go help Ginese for now."

Sirkin followed Lady Cecelia's chair out of her quarters with a mixture of reluctance and glee. It wasn't her fault; she hadn't made those mistakes, and she knew—she thought she knew—who had. But nobody would believe her, she was sure, and she doubted the captain would have the patience to let Lady Cecelia literally spell it out. If anyone came down here, they'd believe the worst of her . . . especially now that she was out of her quarters.

Lady Cecelia's hoverchair made swift, silent progress along the corridor toward the main lounge. Sirkin looked over her head to see Mr. Smith and several of Lady Cecelia's medical team clumped together there. As she watched, they came forward, and Lady Cecelia reversed the chair, nearly hitting Sirkin.

"Weapons," said Mr. Smith. "Where are the small-arms lockers?" Sirkin knew that, but she wasn't sure what they were doing, or if it was right. He grinned at her, that famous grin she'd seen on many a newscast, and punched her arm lightly. "Come on, we've got to get armed, and keep whoever it is from taking the ship away from your captain."

"Skoterin," she found herself saying as she led the way back into crew country. "Joined the ship just before we left Rockhouse . . . old crewmate . . ."

"One of the group that was court-martialed?"

"No—just demoted afterwards. Some enlisted were, she said."

"What specialty?"

"Environmental systems," Sirkin said, almost jogging to keep up with his long legs.

They came out of that corridor into another, which angled downward; Heris would have recognized it as leading to the place where Iklind had died. Sirkin did not; she only knew they should take the turn to the right. The weapons lockers, filled with all those expensive oddments (as Ginese had called them) on Sirialis, were that way, around a turn or two. Sirkin, sure of the way, went first; Mr. Smith came behind her, and then Lady Cecelia in her chair, surrounded by attendants.

Around the last corner . . . Sirkin stopped abruptly, and almost fell as Lady Cecelia's chair bumped into the back of her legs. The weapons lockers were open, and on the deck lay Nasiru Haidar, facedown and motionless, with blood pooled under his head. Sirkin could not speak; her mind ran over the same words like a hamster in its wheel . . . *I didn't do it, I didn't do it, I didn't do it.* Mr. Smith pushed past her, and knelt beside the fallen man; Sirkin edged forward, trying to remember to breathe. And one of the medical attendants rushed forward, opening a belt pack.

"Just stop right there," someone said. Sirkin looked up as Skoterin stepped out of an open hatch across from the weapons lockers. Skoterin had one of the weapons—Sirkin wasn't sure what it was, though she knew she'd seen its like in newsclips and adventure cubes. It looked deadly enough, and Skoterin handled it as if it were part of her body. "How very convenient," Skoterin said. "Just the people I wanted to see, and now you're all here together." She had on a black mesh garment over her uniform; Sirkin found her mind wandering to it, wondering what it was.

"Poor Brigdis," Skoterin said, looking right at her. Sirkin felt her heart falter in its beat. "You must continue to be the scapegoat awhile longer, I fear. Pity that you went mad and murdered Lady Cecelia and the prince—or his clone, it doesn't much matter."

"But I didn't do any of it!" That burst out of Sirkin's mouth without any warning.

"Of course you didn't, though I rather hoped you wouldn't figure that out until whatever afterlife you believe in."

"But you were on her ship! How can you do this to her? To the others?"

Skoterin grimaced. "It is distasteful, I'll admit. I have nothing against Captain Serrano, even though she did manage to ruin my career as a deep agent. It's certainly not personal vengeance for having managed to arrange the deaths of two of my relatives—"

"Who?"

"Relatives I didn't particularly like, in fact, though we do take family more seriously than some other cultures. Who scratches my brother—or cousin, as in this case—scratches me. You were there, Brigdis: surely you remember the terrible death by poisoning of poor Iklind."

"But you—"

"Enough. You two by Haidar—move back over there." Mr. Smith and the medical team member—Sirkin had not even had a chance to learn their names or positions—

moved back near Lady Cecelia. "You, Brig—you stand by Haidar."

She was moving, under the black unseeing eye of that weapon, despite herself. She could hardly feel her body; she felt as if she were floating. Her foot bumped something; she looked down to find her shoe pressed against Haidar's head. He was breathing; she felt the warm breath even through the toe of her shoe. Her mind clung to that, like a child clinging to a favorite toy in a storm. One thing was normal: Haidar was alive.

"Take one of those weapons from the rack, and hit him." Sirkin stared at Skoterin. "Go on, girl. They're not loaded; you can't hurt me with it. I want your fingerprints on it, along with his blood. Whack him in the head with it, hard."

"No." It came out very soft, but she had said it. Skoterin's face contracted.

"Do it now, or I'll shoot your precious Lady Cecelia."

"You will anyway." Sirkin felt the uselessness of her argument, but she also felt stubborn. If she was going to die anyway, she wanted to die without her fingerprints on a weapon which had killed someone else. "Why should I help you?"

"I don't have time for this," Skoterin said, and levelled the weapon at Sirkin. Sirkin panicked, grabbed the nearest object in the rack, and threw it at Skoterin, just as Mr. Smith made a dive for her, and Skoterin fired.

The noise was appalling; Sirkin heard screaming as well as the weapon itself. When it was over, she felt very very tired, and only slowly realized that she had been hit . . . that was her blood on the deck now . . . and she had to close her eyes, just for a moment.

Meharry smelled trouble before she got anywhere near the weapons lockers. An earthy, organic stench that had no business wafting out of the air vents. She knew it well, and proceeded with even more caution thereafter, taking a roundabout route she hoped no one would expect. She had her personal weapons, just as Arkady had—hers were the little knives in their sheaths, and the very small but very deadly little automatic tucked into her boot. If Sirkin thought she was going to take Meharry by surprise . . . She paused, listening again. A faint groan, was it? Real or fake? Scuffing feet, difficult breaths . . . really she didn't know why everyone didn't carry a pocket scanner. Much more sensible than sticking your head around corners so that someone could shoot it off. Carefully, she slid out the fiberoptic probe, and eased its tip to the corner . . . then checked her backtrail and overhead before putting her eye to the eyepiece.

Carnage, she'd suspected. Bodies sprawled all over the deck near the weapons lockers. And on his feet, cursing softly as he applied pressure bandages as fast as he could, Petris. Why hadn't he reported? Then she saw the ruin of the nearby pickups. He must have found this and simply set to work to save those he could. She retrieved the visual probe, and hoped she was right in her guess—because if Petris was the problem they were in a mess far too bad for belief.

"Petris—" she called softly, staying out of sight.

"Methlin! Tell Heris to get the rest of the medic team down here fast. Lady Cecelia's still alive."

"You all right?"

"I got here late," Petris said, not really answering the question. Good enough. Meharry backed up to the first undamaged intercom and called in. Multiple casualties, what she'd seen.

"*What?*"

Just get the medics down here, he says. I'm going to help unless Arkady needs me—"

"No, we only have three ships after us now." Only three, right. "I've put Oblo with Arkady."

Meharry walked around the corner, still wary, and found a situation that didn't fit her theories.

"Here—" Petris shoved rolls of bandaging material at her. "See what you can do with those three; they're alive. The clone's dead; so is Skoterin, and I think Haidar and Sirkin, but now you're here I can look."

Meharry continued Petris's work, glancing at Lady Cecelia—clearly alive, though bloody, but lying against the wreck of her chair as if stunned. She took a quick look at Skoterin, startled to see her wearing personal armor—it hadn't saved her from a shot to the head.

"Damn Sirkin," Meharry said. "I didn't think she could shoot that straight."

"She didn't," Petris said. "I did. It wasn't Sirkin after all."

"Skoterin?"

"Yep. The dumbass wasted time explaining it to them—if she'd gone on a bit longer, I'd have nailed her without the rest of this. But she started to shoot Sirkin, and the clone jumped her, and that's when I arrived."

Meharry shook her head. "I didn't know *you* could shoot that straight." Whatever else she might have said was cut off by the arrival of the others in Lady Cecelia's medical team.

✧ Chapter Twenty-one

On the bridge, Heris heard Meharry's first report with disbelief; she located the rest of Cecelia's staff and sent them down. Meanwhile . . .

Meanwhile the Compassionate Hand ships continued to close, but did not attack.

"What are they waiting for?" Ginese asked. "Do they think we can take them?"

"Nice thought. Let's hope they think so until Meharry gets back up here. Maybe they think we'll surrender if they give us time."

Issi Guar said "There's something coming into the system—something big."

"Not Labienus and the Tenth Legion again," Heris said. They had been dragged through innumerable ancient texts on warfare in the Academy: ground, sea, air, and space. One of the clubs had put on a skit about Labienus and the Tenth Legion—the way the Tenth Legion kept showing up like an adventure cube hero in the nick of time—which they all thought very funny until one of their professors reminded them of Julius's career stats. Nonetheless, it had become a byword among officers of her class.

"No . . . I doubt it." His fingers flew over the board, trying on one screen after another. "I wish we'd gotten that VX-84 you found, Oblo."

"She said nothing stolen," Oblo said, with a sidelong glance at Heris.

"I said nothing *illegal*," Heris corrected. "But you didn't pay any attention to that—what stopped you this time?"

343

"Guy wanted more than I wanted to pay . . . I don't like messy jobs." Messy, to Oblo, could have several meanings. "Let him take care of his own family problems," he continued. Heris let it roll over her and tried to figure out what the Compassionate Hand commanders were doing. The yacht was running flat out, on a course that the gas giant and its satellites would curve into a blunt parabola. They had emerged from jump too close to its mass to do anything else. The two larger C.H. vessels paralleled it, slowly catching up; the signal delay from them was down to five seconds. The third had been unable to gain on them.

Meharry appeared at the bridge entrance, bloodstained and breathless. "Captain—it wasn't Sirkin after all. It was Skoterin. Sirkin's been shot; she's alive—"

"INTRUDER YOU HAVE BEEN WARNED. UNDER THE JUSTICE OF THE BENIGNITY OF THE COMPASSIONATE—"

"Now, Arkady!" Heris said.

"—HAND YOU STAND CONDEMNED OF TRESPASS, REFUSAL TO HEAVE TO—"

"They never said 'Heave to'; they said 'don't maneuver'," Oblo said. "Weapons away, Captain. And it's supposed to be 'convicted,' not 'condemned.' "

"—AND OTHER SERIOUS CRIMES FOR WHICH CAPITAL PUNISHMENT IS THE CUSTOMARY SENTENCE. PROTESTS WILL BE REGISTERED WITH YOUR GOVERNMENT AND INDEMNITY DEMANDED FOR YOUR CRIMES. BY THE POWER VESTED IN ME AS AN OFFICER OF THE—"

"Targeting . . . incoming, live warheads, *much* faster than before."

"BENIGNITY OF THE COMPASSIONATE HAND, SENTENCE IS HEREBY CARRIED OUT. JUSTINIAN IKLIND, COMMANDER—"

"I think those little warts were just testing us before—" Ginese sounded more insulted than worried.

"Get off my board, Oblo, and let me at them," Meharry said.

"Spoilsport." They switched places smoothly, and Oblo returned to his own console. His brows rose. "My, my. Look who's come calling."

"Unless it's half a battle group, I don't care," Heris said, her eyes fixed on the main screen. The incoming missiles jinked, but relocked on the yacht; their own seemed to be going in the right direction but—no—she lost them in the static from the incomings, which had just blown up far short of their target.

"If they thought all we had was ECM to unlock targeting, they're going to be annoyed," Ginese said.

"That wasn't a bad guess, Captain," Oblo said. "Although it's only one cruiser."

"Our side?"

"By the beacon, yes. By behavior—we'll have to see when their scans clear. It says it's Livadhi again."

Livadhi's cruiser had arrived with far more residual velocity than the yacht, and more mass as well—it appeared on the scan with its icon already trailing a skewed angle. Livadhi, it seemed, meant to be in on the action.

The Compassionate Hand ships, on the other hand, made it clear what they thought of his interference. One engaged him at once, with a storm of missiles. The other changed course, angling across the yacht's path to come between yacht and Livadhi's cruiser. The third—

Heris reached out for the tight beam transmitter they weren't supposed to have. "Oblo, get me a lock on Livadhi's ship."

"Why? He's got Koutsoudas on scan one—d'you think he'd miss anything?"

"No, but he's being shot at. Give him a break, can't you?"

"Right." Oblo nodded when he had the lock.

Heris flipped the transmitter switch. "Livadhi—third bogie on your tail—watch it."

As if he'd been waiting for her signal, her own tight beam

receiver lit. "We've got to stop meeting like this, Heris. You got bad data at Rotterdam. You've got a traitor aboard. That's why we're here."

"Not for long if you don't watch it," Heris sent back, eyeing her own scans. But Livadhi, in a fully crewed cruiser, had more eyes to watch than she did, and the first attacking missiles died well outside his screens. She wondered what his orders were— if he had any—because his counterattack was already launched. She had never thought of him as a possible rogue commander, but here he was deep in someone else's territory and opening fire.

"Something else I wish we had," Oblo muttered, watching. "Screens that would stop something bigger than a juice can."

"Wouldn't fit, remember?" Military-grade ship screens ate cubage and power both; offensive armament could be crammed into small ships without room for shields.

Both Compassionate Hand cruisers now engaged Livadhi's ship. Heris began to hope everyone would forget about her . . . given enough time, they could continue their swing around the gas giant, reach a safe jump distance, and disappear. That would leave Livadhi in a fix, but he seemed to be doing very well. His first salvo sparkled all over one of the enemy's screens, an indication that he had almost breached them. And if he had come to rescue them, give them a chance, then the smart thing to do was creep away and let the professionals do the fighting. She didn't really like that, but the yacht was no warship.

"Captain—" That was Petris, on the intercom. "Medical report: We've got three dead, two critical, three serious—"

"Lady Cecelia?"

"Alive, conscious, in pain but she'll make it. Skoterin, Mr. Smith, and Haidar are dead. Sirkin and Lady Cecelia's communications therapist are critical—we may lose them without a trauma team, which we don't have. Three others of her medical team are in serious condition. Lady Cecelia's physician is unhurt, but trauma's not her specialty—she's a geriatric neurologist—and she says she's out of her depth with open chest and belly wounds."

Heris fought down her rage and grief. That wouldn't help. She felt her mind slide into the familiar pattern . . . a cool detachment that allowed rapid processing of all alternatives, uncluttered by irrelevant worries. They had dying passengers; they needed medical care. The nearest source of trauma care was . . . right over there, being shot at.

And of course it was the best excuse for getting involved, although she pushed back a niggling suspicion that that carried more weight than it should.

"Thank you, Petris," she said. "We'll do what we can. Livadhi's out there now, and he has a trauma center. Assuming we win the battle."

Silence for a moment, as he digested that, and calculated for himself the probability that the yacht and Livadhi's ship might be in one piece, in one place, able to transfer patients, before they died. "Right. I'm going back down to check the damage—stray shots hit some circuits around there, and now that we've no live environmental specialists—" It was not the time to tell him that one of the things she loved about him was his ability to stick to priorities.

"I think," she said, in a thoughtful tone that made Oblo and Meharry give her a quick look, "I *think* those Compassionate Hand ships have decided we're not worth bothering with. They seem to think the important thing is keeping Livadhi away from us."

"Yes, Captain?" Oblo looked both confused and hopeful.

"Well, they got between us. All of them—" Because the trailing third ship had risked a microjump—a *huge* risk, but it had worked—to catch up to the battle. Dangerous, but it had worked. "And nobody's targeting us. Now speaking as a tactical commander, don't you think that was stupid?" None of them answered, but they all grinned. "I think they just put themselves in our trap. Oblo, how much maneuvering scope do we have?"

"Not much—but we can close the range on them, if you want. It'll cost us another half hour to a safe jump range."

"Jump won't get our wounded to care any sooner," Heris said. "But Livadhi's got a perfectly good sickbay over there, if somebody doesn't blow a hole in it. Let's make sure no one does."

The Compassionate Hand ships clearly thought they had an enemy cruiser locked in their box; for all that Heris's scans could detect, they paid no attention to the yacht's change of course that brought her swinging out toward the warships. They were too busy pounding at Livadhi's ship, and dealing with his salvos. If the yacht had not existed, it would have been a well-conducted attack, almost textbook quality.

"Of course, when we *do* fire, they'll be all over us," Heris said.

"If they don't notice us another minute or so, we'll be close enough to blow one of them completely," Ginese replied.

"One of them . . ." Meharry said softly. "But the other two will have to acquire us, get firing solutions . . . we have time."

That minute passed in taut silence. Livadhi's attack breached one of the enemy ship's shields, but it neither broke up nor pulled away. Major damage, was Oblo's guess, but he couldn't understand the Compassionate Hand transmissions, which were in a foreign language and encoded anyway. "I think they rolled her, though, to put the damaged shields on this side."

"That's your prime target," Heris told Ginese. "You know wounded C.H. commanders—they get suicidal. How much longer?"

"At your word, Captain."

"Now." The yacht shivered as Ginese sent a full third of its ballistic capability down the port tubes and out toward the wounded C.H. ship. Oblo rolled the yacht on its axis to present the remaining loaded tubes to the fight. Seconds ticked by. Then the yacht's missiles slammed into the enemy cruiser, one after another exploding in a carefully timed sequence. The external visual darkened, protecting its lenses from the flare of light as the cruiser itself ruptured and blew apart.

Heris spent no time watching. "Oblo—maximum deceleration, now."

He gave her a startled look but complied. The yacht could not withstand extreme maneuvers, but a course change like this might be enough to surprise the enemy. And avoid any late-arriving missiles that Livadhi had sent at that cruiser. Unfortunately, it would blur their scans just when they needed them clear, but—

"There they go—Livadhi did have a couple on the way."

"I would hate to get blown away by my rescuer," Heris said.

"I have a lock on the second cruiser," Meharry said. "Permission—"

"Do it." Again the yacht shivered; she wasn't built for this kind of stress. But the salvo was away . . . Heris tried to calculate what that did to their gross mass, and what that meant to maneuvering capability, but at the moment the figures wouldn't come.

The scans had adjusted to their new settings; she could see that the other two Compassionate Hand ships were changing course, the trailing one swinging wide now, losing range to take up a safer position, where Heris could not attack it without risking Livadhi in the middle or performing maneuvers beyond the yacht's capacity. The nearer enemy ship and Livadhi continued to exchange fire, and Oblo reported that the nearer ship was trying to get a targeting lock on the yacht.

With their course change, it took seconds longer for their salvo to reach the enemy, and this time someone had been watching. Heris felt a grudging admiration for a crew that could react that quickly to a new menace. Half their missiles detonated outside the ship's shield, and the rest splashed harmlessly against it. Return fire, already on its way . . . but Meharry and Ginese were able to break the target lock of some, and the timers of the rest.

This time it was Livadhi's crew that exploited an opening—

or perhaps defending against Heris's attack had taken just that necessary bit from the shields—for Livadhi's salvo blew through, and the enemy cruiser lost power and control. It tumbled end over end, shedding pieces of itself to clutter the scans.

"And that leaves number three," Ginese said.

"And their reinforcements. It may take them a while to get here, but they'll arrive."

The third ship now fell farther back. Heris didn't trust that, but she didn't have the resources to pursue it. Instead, she changed course again, returning to maximum forward acceleration, and put a tight beam on Livadhi's ship.

"We have critical casualties," she said. "Can you accept five patients?"

"How's your ship?"

"Not from that—from a fight inside. That traitor you mentioned."

"I see. Frankly, I don't want to risk docking with you while that other warship's untouched . . . I can send over a pinnace with a trauma team, would that help?"

"Yes." It would help, but would it be enough? She could see Livadhi's point—if she'd commanded the cruiser, she wouldn't want to have some civilian ship nuzzled up close when an attack started. "But we have no supplies for trauma, and just empty space . . . send what you can."

"Right away. Stand by for recognition signals—"

"Why not Fleet Blue—I already know that."

He actually laughed. "Of course—sorry. Fleet Blue it is."

The pinnace should be too small to attract fire from that third ship; Heris could barely find it on scans herself and she was much closer.

Time passed. Heris could not leave the bridge, not with a hostile ship out there; she sent Petris to help the pinnace mate with their docking access tube and reported its safe arrival to Livadhi. Was it too late for their casualties? She heard nothing from the medical team—of course, they would be busy. Better not to interrupt. Another hour, and another. The third Compassionate Hand ship continued to fall behind, though it did not turn away.

"Sorry it took so long." That was Petris, as blood-streaked as Meharry. "I wanted to patch up a few things—near as I can tell, nothing really important got holes in it. I'll have to read up on the systems, though."

"And our casualties?"

He shook his head. "Can't tell yet. They brought two trauma surgeons and their teams; Sirkin's the worst, but they're still working on her. Said if they could stabilize them, a regen tank would do the rest, but there's no way to load a regen tank on a pinnace."

"Lady Cecelia?"

"Is spitting mad, near as I can tell. A fragment got her synthesizer, and her communications specialist died, so she's having a hard time making herself understood. She got a shallow flesh wound—probably the same fragment that ruined her synthesizer—but she's fine. Wants to see you, when you've time, but I explained you wouldn't."

"Where is she?"

"In the thick of things. Insists she wants to stay with Sirkin, and the med teams are too busy to carry her out—her hoverchair got a solid hit and it's down, too."

"Have you found out any more about Skoterin?"

"Only what I heard as I came on the scene. She was a deep agent for the Compassionate Hand, before she joined up, and a relative of that mole who died on your first voyage."

"And perhaps that guard who died on Sirialis, the one who shot young George," Heris said. "Iklind—that was the name. Livadhi claims we got bad chart data from Rotterdam Station, which is why we ended up here . . . and Skoterin is the one who fetched the charts from the Stationmaster."

"And altered them on the way? Could be done. She could've

been messing up Sirkin's work, too—we trusted her, old shipmate as she was."

"Lady Cecelia tried to tell me—said it wasn't Sirkin—but I wouldn't believe her. And now three people are dead—"

"One of whom should be." Petris reached out a hand and drew it back. Heris saw the movement, and wished they were not on the bridge in a hostile situation; she needed that touch, some comfort in a bad time. "If it's any comfort, not one of us caught on; we all made the same mistake." The others on the bridge nodded.

"I had liked Sirkin a lot," Meharry said. "So I cut her more slack than the rest of you—kept thinking it was delayed grief reaction or something—but it never occurred to me it could be sabotage. Just like you, and Petris, I trusted Skoterin just because she'd served with us even though I knew some of that crew were Lepescu's agents. I didn't know her before, but— she was military, she'd been a shipmate, that was enough. And that was flat-out stupid."

"That may be," Heris said, "but I'm still at fault."

"That's true." Oblo turned around and grinned. "The great Captain Serrano makes mistakes—what a surprise! We thought you were perfect!"

"I didn't," Guar said. "I always said her nose was too short."

"All right, all right," Heris said, fighting back a chuckle. "I get your point. We're all old friends and we all made a mistake, and we go on from here, sadder but wiser. If Sirkin dies, a *lot* sadder."

"I'd bet on her to make it," Petris said. "With Lady Cecelia sitting there radiating mother-hen protectiveness. She doesn't need speech to convey how much she cares."

Heris's tight beam receiver lit again, and she picked up the headset. "Heris, how close are you to your critical jump distance?"

She looked at Oblo and mouthed "Jump? How long?" He looked at his plot and punched in some corrections, then looked again.

"Less than an hour, Captain—looks like we might make it. Forty-three minutes and a handful of seconds, to be more precise."

Heris relayed that to Livadhi. "Good," he said. "If nothing else lights up, I'll expect you to jump out of here as soon as you can—take my medical teams with you for now—and I'll cover your backtrail. Don't tell me your destination, but do you need any coordinates for a safe jump out?"

"Yes," Heris said. "I'd like to clear the Benignity with one jump—possible?"

"Yes—here—" He read off a string of numbers that Heris passed to Oblo. When she read them back, he said, "Fine. Now—I am authorized to say that the situation we both know about is extremely unstable. The Council would like to speak with Lady Cecelia at her earliest convenience; Lord Thornbuckle has filed a Question with the Grand Table; the Crown asks if you can transport a certain Mr. Smith and his friend back home."

"Medical intervention must come first," Heris said, her mind beginning to buzz with the implications of Livadhi's report.

"Of course. I understand. I would urge extreme caution, and suggest that we rendezvous for your return so that we can provide an escort. You might also consider rearming—"

"Thank you," Heris said. "Give me a contact coordinate." Another string of numbers followed. Then Livadhi broke contact. Minute by minute the yacht edged closer to safety. Heris kept expecting something else to go wrong—another Compassionate Hand ship appearing in their path, another crisis aboard—but nothing interrupted them, and at last Oblo was able to put them back into jump mode, into the undefined and chaotic existence that lay between the times and spaces they knew.

Livadhi's trauma teams had turned two of the guest suites into sickbays. In one, Sirkin lay attached to more tubes and wires than she had arms and legs. Beside her, on a stretcher,

Lady Cecelia lay on her side holding Sirkin's hand. Across that room, two of the less critically wounded were dozing, their bandages making humps and lumps under the bedclothes.

"Lady Cecelia," Heris said. Her employer looked only slightly better than Sirkin, pale and exhausted.

"I . . . told . . . you . . ." Her own voice, with its cracked and uneven tone, was just understandable.

"You did, and you were right. I'm very sorry. I should have listened to you."

"If . . . I . . . could . . . talk . . . dammit . . ."

"I know—you have so much to say—and your people died, too. Must be much worse for you—"

"Thought . . . we . . . all . . . die . . ."

"So did I, for a while there. Let me tell you what happened." Heris outlined the events, and then waited for Cecelia's response.

"Damn . . . lucky . . ."

"It's not over," Heris said. "We have to get you all to Guerni; we have to get you home safely, and survive whatever's going on. And find out who's doing it, and why."

"Lorenza . . . Tourinos," Cecelia said. "Remember . . ."

"I will. But you're going to be able to give your own testimony."

The Guerni Republic's customs were as quick and capable with incoming medical emergencies as with casual trade. Heris requested the fastest possible incoming lane; customs sent an escort alongside to do a close-up scan.

"You've been here before; your references are good; you're cleared with the usual warnings," the escort officer said.

"Thanks. What about a medical shuttle from the Station?"

"We'll arrange it. Actually, trauma cases may not need to go downside; we have major medical available on all stations. We normally handle everything onstation unless that facility is full—saves transport stress and time."

Heris was impressed all over again. It made sense, but in Familias space, most stations transferred serious trauma down to the planet. She had heard it explained as being more cost-effective, but the Guernesi were supposed to be the galaxy experts on cost-effectiveness.

When they arrived at the Station, medical teams awaited them dockside, and the casualties were transferred quickly to the Station trauma center. Cecelia would be shuttled down to the neuromedical center later; she had agreed to have Meharry and Ginese escort her there. Heris would stay up at the Station until Sirkin was out of danger. As soon as she had arranged a private shuttle for Cecelia, her surviving attendants, and her bodyguards, Heris went to the Station hospital.

"Just barely in time," she was told. "That artificial blood substitute saved her, but you really pushed its limits—should have been using exterior gas exchange as well . . . I'm surprised your doctors didn't."

Heris decided not to explain the limits of transferring medical equipment between ships in deep space while in hostile territory. "When they've finished packing up on our ship, maybe they'll talk to you about it," she said. After all, Livadhi's medical teams had already said they wanted to explore the medical riches of the system.

"And we have a newer substitute with a better performance you might want to consider stocking—a license to manufacture would be available through our medical technology exports office—"

Typical. To the Guernesi, every disaster had the seeds of profit in it. "When can I see our casualties?" she asked. "Especially Brigdis Sirkin . . ."

"The two worst, not for at least two days. They'll have two long sessions in regen, but they need transfusions first. The other three will be out of the regen tanks in another six hours, so any time after that—"

Heris went back to the yacht, and found that Livadhi's teams had scoured the areas they'd been using; these now smelled like any sickbay. But one of them stopped her in the midst of her thanks.

"What's this, Captain?" The woman held up an unmistakable cockroach egg case. Heris had a sudden vision of being detained forever on a charge of importing illegal biologicals.

"An egg case," Heris said, trying to sound unconcerned. Inspiration hit. "We had to evacuate Lady Cecelia from Rotterdam in haste; we had no time for proper disinfection procedures. And she was living at a training stable."

"Ah. I presume you disinfected the ship—?"

"Oh, yes. I can't be sure we got them all, but we'll do it again. It was on my schedule, but then we came out of jump in the wrong place—"

"Oh—of course." The woman's accusing expression relaxed. "I'd forgotten about Lady Cecelia's luggage . . . and from a stable yard . . . it's just that contamination from vermin is a serious problem."

You don't know the half of it, Heris thought. At least they'd found an egg case, and not one of the albino cockroaches. She wasn't about to tell this starchy person about the cockroach colonies down in 'ponics.

"They were telling me in the hospital here that they have a newer, more efficient oxygen-exchange fluid for blood replacement," she said. Sure enough, that took the woman's attention off cockroach egg cases.

"Really! Expensive?"

"They said something about a license to manufacture—if you found something the Fleet wanted to use, it might make your time here worthwhile."

"Certainly—thanks. I'll just get the team together—"

Sirkin was asleep, curled on her side like a child, when Heris arrived. She looked perfectly healthy, with color in her cheeks again, and no obvious bandages. Heris had made herself visit Cecelia's attendant first, though she didn't know the man at all . . . now she sat beside the bed and waited for Sirkin to wake. Once an attendant peeked in, jotted down some numbers off the monitor above the bed, smiled at Heris, and went back out. Heris dozed off, waking when Sirkin stirred.

"Captain . . ." Her voice was drowsy.

"You're almost recovered, they tell me," Heris said. "I'm sorry—all of us are. We should have trusted you."

"I—don't know. I didn't trust myself. And I don't know how she could—she had been on your ship—"

"Don't worry about her. Let's talk about you. You know Lady Cecelia stood by you all along?"

"Yes—she came to my cabin and said she knew it wasn't my fault."

"She'd like you to stay with us, Brig, though no one will blame you if you don't. We all want you to."

"You're sure?"

"Of course. I can make stupid mistakes, but I can also admit them. It wasn't your fault; you did good work and someone else messed it up. You'll do good work again. It's more a matter of whether you trust us—if you're sure of us."

"I want to," Sirkin said. "I like you." That almost childlike admission struck Heris to the core. She could have cried. "You were all so . . . so good when Amalie died. Even Lord Thornbuckle's daughter . . ."

"Even? Brun's a remarkable young woman, if she did happen to be born rich. She liked you; I daresay if she'd been aboard she'd have chewed my ears about you, and made a dent in my suspicions."

"I really like her . . ." That was said so softly Heris barely heard it, and Sirkin flushed. Heris mentally rolled her eyes. Youngsters. Meharry had told her privately that Brigdis and Brun were likely to go overboard. Clearly Sirkin had. But they'd have to work that out; she never interfered in her crew members' romantic entanglements unless it endangered the ship. This wouldn't . . . in fact . . .

"Not surprising," she said dryly. "Considering—" Considering what, she didn't say. "One of us will be by every shift, until you're out of here. You're under guard, because we still don't know how much trouble we face, but you can call the ship any time you're concerned. I've got to go down and see how Lady Cecelia's coming along."

"Thank you," Sirkin said. Completely awake now, she had begun to regain that sparkle she'd had at first. Resilience, thought Heris, and wondered again if she would be able to afford rejuvenation someday. And what her employer would think about it.

✧ Chapter Twenty-two

Cecelia had had reports sent up to Heris—encouraging reports, on the whole. Heris didn't entirely understand the medical terminology—she skipped whole paragraphs of multisyllabic gibberish and tried to figure out the "prognosis" sections. Here she hoped the percentages referred to functions recovered, and not permanently lost—87% this, and 79% that, and 93% the other thing. Livadhi's medical teams might have helped interpret, except that they were spending all their time in the station hospital. She would do better, she decided, to go down and find out in person.

The receptionist recognized her now, and gave her Cecelia's room number. When she came out of the lift on that floor, Meharry was stretched out in the visitors' lounge.

"How is she?"

"Better you should see her," Meharry said gruffly. "We're taking alternate shifts now; Arkady's in the visitors' hostel."

"Sirkin's doing well," Heris said, anticipating Meharry's question. "She's staying with us."

"She's a sweet kid," Meharry said. "Almost too sweet for her own good. I think that's what made me so mad—I liked her so much, and she was so good, and then—you know, if Skoterin had been anything but a bland nothing, I'd have figured it out."

"So we look out for bland nothings," Heris said. "See you after I talk to Lady Cecelia."

"You'll be surprised," Meharry said. It was an odd tone of voice, not at all encouraging, and Heris worried all the way

down the corridor. The bright floral prints and soft carpet did
nothing to reassure her.

She found the number and knocked lightly.

"Come in." It didn't sound like Cecelia; perhaps a nurse
was with her. Even more worried, Heris pushed the door open.

The large room opened onto an atrium filled with flowering plants and ferns. Across an expanse of apricot carpet, a
woman in a green silk robe stood by a table set for a meal.

The woman couldn't be Cecelia, Heris realized after a
startled glance. She was only in her forties, and although she
was tall and lean, she had not a single strand of gray in her red
hair. It must be the wrong room. Heris turned to look at the
room number, and the woman chuckled. Heris felt that chuckle
as a blow to the heart.

"It *is*—but how—?"

"Do come in and shut the door. That's better." Cecelia gestured to the chairs by the table. "Here—sit down; you look as
if you'd seen a ghost."

"I—I'm not sure—"

"Vanity has its uses, you know." Cecelia sat down herself,
and grinned at Heris. "I decided to take advantage of it."

"But you—you said you'd never go through rejuv."

"If you'd asked me, I'd have said I'd never be poisoned by
that wretched Lorenza. Here, have a cup of broth. They have
quite good food here."

Heris opened her mouth to say she wasn't hungry, and realized she was. And her employer was looking at her with a
wicked gleam in her eyes. She sipped the broth.

"It was vanity that saved me, actually," Cecelia said. "And
now I'll have to confess it, and you'll laugh at me—"

"No, I won't. I'm too glad to have you alive—and by the
way, thanks for saving us from that mess on the ship."

"I only wish I'd done a better job of it. But—let me tell you.
You remember how smug I was about taking no medicines
and refusing rejuv?"

"Yes," Heris said cautiously.

"Well, I was lying. To everyone and to myself. There was this . . . this preparation. Herbal stuff. Lots of women used it, and none of us considered it medicinal exactly. Or cosmetic, exactly. I thought of it as a kind of tonic . . . of course I knew my skin was smoother, and I felt better, but I didn't consider what it really was."

A pause followed; since a comment seemed to be required, Heris said "And it was . . . ?"

Cecelia laughed. "I was so arrogant about drugs, it never occurred to me that many of them come from herbs—plants. That I was taking quite a solid dose of bioactive chemicals that functioned in some ways like the rejuvenation chemicals." She shook her head. "So there I was, smugly certain that I wasn't like those others—the ones I despised—and in fact I was. I must have known—I didn't tell anyone I took it, not even my maid, and certainly not anyone medical. My doctor just thought I had naturally good genes. Which I do, but not that good." She paused and drank a few swallows of broth herself.

"So when Lorenza poisoned me, she used a dose based on my supposed drug-free biochemistry. It worked, but the damage was not as complete. It required more maintenance drug than expected, which meant that when I came off the maintenance drugs, I could recover with therapy . . . and it also meant that a complete rejuvenation treatment would reverse all the damage."

"And so you thought if vanity had saved you so far, you'd go the whole way?"

"That, and the fact that nothing but rejuv would give me natural eyesight again. That visual prosthesis is good enough for walking around without bumping into things, but it doesn't begin to substitute for real sight." Cecelia looked out at the atrium. "The colors . . . the textures . . . oh, Heris, I thought I would go mad, locked away in that darkness, motionless, helpless."

Heris reached to touch her hand. "Cecelia—milady—I don't know how you did it, but it took incredible courage."

Cecelia gave a harsh laugh, almost a croak. "No—not courage. Pigheaded stubbornness. I simply would not give up. And the advantage of being over eighty when something like that happens is that you have a lot of experience to remember. Not enough—it's never enough—but a lot."

"Do you think this person—Lorenza—intended to kill you?"

"Oh, no. She intended exactly what happened. She used to come visit, you know, and sit by my bed and whisper into my ear. 'I did it,' she would say. She never gave her name, and at that time I couldn't figure out who it was . . . but it told me that someone had done it, and that—that helped. It gave me a target. I didn't remember—the drug I was given was supposed to knock out short-term memory for the event—until one day after a long ride in therapy. I was suddenly there, where it happened, in Berenice's drawing room, with Lorenza handing me a glass of fruit juice." Cecelia stared at the ferns and flowers a long moment before going on. "She said that once, too: *You'll never ride again, Cecelia. You'll never feel the wind in your face, never smell the flowers.*"

Heris shivered in spite of herself. "She must be a terrible woman."

"She's the main reason I refused rejuvenation so long. We knew each other as children . . . and she began to have rejuv early, and often. She was obsessed with her appearance—and I admit, she's a beauty, and always was. But the last time I saw her . . . that smooth young skin and glossy hair, and those ancient, evil eyes . . . I didn't want to become that sort of person."

"You couldn't," Heris said.

Cecelia smiled at her. "Heris, I love your loyalty, but one thing I have learned in my long eventful life is that anyone can change into anything. It takes only carelessness. My mistake was in confusing surface behaviors with the reasons behind them. It wasn't rejuv that made Lorenza what she is—what she is propelled her to that many rejuv procedures."

"Still, you would never—"

"I hope not. Certainly nothing that cruel. But if you put Lorenza and me in the same room? I could kill her. You know I can kill."

Remembering Cecelia as she had been on Sirialis, when she shot the man who would have killed them both, Heris nodded. "For cause, you could. Maybe even in vengeance. But you would not ever torment someone as she tormented you—that I'm sure of."

"Good. So far I feel no temptation that way, though I do have a strong urge to pull her blonde hair out by the roots."

Heris had to laugh then. "So—when do we do just that?"

"I have one more round of neurological testing, and we want to be sure Sirkin's fully recovered . . ."

"She's younger than both of us, and recovers faster even without rejuv—"

"Good, then. Let's go back and . . . er . . . clean house, shall we?"

Heris said, "There is the problem of the prince and his clone, or the clones and no prince. I accepted a mission from the king, as I explained to you—"

Cecelia scowled. "The medical reports haven't straightened anything out?"

"Not really. All the tissue samples are identical. The clones believe—they told me—that they carry markers somewhere. But if these doctors can't find them, who can? As for the mental limitations, both these clones perform at normal levels on tests. Not as high as you'd expect from a Registered Embryo, but not as low as you'd expect from the prince, judging by what we saw on the way back from Sirialis."

"What do the clones say now? Have you talked to them since you got back?"

"No—have you?"

"Once, yes. Heris, I believe in my heart that the young man with us—Gerald A., as you called him—was the real prince. Their prime. I can't give you any reason that would make sense except an old woman's intuition. But remember how he and Ronnie both fell on that gas grenade?"

"If that was the prince."

"It was. Everything that's happened since proves it. Neither the king—nor Lorenza, I believe—would go so far to protect a mere clone; if a clone fails, you get rid of it. My point is that along with Gerel's undeniable witlessness he had great and generous gallantry. A meaner boy, stupid or bright, would not have done what he did. And when Skoterin threatened Sirkin—the moment the weapon swung toward her and away from me—Gerald A. did the same thing. In the same style. Generous, brave, and incredibly stupid. It provoked her to shoot; she might not have fired, and your Petris might have killed her before anyone else got hurt. I think that was no clone; I think that was the prince himself."

"But he had seemed more sensible at times . . . on the voyage with the others."

"Think, Heris. If they were protecting him, if *they* knew his problem, they would shift about, so that you could not be sure which one you spoke to—you'd have to ask. Couldn't that be it? Or perhaps all that time without the drug began to reverse the dullness."

"But if that's true, then I've failed in the mission the king gave me. And what do we do with the clones?"

"I'll tell you what we *don't* do. We don't take them back to be discarded or killed by someone who would let his own son be ruined. Go talk to them. I told them what I thought; they didn't say much. They may to you. If they are the clones, and Gerel is dead, I will not let you take them on my ship. I don't want their ruin on my conscience."

Brun had no intention of staying safely at home on the family's estates. They knew who had poisoned Lady Cecelia; they had figured out that the prince had also been slowly poisoned, and that the same method had been used on George for a short time. She and Ronnie and George were ready, the moment Buttons and Sarah arrived, to do battle with the minions of evil.

"Whoa," Buttons said. "You haven't thought it all out."

"What's to think?" George said. "The woman's a menace: she poisoned me, and then the prince, and then Lady Cecelia, and maybe a dozen others—"

"Why?"

"Why? I suppose . . . I guess . . . she likes poisoning people."

"George, you're sounding about as intelligent as you did in your bad term. I have some missing links you'd better add to your chain of evidence. You mentioned Gerel being excited after visits from his brothers . . . do you remember any more?"

"No." George sounded grumpy. He hated being interrupted.

"I do." Buttons stood and paced around the big library. "It annoys all of you when I remind you I'm older . . . but it matters. You were in school with each other and Gerel; I was in school with Gerel's older brother, Nadrel."

"Who was killed in a duel; we know that."

"Shut up, Ronnie. That's only part of it. Because I was his friend, I got to know the oldest, and don't bother to tell me you know Jared had been accepted as Successor by the Grand Council. That happened our last year in school; it was terribly exciting, and I got to attend, with Nadrel. But what I didn't know—because Jared had said I was too stuffy and priggish and would spill the beans—was that Jared had been groomed by some of the Familias to head a rebellion. Nadrel knew, of course . . . and they dragged in poor young Gerel, who worshipped his oldest brother. And it was Gerel who spilled the beans . . . to you, George."

"I—I don't remember." George looked stunned, as if a rock had landed on his head.

"No—you wouldn't, if they drugged you. I don't suppose you told anyone intentionally—you had a certain innate cunning even then—but your father got wind of it, and he told the king. That assassination—"

"The king killed his own son?"

"No. Nor ordered it . . . but one of the other Familias felt it had to be done. No one knew how far the plot had gone; the military was on alert for months. Nadrel . . . Nadrel was a problem, bitter and violent; I couldn't swear his duel was spontaneous."

"And Gerel—?"

Buttons shrugged. "I would guess—I knew nothing about it, until you told me this—I would guess the king wanted to be sure Gerel could not be the same kind of threat. Perhaps you, George, were the experimental subject, to prove the effects reversible. Then Gerel—I would like to believe the king meant no harm by it."

"No harm!" Brun was so angry she felt her hair must be bristling. "Poor Gerel, everyone thinking him a fool—and then Lady Cecelia being poisoned—and Sarah shot—"

"I didn't say there was no harm, only that he may not have intended it. If Lorenza was the king's arm in this, she may have done more than he knew."

"Then it's Lorenza we have to stop. Now." Ronnie was on his feet now. "What if she attacks my mother, thinking I might have said something to her? Or George's parents?"

"Ronnie, we can't simply walk in and seize her. She's a Crown Minister's sister—another complication, because I for one have no idea how much influence she has with him—or he with the king, for that matter. She's got a vote in the Grand Council in her own right. We have no legal standing—"

"Tell my father," George said. "I'll call him—"

"George, will you listen! Your father's already involved—so is ours. They've filed a Question. But none of us can grab Lorenza; we have no evidence. We need Lady Cecelia alive and well, her competency completely restored so that she can testify; we need the prince alive and well—and both of them are a long way away with a lot of things that can go wrong. Less will go wrong if we all act discreetly."

"Then you didn't need my warning at all—you already knew

about Lorenza, and I could have stayed with Lady Cecelia—"
Brun felt tired and grumpy.

"No—we didn't know about Lorenza. We knew it had to
be someone, but we didn't know who—and that's important.
But we can't afford to lose anyone, so I want you all to agree
to stay calm and follow orders."

"Whose?" Ronnie asked bluntly.

"Mine, for now, and Dad's when he gets here. George's
father will tell him the same. Now will you use sense and act
like the adults you are?"

Cecelia looked around the main lounge of her yacht with
distaste. "I thought the lavender plush was bad, but I have to
admit this is worse." Then she grinned. "Though I must say
I'm glad to see it—really see it. Show me everything." Heris
glanced at Petris, now their new environmental section head
and assistant. "Everything, milady?"

"Every bit of it. I'll be thinking how lovely it will look when
Spacenhance has finished with it." She looked from one to the
other of them. "Come on! What are you waiting for?"

"Well, we have this little problem," Heris said, leading her
down the streaked grayish walls, wondering how Cecelia was
going to react when she saw them. She opened the door to the
'ponics section: stacks of mesh cages held an ever-increasing
number of cockroaches, filling the air in that compartment
with an odd, heavy smell. "This."

"What on—they're *alive*."

"Yes . . . and I don't want you mentioning this to the medical teams, either."

"Where did they come from?"

"Spacenhance," Heris said.

"The decorators? They put *cockroaches* on my ship? On
my ship?" Outrage made her voice spike up; Heris grinned.

"We think they put cockroaches on everyone's ship, to eat
the old wall covering and carpeting, and the adhesives. Illegal, of course. A trade secret, no doubt. We thought we might

need to deal in trade secrets, so we trapped the ones we found and let them breed."

"But what did they do with the cockroaches after they ate the stuff?" Cecelia leaned forward to look at the nearest cage.

"We think . . . mind, this is only our speculation . . . that they converted the cockroaches into a sort of organic slurry, which could then be extruded into fiber or other shapes . . . to make carpets or wall coverings—"

"You mean they put *ground-up cockroaches* on people's floors? Walls? You mean that horrible lavender plush was really nothing but ground-up *cockroaches?*"

"Quite possibly," Heris said, enjoying Cecelia's reaction. "Of course, they would have dyed them—that's why they're white, I'm sure—and they may have added other materials."

Cecelia stepped back. "I have never even imagined anything so . . . so disgusting."

Heris grinned at Petris. "There is something worse . . ."

"What?"

"When they're loose and you haven't noticed them in the sheets." She and Petris both started laughing, and Cecelia glared at them.

"It's not funny. Or—I suppose it is, but—oh, my, have we got a whip hand here."

"That's what I thought," Heris said. "Of course, we're now in violation of half a dozen regulations ourselves, but we've been careful. I would prefer, however, that Commander Livadhi's people not know about the live ones."

"Oh, absolutely," said Cecelia, beginning to smile. "But I suspect that restocking my solarium with miniatures will be well within my budget."

From that beginning, the trip back to Rockhouse Major went smoothly. Heris made the rendezvous with Livadhi's *Martine Scolare*, and his pinnace picked up the medical teams. Heris had braced herself for questions about the clones, but the medical teams were so excited about the new technologies they'd discovered in those few days on the Station that they could talk of nothing else. Livadhi asked, of course, and Heris gave the answer she and Cecelia had worked out. It was not exactly a lie.

"I left the clones behind; neither of them was the prince. As you know, one was killed in the shooting, and tissue analysis at autopsy could neither prove nor disprove that that one was the prince. Perhaps postmortem degradation . . ."

"Or perhaps he's off in a bar somewhere making an idiot of himself," Livadhi said. "I wonder if the king knows how many doubles he had?"

"We may never know," Heris said cautiously. "What's the latest on the uproar?"

"Not quite civil war," Livadhi said. "Fleet's on standby, all the Family Delegates are gathering for an emergency session, and rumor has it the king is considering abdication. The Benignity has filed complaints, and threatens to take action if we don't pay reparations for their two cruisers, which have somehow grown to dreadnoughts; Aethar's World decided this was a great time to try a little piracy . . . oh, yes, and the Stationmaster at Rotterdam says to tell Lady Cecelia that the black mare has foaled. Anything else?"

"No—thank you. What about the Fleet and us?"

"You personally, or you in Lady Cecelia's yacht?"

"Either or both."

"Well, I've had strong representations from senior Familias that my neck is in the noose if Lady Cecelia doesn't get back safely—how is she, by the way?"

"Quite able to take up her duties," Heris said.

"Good. And I've had strong pressure from some . . . er . . . elements in the Fleet that your permanent disappearance would just about guarantee my first star. While others say the opposite. I would suggest the fastest possible course, and I suggest you allow me to escort you in."

"I accept both suggestions." She was not entirely sure of him in all respects, but if he wanted her dead, it would have been easy enough to leave her in Compassionate Hand space without help.

❖   ❖   ❖

The Familias Grand Council met in a domed hall. High above, painted stars on pale blue echoed the carpet of deep blue patterned with gold stars. Each Family had its Table; each voting member had his or her Chair. On the north wall, opposite the entrance doors, the Speaker's Bench had become the king's throne, and the king, wearing his usual black suit, sat there behind a desk with its crystal pitcher of water, its goblets, its display screens, and the gold-rimmed gavel.

For an hour now, the Members had streamed in past uniformed guards and weapons checks and more guards and more weapons checks. The lines extended across the lobby, out the tall front doors, down the steps, to the sidewalk where yet more limousines disgorged yet more Members. A light rain brushed the steps with one slick layer after another, and those who had not expected a wait got damp and grumpy.

Cecelia watched her sister and brother-in-law climb up the steps. She, Heris, Meharry, and Ginese were part of a thin crowd held back by a chain attached to a movable post. From the chain a little tin sign dangled, with the words "Members Only Past This Point." Across from them, on the far side of the entrance steps, another such chain restrained another small clump of observers.

"When are you going?" Heris asked.

"After Lorenza. I want to be sure she's here."

"What if she doesn't attend?"

"Oh, she will. She may not take her own Chair, but she always attends her brother. There—that's theirs—" Cecelia started to look down, then remembered she didn't look anything like the Cecelia Lorenza would recognize. They had docked the yacht over on Rockhouse Minor, where Bunny's shuttle retrieved them. There would have been gossip, of course, but Livadhi, at Heris's suggestion, had docked at the Fleet terminal at Rockhouse Major, and complained loudly to his fellow officers that "that bitch Serrano" had disappeared again.

Cecelia watched as the portly Crown Minister—when had Piercy gained all that weight?—climbed out and offered his arm to Lorenza. She, at least, had prepared for a wait, in a pretty ice-blue raincoat. Piercy had an umbrella; Cecelia felt her lip curling. If you couldn't stand a bit of rain, then carry a personal shield, not an ostentatious umbrella. That was carrying the fashion for antiquity too far. Piercy held the umbrella over Lorenza's head; she looked out from under it with catlike smugness. Cecelia realized she was trembling only when Heris touched her hand. Rage filled her; she could hear that voice whispering in her ear . . . how had she not known who it was? How could she not leap over the chain and strangle that smug little tramp?

Lorenza looked around, as if for admiration. Cecelia stood straight, watching her; their eyes met. Lorenza frowned a little, shook her head minutely, and went on up the steps to the tail of the line. Half a dozen more Members got in line; Cecelia shifted her feet.

"Let's go."

"It's too close," Meharry said. "She'll see you—she'll start trying to remember—"

"Let her!" Cecelia was breathing deeply as if before a race. Heris gripped her hand.

"Milady, we're with you. You have allies; you know that. Don't let her shake your resolution. Even if she does look like the worst insipid tea biscuit I ever saw."

That got a grim chuckle; Cecelia felt her tension ease. "All right. But not much longer."

"No, not much longer." They waited until Lorenza and her brother were near the top of the steps, when the guards at the door recognized them and swept them inside ahead of the others. "Now," Heris said. They stepped around the barrier, and Cecelia clipped her Member badge to her coat. The others put on the ID tags Bunny had arranged; Members could bring their personal assistants, as long as none carried weapons. Heris wasn't worried; Meharry and Ginese *were* weapons.

Most of the delegates had arrived; the line moved faster. At the door, Cecelia moved into the Members Booth for an ID check. The others, with staff IDs, went through without incident. Cecelia came out of the booth and found them waiting. Now, in the lobby, out of the rain, she could hear the steady sound of all those people talking. She felt weak at the knees. She had been alone so long . . . and then with a few friends . . . and now, to face that crowd . . . she had always hated public speaking. She felt the others close in.

"All right, milady?" Heris asked.

"All right. I just—I'm fine." The line they were in snaked slowly forward. She could see in the door at last . . . it had been decades since she'd attended a Grand Council. When she'd been a young woman, first eligible for a Chair, it had been a thrill . . . later a bore . . . later something she delegated to a proxy without a second thought. Now that earlier awe struck her again. That tall dome spangled with stars, those dark polished Tables, each with its Chairs of red leather, all symbols of power that had kept her safe and wealthy all these years, and then had nearly killed her. Across the chamber, as she came to the door, she saw the king on his throne. He stared out, seeming to see no one.

Her family Table had moved since the last time she'd attended; Tables were drawn by lot every other Council. Now it was midway down the right side of the left aisle, almost directly across from the Speaker's Table. A page led them to it, and checked Cecelia's ID again before handing her to her Chair. The Chair itself required her to insert her Member card . . . a precaution resulting from the behavior of a speedy young man who had once managed to vote two Chairs by flitting from one to another while a long roll-call vote dragged on. With the card in place, the screen before her lit. Only then did she look around. Her sister Berenice, two Chairs down, stared at her, white-faced, then glanced at her companions and turned even whiter. Ronnie, at the foot of the Table, started and then grinned happily. Gustav would be at his family's Table; Cecelia had no idea where it was now.

"Good to see you again," Cecelia said. They had not told Berenice; they had not told anyone. Berenice's shock was almost vengeance enough for her treatment of Heris.

"You're—you had—"

"Rejuv, yes. Just as you did." Cecelia smiled. "Where's Abelard?"

"Probably having a last drink," Berenice said. Abelard, their oldest surviving brother, always came late. Ronnie looked as if he were bursting with glee and news both. Cecelia gave him a look she hoped would quell him. They already knew what he knew; Bunny had told her. She looked around. Kevil Mahoney was in his Chair, with George beside him. Bunny, his brothers, and his sons were already seated; Brun, a year too young for her own Chair, crouched beside her mother at another Table. She was scanning the chamber, looking . . . and she saw Cecelia. A grin spread over her face; Cecelia gave a little nod. Now . . . to find Lorenza. The Crown Ministers sat together, at two Tables to either side of the throne . . . but when she found Piercy, leaning back to hand a file to a page, she did not see Lorenza's gold head anywhere near. She let her eyes rove the chamber, but it was Meharry who spotted her.

A nudge—Cecelia leaned over and Meharry murmured, "Top tier, near the right aisle." Cecelia turned casually. There. The ice-blue raincoat had been slung carelessly over the back of a neighboring Chair—unlike the precise Lorenza. But there she was, leaning over to talk to someone else Cecelia couldn't see. Whose Family was that? Not Lorenza's certainly . . . Lorenza's mother had been a Sturinscough, and her aunt Lucrezia should be heading that Table. So she was, an upright old tyrant in black lace whom no amount of rejuvenation could soften . . . maybe, thought Cecelia, it runs in the family.

So why was Lorenza back with the Buccleigh-Vandormers? True, people sometimes got permission to sit in other Chairs— if they had physical problems, if they planned to leave early—

ah. Cecelia felt her smile widening to a dangerous grin. Let her leave . . . let her try to escape. It wouldn't do her any good.

Chimes rang out, and the bustle in the chamber quieted. A last few Members came scurrying in, swiping at their wet clothes. The chimes rang again, and the king picked up the gavel. Grand Council was about to begin.

The king had not recognized Lady Cecelia in the lithe red-head who stalked down the aisle as if she owned it. Not until she sat at that Table, in that Chair, not until her name lit on his screen of Members Present. Then, as if his vision had suddenly cleared, he recognized Heris Serrano with her. Where was the prince? Panic gripped him suddenly; icy sweat broke out all over him; he felt himself trembling. If the prince were alive, she would have brought him; the conclusion was inescapable. Dead.

He could see, as if part of his brain had turned into a tiny viewscreen, the concatenation of errors that had led him to this place. One time after another, he had done the convenient thing, the expedient thing; he had let himself be led from one folly to the next. Jared's assassination, Nadrel's duel, Gerel's drugs, the clones, the secrets and countersecrets, the lies and evasions. He had lost his power; he had lost his sons; worst of all, he had lost the respect of those two women and everyone like them, all the decent men and women in the realm. His former allies would certainly disown him and his policies now, even as they scrambled to save their influence. He had thought Cecelia immature, with her strong enthusiasms, her blunt honesty. Now that immaturity seemed far wiser than the sly counsels he'd convinced himself represented maturity.

He wanted to break into tears; he wanted to throw his gavel down and leave. Tears would not help; he had nowhere to go. If Gerel had come back, he might have stood against the Question already before the meeting, but no longer. He knew what he had to do.

❖   ❖   ❖

Lorenza could not shake the uneasiness that had become her constant companion. That stupid goon on Rockhouse Major had attacked the wrong girl, and thereby raised suspicion. No one had seen Thornbuckle's daughter; no one had seen Lady Cecelia. Berenice had complained that Ronnie was spending all his time with his regiment; he had run out on the opera party over some ridiculous little chit of a girl, and now he never came home. She knew that George, too, had not been home for weeks. The men she hired could not locate them anywhere.

Piercy had come home with vague stories of great unrest here and there. The Benignity was upset, Aethar's World . . . she had tried to listen, but all she could think of was Lady Cecelia. Lady Cecelia awake, alert, able to walk and see and speak . . . worst of all, Lady Cecelia able to remember. She wasn't supposed to be able to remember, but then she wasn't supposed to be able to achieve legal competency, either. Lorenza found herself seeing Lady Cecelia everywhere when she went out. None of them were, of course. The tall woman in the store had had the wrong face when she turned around; the woman with the short graying-reddish hair had been too short when she stood up at the reception. It was just nerves, she told herself. If she comes, then she comes, and then . . . and then kill her. She began carrying a weapon, a tiny thing that fired darts tipped with poison.

Yet no sign of Lady Cecelia—the real Lady Cecelia— showed up before the Grand Council meeting. One informant tried to tell her that Lady Cecelia's yacht had come into Rockhouse Minor—but the database had an entirely different listing, and a more reliable source on Rockhouse Major reported a conversation between Arash Livadhi and another R.S.S. officer, one known to be hostile to Serrano. She had that recording. It could be, she thought wistfully, that Lady Cecelia was afraid to come, that she and that renegade captain had gone off together somewhere.

She didn't believe that for a moment. She had dressed that

morning as if for her last appearance; she had her jewel case hidden in her raincoat; she had her pearls under her dress. If she had to flee, if she couldn't use her credit cubes, she would have something . . .

For a moment, just after getting out of the limousine, she had been sure Cecelia was near. She had looked around, at the little clumps of people who wished they were rich enough to be Familias, to have Chairs and votes. In the rain, it was hard to tell . . . one tall woman with red hair reminded her of Cecelia, but she was forty years younger, at least. And she was prettier than Cecelia had ever been.

Lorenza took precautions anyway. She would sit with the Buccleigh-Vandormers, to whom she was distantly related, claiming an upset stomach. She could leave quickly if she had to; she had a reservation on the noon shuttle to Rockhouse Major under another name, and she knew the number to call when she got there. They owed her plenty of favors.

Even with all her caution, she did not see Lady Cecelia until the king struck for order with his gavel. Her eyes checked the tables: there was Piercy, looking stuffy. There was Abelard, and Berenice, and . . . the back of a red head, a tall woman. The woman turned, and looked her in the eye . . . and smiled, a slow smile of absolute delight. Lorenza almost fainted; her fists clenched on the table before her. Cecelia. The bitch was not only recovered but rejuvenated . . . and she remembered.

She forgot the weapon she carried. She heard nothing the king was saying; in a scramble she grabbed her raincoat and rushed the door, pushing past the row of pages. "Madam!" she heard behind her; she shoved the tall door open and strode across the wide lobby, trying not to run. Behind her she heard the roar of upraised voices, cut off by the closing door. The guards, alert to stop intruders, did not move as she went out the glass doors of the building, down the rain-wet steps. She was on the street, drenched, before she remembered she was carrying a raincoat. She dragged it on over her wet dress and looked for the nearest transportation.

❖   ❖   ❖

Cecelia half-rose when she saw Lorenza bolt; Heris grabbed her wrist. "Not now—she won't escape." Between Livadhi and Bunny, Lorenza would find no transportation farther than the stations. If she bolted that far, they might find out who her allies were.

"Right." The king was speaking, his voice sounding flat and tired. The ritual welcome, to which he had given some grace and humor in years past, sounded as stilted as it actually was. Piercy, at the Crown Ministers' Table, was staring at the door through which Lorenza had left with a worried expression. The moment the welcome ended, Bunny stood for recognition. He was very much Lord Thornbuckle in his formal suit.

"If you'll wait a moment," the king said. It was more plea than direction, and that lack of control released a buzzing hum of conversation.

"There is a Question before the floor," Bunny said.

"I know that," the king said. "But I have a preemptive announcement."

"May I request the floor when you have made it?" That was not so much question as command; the king nodded. Bunny sat down, stiffly.

"Members of Familias," the king said. A long pause, during which curiosity rose again, expressed as a crisp ruffle of subdued talk. "I wish to announce . . ." another pause. "My resignation. Abdication. I . . . am not able to continue."

"Why?" bellowed someone from the far right corner. "We don't want that."

"Yes, we do!" yelled someone else. Other voices rose, louder and louder, in argument. The king banged his gavel, and the noise subsided.

"I cannot—I have reason to believe . . . my last son is dead. In my grief—I am aware of failings that—" He laid the gavel down, shook his head, then put it down on his desk. Profound silence filled the chamber; Cecelia saw puzzlement, anger, and fear on the faces around her. Bunny stood again.

"I was promised the floor to address the Question, which all of you have been sent. The king has indeed preempted that Question, which called for his resignation. I move we accept it, without further inquiry."

"How can we vote, without a Chair?" someone asked.

Cecelia spoke up, without having meant to. "By putting your finger on the little button, the way you always do," she said loudly. A ripple of nervous laughter followed, circled the chamber, and returned. She pushed the voting button on her screen; others followed. The vote carried. She felt a sudden burst of compassion for the king. Had he meant any of the harm he had brought to pass? Probably not. She had not meant him any harm either, but she had been the means of destroying his reign.

After the vote, a long silence, and then confusion. The king—no longer the king, but a man whose Familia name nearly all had forgotten—sat immobile, staring at the desk in front of him. Cecelia watched the Crown Ministers' heads swaying from side to side as they whispered among themselves, exactly like pigeons on a roost. The sound of many voices rose, filling the chamber as if a vast river roared through it. Finally Bunny went to the Ministers' Tables and leaned over to speak to them. One of them rose and approached the ex-king. He looked up, then, and in his expression Cecelia saw a new resolution form. Stillness came as swiftly as the earlier noise. He stood.

"I yield the floor," Kemtre said. "To Lord Thornbuckle." He held out the gavel. And Bunny, grave, unsmiling, took the few steps necessary. The gavel passed between them, and Kemtre stepped down to meet Bunny on the level below the throne. Though his voice was quiet, unaugmented by the sound system, most heard what he said next. "I'm going back for Velosia. If she waits. Then home—" That would be the Familia estates, not the Crown ones. "I'm sorry, Bunny—I hope you have better luck. At least this gives you a chance—"

Then he came up the steps towards Cecelia; she felt

Meharry and Heris tense on either side of her. "It's all right," she muttered; she might as well have tried to calm a pair of eager hounds with the game in view. If he meant her any harm, he was a dead man.

"I'm sorry, Cecelia," he said to her. "I cannot say how happy I am to see you recovered; it was not my plan, but I'm sure it was, in some way, my fault. You did me a good service and I did you a bad one."

Cecelia thought of the suffering of the months—almost two years, in local time—and gave him a stare that made him flush, then pale. "I can forgive you for myself," she said then, into the hushed silence of the chamber. "But the boys? I was never a mother, Kemtre, but I could not have done to anyone's child what you did to your own. How could you?" Before he could answer, her gaze swept the Tables. "Still—I don't blame you as much as Lorenza." Below her, Piercy flinched. "She's the one who poisoned me; I daresay she's poisoned others. She's the one I want."

That brought another uproar. Lorenza's aunt Lucrezia gave Cecelia a glare that should have ignited asbestos at a hundred paces. Bunny gavelled the noise down, and called Kevil Mahoney forward. "The king has resigned; we need not fall into disorder for that, Chairholders. We had a government before we had a king; we can have one now, with or without a king. Ser Mahoney has legal advice for us all; I ask your attention." As Kevil's practiced voice compelled the others to listen, Kemtre looked past Cecelia to Heris. She shook her head, offering no details; all he really needed to know was in that negation. Kemtre seemed to sag on his bones, and then turned away. Cecelia returned her attention to Mahoney, but Heris watched the former king climb slowly to the exit. No one greeted him; no one stretched out a hand to comfort him. She was not sure what she felt; she was only sure it was neither triumph nor pity.

The meeting went on for hours, never quite erupting into complete disorder. Piercy resigned. Two other Crown

Ministers resigned. Cecelia's brother Abelard proposed a vote to restore the Speaker's position; Cecelia had not imagined he had that much initiative. The vote passed, which surprised her even more. She stayed, when she would rather have pursued Lorenza, caught up despite herself in the excitement, until at last the meeting adjourned for the day. She went home with Bunny, despite Berenice's plea . . . she wasn't ready to forgive Berenice yet, not until she'd had her vengeance on Lorenza.

No one on the noon shuttle paid any attention to Lorenza; their attention was on the news being shown on the forward viewscreen. The king's abdication, the surprise vote to abolish the monarchy and restore the Speaker's position, was enough to hold even the most jaded. Lorenza ignored it; she was fingering the pearls hidden beneath her dress and wondering how far they would take her. Although the Benignity owed her favors for her many useful acts, she had no illusions about them. They would do more for pearls or the other jewels than for old times' sake. She slipped into an uneasy doze, missing the interview with Lady Cecelia de Marktos, famous horse-woman and prominent member of her Family, whose miraculous recovery from a coma provided the news program's obligatory "good news" spot.

Rockhouse Major bubbled with rumors and excitement when she arrived. Lorenza put on her most demure expression and made her way to the office whose location she had long ago memorized but had never visited. A lady of her standing did not visit the kind of therapist employed to counsel criminals. Now . . . now she needed to contact the Benignity's senior agent on the station.

She did not like the tall, handsome, self-assured woman in the pale-yellow silk suit. Liking didn't matter, of course, but she felt abraded by the woman's appraising eye, as if she could see through the rejuvenations to her real age, through her carefully groomed exterior to her inner self. She introduced herself with the code words she'd been given long ago. The woman smiled.

"Of course. We'll have to hide you until a suitable ship comes. Come with me, please." She had no choice, really. "Do you have any luggage? Any—I presume you don't want to use your credit cubes—anything to contribute towards expenses?" Lorenza didn't protest.

"Only this." She started to open the jewel case, but the woman took it from her, then smiled.

"You needn't worry—the Benignity is scrupulously honest."

Of course, but why not let her carry her own jewel case? Lorenza had no time to think about it; she was being hurried through back passages, past little cubicles with chairs and mirrors in them, like changing rooms at dress shops.

"This one," the woman said, opening a door at the end of the row. "No one will bother you here. I'll get you something less conspicuous to wear. You might want to take off that raincoat—you must have been seen in it." Under the raincoat, her dress was still damp from the rain. The woman clucked sympathetically. "Get that wet thing off before you catch a chill; I'll get you a warm robe." She went out, the raincoat over her arm, and shut the little door behind her.

Lorenza looked at herself in the mirror: damp, haggard, her gold hair rumpled to one side by that nap on the shuttle. Terrible. She raked at her hair with her fingers. A draft brushed her damp shoulder; she looked up and realized that the walls in this little cubicle went all the way to the ceiling. There shouldn't be any draft . . . but there was, with a whiff of something acrid in it. She grabbed the door handle; it came off in her hand, leaving a slick metal panel. The mirror—as she looked, the upper half blurred, no longer reflective. An image formed; the therapist, with a handful of Lorenza's jewels.

"You ruined it, Lorenza," the woman said, shaking her head. "The Benignity is scrupulously honest, but it doesn't tolerate mistakes."

Lorenza gasped, finding it difficult. "I—please—I still have these—" and she tore at her dress, pulling out the pearls. Their lustrous surface turned a dirty green; she could feel them crumbling.

"Damn!" said the woman. "You had pearls, too! That gas ruins pearls."

"I'm terribly afraid we may have damaged some of your . . . er . . . property," Heris said. She had had no trouble getting an appointment with Spacenhance; at the moment, anything Lady Cecelia wanted was hers to command.

The senior partner looked as if something were crawling over his skin. "Yes . . . ?"

"Some . . . er . . . pets, I suppose."

"Pets?"

"Yes. Unfortunately, they've been somewhat of an embarrassment to us. During a crisis, a medical team member spotted . . . well, let's just say evidence of their presence. They recommended we contact Environmental Control to fumigate the ship—"

He paled; Heris was afraid he might faint. "You told them . . . ?"

"No . . . I decided they represented no present hazard. We could dispose of them appropriately." So they had, she thought with wicked glee. Sirkin, Brun, Meharry, and Oblo had ensured a most unpleasant surprise for a certain therapist they blamed for Yrilan's death. With any luck at all, the discovery of illegal biologicals in her possession would lead to full investigation of all her activities.

His flush was as pronounced as the pallor had been. "Ahhh . . . thank you, Captain."

"No need. It would have benefited neither of us for Environmental Control to come down on *you*." Heris smiled. From his expression, her smile was not reassuring; she hadn't meant it to be.

"Benefited . . . ?"

"Come now—it's clear to me what you do with those . . .

er . . . insects. That is, I presume, an industrial secret of some worth to you. So the benefit to you of my silence is obvious. The benefit to me—" She leaned forward, savoring his uneasiness. "You know, the ship still needs redecorating. The deposit paid to you has been earning you interest all this time—I think you owe me—and Lady Cecelia—a very fast, very special redecoration."

"But—but Captain Serrano—"

"Very fast," Heris emphasized. Then she opened her hand, where an egg case lay. "Don't you?"

He gave in, as she had known he would. "As planned before, or do you have something else in mind?"

"Here are the specifications," Heris said, handing him a datacube. She and Cecelia and the crew had discussed it. "Except for one thing." She dropped the egg case on his desk. "This time, make sure you get all the bugs out."

HUNTING PARTY

Elizabeth Moon

'A highly entertaining adventure . . . thrilling' *Locus*

Heris Serrano was an officer born of a long line of officers.
A life serving in the ranks of the Regular Space Service
was all she had ever known and all she ever wanted
– until a treacherous superior officer forced her to
resign her commission. This was not just the end of
a career path; it was the end of everything
that gave her life meaning.

But even ex-Fleet officers have to eat, and Heris finds
employment as 'Captain' of an interstellar luxury yacht,
working for the eccentric Lady Cecelia de Marktos.
Being a rich old woman's chauffeur isn't quite the
same as captaining a Fleet cruiser, but nothing
Heris will ever do again could compare with that.
Or so she thinks. For all is not as it seems
aboard the *Sweet Delight* . . .

Join Heris and a cast of lively characters on an
action-packed science fiction adventure from the
author of the acclaimed Deed of Paksenarrion
fantasy sequence.

'Over the last decade, Moon has established
herself as one of the best known and most
acclaimed writers of SF adventure'
Publishers Weekly

<u>WINNING COLOURS</u>

Elizabeth Moon

'Once again Elizabeth Moon has crafted a fine, rousing piece of space opera . . . *Winning Colours* is a prize worth taking home' *Starlog*

Heris Serrano thought her life was over when a treacherous superior officer forced her to resign from the Regular Space Service. But captaining a rich old woman's interstellar yacht has proved more exciting – and fullfilling – than she could ever have imagined.

Heris has at last been offered a chance for vindication and reinstatement in her beloved Fleet – and reconciliation with the family she thought had abandoned her. But it means standing alone against the military might of the Benignity, an interstellar criminal cartel more colloquially known as the Compassionate Hand. With only a few small ships and the space yacht *Sweet Delight,* she must become the galaxy's first line of defence and stop a vastly superior invading fleet dead in its tracks . . .

Join the cast of *Hunting Party* and *Sporting Chance* on another action-packed space adventure from the author of the acclaimed Deed of Paksenarrion fantasy sequence.

SHEEPFARMER'S DAUGHTER

The Deed of Paksenarrion Book 1

Elizabeth Moon

Paksenarrion – Paks for short – is somebody
special. She knows it, even if nobody else does
yet. No way will she follow her father's orders to
marry the pig farmer down the road. She's off to
join the army, even if it means she can never
see her family again.

And so her adventure begins . . . the adventure
that transforms her into a hero remembered in
songs, chosen by the gods to restore
a lost ruler to his throne.

Here is her tale as she lived it.

'This is the first work of high heroic fantasy I've seen
that has taken the work of Tolkien, assimilated it
totally and deeply and absolutely, and produced
something altogether new'
Judith Tarr

'Brilliant. Superbly cast with protagonists and
supporting characters that will enchant the reader'
Bookwatch

SASSINAK

Anne McCaffrey and *Elizabeth Moon*

Volume One of THE PLANET PIRATES

Sassinak was twelve when the raiders came. Old enough to be used, young enough to be broken – or so they thought. But they reckoned without the girl's will, forged into a steely resolve to avenge herself on the pirates who had killed her parents and friends.

When the chance comes to escape, Sassinak grabs it, thanks to the help of a captured Fleet crewman. Returned to the Federation of Sentient Planets, she initiates her revenge by joining Fleet as a raw recruit, surprising everyone by her rapid rise to senior rank. And then her vengeance begins in earnest.

Anne McCaffrey and Elizabeth Moon have woven a story worthy of Robert A. Heinlein in its tough-mindedness, reminiscent of Larry Niven and David Brin in its description of human and alien races coming together both as friends and enemies.

DINOSAUR PLANET OMNIBUS

Anne McCaffrey

Dinosaur Planet and *Survivors*: two thrilling adventures from
the bestselling author of the classic Pern series,
now available in a single volume.

On Earth they died out 70 million years ago. But on
the jungle world of Ireta they still rule in all their terrible
splendour. As strange as any in the galaxy, this is
Dinosaur Planet.

When the expedition sent to explore this new world find
themselves trapped on the surface, and the relief ship
disappears, it is only the beginning of their troubles.
For the heavyworlders among them are turning hostile,
and systematically hunting down their colleagues.
Only the frozen sleep of cryogenics offers an escape.
But for how long?

The superb storytelling skills and incredible imagination of
one of science fiction's best-loved writers come together in
THE DINOSAUR PLANET OMNIBUS

THE MARTIAN RACE

Gregory Benford

March, 2015. NASA's first manned voyage to Mars is about to launch.

But disaster strikes. The rocket explodes, killing the entire crew, and the US government abandons the project. What they come up with in its place will change the nature of space exploration for ever.

Businessman John Axelrod and his consortium have every intention of winning the $30 billion Mars Prize for the first successful mission to the red planet. He knows that it will involve far higher risks than the one NASA had planned. But he has no choice. He has to win.

The Martian Race has begun.

The Martian Race is the extraordinary new science fiction thriller from the author of the *Sunday Times* bestseller *Timescape, Cosm* and *Foundation's Fear.*

'Benford is a scientist who writes with verve and insight not only about black holes and cosmic strings but about human desires and fears'
NEW YORK TIMES BOOK REVIEW

BRIGHTNESS REEF

Book One of a New Uplift Trilogy

David Brin

'Exuberant . . . suspense-filled . . . delightful . . .
I couldn't put it down'
Interzone

On the distant planet of Jijo, six exiled races live side
by side. Only ancient relics from their home planets,
fragments of half-forgotten stories and the crumbling
ruins of the mysterious and god-like Buyur remind the
dispossessed of a more noble past, when they were full
citizens of the Five Galaxies. The races of Jijo, it
seems, have been forgotten, along with whatever
crimes they committed. But for how long?

It is at the time of the Gathering, the council of the
sages, when the spacecraft is first spotted. For some,
it offers a new hope. For others, it heralds
a time of reckoning.

Brightness Reef is the story of a world threatened by its
past and fighting for its future. With a gallery of
extraordinary characters, and a wealth of thought-
provoking ideas, it is a novel fuelled by the spirit of
adventure and discovery. *Brightness Reef* is
David Brin at his very best.

Also available from Orbit:

The first Uplift trilogy:
SUNDIVER
STARTIDE RISING
THE UPLIFT WAR

The second Uplift trilogy:
INFINITY'S SHORE
HEAVEN'S REACH

THE RINGWORLD THRONE

Larry Niven

Larry Niven's *Ringworld* burst upon the world in 1970 and immediately became a classic, winning both the Hugo and Nebula awards. *The Ringworld Engineers* followed in 1979 and enjoyed the same popular appeal, becoming a bestseller. Now Niven has returned to the phenomenal world and *The Ringworld Throne* takes its place in 'the most energetic future history ever written' (*The Encyclopedia of Science Fiction*).

Louis Wu is back – but he is now two hundred years old and definitely not looking for any more adventures. Until, that is, he meets an alien Puppeteer who has the power to make him young again. In exchange, Wu must return to Ringworld, to save it from destruction. But, to achieve this, he has first to win the trust and cooperation of the various exotic alien species that inhabit the world. And that is no easy matter.

Niven's ability to create believable worlds and aliens, and his delight in science remain undiminished. The Ringworld sequence is his most significant and enduring achievement.

'His tales have colourful characters and pulse-pounding narrative drive. Niven is a true master!'
Frederik Pohl

THE HOWLING STONES

Alan Dean Foster

The newly discovered planet of Senisran is a veritable paradise, its oceans dotted with thousands of lush islands containing vast deposits of rare-earths and minerals. But Senisran is also the Humanx Commonwealth's problem child, for each island is inhabited by a different tribe of aboriginal natives. Each has to be negotiated with separately for mining rights – and the commonwealth is locked in a race against the vicious AAnn Empire to secure those rights.

The clans of the Parramat Archipelago on Senisran are resisting entreaties by the Commonwealth and AAnn alike. But Pulickel Tomochelor, xenologist and first-contact specialist, is confident of his ability to handle the negotiations.

What Pulickel hasn't counted on is the secret of Parramat: the strange green stones that the natives use to bless the crops, ensure plentiful fishing, heal the injured and ill, and control the weather. For within those stones lies an awesome technology the origin of which is lost in time – a technology that has to be kept from the AAnn at any cost.

Set in the amazing world of the Humanx Commonwealth, *The Howling Stones* is an incredible adventure from one of the most exciting storytellers in science fiction.

THE SEAFORT SAGA
by David Feintuch

Look out for these magnificent adventures:

Midshipman's HOPE

A hideous accident kills the senior officers of UNS
Hibernia – leaving a terrified young officer in command of a
damaged ship with no chance of rescue or reinforcement . . .

Challenger's HOPE

An alien attack and an admiral's betrayal leave a wounded
Commander Nicholas Seafort stranded aboard a doomed ship
of arrogant colonists and violent street children . . .

Prisoner's HOPE

To save the world, Nicholas Seafort must forsake his vows –
and commit an unthinkable, suicidal act of high treason . . .

Fisherman's HOPE

Alone at the centre of a cosmic apocalypse, Nick Seafort
faces his final battle . . .

Voices of HOPE

For Nicholas Seafort, the race to save mankind from destroying
itself has become personal – for to save his son, he must
save the world . . .

Patriarch's HOPE

Seafort has drained the earth of resources in his efforts to defend
it, now orbital assault threatens the future of the entire race . . .

Children of HOPE

The alien war has shattered earth's ecology and the galactic
economy, leaving Hope's colonists with the threat of civil war . . .

www.orbitbooks.co.uk